P9-DGJ-482

Also by Jane Smiley

BARN BLIND

AT PARADISE GATE

DUPLICATE KEYS

duplicate
K E Y S

JANE SMILEY

ALFRED A. KNOPF

New York　　1 9 8 4

NEW HANOVER COUNTY PUBLIC LIBRARY

THIS IS A BORZOI BOOK
PUBLISHED BY
ALFRED A. KNOPF, INC.

Copyright © 1984 by Jane Smiley

All rights reserved under International
and Pan-American Copyright Conventions.
Published in the United States by Alfred A.
Knopf, Inc., New York, and simultaneously
in Canada by Random House of Canada
Limited, Toronto. Distributed by Random
House, Inc., New York.

Library of Congress Cataloging in
Publication Data
Smiley, Jane.
Duplicate keys.
I. Title.
PS3569.M39D8   1984
813'.54   83-47852
ISBN 0-394-53065-9

Manufactured in
the United States of America
First Edition

For Althea Jompen Drew and JTH,
duplicates, with affection

DUPLICATE KEYS

1

"I HAD a key. I was there to water Susan's plants, but I've always had a key. Each of the guys in the band would have one, and other friends, too." Across from Alice, Police Detective Honey jotted something on a pad. When he moved his hand, Alice read, upside down, ? keys out. She said, "Once on the subway I overheard a guy with a suitcase say to someone else, 'Richie knows a place where we can sleep. He's got a key.' I didn't know any Richie, but I can't say I was surprised when the guy on the subway turned up at Susan's apartment a day or so later, and let himself in. He wasn't a bad kid. I mean, he came to Manhattan to take a management trainee job with RCA, but nobody knew him, and he did have a key."

Detective Honey looked at her attentively, but didn't write anything down. In the years Alice had lived in New York, she had never actually spoken to a New York cop. Although reassured by his wide, bland face, she wondered if he was on the take. She coughed into her hand, which was trembling, and went on as if with a psychiatrist. "It took a long time for the implications of that to faze Denny and Susan, and by that time everyone had a key. Then they talked about changing the locks, but it was a lot of money and trouble, and anyway, Denny was afraid of seeming hostile." Detective Honey grimaced and shook his head. Alice said, "I thought it was stupid, too."

"You were watering the plants, Miss Ellis?"

"Mrs. I was supposed to. I told Susan I would come every three days, even if the, uh, men were around, because she didn't really trust them to keep everything watered. Maybe you saw that she has beautiful plants." Thinking of the plants made her think of Denny and Craig. She winced. Detective Honey said, "And Miss Gabriel is where?"

"In the Adirondacks. She should be home tomorrow night."

"In the Adirondacks in May?"

"She usually goes at odd times of the year. There's a cabin she rents, and it's too expensive in the summer."

"Have you accompanied her to this cabin?"

"No one has. It doesn't even have a telephone, and you have to hike in about three miles. Anyway, she hasn't ever really invited anyone. I think she likes the break."

"The break?"

Alice sat up straighter. "Well, getting away. You know. She's a very busy person, dealing with customers all day, and—" Her voice faded.

Detective Honey touched the tip of his pencil to the notepad, then suggested, "So you were there on Wednesday, and came back today?" All of his questions were mere suggestions posed with studied casualness that convinced Alice she was a suspect and made her feel craven. "I was there on Tuesday, actually, but I couldn't get back till today." She cleared her throat. "I left my place about ten or ten-fifteen. I walked down Broadway, and bought a paper at Seventy-ninth Street. The vendor knows me. It's ten blocks from my place, so it must have taken me about twenty minutes. I didn't see anyone. I let myself in, because there isn't a doorman, and went up the elevator to the sixth floor. I've been in that building almost more than I've been in my own, so I'm very familiar with everything about it. Nothing was different. I mean, out of place or anything." Honey drew his left hand across the paper and wrote behind it. "I opened the door. Everything was very neat." With the light streaming in, arrowing among the spikes of succulents, the ivy vines, the heavy, glossy leaves of avocados, the silvered masses of cyclamen, the rosy coleus. Drapes open, skylights blue with sunshine. Alice swallowed, but something in her throat would neither go down nor come up. The detective said, "Did you step into the room before you saw them?"

"They were sitting in chairs. I didn't expect to see them at all. I thought they had a gig somewhere up near Boston." Honey pushed her cup of coffee a few millimeters toward her and said, "As they were found by Officer Dolan?"

Alice nodded. "I said, 'Hi!' Just like that. 'Hi!' I was glad to see them." The cheery greeting had resonated almost visibly in the air of the room, so that Alice had heard it and heard it the whole time she was looking. Somehow the riveting sight was not their ravaged faces, but Craig's foot half out of his boot, so that it looked broken or deformed. It took her a long time to realize that he must have been in the act of pulling his boot off when the shot was fired. Honey flipped back a page or two in his notebook. Alice said, "I didn't touch anything."

"Call received at eleven twenty-eight. That's approximately an hour, Miss Ellis."

"It is?"

"What did you do after discovering the victims?"

"I think I stood there for a long time, but I don't know how long. Then I walked around the apartment."

"And yet you say that you didn't touch anything?"

"I kept my hands in my pockets. I didn't want to touch anything. I didn't even want to breathe."

"You put in your call from?"

"From Broadway, but I had to walk down a few blocks to find a phone that was in order."

"So you were alone in the apartment for approximately half an hour?"

"I suppose, yes."

Honey made marks on his pad, inhaling one large disapproving breath that seemed to drain the small office of oxygen. Alice said, "Maybe you don't understand how shocked I was. I've never seen a corpse. All my grandparents are still alive. We never even had a dog that died."

"Did you notice anything at all that seems unusual? You were there a long time. Try to remember as carefully as you can. Perhaps you can call up a detail that you think you didn't notice. The scene of a crime, Mrs. Ellis, can be remarkably eloquent, but even the well-meaning presence of an untrained or unobservant person can silence much of what it has to say."

Pompous, Alice thought, but, rebuked, she blushed. "I should have turned right in the doorway and left?"

Honey shrugged his assent, but said only, "Please think as carefully as possible."

"I was very upset."

"But what did you see?"

Alice thought for a couple of minutes, but it was impossible to say. When she made herself recall the scene of the crime square inch by square inch, she couldn't tell if she was merely seeing what she knew would be in Susan's apartment. "Nothing comes to me."

Detective Honey cleared his throat. Alice wondered if he were about to run her in. Did the daughters of hardware store owners from Rochester, Minnesota, actually wind up in Women's Detention for stumbling upon murder victims? It was not something you learned about, in the end, from reading Kafka, or *The New York Times.* He said, "Perhaps you could tell me something about yourself, then, Mrs. Ellis."

"The smell was very sharp. I was upset and kind of physically shocked. My bones and muscles seemed like they were vibrating."

"You are not a native New Yorker?"

Alice looked at him for a moment. Was it time to ask for a lawyer, cite Miranda, stand up and refuse to answer any more questions? But when she opened her mouth, she was naming herself, Alice Marie Ellis, divorced, no children, aged thirty-one, librarian, New York Public Library, main branch, 557 West Eighty-fourth Street, native of Rochester, Minnesota, mother nurse, father in hammers and hoses, former husband poet and college teacher. Resident in New York, six years, five of them at present address. No felonies, no misdemeanors, no car.

Detective Honey smiled for the first time, confidently, Alice thought. He was a big man, with the routine confidence of big men. Looking at him was difficult. Conjecture seemed to bounce back at her, like sunlight off the fender of a car. He said, "I'll be in touch with you, Mrs. Ellis," and stood up. Alice stood up, too, and then, almost immediately, she was outside, in front of the precinct station. It was a brilliant day, of breezy clarity and substantial warmth. On the fifth floor of the building across the street, yellow awnings bowed and popped in the wind, as if at the beach and not in the middle of Manhattan. In just this way she had stepped out of her building at ten or ten-fifteen this morning, paused and looked up at gray stone, sharp shadows, azure sky, happy that Susan would be home tomorrow. "Mmmm, what a day!" she had exclaimed, and a man walking by had smiled and nodded. It was the sixth beautiful day in a row.

Alice stood and stood, smack in the path of traffic into the station, not knowing what to think, gazing at the free air of the free city of New York, relishing, even after such a brief time in the station, her present freedom of choice, but also unable to step away from the security of the busy building. To her right, leafy and rolling beyond the tunnel of buildings, Central Park beckoned: the zoo, the Met, the Natural History Museum, vendors of hot dogs and felafel, renters of bicycles, roller skaters, swings and slides. She stood and yearned, stepped forth, turned left toward Broadway.

A S   B E F I T T E D   Denny and Craig's small fame, there were only a few gawkers, and when Alice asked one what had happened, he only said, "Couple of guys murdered in there. On the top floor."

"Does anyone know who they were?"

"Nah. Just some guys."

However, there was a girl, stylishly dressed, with a camera, who could have been from *Rolling Stone*. Alice pretended to be a gawker herself, and didn't ask. As she lingered, more people appeared, shaded their eyes, and stared up at the blank windows of the top floor. No curtains. Behind her, someone said, "Denny Minehart and Craig Shellady, I heard. They had that band, Deep Six."

"Sounds sort of familiar."

"A hit about five years ago, remember 'Dinah's Eyes'?" He hummed a musical phrase.

"Yeah, sort of. Don't you wish you could fly up and look right in the window?"

Alice drifted over toward the photographer, framing a question that she undoubtedly wouldn't ask. She had been party to Denny and Craig's frustration for so long that she knew she couldn't stand to risk the certainty that even after this, *Rolling Stone* didn't care. But they always announced deaths, they always did. Denny and Craig could be sure of that.

"Dinah's Eyes" had brought Denny and Craig to New York, and the rest of them had followed, for various reasons, but mostly because it seemed the natural thing to do, natural even for herself and Jim Ellis to come only out of friendship. A big advance, "real support" from the record company, the sure sense that this was it, and six years ago, not five. A picture in *Rolling Stone*, not the cover and not the center spread, but a half-page shot by the magazine's second most well-known woman photographer, and two pages of print, with Deep Six in fancy type, grossly elongated blue letters dipping into the body of the article. The whole thing was framed and hung on the wall right between those two windows that everyone, including Alice herself, was now staring at. Between the windows was the best place for it, insisted Craig, because then the sun wouldn't fade or yellow it. Sunlight was death to newsprint, said Craig, and although he had his doubts about hanging it on an outside wall, with the sudden changes in temperature and everything, it would be okay for a while. Craig didn't actually live with Denny and Susan, but he might as well have, for he kept all of his instruments there, all of his best photographs, and his scrapbook of performance reviews. It was from that apartment and not his own one-bedroom on Amsterdam Avenue that he expected to rise through a skylight like a great bird into the firmament of rock and roll immortality. Denny didn't mind, having lived with Craig off and on for more than twenty years.

Alice stood so close to the female photographer that she nearly got stepped on. She could have said to the photographer's companion (a reporter?), "I found them, you know. I opened the door and noticed the smell, and there they were, sitting in Susan's orange armchairs, and their heads were so odd and fleshy and red. Do you know how long it takes to realize that you are looking at a dead person, how slowly your mind inches up and over that concept, trying out this speculation and that one, a joke, a trick, a dream, going crazy, wrong apartment, I mean, for a minute I couldn't stop thinking that they'd been hit by cars and come here to recover or something. It was too quiet and clean for such an event to have happened. I wandered around the apartment for half an hour before calling the police, and now I'm a suspect." But the photographer deftly twisted a long lens off her camera and moved off with her companion toward Riverside Drive. And turning the corner from Riverside was Ray Reschley, the sound man. Brightly flushed in the manner of all pale, pale men, and eternally pudgy, Ray caught sight of her and lifted his hand to wave. Then, perhaps discerning from her solitude in the gathering crowd that her relationship to the victims was as yet unknown, he dropped his hand and avoided her with elaborate care, finally glancing around, and then mouthing, "My place, dinner." Alice nodded. Almost immediately a rather drably dressed and very young kid with a notebook stepped up to Ray, and Alice realized that this must be the reporter, a reporter. Ray's perfect pitch and excellent ear had made him rather famous for a sound man, in enough demand so that he could work year-round in New York and never go on tour unless as a special favor. Like Alice, like Susan, like Noah Mast, the bass player, Ray had come here originally just because Denny and Craig were being brought by the record company and it seemed like he might be able to find work, too.

Ray drew himself up, clasped his hands together, and proceeded to give an interview. More people gathered around him. Ray expanded slightly, let his eyes sweep the group, smiled once as if he knew something, and said, "No comment." Simultaneously amused by Ray and sickened by the entire scene, Alice turned away from the group, from Susan's building and enormous problem, and headed up Riverside toward Eighty-fourth Street, although what she would do there she hadn't the least idea.

"YOU heard, then. Isn't it amazing?" The door of Ray's apartment was opened by Rya Mast, black shorts, black French T-shirt, bare feet. She moved backward dramatically, allowing Alice to enter. From across the room, her husband Noah barked, "Alice found them, Rya."

"Noah never tells me anything. How awful for you. I won't even ask you about it. You'd better have a drink."

"She found them this morning, Rya."

"You'd better have a drink anyway. Ray just went out to get dinner at the Chinese place on 105th Street, but he left a pitcher of piña coladas. Let me get you one."

Noah rolled his eyes, but smiled when she returned. Alice took the foamy drink and sat down, resolving not to look up. The ceiling of Ray's living room was a large smoked mirror.

"We're just shocked," said Rya, whose blond hair was wound on top of her head. If she unpinned it, it would fall down in a single shining mass, Alice knew. The only sense of expertise she ever got about Rya was when the other woman was arranging her hair or choosing clothes. "Just shocked, shocked. I can't express it."

"Astonished. Dumbfounded," suggested Noah.

"Noah is shocked, too. Believe me. He teases to cover up."

"Floored. Taken aback."

"Don't make us laugh, Noah. It's awful."

Alice had long ago arrived at a routine toleration of the Masts that enabled her to overlook Rya's irritating coquettishness as well as Noah's sarcastic manner. She was fond of them not only out of familiarity, but also for the countless jokes she had made at their expense over the years. Now she found them annoying, however, and regretted having come. In addition, she was afraid of having to describe what she had seen and of having to listen to the disgust of the others. Really, it was a burden to have to drag herself out of the bathtub, hunt for a cab, and endure an evening going over it all, but she hadn't been able to keep herself from doing it. It was important to know something, perhaps only that it had really happened.

"Have you called Susan?" said Rya. "I can't think of Susan."

"She's in the Adirondacks, remember?" Alice's voice, unused since her conversation with Detective Honey, came out thick and quavering. She cleared her throat. She longed for Ray to return so that they could have the business of eating. Noah resumed rolling joints—tight, uniform, pointed like nails at each end. Alice sipped her drink. Rya's gaze wandered upward, and then, underneath the smoked but revealing mirror, she rearranged her legs to better advantage and plumped her hair. There was no music. Listening to music was distressing to Ray, who heard every wrong note and mechanical waver in pitch. He preferred to save his ears for working hours, he said. Time off meant silence, silence so perfect that it was almost sexual. Sex-u-al. Sex, Ray maintained, was his only other interest besides perfect pitch. When he started talking like that, Alice was irked, knowing it was a pose, for Ray loved to build things and always had some project going, but in the last year or so his friends had changed. Now he went on rather tediously about his passion for sex, pure sex, no complications. Rya stood up as if the mirror were the gaze of God and went into the bathroom, closing the door behind herself. Noah glanced up and said, "How do you think she's reacting?"

"What?"

"Do you think she's reacting oddly?"

"Rya? No."

"Hmp."

Unable to interpret this, Alice said, "Do you?"

Noah shrugged. Alice often wondered why after nearly four years of marriage the Masts still talked as if the interest of their friends in every wrinkle of their relationship was a foregone conclusion. He called out, "Sweetie?"

"Out in a flash!" came from behind the bathroom door. Ray liked the bathroom off the living room, but in the silence Alice found herself listening for the flush of the toilet, the rush of water. Noah, his head cocked, was listening, too, but then caught himself and said, "I can't ever gauge the depths, you know. I think I'm basically sort of a cold person, but she really feels it in her soul." Alice had her doubts. He put one of the joints to his lips and struck a friction match under the desktop. In a moment he gestured with the joint toward Alice, who shook her head. She usually shook her head and then felt rather drab with the Masts. They also always made her reconsider her clothes. The calico skirt and cotton blouse that had seemed perky and brave when she left her apartment seemed dowdy and bland under Ray's mirror, in the same room with Rya's shorts, across from Noah's little grid of reefers. The key turned in the lock and the door flew open. It was Ray with a huge bag of food. In a moment Rya appeared, shooting straight for it, then moaning over the mo-shu pork, the oysters with straw mushrooms, the gong-bao chicken with charred red peppers and cashews, the sizzling rice soup, the shrimp toast. It must have cost Ray twenty-five or thirty dollars. And there were shao-mai dumplings at the bottom. Rya reached into the bag, her red fingernails promising to impale rather than to grasp one of the delicate hors d'oeuvres. Alice stood up. She was hungry, too.

She wondered if the others were thinking constantly of Denny and Craig and Susan, as she was. Of course, they had not seen the bodies there, luminously without life, without even the life of the chairs and tables and rugs, not to mention the growing plants and the lamps and appliances coursing with electricity. But then, Noah and Ray, at least, would have seen Denny and Craig last night or the night before, perfectly alive, completely themselves, annoying, familiar, entertaining all at once. Especially Craig, Alice thought, who managed to elicit from her an exact conjunction of vexation and desire that years of friendship had not gotten her used to. And murdered! Murdered! The shock of it startled her again and again, like random hammering right next to her ear. She placed a pancake on her plate, spread it with hoisin sauce, and spooned on the pork and egg mixture. Ray said, "These oysters are terrific. Craig would have just creamed over them."

"He loved that restaurant," said Noah. A great sigh lifted from the table, and Ray said, "Remember how he wouldn't even taste Chinese food five years ago because it was all mushed together?"

"A very weird guy," said Noah. "I just can't believe it."

Ray dipped his spoon into the bean curd. "I can. You know, I really can. Think about it. Craig Shellady living to a ripe old age? Are you kidding?"

Alice said, "Weren't his folks about this age when they died in that car wreck?"

Ray ignored her. "Denny, yes. Denny with seventeen grandkids in the country somewhere, watching the polls on election days, perfect. Tapping maple trees, building more shelves to store more canned tomatoes, yes, yes."

Alice coughed. "His mother was, I think. His father must have been nearly forty. Craig was eleven or twelve, anyway."

Rya sat back with a stricken look. "I didn't know Craig was orphaned. I mean, orphaned!"

Noah rolled his eyes. "Well, he told you umpteen times that his parents were dead and that he'd lived all those years with the Mineharts!"

"But I didn't realize he was orphaned! Like somebody in an asylum!"

"He never lived in an asylum. He had plenty of aunts and uncles, and the Mineharts, and he was perfectly well taken care of."

"Orphaned! Can you imagine what it's like to be orphaned!" Noah put his arm around her and kissed her on the temple, but with the air of putting his hand over her mouth. "Anyway," said Ray, his chopsticks poised above his plate, "it's weird. I always thought he was doomed, but I can't believe he's dead." Noah said, "Has anyone called Denny's parents?" Everyone looked at Alice, who shrugged. "I hardly know them. I told the police their name and address." She shivered. The Mineharts were crazy about Craig, and Denny was probably their favorite child. No one was warmer or more reliable than Denny. She said, "Lots of people are going to have to know. That's the worst part."

"No," said Noah. "Susan's the worst part. What are you going to do about Susan?"

Alice had rather shunned the thought of Susan all afternoon. Susan had lived with Denny for years, nearly as long as Alice had known her, and, in Alice's view, they had the only nearly perfect relationship Alice had ever seen. Alice felt about it as one might feel living next door to a historic monument. She was proud of it, anxious to show it off, knowing it wasn't hers but as reassured by it as if it were. Susan dazzled with her domestic competence, her way with tax forms and vegetables and hospitality and decor.

Because of Susan, people always wanted to hang around that apartment, partake not merely of the comfort she had created, but also of the comfort between her and Denny. Equally comfortable were her departures, her undramatic efforts to go away by herself, that neither she nor Denny made much of. Perhaps Alice had always envied these even more, since partings from Jim Ellis had been fraught with anxiety and had always ended in arguments, at the very least, about why he hadn't written enough, or why she had written too much. And then, of course, they had ended in parting, possibly their inevitable end, Alice occasionally thought. But Susan and Denny had gone on and on and on, longer than any of their friends, longer than any friends of their friends. Alice put her fork down. "I don't know," she said. "And we haven't done anything, have we? Where are they going to be buried? How will they get there? Is there going to be a funeral? Who's going to take care of the apartment? I don't even know what time Susan is getting here tomorrow. Should I sit outside her building and wait for her? She could come any time."

"And talk to the press," said Ray. "They've been ringing the phone off the hook. I put it on the service for tonight, but I bet when I call there's going to be fifty messages."

"*Rolling Stone?*" asked Alice.

"And everyone else, believe me."

Alice didn't say anything. Noah lit up another joint and said, "I didn't think Craig was doomed for a moment. Crazy, yes, doomed, no. Yeah, he did all that stuff, especially cocaine, and I bet none of you knew that he tried heroin that time he was in California." Alice remembered when Craig was in California. "But he was always looking. Never missed a trick. Once he had me on the back of his motorcycle, that BMW, and we must have been doing about ninety, and he bent down and lit his cigarette on the cylinder casing. I never felt in danger for a moment, but I can't tell you why. That same trip, a bug flew into his sunglasses and broke the lens. We just laughed about it and taped it up."

"Just because you're a fool," said Ray, "doesn't mean he wasn't."

"I don't know about that. I will say, though, that I'd rather be on the back of that motorcycle doing a hundred than in almost any cab in New York." He inhaled deeply from the joint that only he and Ray were smoking and went on, "It just always seemed that if there was anyone with eyes in the back of his head and the reflexes to get out of trouble, it was Craig, you know?"

"That's what was so weird about this," said Alice, realizing it for the first time. "I think the reason I couldn't believe what I saw was that there didn't look like there had been any trouble. That's just the word. Something more subtle than no struggle, no trouble of any kind, as if nothing bad had taken place. When you're little, sometimes other kids have these rubber spiders and things, and you get shocked before you know it. Well, this was just the opposite. I couldn't believe that it wasn't a joke. I couldn't get shocked, even with the smell. And then, this afternoon, I felt funny, but as if I had the flu. Maybe I should have touched one of them."

"There wouldn't have been any smell," said Ray. "Not so soon."

"Well, there was."

"After, what, eight hours? You're imagining things."

"Well, I'm not going to argue about it."

"Oh, God," said Rya. The conversation died.

Taking the last spoonful of bean curd, Noah said, "Just the other day we were rehearsing for this gig. Just setting up, really. That new guy, Zimmerman, the one Craig hired for percussion a few weeks ago, spilled a glass of water on the stage. No one saw but me. He hit it with his sleeve or something. Craig went over to fiddle with the amps. His guitar was on, and he had one hand around the neck, and he reached for one of the dials and lifted his foot. I opened my mouth to call out to him, and shit if he didn't step just to one side of the water, and then he put his other foot just in front of it. I mean, you don't know if he would have gotten a shock, but I thought to myself, there's a lucky guy, there's the classic example of a lucky guy."

"And then he chewed Zimmerman out and practically fired him on the spot, didn't he?" asked Ray, who hadn't been there.

"You know Shellady. Patience wasn't exactly his middle name."

"Not hardly," agreed Ray.

"I just think it's the most awful thing." Rya had thrown herself back against the giant gray pillows of Ray's sofa. "We all do," said Noah. "Shhh."

"Did anyone call Zimmerman?" asked Alice.

"He's been in the studio all day with some guys from the Coast. He probably knows by now, though."

"Did you call Jim?" Noah dropped this rather tenderly into the conversation while Ray pretended to be busy cleaning off the table. Jim Ellis was as long a friend of the others as she was. "I should, shouldn't I?" She glanced around.

"Do you want me to?" asked Ray.

"No thanks. Jim is so determined to be amicable that if I didn't call, he'd assume I was too prostrate to talk to anyone."

"I don't see how you can put up with this by yourself," whimpered Rya.

"Better one than three. I mean, what if he came and brought her? I'll call him tonight. It's only six there now." She looked at each of their sympathetic faces and added, "I don't mind talking to him, really. It's been almost two years, you know."

"Has it been that long?"

"It's been that long since the final split, really and truly."

"Amazing," exclaimed Noah, holding another joint up in front of his face and admiring it, then putting it carefully with the others in his breast pocket. Watching him, Alice felt suddenly giggly, perhaps because after such an odd day, their evening meal hadn't been odd at all, but familiar, usual, with each friend so much himself. They hadn't forced any description out of her and the scene, having not been described, seemed to recede. Other people were dead and she was not. The fragrance of the trees on Riverside blowing in through Ray's window reminded her fiercely that it was good not to be dead. She pursed her lips to stop a giggle, and said, "I'd better go."

"Not alone," said Noah. Rya stood up. "Let's call each other tomorrow," she said. "We should know what's going on first thing, especially about Susan."

"By the time Rya gets up," Noah put his arm around her shoulders, "most first things have happened long since."

"That's not true!"

THE double row of stoplights and streetlights tapered to the vanishing point somewhere downtown, and the few vehicles on the broad expanse of West End Avenue seemed to Alice to roll with the deliberation and elegance of barouches in a park. It was a pretty sight, down the long slope toward Eighty-ninth Street, but there were no cabs. Noah and Rya, who lived nearby on Riverside, discussed walking Alice over to Broadway. Another man, about twenty yards away, appeared to be waiting as well. "Something will come along," said Rya.

"Look. Two just went by going downtown on Broadway."

"Just another minute or two," said Rya.

"Why?"

"I just have a feeling something will come along."

The man had edged closer. Alice didn't mind waiting forever, the western breeze off the river was so gustily warm, practically as firm as another body against hers. "Now," said Noah.

"Just wait a little longer," said Rya. "The longer we wait, the sooner it'll be until a taxi comes."

"That's ridiculous."

The man was almost upon them. Alice stepped closer to Noah. The man said, "Waiting for a cab?"

"Yeah," said Noah, surly.

"Me, too. Going downtown?"

"Only fifteen blocks or so," demurred Noah.

"Me, too. How about sharing?"

By the streetlight Alice could see that he was about their age and dressed in a plaid shirt and jeans, just as Noah was. Noah glanced at her and she shrugged. Noah said, "Might be easier," in a voice of studied doubtfulness.

"I've been waiting ten minutes."

"Why don't you go over to Broadway?"

"Lazy. Prettier here, anyway."

Noah looked for a long second at Alice, then back at the man. "Let me see your driver's license or something," he said.

Unhesitatingly, the other man brought out his wallet, opened it, and presented the license to Noah. Noah said, "Henry Mullet. Remember that, Rya, Henry Mullet. We're not going. It's just Alice. Alice, this is Henry Mullet." Right then a cab appeared around the corner of 106th Street. Henry waved it over, Rya embraced Alice, Noah gave her a kiss and told her to buck up and call him when she got home and any other time, absolutely any other time, they had to stick together, and suddenly she was in the cab and Henry was wiggling around to put his wallet away. Alice said "Eighty-fourth Street" to the cabbie and they sped away.

Henry Mullet smelled wonderful, as if he had been in the sun all day, tanning with coconut oil. Unable to resist, but as impersonally as possible, Alice said, "Have you been to the beach?"

"I was, actually. Fire Island."

"Was it hot enough to sun?"

"It was out there. How did you guess?"

Alice didn't answer.

"How did you guess? I put on clean clothes at my friends' place."

"I'm embarrassed to say."

"Tell me."

"You smell terrific."

Henry Mullet grinned. Doing a perfect twenty-seven miles per hour, the cab made light after light, reds turning to greens like doors opened by footmen. Henry said, "You're Alice? Alice what?"

Alice told herself that she would remember to tell Noah that he had asked her name. "Alice Ellis," she replied.

"Are you kidding?"

"Not kidding a bit." Henry Mullet chuckled with frank enjoyment. They were passing Ninetieth Street. "One of the pitfalls of early marriage."

"It's a nice name. It goes trippingly on the tongue."

"No one could spell my maiden name, so I kept it." They were passing Eighty-seventh Street. The cabbie said, "Where on Eighty-fourth, lady?"

"Halfway to Riverside, but you can drop me at the corner."

"Me, too." As Henry spoke, a little reflexive fear rose in Alice's chest. How could she have been so foolish after all? She crossed the fingers of the hand away from him. But after all, he had heard Noah tell her to call him. And Noah knew his name. Alice coughed. The cab stopped and Henry had the fare; even as Alice was reaching into her purse, he was thrusting it into the cabbie's box, opening Alice's door for her, helping her out. As the taxi squealed away, he said, "Let's walk in the middle of the street. My building's that gray one with the awning, down there." It was just across the street from hers. Suddenly trusting, she said, "Mine's right there. Funny, huh?"

"Maybe." He took her elbow and propelled her down the center of Eighty-fourth Street. "More light, less dog-do," he said.

Alice laughed at the word. At a spot just between their buildings, he said, "I'll stay here till you get in."

"Thank you."

"Wave to me sometime from your window."

As Alice fit her various keys into the front doors, she turned and looked back at him. He was standing gravely in the middle of the street watching her.

2

JUST as Alice stood up from talking to Noah, already formulating in her mind how she was going to greet Jim, what tone of voice she would strive for, what she would say if Mariana answered, whether it would be better to call now, when it was eight o'clock their time, or wait an hour until nine, the phone rang, startling her so that she just stared at it for two more rings. She thought of Detective Honey, and wondered if he might be checking up on her. It was Ray. She thanked him for their generous dinner.

"Don't thank me," said Ray. "Whenever I go into that place, I can't stop ordering."

"It is good."

"Someday I'd like to order a bit of everything on the menu."

"Well, anyway, th—"

"What did you think?"

"Of what?"

"Of the way they were."

"Noah and Rya?"

"I love your innocence. It's so librarianly."

"If I'm so innocent, then you tell me what you're talking about."

"Nothing, sweetie. I'll call you tomorrow, all right?"

"Ray, when did we first meet?"

"Eleventh grade."

"You were dating Julie Zimansky, right? Julie Zimansky was my second best friend. I know you put your tongue in Julie Zimansky's mouth. Don't pull this gay shit on me, Ray. Don't call me 'sweetie' in that tone of voice." She made a little circle with her finger in some crumbs on the table. There was a silence on the other end of the line. Ray was smoking a cigarette. Finally, he said, "It's not shit."

"I'm sorry, Ray. I just think you forget who you're talking to sometimes."

"Maybe."

"Will you tell me what's going on, then?"

"You really don't know?"

"Do I ever?"

"You did in eleventh grade."

"I don't know."

"If I hadn't thought you knew, I wouldn't have brought it up."

"But you did."

Ray puffed a couple more times, then said, "Rya's been sleeping with Craig for over a year now."

"Says who? Ray, you always think that about everybody! Is that the big secret?"

"It's not a secret." He spoke briskly, stung.

"Is this something you've intuited or something you know?"

"Both."

"I really can't believe that Rya has even registered any other man since Noah. In the first place, she wouldn't know how to keep it a secret, and in the second, they are an advertisement for passion, which is why they seem so simple minded."

"In the first place, it was never a secret, or at least, wasn't for long, and in the second, I don't know that they do maintain the hottest fever."

"You're telling me that Noah knew?"

"He found out. I'm not sure when."

"And she kept it up? And Craig kept it up? Noah's been Craig's bass player from the beginning! This is simply preposterous! Did Denny know? Did Susan know? The mere fact that I don't know, and I would if Denny knew, is evidence that this is all a figment of your imagination. Did Noah or Craig or Rya tell you?"

"No."

"Then I don't believe it. I really don't."

"Ask Susan when she comes back." He sounded so distant and cold that Alice purred into the phone, "Are your feelings hurt?"

He said only, "And there couldn't have been any smell. Rigor mortis, yes. But decomposition wouldn't have set in."

"There was lots of blood. It smelled. It was hot. The windows were closed."

"I still think—"

"Why do we have to argue about this? I know—"

"It's been an awful day. I think it's just hitting me. Isn't it odd how it's more exciting than horrifying at first? I really loved Denny. And Craig, too, most of the time."

"Are you going to be able to sleep?"

"Don't know."

She wanted to tell him not to take any pills, but she was afraid to. She settled for saying, "I couldn't stand it if anything happened to anyone else."

"Alice."

"What?"

"You saw the cops today, didn't you?"

"Didn't you?"

"What did he ask you?"

"About the scene of the crime and stuff. I don't know. I don't think he thinks I'm a very promising witness. All I could remember was how shocked I was."

"Did he ask you about the rest of us?"

"You and Noah? Not really. Not even about Susan, really. I couldn't detect any trend to his thoughts."

"You sure?"

"How did he talk to you?"

"No special way." But from the manner in which he pulled deeply on his cigarette, Alice guessed that there had been something.

"They gave out so many keys to the apartment. Something was going on that we haven't the least notion of, Ray. I'd bet on it."

"Maybe. But he didn't talk about me at all?"

"Well, I had to give a list of close friends. He asked me what your line of work is. That's all."

"What did you think about him?"

"I thought his suit was too tight across the shoulders."

Ray didn't chuckle.

"Ray, I was afraid to think about him. I was afraid even to look at him for too long. It would have been like looking straight at the power of the state. I babbled like an idiot, and didn't stay on the point, and felt like I was exposing myself all the time. If he didn't run me in for doing it, then he might just because I was a fool."

"I didn't know what to think, either." Ray was trying to sound normal. Alice pursed her lips, then brushed the crumbs she had been playing with off the table into the palm of her hand. "Can we hang up now?" She knew she was being rude.

"Call me in the morning."

"Good night, Ray."

And then she dialed the number in California. It was only after it began to ring that she realized she still had the crumbs in her hand, and there was a minute jelly stain on the table as well.

Often Alice thought that the break-up of her marriage couldn't have been worse if Jim had planned it to give her as much pain as possible. In the first year after the split, she had even decided, as a kind of protective mechanism, that he had planned it, that his heart was bent on vicious revenge for something she had done, or for her wholesale, and possibly demented, adoration of his aspirations. When she looked back on herself as she had been in the early years with him, she could not help seeing herself with his eyes, seeing the upturned face, the ready leap to fulfill his least wishes, or, better still, to anticipate them, the repeated surrender of her being to his. To all appearances, she had gone around like every other person, doing chores, going to work, drinking in bars, seeing movies, but in reality she had spent years with her forehead to the floor at Jim Ellis's feet. He was a poet. Poetry was a passion that ran through his days like a steel wire. His poetry moved her, good and bad, first to last. It still moved her. Even poems that he now wrote to Mariana, when she came across them in magazines, could draw out of her her best appreciation for love itself, and she automatically responded as Mariana would, with love, pure and brave, in return. The great irony was that she would not have looked for the magazines and seen the poems had she not been a librarian, a profession she had taken up in order to support Jim while he wrote. On her own she would never have become a librarian, never in a million years.

But she did become a librarian, and he, to add to their meager income, taught a few continuing education classes at Queens College and N.Y.U. and City College. Never a real job, but enough to buy the food and pay the phone bill. It was in a night course for City College that he met Mariana. Because he was honest, he kept Alice posted on every twist in the affair: He was attracted to this girl in his class, wasn't that funny, he would just have coffee with her, nothing special, she was a lovely girl, and wanted to meet Alice, yes, they had slept together, but it wouldn't happen again, they couldn't help it, it did happen again, this was something he had to work out, mostly physical, he thought, not a threat to their marriage, they were best friends, weren't they. He did love Mariana, but it was a different kind of love, he didn't see how he could do without either of them, did she understand how painful this was for him, wouldn't she just meet Mariana, as his friend, sort of, to advise him as his friend, he had never

felt like this before, it was sick, obsessive, maybe a trial separation, he couldn't stand doing this to her, he still loved her, but
it was the love of friends, they had been so young and inexperi-
enced when they met, this new thing with Mariana was like life
and death at the same time, he knew she couldn't ever understand that, yes, they could get back together, just to try it out,
but he really didn't think. . . . Three days after getting back together, after moving all his things back into their apartment, this
very apartment she was sitting in now, he disappeared. No note,
no phone call, no message left with their friends, no word, even,
from Mariana, whom Alice had made herself call, out of worry.
"Haven't seen him in weeks," said Mariana, while, Alice later
found out, Jim was sitting right across the table. Then they went
to California, and Alice got a note two months later telling her
to file for divorce, or, if New York laws were too strict and she
didn't mind waiting, he would file. She could have everything,
even the stereo. From the first day of the fateful class to the
arrival of the note, Alice passed the interval of nearly ten months,
she didn't know how. Without Susan, she could not have. As
Jim's phone rang and rang, the receiver began to shake against
her ear, and she realized that she was shivering already. Usually,
she didn't begin shivering until almost the end of a conversation
with him. She was disappointed that they were not at home. In
spite of everything, he was the one she wanted to talk to about
this, before she had to do for Susan, perhaps, what Susan had
done for her.

And then Jim's voice greeted her intimately, in her very ear.
He had to say hello three times before she could speak. He said,
"I thought it was long distance. How are you?" He spoke kindly
and affectionately, but not tenderly. It was apparent he did not
know. "I'm not so good," she said.

"What's wrong, Alice? Did something happen to you? Are you
sick?"

"Denny and Craig were, um, killed last night. We all thought
you had better know."

"My God! What did he do?" He turned away from the phone, putting his hand over the receiver. So she was right there. "Jim!" Alice raised her voice.

"Didn't I always say Craig would—"

"We all always said something. But they were murdered. I found them."

"Jesus, sweetheart."

"That's not important. It's more of a shock now than it was then. I'll tell you about it sometime. But Ray and Noah wanted to be sure that you heard it from us and not over the radio. I should have called earlier."

"The radio's broken and we've been at the beach all day."

"Oh."

"Hadn't we better come there?"

"You don't need to. It would be awfully expensive."

"How's Susan?"

"She's back in the Adirondacks somewhere. I dread that she'll find out in the car on the way home tomorrow. I don't know what we're going to do about it." For the first time that evening, Alice was nearly crying, although she had vowed two years before never to cry in front of Jim Ellis if she had to slit her throat first. "We don't know when she's going to get back or anything."

"I can't understand you, honey."

"Don't call me those names!"

"Alice . . ." But he didn't have anything to say, after all. They maintained a long transcontinental silence while Alice took deep breaths and wiped tears from her eyes. One or two times muffled muttering told her he was talking to Mariana, whom she had never seen but who was always there, it appeared, if the phone rang. Craig had once said, "Didn't you hear about the operation, Alice? They were joined at the waist like a couple of experimental dogs. Medical history made in Orange County." Of her friends besides Susan, Craig had been the most angry on her behalf, the most ready to belittle Jim's claims to talent, good looks, kindness, humanity. She had liked him quite a lot for that.

Finally she said, "I am all right, Jim. It's pretty late here, and all of this began this morning. Don't worry about me."

"I always do."

She decided to get off before she got mad. "I'll let you know what happens, all right? Or Ray will."

"All right, honey."

When she hung up the phone, she stuck her tongue as far out of her mouth as possible at it and said, "All right, honey!" in a strangled, sarcastic voice. Then, with a deep sigh, she got up and deposited the crumbs she had been clenching in the wastebasket. She took a small can of orange juice out of the freezer and set it on the counter by the sink. The cabinets, which she and Jim had stripped and refinished themselves, the vinyl flooring which they had laid, the flowers and vines they had stenciled around the kitchen doorway, all in a delirium of pleasure at having found such an apartment as this one, had long since lost for Alice any heartbreaking significance, although at one time a survey of the place seemed to measure out in completed tasks their three-year march toward the doom of Mariana. Nonetheless, the apartment, rent-controlled, was too good to give up for sentimental reasons. For seven rooms, five of them overlooking the street, Alice paid $375 per month, probably no more, these days, than mainte-nance. It was a gem of an apartment, and Alice loved it quite personally for the quite personal blessings she received from it. As she came out of the kitchen tonight, for example, her gaze automatically caressed the oak floor, laid in chevrons, forty-four feet by three feet, that washed from her toes and broke against the bedroom door. A huge apartment. Every New Yorker, Alice thought, loves to toss off the remark, "I've got this huge apart-ment."

When she opened the door to her bedroom, fondling for a mo-ment the molded brass doorknob, Susan sat up in her bed, saying, "Alice! You're home." Alice was paralyzed with astonishment, so shocked that what might have come out as an exclamation came out as a groan. The accumulated experiences of the day seemed to drop on her at once, exploded by this insignificant surprise into pure horror, and even a kind of terror. Susan declared, "I frightened you. Are you okay? Didn't you see my backpack in the living room? There's dirty laundry in the laundry room, too. I was sure you'd notice my junk all over the place and be annoyed."

Alice closed her mouth.

"I had a wonderful time. Hardly any rain, but this afternoon I was just ready to come home, so I came home. Denny must have a gig somewhere, because I called over there and there wasn't any answer, so I stopped here and let myself in. I figured that if you hadn't fallen in love in the last two weeks, you'd get in sometime, and here you are!" She bounced across the bed and reached for Alice's hand. "Are you all right?"

"There were crumbs on the table."

"I made myself some toast."

"I saw them, but they just didn't register. I'm all right. I missed you."

"Was I asleep? I must have been asleep. What time is it? Jesus, it's after twelve. I must have been asleep. The cabin was lovely. This is the perfect time. There were tons of wildflowers and deer and badgers and chipmunks, it was almost warm, no summer visitors. Is something the matter?"

Alice shook her head.

"Well, it was great!" But her enthusiasm had begun to sound a little hesitant. Alice said, "I'll bet!" and wondered if she could avoid delivery of the news until morning. "I just lay down here so I'd be sure not to miss you, or him, either, if there was one."

"No him. I was up at Ray's."

"He's not with Denny and Craig, then?"

"No."

"It's been a long time since he's had anyone over. I'm sorry I missed it. Did you go out to that Chinese place?"

"He got it in."

"What was the best thing? You don't have to tell me the whole menu, just the best thing."

"Um, well, I always love the mo-shu pork."

Susan began gathering her things off the nightstand. Alice exclaimed, "No! Stay here. I'm going to brush my teeth. We haven't slumber partied in years, okay?"

N O W Alice ached to tell her and have it over with, but it was impossible to come out of the bathroom. When she did, the light beside the bed was on, and Susan was sitting up, putting a pin in her straight, collar-length, reddish blond hair. She had Alice's favorite face, pale, peaceful, and good, unglamorous, a face that never fell apart with animation like Alice's own, a face that Alice was used to staring at and analyzing, wondering if Susan was pretty or beautiful, wondering if the fascination of it came from Susan or from herself. "Who do you think you've looked at most in your life?" Craig once asked at the dinner table. "Denny," said Susan. "My dog," said Noah (having only just met Rya). "My mother," said Alice, ashamed to tell the truth. "Think of all that time at the breast, before you can remember." Nonetheless, the truth was Susan. Alice walked around the bed, turned back the coverlet, and got in. Susan said, "I'm glad I have one day before going back to work. Do you think it's stupid to take my vacation so early? Maybe by August I'll be going crazy."

"I don't know."

"I wish you'd tell me what's eating you."

"It's hard."

"To tell me?" She emphasized the "me" in disbelief.

"Especially you."

Alerted, Susan looked at her suspiciously.

Alice squirmed under the comforter. "I missed you. Snuggle up."

Susan snuggled up.

And then, when Alice had her securely in her arms, she told her. After a minute or so, Susan disengaged herself and got up, went into the bathroom, and closed the door.

If she had expected wailing, she should not have, for Susan was not that way. In fact, her silence in the bathroom rather frightened Alice, while also pinning her to the bed, where she lay hardly breathing, listening with her whole rooted body for a crack in Susan's reserve, even the sound of the toilet flushing or water running. Susan was better at giving sympathy than receiving it. Hadn't Denny said so himself? Taking care of Susan when she had the flu or her wisdom teeth out was like looking after a hedgehog, Denny said. "I just put the food by the bedroom door and knock," he laughed. At once Alice could see Denny alive for the first time that day, leaning at you, teasing, intimate, his eyes bright with affection and a joke at your expense. The vivid image made her catch her breath and ache for some sound, some breakage or flow from the bathroom. But there was none, and Alice, perfectly still in her warm bed, the covers up to her ears as Susan had left them, went to sleep.

Must have gone to sleep, for she had the sense of waking sometime later, or partly waking. At first she felt delicate and victimized, as she had earlier in the day, ill but with a safe and definite disease. The door to the bathroom was open now, and Susan was moving about like a mother in Alice's room, folding clothes, picking up shoes, putting caps on bottles and taking them into the bathroom. In the bathroom the light was full upon her as she went back and forth past the doorway, in and out of Alice's sleepy gaze. Always well groomed, she was even more so now, two long bobby pins like arrows in her straight shining hair, her nightgown buttoned to the throat, her face absolutely clean, splashed thirty times with lukewarm water. How typical of Susan, she thought, to face devastation with cleanup. How typical of herself to face it in bed. The light in the bathroom went off and Alice heard Susan go out the other bathroom door and walk down the hallway toward the kitchen. "Are you all right?" she called out, but there was no answer. Now, Alice foresaw, would come the test of friendship, the great task of taste and tact that she, always indulged by Susan, always advised, encouraged, and strengthened, might or might not accomplish. For this they had no practice, no trial runs of adversity in which Alice could take the role of comforter, Susan be comforted. Susan never needed comfort, avoided it, in fact. Alice could too easily envision a kind of well-meant estrangement, in which Susan turned in and in on herself and Alice reached out only clumsily or imperceptibly.

Jim had often said about her that she had no sense of timing or nuance; in her desire for him she was afraid to touch him and then elbowed him in the ribs. Driving their old car, she waited forever to make left turns, and then, nervous because of the cars accumulating behind her, darted into traffic. A sense of rightness she did not have, never had, could not learn. Alice sighed with love and sympathy for Susan, knowing that if she left the expression of it to her instincts she was bound to fail, bound to go too far, or, more likely, fall short. After a while, after thinking that the best thing to do would be to stay awake so that Susan could come in and talk if she felt the least bit like it, Alice fell again into a sound sleep.

In the brightening glimmer of the sun rising on another perfect day, Alice awoke to Susan's quiet exhortations. A warm breeze off the river fluttered the spider plant and the grape ivy hanging in the window. Alice pushed her hair out of her face and sat up in bed. "What?"

"Are you mad that I woke you?"

"Of course not. How are you?"

"I don't know. I've been up all night. It's been two weeks since I've seen Denny, so it's all sort of abstract. I think I have to go there and look for myself. Basically, I feel awful, I guess."

"Don't you want to get some sleep?"

"I can't right now. I want to go home and be there."

Even having seen the bodies taken away, Alice could only

imagine another shock like she'd had the day before. She said, "You don't really."

"I really do!"

"Susan, it's awful to go in there. I don't think you quite understand."

"I understand."

"Please don't be mad."

"I'm not mad!"

"I found them! I know what it was like!"

"But they're not there to be found. I'll go by myself."

Biting her lip, wondering how she had gotten off the track, Alice threw back the blanket, put her foot to the floor, and remembered the police barrier she had seen them nail over the door and lock after taking out the bodies. Afraid to mention it, she let herself get dressed, brush her teeth, hurry as if they actually had some goal. She hated this clumsiness of hers. She could have remembered the barrier the moment Susan broached the subject, told her calmly that they couldn't go in, would have to wait for Honey to let them in, would have to apprise him, probably, of every move they made. Here she was, rushing down West End Avenue at dawn, afraid to speak, afraid to tell the truth. High cirrus clouds skated east over the roofs of the clean buildings and their clean shadows. In the vestibule of one building, a wino sat up and ran his fingers through his stiff hair, smoothing it down, as if even for him it was a new day. The wooden soles of Alice's clogs rang on the pavement, and her spirits, once again in spite of themselves, lifted. After all, how was she to know what would be there, what would happen? Anything could happen.

It was there. Susan looked at it for a long time, reading and rereading the black stenciled words, not speaking. Alice made herself wait patiently the whole time, not offering breakfast, not offering any solace, until Susan really and truly had had her fill of the familiar hallway and the well-known door with its strange accessory. Alice didn't know what to expect. Perhaps not tears, and, at first, Susan seemed to have no reaction, except ravenous curiosity. Alice looked tactfully away. Finally, Susan said, in a soft, pressed-out voice, "I'm furious, you know. This is enraging."

Alice made the appropriate wordless response. She hadn't thought of it that way.

When they came back out on the street, the bustle of church goers, newspaper readers, bagel eaters, dog walkers, and parking place hunters had begun.

Over breakfast Alice tried to ease into the topic with a description of Detective Honey. Susan was calm now, and Alice wondered if she was really paying attention. "I don't know what he thinks, Susan. He's got that enigmatic cop shit down to a T. Half the time I'm with him, I think he thinks I did it, and I wonder if I did. Trying to figure him out is like staring at a bright light. Afterwards you see a lot of things that aren't there."

"Does he seem very smart, as if he'll be able to solve it?" She sounded almost indifferent.

"I can't tell that either. There's a kind of structure to the whole experience of being with him, like going to the doctor. You sort of do what's expected."

"How did he refer to Denny and Craig?"

"Let me see. Mostly as Mr. Minehart and Mr. Shellady, and a couple of times as 'the victims.' "

Susan wrinkled her nose.

"It's very public, isn't it?"

Susan nodded. Alice thought that here she was eating again, eating a good breakfast of bagels and fresh cream cheese and smoked whitefish, eating with relish as she had at Ray's the night before. It was strange but reassuring to eat this way, to love her food with conscious appreciation. Continually on the verge of losing her appetite, she savored every morsel, considering how odd it was that in such crises she and Susan, and Ray, and Noah, Rya, Denny's parents, and Detective Honey, would make time for this eating two, three, or even four times a day. She said, "He doesn't think you're coming home until this evening. You don't have to call him until then."

"What would that look like? Besides, I want to find out what they know."

Alice licked her lips. "That's one thing I don't think we're going to find out, sweetie."

Susan lifted her own bagel, blushing with lox, and said, "Oh, my God," and put it down again.

"What?"

"Nothing. I'll tell you later." She glanced around the deli. In a moment she said, "How carefully did they search the apartment?"

"I don't know. They looked everywhere. They probably came back later. Why?"

"Not here." Then, "Tell me some more about Honey."

"I don't think he's much older than we are, but he seems a lot older. He's sort of paunchy, I guess."

"Did you like him in a human way?"

"I sort of did. But I couldn't tell if that was because I was supposed to or because I really did."

"Did you feel like co-operating with him?"

"I felt like there was no question about that."

Susan breathed a deep catching sigh and said, "What are we talking about? This is so impossible." She put her face in her hands. Almost against her will, Alice continued to eat.

When they left the restaurant, it was nearly nine-thirty. Susan said, "You know, I have to call the Mineharts. They're expecting to hear from me. It's been nearly twenty-four hours. I'm ashamed of that," but when Alice turned up Broadway, Susan steered her instead down Seventy-sixth Street toward Riverside Park. Joggers and dog walkers were out in fleets. After a full week of adamantine blue skies, the grass along the river had lost the freshness briefly attained during a damp April, but the trees swayed in full, sybaritic leaf. They walked along the river toward the boat basin, and Alice said, "Does the weather make you feel better or worse?"

"Better, but strange. I don't know."

"What is going on?"

Susan glanced around them, and waited for a pursuing jogger to pass. When there was not even a tree within ten yards, she stopped, looked at Alice, and said, "When I left New York two weeks ago, there was ten thousand dollars' worth of cocaine in a box in the kitchen."

"Ten *thousand?*"

Susan nodded.

"Is that a lot?"

"It didn't seem so to me, but I was told it was very pure, etcetera, blah blah."

"Whose was it?"

Susan didn't answer, instead bent down and picked up a chip of broken pavement and tossed it over the fence at the river. Finally, she said, "It wasn't all paid for."

"Who was supposed to pay for it?"

"Craig." She looked at Alice piercingly, then looked away. Finally, she said, "Denny, too."

"I didn't think Denny did a lot of cocaine."

"He didn't. Neither of them could afford more than the occasional hit." Susan inhaled deeply, perhaps at the use of the past tense. "This time they were going to sell most of it, and give the rest to the band at that Providence gig." She picked up another piece of the pavement and began to crumble off tiny fragments between her fingers. "They thought they would sell enough to pay for it, and then have a party with the rest."

"Ten thousand dollars?"

"Denny and I had a tremendous fight about it before I left. They weren't making any real effort to sell it, and I was afraid it would just go right up their noses."

"Ten thousand dollars!"

"You know how much they were getting paid for that Providence gig? The whole band, five hundred per night, not including expenses. And the one before that, up in Irvington, that one-night deal, was only seven-fifty. Split four ways, with something for Ray to help set them up? Shit."

"Who did they owe the money to?"

"I was afraid to ask. They got the cocaine through Ray."

"Ray Reschley?"

"None other."

"Jesus!"

"Ray could have gotten it anywhere." Susan spoke bitterly.

"I think he just talks big, don't you? He's really just our boy from Minnesota. You know that."

"No, Alice, I don't know that any more. All I know is that two weeks ago there was ten thousand dollars' worth of cocaine in my apartment, and yesterday Denny and his best friend were found murdered in the same apartment. Murdered!"

"Ray couldn't have anything to do with that."

"Not intentionally, maybe. But maybe those contacts he had have a way of getting out of hand."

"Oh, Susan!"

"Oh, Alice!"

They turned and walked up the pavement, avoiding, by instinct, the various viaducts and secret places of Riverside Park. "Another thing," said Susan. "If the stuff was there, maybe the police found it, and they are going to think it was mine. I'm an official resident of the apartment, not Craig. Damn him! He always wanted to be the big guy! After Ray took him to all those parties for those tours that were coming in last Christmas, and he saw for himself all the weed and cocaine floating around, he just had to do the same thing, had to have a party like that, had to treat his band the way those people treat their bands. Do you know how many rock stars he referred to by their first names after that? As soon as they brought that stuff into the apartment, I knew the shit was about to hit the fan, and here it is."

"Was there anything else they might have found?"

"No. Denny was kind of off dope, and didn't want it around, so that was the only thing. As if that wasn't enough."

Alice thought of Detective Honey. A definite man who filled out his dark suit, Detective Honey would not approve of cocaine, not even overlook it. She glanced at Susan, another definite, substantial person. Ignorance was something a man like Honey, with at least some powers of perception, would never believe of Susan. Alice said, "If he asks you, you've got to tell him the truth."

"Who?"

"Detective Honey. If he asks about the cocaine, then you'll know they've found it, and you'll have to tell them exactly what you've told me."

"But I disapproved of it! I didn't want it in the house, or anywhere near me!"

"You've just got to tell them that."

"They aren't going to believe me."

"They aren't going to believe that you don't know anything about it."

"I've been gone for two weeks."

"Well, that's true. Yes, that is true, but you don't know what the police know, do you? They might be in touch with people who could tell them that it came into your place three weeks ago."

"A month."

"It's impossible for people like us to know what the police know. I'm just afraid you'll trap yourself for no good reason."

"Oh, hell!"

As they turned at Eighty-fourth Street to leave the park, Susan looked at Alice and declared, "I always knew Craig Shellady would get me into real trouble. Something I couldn't get out of by dipping into the savings account or putting my foot down. I've known that for twelve years. Now I don't forgive him. I blame him for all of this. That's what enrages me!"

"He's paid for it."

"No, he hasn't! I'm the one who's going to pay for it. You don't pay for anything by being dead. That's when you stop paying for it."

"Honey, he's dead! Really dead!"

"And Denny, too! However it happened, you know, Craig is to blame. He's the guilty party here. Nothing is ever going to change my mind about that." The light turned and they stepped off the curb into Riverside Drive.

3

T H E momentum of her daily life had carried Alice through the discovery of the bodies and past it, but when she unlocked her apartment to the ringing of the phone, she realized that the momentum was played out, and the real chaos of such an event as a semi-public double murder was about to crush them. For the time being she didn't answer the phone, but unplugged it. Ray would be trying to reach her, and Noah or Rya, possibly Jim, certainly Detective Honey, and any number of others wondering where Susan was. Susan turned without speaking and shuffled down the hallway toward the bedroom, visibly fatigued. There would be so much business to attend to—the burials, the services, the parents and other relatives, so much talk on the phone to be gotten through. She followed Susan, and found her flung across the unmade bed. Afraid to push, she said, "What are you going to do?"

"Sleep. Call the Mineharts first. God, I hate to make that call."

"Funeral home?"

"Oh, Jesus."

"We've got to do all that stuff."

"I know."

"What are you going to do with them?"

"His parents will want a complete funeral with priests in purple, open coffin—"

"They can't have *that*."

"Oh, Lord. Catholic cemetery, black limousines."

"What did Denny ever want?"

"The usual. Cremation over a bonfire with only his friends in attendance, then flinging his ashes to the four winds."

"Was he serious?"

"We only talked about it once, five or six years ago."

"Is there any will or anything?"

"I'm so tired I can't keep my eyes open. I have to call them. Will you dial? If a child answers, then ask for Mrs. Minehart. I couldn't stand hearing the voice of one of those kids." Denny's youngest sister was only six. Alice picked up the bedroom extension, plugged it in, and dialed the numbers Susan dictated. A youthful voice did answer, probably the ten-year-old. Alice asked for Mrs. Minehart, and when she came to the phone, anxious but polite, her voice clear and questioning, Alice gave the phone to Susan and left the room, closing the door.

In the kitchen she put the teakettle on to boil, found her favorite china teapot and her favorite cup, and sat down to wait. After a few minutes, she got up, went into the bedroom where Susan was now asleep, and threw a blanket over the shoeless, prostrate form of her friend. Looking at Susan, she tried not to panic, tried not to imagine the shambles Susan's affairs were now most certainly in. Of course there would be no wills, no insurance, no agreement on the final disposition of the bodies, of course there were debts, and not just illegal ones, of course there would be suspicion, and possibly trouble, from the police. All of this in addition to grief. Alice pulled the blanket down over Susan's feet, and Susan's head turned and her beautiful straight hair that shone like new pennies curved smoothly over her cheek. Grief would hit her hard, Alice thought as she went back to the kitchen, where, with her pot of tea and her window onto Eighty-fourth Street, she would sit in perfect silence for no less than two hours. Then she would plug in the phones again and answer the buzzer for the downstairs door.

She thought she should make a list of practical matters, things like people to call and arrangements to make, items that had been flooding her mind all morning, each with its attendant mental note that she couldn't forget that, but when she got up to get paper and to find a sharp pencil, every notion vanished, and she found herself staring out at Eighty-fourth Street, at the happy bustle of New Yorkers in shirt sleeves and backless dresses heading for Riverside Park and a walk in the sun, or for Broadway and a little harmless buying. Across the street and down a ways, an older woman in a bonnet was bedding plants in the three-foot strip of earth in front of her brownstone, and three floors above her another woman, in a bathrobe, was leaning far out of her apartment window, also bedding plants, in a window box, something flame colored, perhaps geraniums. At that height and facing south, she would have the sun for them. It was thought in the neighborhood that the brownstone one up from the corner of Riverside had a large roof garden. At least, trucks with huge redwood troughs had pulled up one day, and another day men had carried giant bags of soil and gravel and composted manure into the building. Alice did not think with envy of the fresh spinach and perfect tomatoes those roof gardeners undoubtedly enjoyed. After all, set like brooches along the sweep of Broadway were vegetable markets that presented to any city dweller with a few dollars the pick of East Coast crops. What she envied, and what she would have paid for those countless home deliveries to have, was the vista of sun-drenched green under the bell of heaven, and the silver plume of the river waving in the distance. On Eighty-ninth Street, some top floor resident had erected a solar collector that Alice felt proud and proprietary about, as, she suspected, did everyone who knew it.

That made her think of Ray Reschley's father, who, Ray said, was building a pair of windmills, one on top of the house and the other on top of the garage. He had gotten rid of the second car and filled half the garage with batteries to store the excess power. Average wind speed in Rochester, said Ray, was 12.8 miles per hour. Ray was a tinkerer, too, and as long as Alice had known him, he had been refining some project. Now he talked about selling his apartment and finding himself a top floor place. Average wind speed on the West Side was nearly ten miles per hour. He could find himself something with three bedrooms and have plenty of space to store the batteries. Alice wondered if he had the money for it, and then she wondered how much money he had. In that sense, Ray had obviously done better than any of them, no Hamlet, but a technical Horatio whom Craig, the very image of a Hamlet-to-be, had convinced to drop out of optometrist school. Now one of the most dependable sound men in New York, Ray earned more outfitting studios and working for record companies than any number of handsome guitar players. So what if his life was a confusing round of sexual passion and frustration, no domestic homosexual bliss but repeated cravings for men who didn't crave him. In a world of beauties, Ray, with his pink skin, pointed fingers, tiny feet, and swelling middle, was not even pretty. For the past year or eighteen months, he had found himself a new crowd, or so he said. Unlike most peer groups, this one carried knives, razor blades, even guns. Ray did not introduce them to any of his old friends, and Alice didn't often think of them. Once, angry, Craig had called them Ray's "imaginary playmates." Craig, in fact, had teased Ray a lot over the years, even after Ray's work for him had become a kind of noblesse oblige. Alice thought of Ray's remark that he had loved Denny and "even Craig, most of the time." He probably did.

They had all known each other for so long! Julie Zimansky had first whispered to her that this guy Ray Reschley kept calling her up all the time almost sixteen years before. Two years after that, Susan had lived down the corridor from Alice her first semester in college, and Christmas of that year, Susan had introduced her to Denny and his adopted brother, Craig. During her junior year, she had met Jim Ellis on her own, but he rapidly joined the group, and that summer the band had formed, stretching to include Noah Mast and his dog, Fred, both already graduates, since Fred accompanied Noah to classes and even into restaurants. When Fred was hit by a car, the whole group mourned, and when Rya came along, the whole group groaned, but eventually expanded to include her, like any family with marriageable children. When Jim ran off with Mariana, he lost all his friends as well as his wife, and Alice sometimes wondered if that might not have been his hidden purpose all along. He called them on Christmas and said everything was just great, like a dutiful prodigal son, but they only heard third or fourth hand about the stillbirth of Mariana's baby. Alice looked out the window to where the woman in the bonnet was tramping down her flower bed—*Impatiens*—and began again to panic. How was it that they had jogged along from day to day, from dinner to dinner and gig to gig and apartment to apartment never comprehending the dangers around them? Why did Denny hand out keys to his apartment, why did Craig sleep with Rya and sample speed and heroin on the Coast, why did Ray flirt with wielders of knives, how did ten thousand dollars become so debased a sum that Craig and Denny didn't even worry about owing it, and how was it that this life seemed still continuous with the rest of their lives, and the lives of their mothers and fathers on the slow, spacious northern plains? Even Craig spoke of the death of his parents as a strange anomaly, not a symptom of some evil reality. Yes, they died, but numerous aunts, uncles, and friends flowed into the breach, and that kindly, God-loving and God-fearing, happily populous family, the Mineharts, enveloped him, adored him, admired his edgy difference from themselves. "Oh, that Craig!" was what Mrs. Minehart said ten times a day when Alice spent the weekend there once. It was as if they had rolled into Minneapolis and then into New York without ever losing the sublime Midwestern confidence that if you left the doors unlocked while you slept, the neighbors down the road might stop by and drop off the tools you needed to borrow. If they had grown up in New York, would they have been more wary of the dangers or more tempted by them? The drop from the middle class that was a little slope in Rochester was a precipice in New York City. How had they not known that? Unlike some of the others, Alice had never spoken contemptuously of the middle class. A job, an apartment, a washing machine, some money to spend, these were goods, not evils.

Alice stood up and stretched, thinking of her job, her apartment, her washing machine, her spending money. Of course they were secure, of course they were. Ray and Susan and Noah and Rya and all the rest of them had no claim on her tight little life. Whatever the police did or Ray's friends did, the library would go on, employing her to catalogue and do reference. But as she thought of them one by one she loved them one by one, yearned to embrace them, to take each one into her tight little life and divvy up the library proceeds, share out the rooms, feed and embrace and reassure. Briefly she fantasized some fending off of the police with weapons, but then she looked down on Eighty-fourth Street, at people walking around, going in and out of apartment buildings, people she had seen so often in the last five years that she almost knew them; wanting to stay a part of that bustle, too, she did not know what to think. That was her usual frame of mind now, not knowing what to think. She picked up the phone jack, flipped it a few times with her index finger, then plugged it in. It rang at once.

PAUSING outside the police station on Eighty-second Street, Susan ran her hands down the front of her dress and said, "How do I look?"

"Respectable. Neat. Tired."

"Still?"

"Aren't you?"

"Beat."

"Don't worry. You might even like him."

"I might."

"He ought to love you." Alice kissed Susan on the cheek for confidence and followed her into the station.

Detective Honey, whom they had called beforehand, came out to meet them, extending his hand congenially. He reminded Alice of a farmer, a friend of her father who was now dead. As a gesture of affection, he had been in the habit of putting his big hands on Alice's eleven-year-old shoulders and cracking her back. His hands were like rocks from years of farming, and the pain of his affection hadn't been eased by his cheery, teasing words.

As Honey placed the chairs and offered them coffee, as she herself smiled warmly in response to his inquiries, she assumed that he suspected them, innocent as they were, and that if he could get evidence on them of any kind, even the most circumstantial, he would use it against them rather than pursue further investigation. Wasn't it well known that the police were simply overwhelmed with work?

"You've been in the Adirondacks, Miss Gabriel?"

"I got back last night."

"How was the weather up there? Isn't this rather early in the season for the Adirondacks?" He looked up at a wall calendar and Alice's gaze followed his. May 11.

"The weather was quite good, actually. I can't afford to go during the season." Susan finished with a smile, and set her purse on the floor beside her chair.

"You are employed at?"

"I manage Chops, on Broadway."

"Chops?"

"It's a boutique specializing in imported clothing, mostly from France and Italy."

"Expensive?"

"Very."

"And you can't afford to go to the Adirondacks during the season?"

"I don't buy my clothes at Chops, either."

Alice smiled and bit her lip. Honey chuckled, then settled more deeply, more intimately into his seat and tried again. "You are aware that Miss Ellis here found the bodies?" He smiled at Alice.

"Mrs." This time Susan said it. "Yes, she told me all the details. I was hoping that you would have something more to tell me."

Alice marvelled that Susan was hardly susceptible to Honey at all, that his very presence didn't call from her a stream of talk, as it had from Alice, as it did even now, when he attended Susan, and remarks, questions, conciliatory observations piled up behind Alice's teeth. Honey said, "Let me just get a few facts down here, then I can let you go." He coughed. "Your name is Susan Gabriel, you live at 523 West Seventy-fourth Street, you manage the clothing store 'Chops' at where on Broadway?"

"Seventy-eighth Street. I've been the manager there for about four years."

"Before that?"

"I managed a housewares shop on Seventy-second, near Amsterdam."

"Your duties?"

"Hiring and firing, watching over, but not doing, the books, helping the owners decide what to buy, making daily decisions about damaged merchandise, shoplifting, window design. Maid of all work."

"You've lived in Manhattan six years, like Miss Ellis?"

"We came together."

"With Mr. Minehart and Mr. Shellady?"

"And Mr. Mast and Mr. Reschley and Mr. Ellis."

"Yes, the other members of the band."

"Jim Ellis wasn't a musician," offered Alice. "He is my former husband."

"A wholesale migration, then?" Honey smiled. Alice could not help smiling with him, but Susan remained sober faced. "In those days," she said, "it seemed perfectly natural. We lived in Chicago for about a year, and before that we were in Minneapolis."

"You have been close friends for a long time, then?"

"The band formed in the summer of 1968."

"There have never been any falling-outs in all those years?"

"No," said Susan.

"What about—" Honey flipped back a couple of pages in his notebook—"Mr. Dale Nolan?"

"Dale was the original drummer in the band. He moved to California some years ago, to be with another band. He wasn't a particularly close friend, though."

"There was some friction between him and the band?"

"Some."

Honey waited for Susan to go on. So did Alice. She did not, until at last he prompted her. "What sort of friction?"

"He couldn't get along with Craig. Craig thought he dragged the tempo."

"Did he?"

"I don't know."

"And was he successful in this other band?"

"Very."

"More so, for example, than he would have been if he had stayed?"

"Probably."

"But he wasn't a close friend?"

"No. He had other friends all along. He saw the band as just a job."

"There have been other drummers?"

"Countless."

"How did they get along with the band?"

"Fine with Noah and Denny. Craig had his ups and downs with them."

"The latest is Mr. Jake Zimmerman?"

"Yes."

"How long has he been with the band?"

"A couple of months."

"How did you get along with Mr. Shellady, Miss Gabriel?"

"Fine."

"Did you have your ups and downs?"

"Craig was a very moody person, with a hot temper, but also rather charming."

"Did you see much of him?"

"Yes, he was at our apartment most of the time."

"That was a satisfactory arrangement?"

"We were used to it, and it is a large apartment." Susan took the long bobby pin out of her hair and replaced it with deliberation. "Do you have brothers, Detective Honey?"

"Yes, two." Alice tried to imagine them.

"Craig was very much my boyfriend's brother. I had to accept that a long time ago." She paused, thinking, and then, apparently, decided to go on. "I liked Craig, but I understood his limitations. Denny loved him in spite of them, or maybe because of them, and I had to accept them, too. Denny and Craig were a package deal."

"What were these limitations?"

"His hot temper wasn't just a hot temper. It was a kind of psychotic interlude. He would become very, very abusive and paranoid. And he couldn't manage his money very well."

"Did he give rein to his temper physically?"

"If you mean, did he hit people, no, he didn't. He was very eloquent. He didn't need to hit people."

"Did he take drugs?"

"Drugs weren't the reason for his problems. Alcohol made it worse, though, and in the last few years he's pretty much quit drinking."

"What do you think was the reason for his problems?"

"His parents were both killed when he was twelve, for one thing. I've heard that his father had some problems, but I don't know. They were killed in a car accident."

"Mr. Minehart remained loyal to him? To the point of practically living with him?"

"Craig loved Denny, like everyone else. Denny could calm him down, and he never really got mad at Denny. Craig lived with

Denny's family off and on after the accident, except for a couple of years when his aunts and uncles sent him to a military school."

"He didn't stay there for long?"

"He attempted suicide, I think."

"In other words, Craig Shellady was a very troubled person?"

"Not exactly. Not day to day. It sounds worse than it is just listing it like this. He was very charming most of the time. Ask Alice."

Suddenly both their gazes turned on Alice. She nodded immediately, without thinking. "He was very compelling," she said, wondering if someone like Honey could understand limitless warmth, limitless oblique and edgy insight. "I can't describe it."

"Did he ever abuse you, Miss Ellis?"

"Mrs. No. He hardly ever got mad at women."

"Sometimes?"

Alice looked at Susan, who said, "He threatened to kill me once. And there was a woman he was deeply involved with a few years ago who brought it out in him."

"Her name?"

"Iris North."

Honey wrote the name down. Alice detected a certain elevation in his level of interest, and said, "She's dead. She died of a drug overdose about six months after they broke up."

"Did Mr. Shellady take drugs?" This time he meant to be answered. Susan inhaled deeply, to Alice's dismay. Finally, she said, "Sometimes. Once more than now."

"What kind of drugs?"

"Marijuana. Speed for a while in California, and heroin, actually, there, too."

"Cocaine?"

Alice felt Susan's head turn in her direction, but did not lift her eyes from her lap. "Yes." She spoke firmly. Alice began to be afraid. Honey shifted in his seat, which creaked loudly. He said, "I understand that the bodies are still at the morgue."

"I've contacted a funeral home."

"Work on them has been completed, so they can be released to you or to Mr. Minehart's parents any time. May I ask what will be done with them?"

"I don't know. The Mineharts are Catholic, but I would prefer cremation. The kind of funeral they want, no one can pay for, I'm afraid."

Honey made a little noise of sympathy, then went on, somewhat expansively. "We also have finished with your apartment, Miss Gabriel, and the police lock will come down tomorrow morning. If you would prefer not to clean it yourself, I can give you the names of firms who would do a good job."

"Thank you."

"Thank you for coming over." He made it sound as if they had had a choice. Alice wished he would chew cigars and snarl at them. Then she might trust him.

On the street, once again, she was tempted to turn toward Central Park. As if reading her mind, Susan said, "Let's go to the zoo."

It was like coming out of a powerful movie with a date—while yearning to ask what Susan thought, she was afraid to appear so unperceptive that she didn't already know. To make conversation, because any talk might lead into the subject, she said, "Ray and Noah will be there in an hour."

"Don't they have keys?"

"No. You have the only keys to my apartment."

"I wish I could say the same."

"Me, too."

"They can wait. It's a nice day." She fell silent. After a moment, she sighed deeply. Impulsively, Alice put her arm through the other woman's and drew close to her. At last she could say, gently, sympathetically, "What do you think?"

"Have you told him about that thing you had with Craig when Jim first moved in with Mariana?" Susan's arm, which had pressed softly into her soft side, seemed to Alice to grow angular and awkward. Nonetheless, she tightened her grip around it, saying, "That wasn't a thing. It was just craziness."

"Have you told him?"

"We only slept together three times."

"The more he knows, the more chance that he'll solve the murders."

"What would that tell him?"

Susan extricated her arm, but didn't say anything. The light changed as they approached Central Park West, and without hesitating they crossed the street and entered the park. When they had walked a short distance, Susan said, "I think the zoo is this way."

Alice could not help saying sharply, "I don't think I would call Craig's tempers 'psychotic interludes.' I think that's awfully strong." When Susan didn't answer, she said, "You made him sound like he should have been in an institution or something, as if you and Denny were his caretakers." Susan looked at her as if to say, Well, weren't we? and Alice raised her voice. "His temper was uncontrollable when he really lost it, but he didn't really lose it that often. He was a volatile person. He was also very charming and lots of fun to be with, and he paid attention to how people were feeling and could be very sympathetic."

"Really?"

"You know that!"

"When he was seeing Iris, he was in a state most of the time."

"Iris was crazy. She really was. I don't think you can blame most of that on Craig."

"He fell for her. He stayed with her for over a year."

"She was beautiful and she was smart. You said so yourself at the time. After that he was more or less trapped."

"Now there's something you can tell me all about."

"He thought he could help her."

"By beating her up?"

"Susan, she was picking guys up on the street that nobody knew and bringing them back to their apartment."

"So she needed to be slapped around a little?"

"I didn't say that! I don't know that." Alice was panting. She pushed her hair angrily out of her face and tried again. "Look, I admit Craig was different from other people. He was a jittery person. A feeling didn't go by that he didn't express. It could be irritating."

"You know what Craig did? He did the same thing all his life. He got a death grip on someone with one hand, and then he beat them up with the other. Or gave them a kiss. You never knew what to expect. The signals were never consistent. I think that's psychotic, not volatile."

"Why do you make him into this monster? He was just a guy. He was nice to me."

"Yes, I know." They entered the zoo through the back, picked up in the trickle of families with folding strollers. Through her own anger, Alice saw that Susan was angry, too, and she felt thoroughly compromised. Really, so what if Susan was wrong about Craig? If that was the way she had to take the death of her boyfriend, then she should have the right to take it that way. Alice made herself look at the brown bear in his cage. No amount of money, she always thought, could transform this menagerie into a zoological garden. She thought of Craig and their "thing." It was a pleasant thought. He had been very handsome and very kind when she needed it. As she stood in front of the bear, a shudder of desire closed her eyes, stopped her breath, constricted the arteries streaming from her heart. The soles of her feet prickled and she smiled, loving Craig briefly again; but she was used to thinking of that time in her life as madness. Every memory brought with it the fatigue of unceasing labor. The effort not to call Jim, not to walk past Mariana's building, not to cry at work, even to go to work rather than stay in bed all day, the effort not to talk about Jim and "it" hour after hour to every ear nearby had almost submerged her. With Craig, there had been a kind of mad relief to the madness: food and sex and skipping work to see morning movies at the Modern and talk of astrology and self-healing and The Eck and anything else that made the end of her marriage seem trivial. She turned away from the bear, following Susan through the gate into the main quadrangle. Knowing what she knew, how could she fight with Susan, who could have no idea of the tide of pain yet to come? She ran and caught up with her friend. "Susan," she said, "I didn't mean to fight with you."

"I know. I'm sorry. Let's go home."

"I have money. Let's take a cab." She reached into her pocket and extricated a five-dollar bill, opening her hand and holding it out to Susan as an offering. "Let's," said Susan.

AT DINNER, Susan told them that she would be arranging for a large Catholic funeral with limousines, then for the bodies to be flown to Minnesota. She told them how much it would cost. They gasped. After a moment, Ray said, "How are you going to pay for it?"

Susan looked around the table with a grimace and a jut of the chin and said, "Go into debt."

"Can't his parents help?" suggested Rya.

"With eight kids and two in college? They're going to pay for the shipment of the bodies and the cemetery plots."

"No insurance, huh?" said Ray.

"They were self-employed. Do you have insurance?" Susan grimaced again and picked up a tiny fragment of lettuce from her plate.

"As a matter of fact—"

"I found a funeral home up in the Bronx with a time payment plan. They've already picked them up." She looked around the table again, as if daring herself not to cry, or scream, or throw something. Soon, when it was still light, Rya and Noah and Ray

had gone. Alice said, "Susan, why do you think you have to—"
Susan turned away from her and walked down the hall to bed.

Alice cleared away the dishes and threw out cartons from the
take-out food. Tonight it had been Italian. Except for the anchovy
that Alice retrieved and stuck in her mouth, every morsel of
pasta, every drop of oil and sauce had been eaten. After wiping
the kitchen table, she turned resolutely from the dishes, got out
her list of things to do, and spread it out. At the top was that
command, "Call home." How, after hearing the sum of money
Susan had quoted at the dinner table, could she persuade her
father and mother that she was not in trouble? She looked out at
Eighty-fourth Street, where her parents had never been, basking
in the long vermilion rays of the late sun. A cab slid beneath her,
but only one. Eighty-fourth Street, neatly squared off and deserted,
grew blue and then black. Then the streetlights came on, and
across from her, a scattering of windows. Her parents never trav-
elled, wouldn't leave Rochester. When they thought of Alice,
they thought of her in her bedroom at home, not in her home in
New York City.

During her childhood, they hadn't taken vacations because her
father couldn't get away from the hardware store, and there was
so much to do around the new house (which he built). During
her adolescence, her mother, a pediatric nurse for a private clinic,
hadn't felt right about leaving "my babies," even for two weeks,
and now that all of Alice's grandparents were in their eighties
and nineties, there was just no telling what might happen while
Doreen and Hugh were away. In fact, between the lettuce season
and the raspberry picking, spraying the apple trees at ten-day
intervals, and then the harvest of tomatoes, peppers, and beans,
not to mention keeping the roses watered, sprayed and mulched,
there wasn't time to get away in the summer, they didn't like
what they'd heard about Florida in the winter, and there was too
much to do in Rochester during the rest of the year. Although
Alice would have liked to show off for her parents—to call a cab,

to take her mother to Saks and buy a dress for her, to order in French at a midtown restaurant, to sit in overstuffed chairs with her father at the Algonquin Hotel, Alice really didn't mind that they would never visit her, except that now they wouldn't know how to think about the recent events. They would imagine her living alone in New York, avoid telling her grandparents, and then spill it to them one by one, so that the clamor about her coming back to Rochester, or at least to Minneapolis, would be deafening. All six of her progenitors would call her secretly, without telling the others, just to let her know how much her safety meant to the other five, how, in spite of the confidence the caller had in her, the others were worried, shouldn't she come home, a good job couldn't be that hard to find. The only child of two only children, Alice considered herself the tip of the iceberg breaking the surface of the dark sea into the light of Manhattan. Truly she loved her miraculously surviving family tree (and two great-grandmothers had lived into Alice's teens) but she didn't want to live with them. And now they would think she was in trouble.

Her mother answered, even more whispery than usual. They talked about the weather in Minnesota (very changeable, that's the worst kind), about the garden, about the grandparents, about her father. "You must be psychic," said Doreen. "He wants to send you something."

"Uh, oh."

"I'll let him tell you."

"Do you want him to send it to me?"

"I don't have an opinion." That meant he had overridden Doreen's basic practical objection; now she simply thought it wasn't a good idea. "I'll get him."

"Ma!" But Doreen had turned away from the phone already, and Alice could hear her calling in the distance.

"Did she tell you?" Her father never greeted her, either in letters or on the phone. He always simply talked, as if she had just gone out of the room for a minute and returned. Alice said, "No, but I can imagine."

"Honey, you'll like this a lot, really you will."

"What is it?"

"It's all boxed up and ready to go."

"Good, Daddo, what is it?"

"A microwave oven. Radarange. It got to the store with a couple of big scratches in the finish, so rather than sending it back to the factory, I just thought I'd send it to you. Now look, honey, you just set it on the counter and plug it in."

"Thanks, sweetie."

"Sure. Say, have you seen this show called *Ain't Misbehavin'*?"

"No, but some friends of mine have tickets."

"I bought the records. Pretty good."

"Daddy, come to New York. We'll go see it." Guaranteed to get him off the phone. In a moment, she said to her mother, "Don't let him send it. I'll have to pick it up at the post office in a cab. It'll be a mess."

"I tried to tell him that, but the ball's rolling. Can you give it to some daycare center, or something?"

"I don't know any daycare centers. I'll ask the police what to do with it." But Doreen didn't perk up, didn't wonder what Alice might have to do with the police. The police in Rochester would know what to do with it, and have time to do it. Alice sighed. After talking for a moment about the new strawberry bed, a kind of earthen ziggurat in the middle of the garden, Alice hung up, unable to tell them after all.

She went into the living room. She was terribly ready for bed, but somehow afraid to go. It was better to stay near the still-warm phone, imagining her parents in Rochester. Her mother would have turned on "Masterpiece Theatre," and her father would have stuck his hands in his pockets and gone out to inspect the new ziggurat yet again. After "Masterpiece Theatre," Doreen would call her mother to say that she would call in the morning, then Alice's father would go through the house, locking doors and windows, buzzing the smoke alarms, sniffing all around the gas stove, turning down the heat if the day had been chilly. Then he, too, would go to bed, and sleep would come to them at once, and stay with them hour after hour. They were excellent sleepers. Alice stood again by the window, wondering if any relative of hers ever had insomnia. Was sleep the clue to their longevity? She sat down on the couch and rested her chin on the arm, gazing idly down Eighty-fourth Street toward West End. She almost never sat in the living room. The couch, a convertible, did not wear its machinery very comfortably, but still, from one window or another, she had probably gazed pensively down Eighty-fourth Street a hundred thousand times in the last five years.

A figure came down the other side of the street, and she recognized it as it stepped into the light of the building across the way as the man she'd shared the cab with the other day, last night? Henry. Henry Mullet. He pulled open the big door, reached with his key to the inner door, and disappeared. Alice imagined him crossing to the elevator, pressing a button, getting into the elevator, pressing another button, rising slowly in the shaft, getting out, crossing to his own door, fumbling with his keys, unlocking two, maybe three locks. Sure enough, the light went on in a window one floor above hers, and then in the window next to that one and the one next to that. After a moment, in the middle window of the blazing apartment, Henry Mullet himself appeared, with a beer, yawning. He looked out at Eighty-fourth Street, too, out at her in her dark window. He was handsome. Had she noticed that the night before? He unbuttoned his shirt and took it off, revealing a ribbed sleeveless undershirt. Alice wondered if he had ever seen her unconsciously naked, scooting down the hallway, secure in being alone. He drained the can of beer and, turning, threw it toward some invisible wastebasket. Alice reached for the overhead light, pulled the string, waved vigorously at Henry Mullet, who waved back, then pulled the string again. Henry Mullet laughed and turned away from the window. She could see the moldings of his walls, painted a dark color, possibly blue, over cream. Looking at them made her feel funny—contained, as if her apartment were a vessel in which she and Susan floated from one horror to the next. The lights went off across the street, and Alice sat back on the couch. She let her head slip back, and felt her mouth open. Soon she was asleep.

IN THE middle of raucous buzzing, she awoke with a start and kicked her shin into the coffeetable. There was silence, then, as she realized she was in the living room, the buzz, flat and blaring, came again. Her shin throbbed, and she sidled carefully around the table, also avoiding the sharp, high runner of her rocking chair. She had just enough wits to press "talk" instead of "door." "Who is it?" She cleared her voice and repeated, "Who is it?"

"Ray."

"Shit, Ray, it's the middle of the night."

"It's not that late. I need to talk to you."

She buzzed the door.

He appeared in a moment, oddly apparelled, a different incarnation from the one who had eaten dinner with her a few hours before. His very nice shirt and very tight jeans looked binding and uncomfortable. The shirt was unbuttoned nearly to his waist, revealing a few red hairs and a prominent breastbone. She stepped back into the apartment, and Ray followed. He obviously wasn't going to take time for preliminaries. He said, "Some people are waiting for me. Listen. You were the last person in Denny's apartment. What did you see there?"

"I saw dead people. Plants. Furniture. All the usual."

"Anything unusual? I mean, besides Denny and Craig?"

"I don't know. Honey asked me that. I don't remember."

"Just think about it."

"It's the middle of the night! You woke me up."

"Please. Think, okay?"

Alice inhaled deeply and rubbed her eyes. "I didn't see it, Ray. I don't know what it is, and I didn't see it."

"Think again. Did you look in any closets or cabinets in the kitchen or anything?"

"Of course not! What do you think I was doing there?"

"A box maybe, a tin box with poinsettias. On the coffeetable or on the floor, or on one of the other tables."

"You don't have to be so cagey, Ray. I know what you're talking about and I didn't see it. It was probably gone."

"Did Honey mention it?"

"No, Susan. She said it was supposed to have been gone two weeks ago."

Ray sighed doubtfully and buttoned one of the buttons on the shirt. "Maybe it was gone. Maybe they did sell it. Craig was sure he had a deal. You don't think—"

"What?"

"That the guy he was going to sell it to just killed them instead of paying—"

Alice smiled. Surely that was it. "Well, there wasn't any money there. I would have noticed that, I'm sure."

"I just wish I knew—" Ray, pacing around the room, looked out the window, then came back and said, "Listen. This is too important for you not to remember. It's got to come to you at some point, it just has. I'm sure it was the box with the poinsettias—"

"Are you going to tell Honey about this idea, or am I?"

"Does either one of us need to? It's just a theory. Craig didn't say anything definite. I don't want—"

"I can imagine."

"Are you going to tell him?"

"If he asked—"

"Well, obviously, if he asked, you'd have to, but you don't have to let him know that there might be something to ask about."

"Unless you have a sense of responsibility."

"Does a sense of responsibility have to include every little notion?"

"I don't know. I think maybe you should—"

"Don't say it. Leave it to me." He turned and kissed her on the cheek. "Let's talk about it tomorrow. Don't even think about it until tomorrow, okay?" He opened the door and disappeared down the stairs. Alice locked up carefully behind him, put up the chain, and went to the window. Although he must have left, he was too close to the building for her to see him. It was tempting not to think about it. A life of never thinking about it was quite easy to imagine. She thought of how the police had their own methods, much more reliable than gossip or speculation. She shivered, then walked down the hall toward her room.

4

ALICE'S Monday morning at the library was well advanced by the time Susan called, her voice furred with sleep. Alice had been cataloguing, rather peaceful, impersonal work that gave her a spurious sense of distance from the events of the weekend. On her coffee break, she could not bring herself to mention the murder to Laura, Sidney, and Howard. When they asked her what she had done during her two perfect days, she didn't answer.

At the very sound of Susan's voice, her heart swelled painfully in sympathy. Didn't she remember with absolute clarity how the moment of awakening was the worst moment of the day, a hole of a moment out of which, some days, one never even climbed? Susan, however, said that she felt much better, strengthened by her fourteen hours of sleep and by the task Detective Honey, who had just called, had given her. She needed Alice's help in remembering everyone who would have or could have had access to a set of keys. Alice groaned.

"I know," said Susan. "Can I meet you for lunch so we can brainstorm it? He sounded so disapproving. I have this vision of us flinging keys out of a basket like flower petals at a wedding."

"Bring some pastrami sandwiches," said Alice. "We can eat on the steps of the library. I only have half an hour today."

The list filled two pages of lined secretarial paper. Two pages! thought Alice. "Only two pages," said Susan. It included people Alice had never heard of as well as people she had not only heard of, but whose records she owned and played. "I didn't know he was a friend of Denny's." She pointed to a name on the first sheet of paper.

"He wasn't." Susan pursed her lips angrily. "Craig met him in California and gave him a set of keys, in case he ever needed a place to stay in New York. As if the record company wouldn't put him up at the Waldorf. Craig just wanted to be able to say that 'Kenny had keys to my place.' Except that it wasn't his place."

Alice counted the names on the list. "Do you really think you gave away forty-seven keys?"

"There were only six or eight sets that we ever had made, but any key can be duplicated. Honey said we should write down the names of anyone who might have had one or might have borrowed one." After a moment of regarding the leisurely lunchers and eager pigeons on the steps of the library, she went on, "And I don't even know who Ray's friends are. Talk about a doorway into the void."

"Say!" exclaimed Alice, but then she hesitated. Had Ray really been to see her in the middle of the night? The incident was so brief that until Susan started talking about him, Alice had forgotten it. She said, "Ray wouldn't give away keys to your apartment, would he? He's always kept those people separate from us. He's not crazy. I mean, he may like the sense of danger he feels with them, but he does recognize the danger. Anyway—"

Susan interrupted her distractedly. "That's the way it seems, or at least, it did seem."

"Listen to this—" How would she state it? Alice paused.

Susan filled the pause, warming to an angry glow. "I know that's where he got the cocaine. Who's to say that somebody didn't get impatient about waiting for the money? Who's to say that Ray, having failed as the go between, didn't hand over the key for an evening, so that the dealer could impress upon Craig how much he wanted his payment? It's not exactly Ray I distrust. But Craig was always dismissive and belittling with Ray. He liked him, but he always teased him and patronized him, and he never saw that it hurt Ray's feelings. So, what if some guy was pressuring Ray and threatening him, why should he put up with it, when he could just lend the key for a few hours? It might be good for Craig to be taught a lesson." She was bitterly sarcastic.

Alice said, "It all seems to revolve around the cocaine, doesn't it?"

"What cocaine? That's the question. Maybe it was really gone. Maybe they did what Denny said they were going to do two weeks ago."

"What if we told Honey all this?"

"What if? I don't know. Do you ever talk about drugs to a cop, voluntarily?"

"What did they keep it in?"

"What?"

"The cocaine. How much is that much? A salt shaker full? A breadbox full?"

"In between. They kept it in various containers. Fruitcake tin, plastic box, that kind of stuff. Craig talked about having a brass-bound cherrywood box made, all lined with some special metal."

"Was he doing that much coke?"

"No! That's what made me so mad! He just spouted these ideas. He had this vision of himself surrounded by all the best accouterments. There might not have been money to put gas in the car, but Craig and Denny were always discussing these huge purchases—land in New Mexico, beach property near Big Sur, three- and four-thousand-dollar guitars, custom-made oak wall systems, thousands of dollars' worth of quilts that we were going to buy in Iowa and Minnesota and bring back East, or take out West."

Alice was determined not to get off the subject. "Would the coke have been hidden away? Would the cops have looked for it? Honey said the autopsies showed no suspicious indications, didn't he? That must mean no sign of drugs."

"Possibly."

"Maybe we should talk to him about this."

"Well, what do you remember? You were there before anyone else. Any boxes on the table—that fruitcake box, or something about that size?"

Alice closed her eyes, conjuring up the scene, the coffeetable in Susan's apartment. But it was too easy. She had been there so many times that the scene, with and without the box, or another box, or all sorts of debris on the coffeetable came readily to her. She shook her head. "Maybe it will come to me when I'm not thinking about it. We could just ask Honey, you know."

"Could we? It scares me just to think about it. In fact, it enrages me to think about it! It's unbearable! Everything is unbearable."

Alice looked away. After the proper amount of time, she said, "What shall we do tonight?"

"I'm going to clean the place up. There are locksmiths and cleaning people there right now, but they'll be gone by four."

"I said I would help."

"You don't have to."

"I want to, really." Alice knew that she should tell about Ray's late night visit, but she felt oddly protective of him, with his pale prominent breastbone and tight clothes. She said, "Was Rya sleeping with Craig?" The instant denial she expected did not come. "I don't know" was what Susan said.

"Then probably not, huh?"

"I couldn't say yes, I couldn't say no. Denny couldn't either. They got close in some way, and it's hard imagining a platonic friendship"—in spite of herself, Alice chuckled—"but it's even harder to imagine her cheating on Noah, don't you think?"

"That's what I thought."

Susan did not ask her when she thought this, and Alice was

unwilling, for the moment, to tell her, even to mention Ray's name. Although she hadn't seen too much of him in the last year, there had been a time when the two of them, apparently unable to stand by themselves, had leaned against each other like a couple of playing cards, not solid, not capable of supporting any weight, but at least upright. She had listened to the tale of his many loves, he had told her that she really was pretty, distinctive looking, unusual. She had knitted him a sweater, he had built her a desk, with a drawer, his first piece of dovetailed work. Together they had gone to bars. When someone unattractive came over, they sat closer together and held hands. When someone attractive came over, whichever of them not under scrutiny excused himself or herself and went to the bathroom. Alice had met George Hellmut that way, and Ray had met Lonnie and Rick, whose last names Alice never knew. She wrapped up the flavorless remains of her sandwich and said, "I've got to get back to work."

"I'll take this to Honey. He wants to see me anyway."

"When do you have to go back to the store?"

"I told them Wednesday."

"Surely they wouldn't mind if you took another day or two?"

"They offered me the whole week." She stood up and brushed crumbs off her skirt. "But look at you. I envy you." She waved her arm across the facade at the top of the steps. "A mighty fortress is our library."

"Meet you after five?" Alice leaned forward to kiss Susan on the cheek.

"Your place."

"I'll think of you all afternoon."

Susan departed briskly, pausing only at the trash can to balance the crumpled bag containing Alice's half-eaten sandwich on the crest of all the refuse. At the corner, Alice lost sight of her.

THEY spent the evening cleaning Susan's apartment, because she was bound and determined to move back into it. The firm Susan had hired to take the blood out of the rug and the orange upholstery of the two chairs had done a fair job, at least on the two chairs. On the rug, Alice was not sure. Perhaps she saw faint, translucent smears, but perhaps they were hallucinations, or spots before her eyes. Susan put on her rubber gloves and began in the bathroom. Alice saw at once that it was not to be specific spots they would be scouring away, but as much as possible of the whole experience, the whole interval during which the murderer had come and inhabited and left, the interval of the resting, stiffening corpses, the interval of the police boots and police investigation. By cleaning, they were going to take a little tuck in time, and after neatly seaming together Friday night and Sunday night, they were going to cut the rest away and throw it out.

Alice began on the kitchen. In a cloud of ammonia, she washed down cabinets and windows and walls and floor. Twice she called to Susan, "Are you all right?" and twice Susan answered, clearing her throat and with a catch in her voice, that she was. Otherwise, the only sounds in the apartment were Alice's own rubbings and swishings. Although she had looked steadily at the orange chairs in the next room, and knew that they were empty, it was hard to believe it. After the counters were dry, she set all of the dishes upon them, and changed the shelf paper. She found herself panting, and made herself drink some juice that they had brought from her place, standing in the kitchen doorway and staring at the empty, certainly empty chairs. But as soon as she turned away, it was impossible, once again, to shake the notion that they were out there. She washed all the dishes, put them back, all the cups, all the glasses, all the pots and pans and tin foil baking utensils, all of the pieces of silverware, one by one. Craig's head, especially, had been grimly raw and bloody, dropped back, but violently turned with the force of the shot. Dish towels and aprons and tablecloths and placemats she wadded into a large ball and stuck into a garbage bag, to be taken to her place and thrown into the washing machine. At least Susan had not seen them, had not even seen the stains, had certainly not had to endure the odor (was there an odor?). She rinsed off jars and cans of food, working faster, pouring more ammonia every time she thought of the odor. What if it got into walls and floors and furniture? What if, after the cleaners and solvents faded away, it was there, always? She wiped with a damp sponge boxes of cereal and bags of sugar and flour. Denny was not a cook. He and Craig had sat in those chairs countless times, laughing, arguing, waiting for food that she and Susan were fixing. At the thought, Alice felt the stirrings of a constricting pain at her breastbone, a pain that, along with these shallow, quick breaths, was familiar from the months of Mariana. She sat in one of the kitchen chairs, put her head between her knees and tried to breathe as slowly and as deeply as she could. If Susan came in, she would send Alice home and finish alone. Alice pressed her fingers into her temples and sat up. Finally, she got up and began to scour the sink. This time, the image that floated into her mind and fastened there was of herself and Susan, axed to pieces, in the bathroom, in the kitchen. Neither had spoken in at least half an hour. Perhaps, in the flurry of cleaning sounds, someone could ease into the apartment and pick them off one at a time. The real horror would be to turn and see, for the first time, a grinning stranger in the kitchen doorway. The ensuing dismemberment—

"Didn't you hear me?" said Susan. "I'm finished." Right in her ear. Alice put her hand over her mouth and closed her eyes. Finally she said, "I've been having the willies."

"It's not hard. I don't think we should split up."

Once the bathroom and the kitchen had been done, and the hallway both dusted and mopped, they were faced with a painful choice. Susan had to clear her throat before asking, "Well, what now?"

The bedroom she and Denny had shared? Where all of his clothes were hung or thrown just as he had hung or thrown them? Where his pennies sat in a pile on the dresser and his shoes lined up under the bed? Where the book he had been halfway through reading lay facedown beside the bed, its back broken?

The spare room? Where the boys kept the amp and the speakers and the preamp, and all the other stuff they practiced with and carried, at times, to smaller gigs, not to mention their guitars— Guild F50 twelve-string, Martin D28 six-string, a little Alvarez, cheap but with a sweet tone, Craig's big old Fender, the Ovation they'd bought for fun once and abandoned, Denny's electric Gibson, Craig's "investment"—an ornate Washburn banjo that he didn't know how to play, but the price of banjos was rising faster than anything, and this one had musical notes inlaid in mother of pearl all up the neck. And wasn't there a dobro in the closet?

The living room? The unspeakable living room, where faint salmon smears on the beige rug smote even the eyeless backs of their heads and the insensate soles of their feet?

Alice said, "It's after ten. Let's go back to my place and then do this tomorrow."

"You go on," said Susan.

"Let's do the living room, then. When I'm in another room, I keep thinking that they're in here."

"When I had the water running in the bathroom, it was like I could hear Denny moving around the apartment." She got out the vacuum cleaner, and Alice pulled back the chairs. When the whole carpet was thoroughly swept and Susan was rewinding the cord, Alice said, "Don't live here! This is too grisly! Live with me! I've got scads of room!"

Susan shook her head, and began lifting the couch cushions. There were pennies, crumbs, bobby pins, two flat picks.

"I want you to. I can't imagine anything better. There've always been men and we've never done it. We should do it."

"I don't want to run away."

"I knew you were going to say that. It's not—"

Susan stepped back, her eyelids dropping briefly, a stubborn sign. "Besides, I want to live alone for a while. I can afford this."

"How can you want to live alone after—"

"The locks have been changed. I even had them put in one of those French ones that haven't ever been broken into."

"I saw, but—"

Susan lifted up the cushions of the orange chairs. As clean as new.

"It's not rational to want to live here. Besides I want to be with you."

"Now I have to be rational?"

"No, but—"

"It is rational to live here. That's exactly what it is. This is a wonderful apartment. We were lucky to get it and I'd be stupid to give it up, at least before they decided whether or not the building was going to go co-op. It's too rational. That's the problem."

They went into the bedroom.

In her wanderings about the apartment that Honey found so suspicious, Alice had gone into the bedroom once or twice. Going into it now, she recognized that it was just the same as it had been, except that now she saw it. She saw that more than any room in the apartment, it bore the signs of Denny's last days. Without trying to, Alice could see him throwing back the bedroom door, kicking off his sneakers (one rested on its heel behind the closet door, the other had slid half under the bed), unbuttoning his shirt. He would do it energetically, with a kind of hasty fatigue, it would be late, he would be anxious to get into bed. His shirt hung from the back of the rocking chair. His pants, the belt still run through the loops and his underpants still folded in the crotch (he had taken them off together), fell over and bunched next to his side of the bed. When Susan picked them up, a sock fell out of each leg. His T-shirt, perhaps, he had worn to bed. It was not with the other clothes. On the table beside the window that looked down into the air shaft, he had left the contents of his pockets—a St. Christopher medal on a broken chain, three quarters and a dime, a few pennies, two tortoise shell flat picks and a set of finger and thumb picks pushed together in a little clump. Beside these things there was a little brochure from an art gallery in Providence, once wadded but now cupping upward.

Alice imagined Denny asleep, the stiff paper of the brochure un-
folding in the dark. Alice wondered if Honey and his men had
looked at these items and considered the evidence. They gave up
no mysteries to her, except the mystery of life and motion. She
must have sighed deeply, because Susan looked at her. Alice took
the other woman's hand and squeezed.

"There's not enough of my stuff around," said Susan. "That
would be some relief, just to pick up my stuff and put it away.
Let's change the bed." She went to the closet and got a new set
of plaid sheets, these blue and green. Those on the bed were red
and orange. Alice felt skittish, in spite of knowing that Denny
had probably not even been in here that last night. She could not
help imagining herself touching something stiff and dry, cam-
ouflaged by the color of the sheets. But they folded from the
corners, and, as if thinking the same thing, patted the red and
orange sheets into a ball and rolled them off the bed. With a rather
more determined air, Susan flipped and snapped the clean sheets
into place. When the bed-making was finished, her hands were
shaking.

"You're not going to sleep here!" exclaimed Alice.

"I've got to."

"It will be torture to stay here."

"It would be torture just to clear out."

"Susan!"

But Susan interrupted her, picking up the pants again and saying, "Thirty-two! I never could believe that such a big guy wore
a thirty-two. Thirty-two, thirty-six. Amazing size. But he never
looked skinny, did you think? He always thought he was too
skinny, but I never did."

"He had big shoulders and a big chest."

"He really was handsome, wasn't he?"

"Yes."

"In his own way, I mean. He wasn't model handsome like Craig
or anything. I loved to look at him, though. He looked so benign,
and his cheeks were kind of chipmunky and his eyes were so

sparkly. He looked like a good person. That's really what he looked like. Even when he was angry, he looked like a good person who'd gotten angry. I never could get over that."

"He was a good person."

Susan seemed to ignore her. "I remember after I first got to know him, I used to always say to myself, What a nice man, he's really a nice man, isn't he? That seemed so sexy at the time. Very rare and unusual." She picked his shirt off the back of the rocking chair and held it against her chest, smoothing her hand down it. "At first I was even touched by his loyalty to Craig."

"Craig was loyal, too."

Susan glanced at her. "What should we do with these clothes? I hate these clothes."

Alice reached for the shirt, but Susan would not let it go. Feeling that she had pushed, Alice blushed, but tried to speak firmly. "Why don't I pack everything up? I'll put what you don't want to keep in boxes, and you can send them to his mother. Maybe some of the kids would like to have things."

"Maybe."

"Shall I do that?"

Susan sat down on the bed with a large sigh. "Remember when Denny and I took that vacation in California? We decided to drive out there and travel around for a couple of weeks up north before Craig got out of that place in L.A."

Alice nodded.

"Did I tell you about the time I nearly fainted in the car?"

Alice shook her head.

"It was pretty far up north, north of Santa Rosa, anyway, and we were east of the coastal mountains. As soon as we crossed them it got desperately hot. I don't know why I reacted so strongly, but there I was, just sort of lolling in the car. I could barely open my eyes, and I couldn't make any sense talking. Denny never got panicky. He just drove along making light conversation, until we got to this river, the north fork of some river. He pulled over and made me get out of the car, and then half carried me down the bank of the bridge abutment and into the water, which was very shallow, and he made me stand there with my ankles and wrists in the water. I was completely revived after about five minutes. It was a beautiful spot, too. No beer cans, if you can believe that, no McDonald's wrappers. We just dug our toes into the sandy bottom and let the water cool our blood. I adored him." She paused, then went on. "Later, when we were driving south to pick up Craig I remember that we were laughing about something, and I got hysterical, really hysterical. I couldn't stop laughing, and then I started to cry and laugh at the same time. We were driving through some hills somewhere north of Santa Barbara. It was late afternoon, and the hills rose all around us, this beautiful liquid golden color. They were so beautiful that they made me start laughing and crying harder, until I really couldn't control myself. I thought I would wet my pants, which made me even worse. Denny just leaned across me and rolled down the window and practically pushed my head out of it. He made me ride with my head and neck completely out the window for about five or seven miles, until the blast of air brought me to my senses. And it did, just like he said it would."

"Sometimes I think that the best thing you can say about a person is that he knows what to do."

"Then we got Craig. Boy, was he a mess. When I look back on the trip, I always think of the first two weeks, never the drive home, although we stopped at the Grand Canyon and in Taos." And then, "Oh, Lord!" She hid her face in her hands. Alice began to take things out of the closet—shirts, mainly—one by one. She folded each with delicate neatness, as if she were about to stop, as if she weren't really doing anything final. Denny had lovely big shirts, mostly cowboy shirts in flannel and pure cotton plaids. They were an indulgence. Almost thirty of them, old and beloved, new and prized, were stacked on the bed. Susan wiped her eyes and said, "Noah might like some of those."

"Do you want me to call him?"

"No. I want to call him. I want to do all of this. I think it's shameful that I don't."

"You're doing fine. Better than fine. None of us helped you make the funeral arrangements."

"Oh, don't talk about that. I think that's a chute that you simply slide down. It's all very well oiled by the funeral home. I shudder to think of it. I hate being a sucker. Denny would have shrivelled up with embarrassment."

"But he doesn't care and his parents do."

"What am I going to say if they offer me money?"

"Say you'll take a little of it. Say the record company helped pay."

"The record company! Hah! You know, no one from there has even called me?"

"His parents don't know that."

"At least I'm glad they think the band made it."

"Didn't they, at least in some sense? I mean, they managed to support themselves."

"Well, if you'd talked to Craig Shellady for more than five minutes in the last year, you'd know what making it is, and it's not supporting yourself, believe me."

"But Denny didn't think that way, did he?"

Susan shrugged and pushed her hair out of her face. "I said it once and I'll say it again. I blame all of this on Craig. I don't forgive him, and I'm furious that once again I have to clean up the mess!"

"Susan!"

"I don't care."

Alice shook her head, annoyance stinging her in spite of the stack that Susan was making of Denny's underpants, in spite of her unconscious smoothing motion as she laid each new pair on the pile. The conflict of sympathy and irritation was so uncomfortable that she turned and left the room.

. . .

W H E N they finally got back to Alice's place, where Alice had prevailed upon Susan to stay at least until the boxes were sent, it was nearly 4 a.m., but Alice could not envision sleeping. The cleaning, which had been for Susan an act of love and purgation, had been for Alice a horror, even after the boys' shades were exorcised from the orange chairs. Susan went to bed. Agitated, Alice went into the kitchen and made some herb tea reputed to induce slumber. All up and down Eighty-fourth Street, buildings rose dark into the darkness. From her window she could see only one light on, and that one, behind frosted glass, probably a bathroom light left on for children. Even most of the building entrances were dark. Alice wondered if the contemplation of dozens, or hundreds (what would be the population of Eighty-fourth Street?) of sleepers could bring her sleep.

Her gaze settled on what she thought were Henry Mullet's windows across the way, and, as if by magic, the center one of them lit up. In a moment, the figure of Henry Mullet himself was silhouetted in the light, and then disappeared again. Alice saw enough to see that he had no shirt on. He looked wonderful. Entirely alive and possibly immortal. He reappeared, still without a shirt, then disappeared again. She thought he had looked at her. A few seconds later, the phone beside her rang. It was Henry Mullet. He said, "What are you doing up so late?"

"Can't sleep yet. How about you?"

Across from her, he dragged the phone and its apparently long extension cord into view and waved. "Can't sleep any more," he said. "Is insomnia a recurrent problem with you?"

"I don't think I've ever missed a full eight or nine in my life. Tonight is different. I haven't been to bed."

"A woman to be envied."

"Maybe. All my grandparents are in their eighties and nineties. They've been sleeping for years."

"Comatose?"

Alice laughed. "No! Peace of mind!" Across the street, Henry laughed in the window, silently but merrily. Alice said, "Have you done this before? You're so near and yet so far."

"Never."

Feeling the conversation die in her ear, Alice offered, "Did you go to the beach today?"

"No. I went to work. Didn't you?"

"I guess I did."

"Where do you work?"

"Public Library. How about you?"

"Brooklyn Botanic Gardens. Did you catalogue all day?"

"How did you know?"

"It was Monday. I catalogued today, too."

"I do little poetry magazines."

"I do plants from mainland China."

Alice's breath caught with envy. "And what did you do with them after you catalogued them?"

"They went off to be planted."

"I'm envious."

"You should be. They were rather exotic."

"Are you a botanist?"

"Yes, indeed."

"I've always meant to get out there, but Brooklyn seems so far away."

"It is. I'm considering moving out there because of the subway ride."

Alice wondered how she could hang up gracefully. It was nearly four-thirty and, though she didn't have to work in three hours, she grew suddenly afraid of the day ahead. Henry said, "I'll take you out there sometime, on my day off."

"You wouldn't mind?"

"I love it there."

"I can't say the same about the library, I'm afraid."

"Are you tired yet?"

"I am, as a matter of fact."

"Good night, then." In the window he waved and, perhaps,

blew a kiss. Then he turned away, the phone disconnected, and in a moment the light had gone off. Alice smiled, as if she had gotten away with something secret.

A T   T H E   two o'clock funeral, Alice mostly watched the photographers jostling for position. One or two of them, including the woman who Alice liked to think was from *Rolling Stone*, recognized Susan and, noticing Alice beside her, blatantly studied Alice's face, as if to memorize it for future reference. But maybe they were merely curious. There hadn't, after all, been as much attention to the story as Craig might have wanted. Rya sat between Alice and Noah. As the church, Mount St. Ursula's (chosen by the funeral home because it was nearby), filled with sightseers, Rya said, "I want to tell you that Noah and I went to see *Ain't Misbehavin'* last night."

"How was it?" Alice could not help noticing Rya's shoes, which had pointed toes, four-inch heels, and were made of black satin, although, on the other hand, she had dug up one of the most subdued black suits Alice had ever seen to wear with them.

"Do you think it's terrible that we went?"

"Why should it be? You got the tickets ages ago."

"It seemed terrible."

"Don't worry about it. Was it good?"

"Wonderful. There was even a song in it just for Noah. It was about a five-foot reefer."

Alice chuckled shortly. The priest, perhaps (Alice read the names over the confessionals) Father O'Brien, perhaps Father Angelini, perhaps Father Becker, bustled in with his purple robes trimmed in black and his two little boys. Alice was surprised at how nervous they made her, at how well the Lutheran prejudices of her grandparents had taken hold. Instead of watching them, instead of kneeling and sitting and standing up with the faithful, she perched on the forward edge of her seat, in a compromise between kneeling and sitting, and gazed around. One photographer, a lanky, pale, and soberly dressed kid, hardly in the employ of any newspaper or magazine, glided around the church, flashing his bulbs at the priest, the little boys, the (closed) coffins, the audience, the stained glass, the crucifix. Next to Alice, Susan glanced at him, too. Susan was "bearing up." The church was "lovely." It was hard not to think in funeral lingo. Alice thought of the priest suggesting a "guitar Mass" and suppressed another harsh chuckle. She reminded herself that he hadn't had to agree to memorialize two non-parishioners at all. She thought of the twenty dollars folded in her pocket that she was to slip him after the service. She thought of everything the undertaker had done for them and the money it would cost. In a shaft of yellow light from the stained glass, Susan's copper hair blazed up. Rya squirmed. The young photographer glided down the side aisle into something, the apse, maybe, and took an oblique shot that included St. Ursula, the crucifix, and the purple-draped coffins bathed in colored light. Noah, Ray, and some other men Alice barely recognized stood up and went forward. Susan fetched up a sigh so deep that Alice could feel the air vibrate.

DINNER, because everyone sensed it would be the last official communal meal, was taken in a French restaurant. Susan ordered extravagantly. Alice got the distinct impression that Susan no longer considered the four of them supportive. "Ray," she said, "I want my key. And Noah, too. Do you have a copy of Noah's key, Rya?" Rya nodded her head. "That, too. And I want a list from each of you stating to whom you have lent or given your keys to my apartment for as long as you can remember."

"But Susan, you had the lo—," began Alice. Susan glared at her.

Rya said, "Do you think—"

"What do *you* think?"

Rya shrugged. Noah didn't say anything. Susan said, "Alice knows she can keep hers, and besides, she would never lend it or give it away." With her tiny fork, she dug a garlicky snail dripping out of its shell and popped it into her mouth. Alice's own mouth watered. Rya began to sniff. Susan helped herself to another snail. "Everything's going to be different now," said Rya. "Different and worse." Alice said, "Maybe not." Susan glared at her again. "I mean, it is different and worse already," she amended, "but—" Susan seemed to grow larger before them, as if Rya's complaints expanded her into anger. Still, though, she didn't say anything, and finished her snails with her usual neatness, wiped up some of the butter sauce with a crust of bread, patted her lips, and cleaned her fingers on her white napkin. She had gone out before the funeral. Thinking of it now, Alice wondered if she had gone to see Honey, for she seemed to look at them with Honey's eyes. To speculate about them. Over and over, her gaze dropped on Noah and Ray. Alice's response to this was to wish she could eat everything on the table. The waiter cleared their dishes.

In addition to Susan's green-peppercorned fillet and Alice's golden slices of roast chicken napped in a smooth pale sauce, he brought medallions of veal for Noah, chicken Kiev for Rya, and lapin à la moutarde for Ray, which everyone stared at when it was set before him. The vegetable of the evening was spooned onto each of their plates. After the waiter had departed everyone seized their utensils and dove at the food, as if, Alice thought, it were trays of Big Macs and fries. Her own fork she dipped in the sauce embracing the chicken and touched to her tongue. A flower, savory and sharp, seemed to open in her mouth. Rya snuffled deeply, wiped her eyes, and drove her fork into the little balloon of chicken on her plate. Susan, who rarely drank, poured herself a second large glass of wine.

"The service was nice," said Ray.

"Don't even talk about it," ordered Susan.

"I want to talk about it," he began, in his wise mentor manner. "We should talk about it. It's a horrible thing."

"We keep having these dinners," said Susan, "as if they were killed in a car accident or died of pneumonia. We keep embracing each other, and wiping away each other's tears and calling each other on the phone and saying, significantly, 'How *are* you, dear?' "

Ray reddened.

"Who did you give the keys to my apartment to?"

Ray twisted a bone out of some meat on his plate and laid it aside. Indignant? Alice wondered. Afraid? Would a trained observer, like Honey, draw a conclusion or only leap to one? Ray said, "That's a valid question for you to ask and I'm trying to think. I sent one of the kids from Studio Midtown up there a few weeks ago to pick up Noah's bass, but he gave me the key back that day. Zimmerman had the key for a few days last week. I was negligent there, I admit. That's all I can think of. But didn't Alice say something about the locks being changed?" Ray opened the clip of his key ring and put two keys on the table.

"Who else might you have loaned them to?" Susan picked up the keys.

"Like I said. Nobody."

"Well, what were you doing that night? Where were you at zero hour?"

Ray was casual. "With some friends."

"You don't think any of your other circle of friends might try to force himself on someone in our circle, do you?"

Delicately, Ray allowed, "You could say there's been contact. Hardly more than that."

"So you were with your friends."

"With one friend, yes."

"Who?"

"You don't know him, I believe. Honey talked to him."

"I'll bet," said Susan.

"What are you saying?" Noah tried to speak judiciously.

"You always leave your keys lying around, don't you, Noah? Once you even lost the whole bunch and Denny gave you a brand-new set to our apartment."

"I used to keep a lot of stuff there."

"Didn't everyone?"

"Any band—"

"So, who's had access to your keys?"

Noah shrugged. "No one, I don't think."

"But you don't know! Very careless! People get hurt!"

"If you—"

"Anyway, you were there that night, weren't you?"

"Where?"

"At my apartment, the night Denny and Craig 'got killed,' as it were."

"Of course not." Noah met her gaze.

"Well, where were you?"

"I was at home. I answered all these questions from Honey, Susan."

"With Rya?"

"Rya didn't get home till late that night."

"By yourself? No one there to swear to your presence?"

"Well, where were you?" His voice came out too loud, and diners at the table behind him turned slightly and leaned over their plates. "Where were you? Alone in the woods?"

Susan smiled and shrugged.

Alice piped up. "Where was I? I was asleep in my bed. None of us has an ironclad alibi, if that's what you're looking for. Most people don't three-fourths of the time. So what does this prove? Susan, I think—"

Susan poured herself another glass of wine. "I know you were in bd. I know you had nothing to do with it."

"How do you know? You can't know."

"You're drunk, anyway," said Ray.

"Fuck you," said Susan. With an exchange of significant glances around the table, Ray, Noah, and Rya all stood up in unison, laid down their napkins, and turned from the table. Susan said, "Don't bother to finish!" Alice saw Ray step up to the captain. She speared Noah's last medallion of veal and lifted it onto her own plate. Susan was panting. The diners at the tables around them were resolutely attending to their own business. Alice's head began to throb. "Hey," she said. "What's going on? They're our oldest friends!"

"Sometimes I don't think you understand what's happened."

"I admit it's rather hard to take in." She raised a bite of veal to her lips, paused to inhale the aroma, then put it on her tongue. Lemon, pepper, parsley, the tender, milky flesh, a velvety sauce mysteriously seasoned. Susan said, "You act as if things haven't changed, as if nothing has taken place. Where do you think Denny and Craig are? How do you think they got there? Our group of friends isn't just going to roll supportively along, patting and kissing and eating together."

"All kinds of people had those keys! Honey seems to think— Well, you can't tell me that Ray or Noah or Rya—"

"That's what Denny always wanted, too. Lots of patting and kissing and holding hands. Nestled in the bosom of the family. Craig on one side, me on the other, everybody embracing."

"You didn't seem to mind."

"What do you know?"

"I know that I can't stand this. I think I'd better leave, too."

"I bet you think I don't cry enough. I bet you think I'm wonderfully brave. That's what Denny's mother said I was. My mother, too. Those exact words. Did I want her to come and I was wonderfully brave. I bet you think that after all these years together, I'm not reacting to Denny's death quite right, that I'm a real bitch to recognize that my apartment's a good deal even after this."

"In New York, any apartment—"

"I bet you think there's something wrong with me, you can't quite put your finger on it. I'm doing all the proper things, but, well, you don't want to say it. Even think it. You're a very loyal person. I bet you're remembering how you could hardly walk or talk after Jim left you, couldn't even write your name. Remember how you called me on the phone the night you got the letter, and you said that you were trying to write back, but your hand didn't work, and the pen wouldn't work, and you couldn't write his name or your own, or even simple words like 'is' and 'chair'?"

"I haven't thought anything about it."

"You know what my mother did when my father died? She bought a new living-room suite! You better believe that shocked the neighbors. It even shocked me. The day after the funeral she went out and got a sectional sofa, a glass-topped table made of a redwood burl, a La-Z-Boy Chair, new drapes, and a music center." It shocked Alice, too, although she didn't want it to. "Then she hired a trash hauler and took all the old stuff, my father's chair and his record player and everything down to the Salvation Army and dropped it off."

"Maybe that was the only way she had to be desperate."

"Maybe."

"Let's go."

"I haven't had dessert. I want crêpes Suzette."

"Let's have something on the way."

"I want crêpes Suzette!"

"Okay, sweetie." Suddenly what Alice wanted was to put her head down on the beige tablecloth, or to lie down on the toast-colored banquette. How was she going to deal with this? The restaurant was very warm. She felt trapped and terrified of leaving at the same time. She could hardly hold her head upright. Weakly, she said, "Why did you send our friends away?"

"We don't know anything about friends," said Susan, beckoning the waiter.

5

S U S A N wanted to sleep in her own apartment that night, and Alice did not try to dissuade her. They parted at West End, exchanging tentative and promissory kisses on the cheek. The late dusk was still pale and shot with rose. Alice tried to take solace in it as she walked uptown, to smile at passers-by who smiled at her, to mention the weather to the occasional doorman who mentioned the weather to her. What she yearned to do upon reaching her place was to call Jim Ellis and to cry and cry and cry, to beg for his help, to plead that he leave Mariana, to insist on a return to three years before. Even while rolling these desires through her mind, she recognized them as her habitual response to trouble. Of all the things his departure had done to her, wasn't that one of the worst? Opening her door, setting down her bag, taking off her jacket, she let herself plan out what she could say, what her tone could be (easy but serious), how much need she could show (fatigue, strained loyalty). She unplugged the kitchen telephone resolutely, but then not so resolutely went into her spare room and found her copies of his poems, both old and new, in his hand and Xeroxed from journals in the library. This was one of her most craven habits, that made her feel worse, not better. She turned on the light as the dusk thickened and opened the folder. "Chinese Chestnuts" lay on the top, about a year old. In it he likened his love for Mariana to one of those spiked chestnut cases, the very thought of which made Alice's palms prickle as she read. It was of course with her, in Doreen and Hugh's fruitful backyard, that Jim had first gathered chestnuts and pricked himself on the hulls. He probably didn't gather chestnuts in California, having never cared for agricultural endeavor. By the end of the poem—"the satiny sweet lodged within—" the phone rang. Thinking at once that it might be Susan, a different, sober Susan, who did not suspect their friends, Alice went into the bedroom and picked it up. It was Henry Mullet.

"What are you doing?" he said.

Annoyed, Alice replied, "Reading poems my ex-husband wrote to his second wife."

"Sounds self-destructive. How about a movie instead?"

"Not tonight."

"What are you going to start on after the poems, old letters?"

"I thought of it."

"I think you'd better put on your sweater, put your keys in your pocket, and meet me on the sidewalk."

"Not tonight."

"It's a beautiful evening."

"That's not so rare any more. Look, I feel really bad. I've got a headache—"

"Am I being too forward?"

"I don't know. I've had a bad day. I've had too much to eat and drink and think about already this evening."

"So who's going to eat or drink or think. Hang up the phone, take your keys, come downstairs. You'll be back with your ex-husband and his wife by nine-thirty."

"Please, I— All right."

When she got down to the street he was waiting for her. Without speaking, he put his arms around her and hugged her tightly.

Once again he smelled wonderful, this time of laundry detergent and clean warm skin. After a few seconds, she reached around him and returned the pressure. When he seemed about to release her, she broke away and said, "Yes, that was very forward. What now?"

"I'd still like to go to the movies."

"It's too late for me."

"Work, etcetera?"

"You bet."

"But what will you do if you go back in there? You won't go to bed."

"Probably not." The apartment did seem an arid cell when she thought about it. "Let's walk around the block," she said, "and smell those trees on Riverside."

"The silverbells."

"Is that what they are?"

"Carolina silverbells, *Halesia carolina* and so forth."

"That's right, you're a botanist."

"And you are a librarian."

"Not your glamor careers."

"Definitely on the side of preservation rather than creation."

"Do you consider yourself dull?" she eyed him.

"No, do you?"

"Not yet. I wonder, though."

"I spent three years in Taiwan and six months in Japan."

"Maybe I have a monopoly on dullness, then."

"That's when I thought I was getting dull, actually. Abroad is duller than home in a lot of ways, even a place like Japan, which is often perfect, especially for a botanist. I couldn't wait to move to Manhattan. Champagne and satin, you know."

"I've heard. I usually think in terms of Rheingold and wool."

"Twenty-One? Elaine's? Zabar's? Lutèce?"

"You know Elaine, too? She's only been at the reference desk for about a month."

"I'd stand in line for her."

"*In* line?"

"Wisconsin."

"Minnesota. That's why you hugged me rather than mugged me, I suppose."

"Maybe." After a moment, he said, "How long since this presumed husband?"

"Presumptuous is more the word. Two years."

"And you're still reading his poems?"

"He's still writing them. Actually, they're beginning to get good." She thought of telling him about the one in *The New Yorker* over the winter, but didn't. Henry said, "Two years ago I had just gotten to Japan from Taiwan. I thought it would never end."

"Two years ago I thought it would never end, either. Did you come back any while you were away?"

"Not once."

"Amazing."

"I thought so, too. Do you want to go around again?"

Alice took a deep breath of the refreshing air. "Yes. I forgot to smell the trees."

"This time we won't talk. We'll just smell, like dogs." Halfway around he bumped her and then took her arm above the elbow. When they got back to her doorway, he said, "Did you smell anything good?"

"Lots of things. I couldn't distinguish the odors, though. Surprisingly few bad things, even this close to the river. I think it's always strange how good mere inhalation makes you feel."

"Would you go inhale with me out in Brooklyn on Saturday?"

"What time?"

Not until she had turned to go did he relinquish her elbow.

I N T H E morning, when they were dropping off the boxes at UPS, Alice wondered why, although she had been with Susan for nearly an hour, and on fairly good terms, she hadn't mentioned, or even thought to mention, her walk with Henry Mullet.

A botanist would interest Susan. If she met Henry, Susan would have something intelligent to say to him. She wouldn't have to ask questions simply to dredge up something to talk about. Oriental plants or Japanese gardening would be something she had read about not too long ago. Still, just as she could not bring herself to tell her parents about Denny and Craig, she could not bring herself to tell Susan about Henry Mullet. The boxes, neatly addressed, rolled down a conveyor belt out of sight and Susan heaved a large sigh. "Want to eat?"

"All of this does make me famished all the time, but I'd better get to work."

"Shall I drive you before I put the car away again?"

"You don't want to go to midtown. It would probably gridlock."

"Then I could abandon the car for good."

"I wonder if you'd have to. If the whole island of Manhattan would be a pedestrian mall forever after that."

Susan was smiling. With a start, Alice realized that days had passed since their last smiles. Warmth, banked since the night before, kindled again, as always. "Dinner?" she said.

"I may just be able to afford two cartons of yogurt if you'll bring the bananas."

"Your place?"

"Why not?"

Smiling as broadly as she could, Alice said, "About six, then. Bananas. I'll stop at the Fairway." She got out at the bus stop and Susan rolled away. On the trip downtown Alice put her purse between her feet, stepping firmly on the strap, and used her hands to count up her friends. With Laura, Sidney, and Howard, to whose homes she had never been, and Janet O'Connor, who had so many children, in Minneapolis, that she never had time to write, Alice still could not fill up two hands. Denny and Craig, of course, could hardly be so soon replaced, and it was hard to tell if Jim Ellis should be called a friend or not. There was no one else, no lover from the years since Jim that she could even telephone. The fewness of them shocked her, and what shocked her even more was that until now they had seemed plenteous, a wealth of friends. Of course, she had spent her whole childhood with her parents, not understanding the occasional sympathetic query, "Wouldn't you like to have brothers and sisters?" To share Doreen and Hugh? Wasn't seven at the table, plus friends, for holidays, an enormous number? Riding downtown on the Fifth Avenue bus, Alice felt for the first time in her life depopulated. She tried to think that Susan's suspicions of their friends didn't have to influence her, but posing the unanswerable question, to whom would she go if she had to, she saw that already the influence was felt. Her brief, nearly involuntary mental images of Noah killing Craig out of a jealous passion (and Denny because he entered the apartment at the wrong moment?) and of Ray lending out his key to thugs and of Rya teasing Noah with the rivalry of his best friend distanced her absolutely from them no matter how she regretted it. Of course, there was Susan. Alice smiled at the richness of the friendship: its length, its intimacy, its comfort, at her own deftness in handling Susan's porcupine periods and at Susan's skill with her jellyfish periods. There would always be Susan, but still— She jumped off at the library. She rarely came in this late, and when she looked up toward the grand sunlit facade with its rising pigeons and tranquil lions, she thought it beautiful. Susan's phrase, "A mighty fortress is our library," recurred to her. Just then it did seem that a dozen acquaintances and one beautiful building might indeed equal a friend.

Nevertheless, when she got inside she was not disappointed that the day's assignment, to bring the card catalogue in line with losses in preparation for the programming of all materials that was to begin over the summer, paired her with Laura, whom Alice especially liked, perhaps because at thirty Laura was nearly all gray, as Alice's mother had been as early as Alice could remember. And Laura was a gossip. Her flow of anecdote about her family, her friends, their co-workers, and anyone else who crossed her mind reminded Alice over and over of all the friends there were to be made. Laura's gossip was redeemed by its lack of spite. She was warmly objective about every event, taking endless delight in action and complexity, as if she had been bed-ridden in a small windowless room for years and was just now discovering the dramatic possibilities of daily life. She sang Alice through the day.

On the bus up Sixth Avenue it seemed to Alice that she had caught her life in its downward plunge, that she held it, although with difficulty, and that with only a little luck she could turn it. What did the lives of her four ancient grandparents prove if not that life itself would go on? Wouldn't such a crisis as this one appear almost invisible from the perspective of sixty years on? An anecdote like one of Laura's that she could hardly remember.

On Thursday Roger Jenks sat down with them. Alice barely knew Roger, but he had a strange fame among the librarians, and although he was a nice man, his sitting next to them seemed ill-omened. It was Roger who, the year before, had wrestled a distraught attacker to the floor of the main reading room and held him pinned in a pool of the victim's blood until the guards and a policeman could get there. Perhaps it was just a minute, but afterward Roger had looked like a walking corpse. None of the library staff ever talked about the incident, and both the victim, stabbed from behind in the neck and shoulder while reading a German grammar, and the attacker had never been heard of again. It was thought the victim had survived. Laura, who knew Roger fairly well, said, "Hey, you two have something in common! Guess what it is."

Alice didn't dare. What could it be besides gore? Fixing a smile on her face, she did her best to look intrigued. She had not known Laura knew about her.

"If you're referring to the L-Two trap," said Roger, "we have that in common with everyone here."

"Nope!" said Laura.

"Shoe size?" Roger picked up his feet and looked at the soles of his oxfords. They were at least size fourteen. Alice laughed.

"No. Aren't you from Minnesota somewhere, Roger?"

"Bemidji."

"That's not much in common," exclaimed Alice.

"Thanks," said Roger. "You sound relieved."

"I didn't mean to. Where did you go to school?"

"Iowa."

"Oh."

Roger put his elbows on the table and looked at her. "But maybe we have more in common than that."

Just then Sidney appeared with the news that Alice had a phone call. Alice got up reluctantly. It was Ray. "Can you come over to Studio Midtown on your lunch hour?" he demanded.

"Half hour. I don't know. Let me think."

"You've got to."

Alice was annoyed by his tone. "You come here."

"I can't. I'm watching the board for someone. She considers herself a big star. If she were, she'd probably be more easy-going."

"Ray, I've had too much time off this week. Let me come after work."

"I need you before that."

"What for?"

"I'll tell you when you get here. I'm in room—"

Alice had a sudden vision of Laura, Sidney, Howard, and now Roger sitting cozily at lunch. Friendly. Funny. Not guilty for sure. "Don't assume I'm coming!" she barked. "I have a job, too. That's an hour and a half or two hours with traffic."

"A half hour each way, tops, and I just have to talk to you for a minute."

"You want me to walk up there, or pay for a cab, just to talk to me for a minute? I've got work to do!"

"It's important!"

"Then you come here. If you can't make it, then I'll meet you there at about five-thirty, all right?" Annoyed by his imperious attitude, she couldn't help sounding sharp.

"I wish you understood."

"I'll be there before you know it. You said you're stuck there. I'll come right after work." After hanging up, she realized that he hadn't mentioned the room number after all, or the name of the "star." But the studio would know Ray. Everyone did.

Except the boy in the booth, who was not only gigantically mellow, but new on the job as well. And he didn't know how not to answer the phone while he was talking to her, and in the middle of the third phone call, when he was running his finger down the schedules looking for an empty room, he knocked everything off his desk, including his cup of coffee. Still, she found out from asking passers-by that he was the only person who even might know something. Everyone else had gone on a delivery or out to dinner. Alice looked at her watch. It was nearly six. Her trip from the library had been a chain of time-consuming mistakes—getting into a cab that got stuck in traffic, getting out of it just before the jam eased, bumping into people, turning down wrong streets. The boy got off the phone again, looked at the mess on the floor, and said, "Oh, shit. Shee-it."

"If you'd just think a minute," Alice pleaded, "you might remember who Ray Reschley is. He comes here all the time. He mixes sound and stuff like that."

"Who's he working for again?"

"I don't KNOW. I told you that."

"Well, it's all listed under whoever's playing."

"Well, read me the names. He said she was a big star."

"Can't do that."

"Point me to where the rooms are, and I'll just look for myself, okay?"

"Lady!"

"I won't disturb anyone."

"If there were windows in the doors, you'd disturb people just by looking into them. That's why there aren't any windows on the doors."

"But even if I disturbed people, I'd only disturb them for a minute."

"Hey, that's why people come here. That's why they *pay.* So they won't be disturbed for even a minute."

"This is an emergency."

"Who says?"

"Do you have a manager?"

Now the kid was beginning to get annoyed. "He doesn't like to be disturbed, either."

"Look—" Alice didn't know quite what to do. The boy's tentative look of annoyance widened into a smile of victory as Alice stepped back from the booth. Alice smiled herself, pretending to be about to leave, but then she threw back her head and screamed as loudly as she could, "RAY! RAY! RAY!" Her voice broke. The kid in the booth was shocked. No manager, however, came gliding out of any of the closed doors. Nothing at all happened, except that another truck came in and the boy in the booth picked up the phone. Alice felt her throat with her hand, wondering if she would ever speak again. After dialing two or three times, the boy beckoned to her. "I found the people he was with. Mixing sound, right? That band's gone home."

"I don't want the band. I want Ray Reschley."

"Hey, they've gone home. They've all gone home. Now you go home."

"See if they went out somewhere."

His hand didn't even touch the receiver. "He's gone home."

"Okay," said Alice, turning away. When the boy bent his head to pick up the rest of his papers, she scurried around the booth and ran toward the closed doors and the stairwell. "Hey!" shouted the boy, but only once. He probably didn't dare leave his booth, especially since he was new on the job.

Alice stood between two doors, with her eye on a third, waiting for someone to come out. No one did. At last, she opened the door to her right and saw that the room, cavernous and completely insulated, was empty. So was the room to her left. Across the hall, a man with a guitar looked up and scowled before she could get the door shut. She crept toward the stairs. Her own behavior was making her afraid. Surely it hadn't really been an emergency. Ray hadn't called it an emergency. He had wanted her, but he hadn't needed her. If he needed someone, wouldn't he call Noah, or some friend that Alice didn't know, someone who'd seen him more frequently over the last year? Thinking of how they had drifted apart rather reassured Alice. At the top of the stairs she stood up straight. A face she recognized came out of one room and went into another, but she barely had time to remember the name, much less ask him if he knew Ray Reschley. The emptiness of the high-ceilinged corridor made her jumpy. She looked at her watch. It was six thirty-three. She opened the door next to her. Inside, someone very famous, judging by his resplendent clothing and his entourage, was practicing. No Ray. Five chords boomed over her before she got the door closed. After that she knew that she couldn't open any more doors. Shortly after that, she began to view favorably the notion that Ray had gone home. Why should the kid lie? Ray was probably in his apartment right now, wondering what had happened to her. She should go home, too, and wait for his call. Call him, even. The door in her distracted gaze opened, startling her. A Rastafarian sauntered out. Alice squeaked, as she had planned, "Do you know Ray Reschley?"

"Shit, man," said the Rastafarian.

"Thanks, anyway," said Alice.

But Ray wasn't at home, or else his phone was unplugged. When at last the answering service picked up, they wouldn't give Alice any information. She could not help thinking of Roger Jenks, thinking he had been ill-omened, for now she was a little worried, and felt a little like she had betrayed an old friend in order to make a new one. And Roger Jenks hadn't even sat with them at lunch.

DETECTIVE Honey was waiting for her on the sunlit steps when she came outside with her peanut butter sandwich on Friday. She had never expected to see him outdoors, somehow, and she didn't recognize him. He hardly looked imposing at all. When he saw her, he took off his sunglasses. Alice dropped her sandwich while opening it, and he picked it up for her. "Another beautiful day," he said.

"Almost two weeks, now." She smiled as well as she could.

"Mind if I take up a few minutes of your lunch hour?"

"May I?"

"May you?"

"May I mind?"

He smiled politely. "No," he said. He flipped back the cover of his notebook and gestured for her to sit down. He was dressed in plain clothes, but he looked very coplike; Alice prayed that Laura wouldn't come out.

"How've you been?" said Honey.

Alice shrugged.

"I saw you at the funeral."

Alice hadn't seen Honey. "I didn't expect it to fill the church, but it seemed to."

"More friends than you thought?"

"I suppose."

"Would you say that either of the victims was closer to Mr. Mast, say, than to Mr. Reschley? Or vice versa?"

"Noah would have been with them more, I suppose, because they all played together, but Ray might have been around more in off hours, except that he's a pretty busy person."

"You would say that Mr. Reschley is successful in his job, sought after?"

"I've gotten that impression."

"And Mr. Mast?"

"He's probably a fair bass player. No one has ever lured him away, but I wouldn't know if anyone ever tried."

"How would you characterize Mr. Mast?"

"He's a nice guy."

"Could you be more specific?"

Alice lifted her gaze, and shading her eyes against the glare, looked into Honey's face. He looked merely curious, pleasant. She thought of Noah's habit of carrying a bag of dope or a few joints with him wherever he went. He had done it for so long that he probably no longer remembered that it was illegal. "He's very relaxed," she said, "generous, dependable, loyal."

"Could you characterize Mrs. Mast?"

"Harmless."

"Compared to?"

Alice started. For a moment Honey seemed just the least bit predatory, but then he veiled his interest. Alice shrugged. "Not compared to, or maybe, compared to what she seems. She wears a lot of make-up and usually dresses in revealing black clothes."

"Intelligent?"

"I don't know."

"Your friend?"

"Sort of."

Honey settled himself. "Is Mr. Reschley your friend?"

Alice nodded.

"You've known him for a number of years, I believe?"

"Almost sixteen."

"You've known him longer than the others have?"

Alice nodded.

"Was Mr. Reschley ever married?"

"No."

"Does Mr. Reschley have any unusual habits?"

"Not strictly unusual, no."

Honey pursed his lips. "Is Mr. Reschley a homosexual?"

Alice nodded.

"Completely so?"

"Yes, as far as I know."

"Any of this sort of involvement with the rest of the band?"

"No!"

"Have you met any of Mr. Reschley's homosexual associates?"

"Not really, no."

"But?"

"Once we were in a bar. I saw a guy he later went out with, but I didn't actually meet him."

"Named?"

"Lonnie something. I don't know any others." Alice looked at her watch.

Honey leaned forward. "Let's be perfectly clear about this, okay?" he said. "You have never met and know nothing about Mr. Reschley's present friends and associates?"

"I've never met any of them and Ray never talks about them."

"Docs Mr. Reschley take drugs in any form?"

"I've never seen him." But of course she had seen him reach for joints, inhale, pass them on. She had seen herself do the same thing. Lying. She bit her lip.

"Have you seen Mr. Reschley lately?"

"He called me on the phone yesterday, but I didn't see him. I went to meet him, but he had gone home."

"You haven't heard from him since?"

"No."

"Have you seen more of Mr. Reschley since the incident than you were accustomed to seeing him before the incident?"

"Yes." Why evade the question? "He's the most used to the public eye, so he's been taking care of a lot of things having to do with newspapers and magazines. He's been very kind."

"Miss Gabriel and Mr. Reschley and the Masts and yourself have, would you say, sort of drawn together for mutual support?"

"I would say that." How much did he know? Did he need to be advised of every little angry exchange, every suspicion? Did five minutes of suspicion balance years of trust? Honey stifled a yawn. Alice wondered if the case bored him. An old phrase from the Sherlock Holmes she had once been in the habit of reading occurred to her, "features of interest." Did this case have any features of interest for Honey? Could she herself be a "feature of interest," or mistaken for one by someone tired, overworked, underpaid, furnished with a certain moral blindness? Would he hold lies against her? Alice realized that her fingers in her pocket had shredded the napkin around the remnant of sandwich she had put there and that a red stain of strawberry jam was beginning to spread in the weave of her skirt. She took her hand out of her pocket and placed it inconspicuously over the stain. Honey continued to glance alternately through his notes and out toward Fifth Avenue. A sigh, perhaps a companion to the yawn, escaped him. Alice said, "Detective Honey, is the investigation proceeding pretty quickly?"

When he smiled she resigned herself to being palmed off. "Quickly enough," he said. Just as she would not confide in him, he would not confide in her.

But there was one more question she had to ask. "Do you think that the deaths were, what, anomalous?"

Perhaps he took her meaning more clearly than she did. "Do I think anyone is in danger, do you mean? Like a plot or a pathological killer? No, I don't think so at this point."

The words "killer," "danger," and "pathological" startled Alice. She hadn't been thinking of the peaceful still-life of the previous Saturday in such dynamic terms. Instead of reassuring her, Alice could feel Honey's words dropping into her like acid, beginning to burn away her Midwestern sense of safety. And, she reflected, he didn't simply say, No, or Of course not. He said, "I don't think so at this point." Alice shivered. Honey said, "We've lost the sun, I'm afraid. You'll be wanting to go back to work." They stood. "Thank you for your time."

"Any time," said Alice, suddenly afraid for him to go, afraid even of the ten or twelve feet of open pavement before she could gain the preserve of the library. Honey shook her hand. She was hard put to release it at the proper moment. That afternoon she hid in the labyrinth of stacks, looking for lost books.

SINCE Tuesday she had been even more unsure with Susan, more tentative but more helpful, unable to decide, or rather to know instinctively, just the right degree of intimacy. It seemed to her that the merest breath of a wish not to have her around would make her vanish, but at the same time, it often seemed to her that Susan had just grimaced at some clumsiness of hers, or just suggested, subtly, that she leave, and she hadn't understood until it was too late to do anything gracefully. They were spending a lot of time together, each night eating something at one or another's apartment, doing the dishes, going for a twilight walk at the end of which they stopped for ice cream, coming home, reading or flipping through the channels on the television. It was the sort of intimacy Alice had desired, as co-operative as two feet walking, and yet she was unusually uncomfortable, too, terribly desirous of pleasing.

Sometimes Alice could not help staring at Susan, admiring the liquid copper hair that stopped so abruptly at her shoulders, the strong high cheekbones and wide mouth, the eyes set deeply under great arching brows. Peasant stock, Susan said she came from, and it was true that she would never be thin. Broad shouldered, wide hipped. Alice thought over and over that she was beautiful. On Friday, they were at Alice's, handing across the salad dressing, and Alice felt everything shift, as a driver feels a long line of stopped cars begin to move before it actually does. Suddenly, for no apparent reason, the discomfort drained away, and they were simply two friends eating together at a kitchen table. Alice could not help smiling, but it was Susan who began to talk. "Do you remember when I met Denny?" she asked.

"Of course. You barged into my room at three in the morning and said you'd met the man you were going to marry."

"Did I say marry? I wasn't so prescient after all, then. But I've been trying for days to remember the name of the guy I was with that night. Jerry something."

"Jerry McMann."

"Jerry McMann! Right! It seems to me that he spent the evening talking about all the other girls in the bar, what they looked like, what they were wearing. Anyway, these two guys got up on stage and sang a lot of folk music. Kingston Trio, the usual. But every set they sang two songs, 'Don't Think Twice, It's All Right' and 'That's What You Get for Lovin' Me.' I was entranced. I didn't even realize that Jerry was boring, and I loved watching Denny and Craig. Those two songs made them seem so mean, and then they'd sing something like 'Early Morning Rain' and instead of seeming mean, they'd seem tormented. We sat there for hours. Sometime in the last set, they sang that old Ian and Sylvia thing called 'Song for Canada' and I just knew they were Canadians. Denny was completely hairy, as if he'd just gotten in from the Arctic, and Craig simply looked exciting. He could have been from anywhere far away and difficult. Then Jerry said we should buy a pitcher and get the singers, who he knew slightly, and the girls at the next table, who he kept talking about, to join us. It worked like a charm, except that the funny thing was that I angled to sit next to Craig, and then one of the girls just shot in there and grabbed the seat, so I was stuck sitting next to Denny, who looked almost normal rather than in the advanced stages of some Romantic agony. The first thing he said to me was 'I was watching you from the stage,' which of course sounded thrilling and so-phisticated. These two guys just moved in on Jerry, and it was so graceful and worldly and perfectly cruel that it seemed marvellous to me. There was a teasing sexual innuendo in everything they said that flattered us and made us laugh and made adulthood seem very possible and desirable. I'm sure I was arch and joking and rather distant, I mean, you had to be, but inside I was leaning and melting, and when Denny told me he was from Minnesota after all, and then when he talked affectionately about his family and all the other kids, he somehow didn't get any less exotic or cruel, he just got exotic and cruel and familiar and kind and desirous and experienced all at the same time. We left Jerry at the bar, which seemed to be what he deserved, and went to their apart-ment, which was furnished entirely with mattresses on the bare floor and with their record collection, and of course Craig got out

the dope and the unfiltered apple juice, and there was Country Joe and kissing on the Indian bedspreads and discussion of whether marijuana enhanced or dampened sexual desire, and then some friends came over to play music, and that was what really struck me, that friends who rode motorcycles could just walk in at one in the morning. Exotic again! I shook his hand in the doorway, but there seemed such a terrible lack of compromise between never seeing Denny again and becoming his slave."

"You always seemed much cooler than that, somehow. As if you thought you might allow this guy to take you out."

"Did I?" She pushed herself away from the table.

"So how come you never got married? It seems irrelevant. I mean, you always seemed married in a way that Jim and I weren't, as if nothing could hold us together and nothing could drive you apart."

Susan ran her hands under the back of her hair and lifted it out of her collar. "Really? I always admired you for committing yourselves in public, for not keeping anything in reserve. I always wondered why you and Jim and Noah and Rya were freer than I was, or more grown up, or less suspicious."

"Or more benighted. I think having gotten married means more in retrospect than it did at the time. I don't know about Noah and Rya, but I'm willing to admit that my marriage was just a fruitless attempt to have something I couldn't have, another bent nail in a very ramshackle structure." She shrugged.

Susan was looking out the window. "Denny would have done it, I think. In spite of his rock and roll image. Something held us back." She paused, tipping the chair up on two legs. "No, something held him back and something else held me back. Do wives go away by themselves every six months or so? Do husbands come and go unannounced? Everyone thinks beforehand that they're going to have that kind of free, creative marriage, but does anybody? If I'd ever seen somebody like me who was married, I might have done it."

"But you're amazingly domestic. You make good homes where people like to be. I feel like I specialize in The Virgin's Retreat."

"Now I wouldn't say domestic. I wouldn't say domestic at all. I would say competent, or good at business, never domestic."

Alice opened her mouth to protest, or at least to exclaim at Susan's misinterpretation of herself, but the phone rang. Susan, closer, reached for it. After a moment of listening, she looked up at Alice and said, "They can't find Ray. Ray's disappeared."

6

I T W A S Alice who called Noah, half expecting to ease into
the bad news, but Noah greeted her with, "I just got back from
Studio Midtown and I talked with most of the guys who were
there yesterday. No one's seen him since they packed the band
up about five—"

"Why didn't they tell me that!" Alice couldn't help exclaiming.

"And I called Murray, too. He plays bass in that band. He says
Ray didn't go uptown with them, and the last he saw him, he
was going into that Greek place across the street. They're all
pissed, too, because he made a deal to be there today and tomorrow."

"I thought Ray was the most dependable guy in New York."

"So did Ray."

Alice could hear Rya's faint shout in the background, "Tell her
about—" but then it was garbled. Noah ignored her. Alice said,
"Tell me about what?" but Noah was already talking. "The police
went over to his apartment this afternoon, when he didn't show
up for the job and nobody could reach him. Clean as a whistle."

"Tell me about what?"

"What?"

"I heard Rya say for you to tell me about something."

"Did she?"

"Come on, Noah."

"I'm sure he's all right."

"Are you?"

"We don't have any evidence that anything has happened to him, or that he's left town on his own, do we? He probably met someone last night. If it weren't for this other thing, nobody would give it a second thought."

"Yeah, but when was the last time he missed a job? He never does. That's the point. He always told me he was very careful about how his personal life mixed with his professional life. He always said that if he forced anyone to think about his being gay, that would be it in the music business. He was very aware of that."

"I know."

"So what's your answer?"

"Nothing. Don't worry." He hung up before she could press him again to tell her whatever Rya had been referring to. Susan came in from the bedroom, where she had been listening on the extension. After looking for a long moment at Alice, she said, "No relief in sight, huh?"

"Doesn't seem to be. Did Ray—"

"What?"

Alice bit her lip. "Has Ray seemed weird to you lately?"

"He's been weird for the last year!" Her tone was hard and dismissive, which shocked Alice in spite of herself, and evaporated her wish to confide what she'd seen of Ray in the last week. "Are you still mad at everyone?" They hadn't spoken of this since the night in the restaurant.

"It's not a case of being mad. Be realistic, Alice!"

To forestall an argument, Alice said, "What time is it?"

"Almost twelve."

"Are you working tomorrow?"

"But of course! Zut! We got a whole shipment in from Paris yesterday, les jupes, les chaussures, les bleujeans, le deesplay pour Madame et Monsieur, chop chop."

"I'm almost envious of you working."

"Come sit with me behind the counter."

But when they got up late and Susan hurried off in an unaccustomed cab to unlock before the clerks arrived, there was no talk of Alice's accompanying her. Alice remembered Henry Mullet and their date. A whole day, no matter how pretty, in some garden with some guy? Henry was handsome enough, she thought, and not without wit or conversation, but there was nothing compelling about him. You might date him for a while, and recite his virtues to your friends with dutiful respect, but at some point you would realize that you had stopped going out with him. Had Susan said a word about coming to the shop, Alice would have cancelled, but she had not. Alice sighed and picked up her keys a moment before she was due to meet him. Out the window on Eighty-fourth Street, he was already there. In a flash, for some reason, she took against him.

Nothing about the rather awkward walk to the subway or the ride itself on the uncrowded Saturday morning train challenged her predisposition. In fact, even the pleasant banter they'd achieved before failed them, and Alice could see that Henry was looking forward to the morning, and oh, God, the afternoon with the same discouragement turning to despair that she was. A mesomorph. She had never liked mesomorphs. Jim Ellis was over six feet, and wiry, with lightning reflexes and limitless energy. On the subway, he never sat, never let the ride shake him down into a lump, a passive lump. And his ancestry was not definable by looking at him. You couldn't help wondering where the dark, coarse, curly hair came from, the tyrannically beaked nose, the startling blue eyes. WASP to the core, according to the names of his progenitors, and yet Alice had found him exotic. He found himself exotic. Henry Mullet looked about as exotic as hashed brown potatoes. Between stations, she caught her own reflection in the dark window across from her. At least she was slender. No one could say that she didn't have a pleasing figure. She put her hand to her hair. Her hands were good, big, long fingered, graceful. But why had she worn a white blouse, and, she looked down, green slacks? She stared steadily into her reflection, and dared to be honest. Yes, she looked neat and thin. And pinched, prim, without chic, entirely thirty-one and absolutely a librarian. She sighed.

Henry said, "We'll go in the museum entrance. Some of the Oriental fruit trees are still in bloom, but the best thing now is the lilacs. You can smell them all over the garden. Are you interested in native plants? In the last few years the botanists and horticulturists have been cleaning up the native plant collection. The public isn't allowed, but it's one of my favorite parts of the garden. And the roses are starting, if you like roses."

"Wonderful," said Alice, smiling a good enough smile. In spite of himself, Henry, too, sighed. Alice wondered if he hoped that she wouldn't know how to interpret it. When she looked at her watch it was only ten thirty-five. She nearly groaned aloud. Only a week had passed, exactly a week. At Grand Army Plaza, Henry Mullet forgot himself, took her hand, and ran her off the train. He was physical in a way that Jim Ellis was not. Although Jim hovered around you, desire shooting out of him like sparks, either the desire to do something, or, more uncomfortably, the desire for you to do something, he hardly ever touched. When he did, it was a stroke or a prod or even a glancing light blow. Henry Mullet was a grasper, a holder-in-place, a propeller, a preserver from traffic. Alice wasn't sure she liked it.

At the turnstile set into the wrought iron gates, he began to fidget, and then grin. Alice realized with some surprise that he was getting excited. "Been here in a while?" she teased.

"Just go that way, to the right, we'll come back the other way. I was here until dark last night. Why?"

"You seem excited to be back."

"Do I?" His eyes swept down the long formal promenade toward the fountain and then back to her, with a warm smile.

"Maybe I am. I suppose I am. Here, look. These are the Oriental crab apples and the European crab apples. *Malus* is the generic name. Beautiful blossoms."

"Hmm," said Alice politely, beginning down the promenade, but he wouldn't let her go. Although he was all set to escort her down the walk, to point out the beautiful shapes the trees had been trained and pruned to, he could not help stopping at nearly every tree and inspecting something—a black spot, an ooze of sap, a fissure in the bark. Alice, who was used to drifting through museums and parks, appreciating the beauty by a kind of ambulatory osmosis, felt impatient at first, imagining herself conducting a tour of the library and stopping to pull damaged or inaccurate cards out of the card catalogue, but after a few minutes he began to point things out to her, to identify insects and incipient diseases, especially of age, since many of these trees had by now lived ten or fifteen years longer than they had been expected to live. He saw everything—not just the robins and bluejays that Alice would have recognized, but also two phoebes, a group of orioles, a house finch, and a pair of large green birds that looked like, and actually were, parakeets. "They don't eat here," said Henry. "We think they steal fruits and vegetables on Park Slope. There's another pair in the garden, too." He saw shoots and leaves and buds that were out of place, he saw spider webs that only shone when the sun struck them at one angle. Alice saw that he could not look without noting work that had to be done, situations that had to be looked into, but she saw also that he loved looking. After they had listened to the distinctive calls of the birds, the distinguishable snaps and buzzes of the insects, after they had noted the various herbaceous specimens that Alice would have called weeds, or perhaps not seen at all, after they had walked around most of the trees, looked up, looked down, looked near and far in every direction, Alice felt that she had never really taken a walk before. "And everything lives so effortlessly and plentifully right in the middle of the city?"

"Why not?"

They stepped down from the formal promenade into, and among, the more spacious spreading of grass and lilac bushes covered with white, lavender, and magenta blossoms. Alice gasped, both at the sight and at the sweet fragrance. "The Botanic Garden," he went on, "is actually a fairly thriving ecosystem."

"It's like heaven."

"Yes," Henry said, "it is. The funny thing, to me, is that there is very little vandalism. Sometimes people pick the flowers, but no one writes on the trees or defaces them or hurts them. And there are days when you can walk around here and not see anyone. No gardeners, no botanists, no police, no one to stop you if you wanted to break something or spray paint it." He had her arm and walked her comfortably past the lilacs (always stopping, always pointing out to her the differing perfume of each variety) around behind the roses, which were beginning to bloom, and Alice felt her good nature, and her very flesh, warm and spread beneath his grasp, beneath his detailed, observant, and passionate knowledge.

She hadn't dated anyone who was particularly informative in a while, and she had forgotten the pleasures of such companionship. Henry Mullet was good at it. For one thing, he wouldn't let her back away from the plants. He made her kneel close to them and smell them, look at their tiny parts, turn the leaves over gently, take insects (ladybugs, Japanese beetles) on her finger. For another, he loved, not his own talking, but what he was talking about. After a while, every time he paused to scrutinize something, Alice grew anxious to know what he was seeing, not bored with the wait. And he talked in a normal tone of voice, unlike men she had known, most men, perhaps, who tended to switch into Public Speaking rhythms about three sentences into any dissertation. She imagined herself coming here often with Henry, his good friend, a dependable companion for all seasons, if nothing more exciting was going on.

In the administration building, everyone greeted him jokingly, asking if he'd wiped his feet, what was that smell, was Alice really not his sister or his cousin, but an actual date, didn't he know there were other things to do on your day off than come to work. The women did not come from behind barriers to greet him, but they all looked up and smiled indulgently. While he ran up to his office to pick up some papers, Alice surveyed the rack of cultivation guides, choosing for Hugh and Doreen one on herbs and one on small fruits. The woman behind the counter put them in a bag and stapled it shut without accepting Alice's five dollar bill. "It's a lovely day," she said kindly. "There." As Henry returned she raised her voice. "Now you make him take you to some nice place for lunch." She grinned. Across the room, another woman called, "Think he can pay for it?"

Henry laughed. "I was thinking of your place, Helen. About two?"

"You'd be out of luck there, Dr. Mullet! Unless you'd like peanut butter and grape jelly on saltines like my kids."

"We'll bring the wine! Got what you need?" As he opened the door and let her into the bright sunlight, Alice felt both privileged and impressed. The most she ever got at the library was a hello or a friendly smile. Administrators were rather trembled at or scorned than teased. She said, "You must like it here."

"Who wouldn't? 'All that in this delightful garden grows, should happy be and have immortal bliss.' Go left. I'll show you the bonsai collection."

And the cacti that looked like rocks, the banana tree, his plantings of day lilies, the flourishing Shakespeare herb garden (he pinched off leaves when no one was looking and put his fingers beneath her nostrils), the lilacs again ("I can't bear to leave them," exclaimed Alice, inhaling deeply), and then the wilds of the native plant collection, which looked not unlike someone's uncultivated backlot. Native American ecology made good talk, nothing personal that might ambush her into the news of Ray and Craig and Denny. Tales of her parents and their enormous garden, of the apple tree and pear tree her father had grafted together, of her grandmother Bovbjerg's pickled peaches and her grandmother

Gustavson's preserved chilis that her father ate by the bottle on toast served to represent her private history well enough. In return, he told her about what all those Scandinavians would have had to do upon reaching Minnesota, breaking the sod with axes, burning back the chest-high native grass; Alice had never enjoyed the thought of agriculture so thoroughly. Over lunch he talked about his special interest in Chinese plants and his increasing fluency in the identification of mainland species that no one had seen in thirty years, if ever. It turned out that he had an application in for a visa to the People's Republic. He asked, suddenly, about Jim Ellis, wasn't that his name? He had found a poem by him in an anthology.

" 'I Said Mistaken Descent'?"

"Something like that."

"That poem is anthologized fairly often. It's a villanelle. Did you notice?"

"I noticed that the first line was repeated a lot. I didn't understand it."

Alice opened her mouth, possibly to recite or interpret. It was a favorite of hers, as rich in her memory as a bowl of ripe fruit. But she closed her mouth without saying the first juicy lines, afraid suddenly to appear obsessed with her former husband. "He wrote it after a fight with me, but it even took me a long time to make sense of it."

"Hmmp. Did he write a lot of poems to you?"

"None. I think sometimes, though, that I was sort of the grain of sand that the pearl formed around."

"None?"

"Nothing 'for Alice,' or 'to my wife.' Nope."

"Did that hurt your feelings?"

Alice lifted her fork out of her salad and inspected the oily lettuce leaf sanded with Parmesan impaled thereon. "Frankly, hurt feelings were such a normal condition that I'm sure I didn't notice."

"How long were you married?"

"Married, four years. Obsessed, almost nine. I mean, me with him."

"Still?"

Alice shrugged. "What about you? Any long-term obsessions?"

"Two short, one long. No marriage, though. And I shouldn't really call them obsessions. I'm not the obsessive type, at least with relationships, which is maybe what went wrong. I was always going off to the Orient or staying at school until all hours. I'm a chronic forgetter of plans."

"I'm the type who chronically takes that sort of thing personally."

"I've gotten better about it. I almost got engaged once. I spent the night of the party studying for an exam."

"That kind of forgetting, huh?"

"I have no excuses, but I don't do it so much any more, really. I've changed. I'm ready to move out to Brooklyn in a big way, sometime."

"I thought you were going to China." She was only twitting him, but he seemed to take it seriously, and sighed. He replied, "Once I went straight from the post office, where I was mailing a travel grant application, to a realtor, who was showing me co-ops for sale in Park Slope. Maybe a sign of age is wanting to do everything at the same time."

Alice smiled. Such a desire seemed much more refreshing than a sign of age to her. "Isn't it funny," she said, "the way people trade this sort of personal information on the first date: this is the way I am, this is who I've been involved with and what I did to them? Every time I start doing it, it feels like a ritual exchange. I wonder if I even say the same sentences over and over."

"Don't you think a date is a fairly personal event?"

"If that's your main experience, you're lucky! Anyway, it is with you." Alice smiled, then blushed, afraid she had implied something beyond incipient friendship, but one of Henry's virtues was apparently tact. He smiled, but slightly, without making eye contact. It was nearly five when they left the restaurant.

Although still not compelling, Henry was not like any other man she knew. She walked in his aura of safety and enthusiasm as under an umbrella, certain, among other things, that Ray was okay and the murder well in the past. Although he himself did not fascinate her—she didn't care to hear, for example, about his family in Wisconsin or his experiences in grammar school—in his company, many things were interesting, and while Alice felt dull by contrast, Henry did not seem bored with her, and so the familiar worry about being good enough company did not nag her. He talked of books he had read and books they had both read. There were books she had read that he had always meant to read. While he had been to the Orient, she had been to Mexico, and he quizzed her enviously. In his talk there was a vivid sense of the populous, busy world. It was enormously agreeable, and Alice found herself kissing him on the cheek as they waited for the subway train back to Manhattan. Henry squeezed her shoulders. By Eighty-sixth Street, they were holding hands.

And physical contact, she realized, had its own dynamic, especially with Henry. "What's a taxonomist?" she said. His hand was rough and dry, larger than hers. "Is that like Linnaeus, or what's his name, van Leeuwenhoek?"

"Very good! Both, actually, in my case. Linnaeus was the father of botanical taxonomy and van Leeuwenhoek invented the microscope."

"You just sort of decide what things are?" Alice felt him switch his grip, putting his fingers between hers. In spite of herself, she squeezed his hand.

"You don't sound impressed."

"I thought that part was all done."

"Most of the work has been done on plants of fashion, like roses and apples. But we're only beginning to realize the real variety and complexity of the world, especially the non-European world. And getting less so every day." He said it with a rueful smile that made Alice wonder if botany was a sad science in 1980. They crossed West End. Alice had forgotten to prepare for this moment, the moment of parting or not, a difficult moment on any date.

Henry said, "Did your family have big Sunday dinners when you were growing up?"

Alice nodded.

"Always at one or two in the afternoon?"

Alice smiled.

"Remember sitting around early Sunday evening, the main event of the day already over and nothing left to do but homework?"

Alice made a face.

"Let's go to the movies."

Alice took her hand out of Henry's and put it through his arm, turning him up West End Avenue. She was a little frightened and a little exhilarated, both at the decision that seemed to have been made to stay with him, and at the decision that seemed to have been made to avoid her apartment and all the responsibilities it represented. She shivered and he said, "Cold?" but she didn't answer.

THEY had been together for twelve hours. Alice thought that might be equivalent to three regular dates, a week of acquaintance, even two. Upon crossing West End they hadn't even looked in the direction of her apartment, and now here they were, in his building, flat, and bedroom. Or Alice was. Henry was in the bathroom. She had no clothes on and her lips still felt impressed upon, taken by surprise. His physical virtues continued. Along with dry, strong hands and vigorous hugs went a searching pucker that made Alice feel kissed and wanted and sought after. She slid between the clean flowered sheets. The bathroom door opened, and Henry came out, smiling, turning out the light, taking off shirt and underpants. Blinded by the sudden darkness, Alice put out her hand, laughing. "I had a boyfriend in college who always turned out the light before taking off his underpants. He said it was because he was Catholic."

Henry took her waving hand. She could almost see his face. He wasn't laughing. "Not Catholic," he said. He kissed the tips of her fingers and the ball of her thumb. "I was burned as a child. It embarrasses some people."

It embarrassed Alice. She was suddenly conscious of the inside of her mouth, the way there was too much saliva there. She swallowed. Henry took the hand he was holding and placed it flat against himself. Alice's fingers sensed the shiny corrugated scar tissue. Its area was at least larger than her hand. She said, without coughing, "Does it embarrass you?"

After a pause, Henry replied, "Yes."

Henry was right. It might have struck Alice more forcefully if the light had been on, but with her hand on his side, his left side, she could feel beneath the surface mutilation solid warm flesh, the vibration of his heart beating. She could see his face more plainly now, as she knew he could see hers. She felt herself begin to smile. Henry put his arms around her and she slipped into them. In a moment, she said, "Can I just ask how it happened?"

"Of course. My cousin was chasing me around a campfire. I was wearing a bathing suit, and I stumbled and fell into the coals. My father was on the other side of the clearing, and my mother, who had been after us to get away from the fire, had my baby sister at the breast, and so, somehow, it took a while for me to get extricated." He shrugged. His eyes drifted down from her face to her breasts, rounded in the moonlight, and Alice shuddered, suddenly seized with desire. Immediately, Henry was embracing her, kissing her chin and neck and shoulders and chest. His instantaneous erection bobbed against her thigh, her hip, her stomach, her other leg, scorching her each time. She put her hands in his hair, feeling for the shape of his scalp, then for the tendons in the back of his neck, then for the muscles in his shoulders, his well-padded scapulae, to either side of his backbone. The small of his back. When she came to his buttocks, which seemed great and hard, islands under her palms, he had already taken his penis in his hand and guided it toward her, through the thicket of hair.

She felt it butt once and then slip. She pulled with her hands on his buttocks and let out a large groan. His was muffled in her neck. They were still for a moment, as if astonished, and then Alice moved against the bed. Usually she yearned for hard endless pounding, but Henry probed inquisitively at first, with molasses slowness, easing moistly out and in until Alice's own body felt like liquid. When the pounding came, it came with little shocks that Alice couldn't get away from. He hugged her tightly. A final shock broke over her, and then, apparently, over him. Alice was panting. She closed her eyes and opened them. By now she could make out everything in the room, which was actually quite light from the street. Henry lifted his head with a groan, and put the palms of his hands under her head. His face, Alice noted with relief, was perfectly familiar. For that more than anything else, she kissed him affectionately and pushed his hair off his forehead.

When she awoke, it was still dark, although she had the sense that most of the night had passed. Beside her lay Henry Mullet, asleep on his back, his arms crossed over his chest. He was not snoring, but he might have been. That might have been what woke her up. Alice adored him.

Exactly coincidental with her adoration came the realization that it was now Sunday and soon she would have to go back to her apartment, and to Susan, and to the impossibly huge difficulties of Craig, Denny, Ray, and Detective Honey. Her visits to the Botanic Garden and the movies that seemed so present were actually over, and in the expected course of events, Henry would return there alone next, even were she to inspire in him the worship he inspired in her. When she sat down on the toilet, the odor of his semen ravished her again, and it took her a moment, a long moment, to gather her thoughts. Even gathered, they made up no system. Henry by himself, intruding upon an ordered and willing life, would have been complex enough. She marvelled at how she had forgotten the chaos of beginning an affair, and at how clearly it now came back to her—the mad rotation of elation and despair, longing, fear, content, desire, the impossibility of work, routine, customary pleasures such as reading or visiting museums. She remembered thinking the last time, the one time since her marriage, that nothing was good about it, even the feeling of being alive, excessively alive. Or she didn't know what it made her feel except full of craving. And that one, George his name was, hadn't lasted a month.

Henry entering her present circle, however, was a complication of cruel proportions. In the first place, she had said nothing to him about Susan or Craig or Denny. He had no idea they even existed. Presenting herself as any old librarian, she had led him to believe a sort of innocence about her that she no longer believed of herself, and yet how could she have said, One thing you should know about me is that I discovered a murder only last week? To do so would be ridiculous and repulsive. She opened the door of the dark bathroom and looked out into the room. Henry had turned over on his side. Nothing had changed in the previous ten minutes. She still adored him. She closed the door. She had pretended to Henry that her abandonment by Jim Ellis was the largest event in her life, but she could now clearly see that that was no longer the case. In the dark, in a stranger's anonymous, coldly tiled bathroom, it was nearly possible to imagine herself across the street, wedded to Susan and as devoted to surviving this crime as the fairy tale princess who must sort seven bags of barley before sundown. Did such a princess take on another task, the task of spinning three bales of straw into gold, say, with the barley tumbled at her feet? It was a helpful thought.

And it was not necessarily Henry Mullet who had swept her away in the first place. Clearly, as through a pinhole, she could see that he was a nice man with a stock of information and a pleasant expertise in bed, but still not compelling, although she was compelled. What she felt for him now (she inhaled sharply, visualizing him) had been plucked from a hat, like a large feather duster. She leaned her warm shoulder against the cold tile until she was shivering, but calm, ready to put on her clothes and cross the street.

She was fond of Henry as she crept around the bed. He had stretched automatically to fill her place with his knees and fists. She sat as lightly as she could on the very edge of the bed, and felt on the floor for her underpants. His warm hand slipped beneath her buttock, electrifying her, and she fell into the welcoming bed as into a bowl, her underpants clutched in her fingers. "Where were you?" whispered Henry, his face ablaze with the light from the street. His eyes dipped at the inside corner, his matter-of-fact nose jutted at her, the peaks of his upper lip flattened to hills when he smiled, his chin was square across the bottom. Had he not looked like this, would she be more resolute? Her body seemed to smooth itself against his. Alice closed her eyes, panting. "In the bathroom," she said.

Her resolution had withered away by the time they awoke to the well-risen sun and the scattering of clothes around the room. Fortunately Alice recognized her yearning to stay in bed as an old and familiar opponent. Henry appeared to be an eager riser. "What shall we do today?" he demanded, thrusting himself into a T-shirt. His derriere as he crossed the foot of the bed was muscular, each buttock hollow at the outside. Alice thought how large they had seemed beneath her palms and grinned. "Breakfast?" said Henry. "A marathon of Polish movies at the Modern? Do you have a bike?"

Alice threw back the covers and stood up, feeling, under his gaze, tall and slow limbed, but not in the least modest. "What would you have done today?"

"Gone to work, probably. We're always a week behind in May. Looking at you, I'm sorry I hate to make love in the morning."

"Do you?" Alice attempted to extricate herself from his embrace.

"I used to." He was whispering. "I've always hated to be indoors. Alice."

"I think you should go to work, then." She made herself smile with mere affection and good humor, made herself relinquish the feel of his smooth back, made herself push him away.

"What are you going to do, then?"

"Come to my senses."

"Don't you dare."

"Call me tonight and I'll let you know." She sat on the bed and buckled on her sandals.

"Alice."

"Don't Alice me, or I'll stay in bed all day."

"Why not?"

"Because you hate to stay in bed. Really."

"Don't you want any breakfast?" Alice shook her head. "Will you walk me to the train, then?"

Returning from the subway stop with two bagels and four ounces of chive cream cheese, she found Noah at her door, leaning on the buzzer for her apartment. He saw her before she could greet him. "Alice!" he roared. "Where the fuck have you been?"

"H and H hot bagels." She flourished the bag.

"All night? We were worried sick! Rya was afraid to come over!"

"I did go to a late double feature last night." She said it tentatively, exploratively.

"Why didn't you tell anyone? Susan called and called, then I called and called."

"Why didn't anyone just come over?" Had he been listening carefully, he would have noticed the tiny shake in her voice.

"Susan did, about ten. I was going to later, but I couldn't make it."

"Did anyone think that I might like to be alone?" She raised her voice self-righteously. "That I might like to go to a bunch of movies, and then just unplug the phone? I haven't been alone, or away from all this for a week! It's hard on me, too!"

Successfully intimidated, Noah put his arm around her and eased her into the vestibule of her apartment building. "You just have to say something, you know. Everyone's ready to be worried, especially with what's happened to Ray."

"What's happened to Ray? Let's go upstairs."

"Nothing new. Except that Honey says he may have been seen in Miami, at the airport. He asked me if I knew if Ray had friends in Miami."

"Was he all right? Was he with anyone?"

"He was all right, if it was Ray, and they couldn't tell if he was with anyone."

"Miami!"

"Maybe it wasn't him." Noah stepped off the elevator and un-snapped the pocket of his shirt. He twirled the joint absently between his fingers as she unlocked her door, and lit up as soon as they got into the apartment. Alice handed him an ashtray. Alice had always liked to look at Noah, who was tall and thin, with dark thick hair and regular features. His mouth, especially, was straight and perfectly shaped, like that of some founding father known for absolute integrity. She had never felt, though, that she was his particular friend, as she had with every other member of their group, even Rya. There was something either reserved or simply boring about Noah. He perhaps felt the same way about her. She understood that he was a good, even excellent bass player, with a tenacious hold on the beat. In astrological days, Craig had sometimes called him a "closet Taurus." Alice had wondered more than once whether drugs had destroyed his mind. He was older than the rest of them, and even twelve years ago, at twenty-three, Noah smoked marijuana the way some people smoked cigarettes. "You want some juice, Noah?"

A seed popped at the end of his joint. "I'm not that worried any more about him. Ray's pretty good at taking care of himself."

"Noah, you know that's not true. Remember that guy who beat him up a couple of years ago, then came back two weeks later and Ray actually let him in his apartment and he had a knife and he took something, what was it, Ray's tape deck?"

"That's so."

"I'm more worried that they found him in Miami. I wish they'd found him in Toronto or London. Someplace English."

"They may have seen him. *May*."

"Okay."

"Why don't you call Susan and tell her you're safe and sound?"

When she came back from the phone, Noah had stretched on the couch and put his booted feet up on the window sill. Alice set a glass of orange juice in front of him. In the ashtray was a large roach. Looking at him, Alice could not help imagining Henry Mullet, who had kissed her for five minutes before getting on his train. Noah's conjugality, which had always seemed rather funny to Alice, assumed new interest. She visualized Noah animated with desire as Henry had been not twelve hours before. Even as he sat there, he gained depth. "Actually, I should tell you that I—" It was out before she knew it, but as Noah's head turned toward her, she chose not to go on. What if nothing came of Henry? There would be time to bring him up later. "You're speaking to Susan then?"

"I was never not speaking to her. That dinner was just a bad scene. I don't blame her or anything. Rya was hurt, but you know Rya."

Alice nodded. "I've been wondering how you guys were feeling."

"It's hard, man. Nobody said it wouldn't be. And Rya was pretty close to Shellady."

Alice made a circle of orange juice on the table with her finger. "Not closer than you were, Noah?"

"Lately, maybe. I don't know. Maybe lately." He seemed uneasy.

"Noah—"

He surprised Alice by looking at her expectantly, almost eagerly. Alice realized that he may not have had anyone to talk to all week. She grew frightened, then with her bad sense of timing, waited too long. Noah turned back to the window. At last, she said, "Noah, was there something between Rya and Craig?"

He opened his mouth and closed it, continued to look out the window. Alice's thought returned to Henry Mullet like a wave to the ocean. "Yeah," said Noah.

"I can't believe it."

Noah shrugged.

"How long?"

Noah sat up and picked up his orange juice, looked at it, then chugged it down. "Too long," he said.

"Didn't it drive you crazy?"

"Yeah."

"Why didn't you do anything about it?"

"I did. I tried, anyway."

"What happened?"

"Remember that old Jefferson Airplane song, 'Triad'? 'Why don't we go on as three?' " He hummed a few notes. Alice nodded. He shrugged.

"It must have been very painful for you."

"It wasn't, in a way. They were very affectionate."

"Oh, Noah."

"Shellady had this theory. He said that he and Rya would have to go through a kind of breaking-in period, that when you were new with somebody, you couldn't avoid that." Alice nodded in vehement agreement, then looked at her watch, wondering if Henry had gotten to Brooklyn yet. She glanced out the window. It was a beautiful day for it. She imagined him excited at the gate. "He figured that after that period was over, then we could go on as three, in fact we would have to, since none of us would be able to do without the other two."

"Did you believe that?"

"I couldn't do without Rya, that's for sure."

"Noah, I'm really shocked."

"Maybe not without Shellady, either. I thought of finding myself another gig, maybe something on the Coast. I even called Dale Nolan. Remember him? There wasn't much. Anyway," he paused. "It scared me to move." He said this shamefaced, as if,

Alice thought, a real man would have moved. "Shit," he said. "I loved the guy. You loved the guy, too. How could Rya not? How could she? That's the thing that's kept me here. It was all completely inevitable. I think about Shellady and he seems like this bright light to me. Sooner or later the moth has got to give in."

"That's not true! We didn't orbit him! He wasn't the sun!"

"Do you think?" Noah let his head drop on the back of the couch. He sighed. Alice's hands were trembling.

7

A L I C E hated her responses to things. Always amazed and respectful, she never managed to find anything out, or even to see what had to be found out. After Noah left, Alice stood in the shower regretting over and over that she hadn't picked up on one of their exchanges: "Why didn't you do anything about it?" and "I did" or "I tried." (So unobservant was she that she couldn't even remember his exact words.) It would have been perfectly natural to ask, What did you do, when did you do it? Wouldn't Honey have asked that? Wouldn't Honey have secured dates and times, details about Noah's present relationship with Rya, alibis for the evening and the night of May 9?

Honey intrigued Alice the Citizen. He could perceive the murderer in everyone, she thought, whereas she was only able to instantly sympathize. He was trained to make judgments, while judgments were the last thing she could make. As soon as anyone spoke, she saw his point of view, and it was hard for her to rate points of view or to decide between them. She was a liberal who voted in Democratic primaries, addressed envelopes, and even canvassed from time to time, but she had come to suspect that a vital body politic couldn't really stand such tolerance as hers, widespread. She wondered what Henry was doing. The door of her bedroom opened. It was Susan, who said, "Yoohoo! Didn't you hear me shout?"

Alice, momentarily transfixed by surprise, shook herself and smiled. "I was in the shower. I hate this paranoia! Noah just jumped all over me about being out of touch last night, and every time the door opens or a curtain moves, my heart starts pounding."

"Yours!"

"You probably want to pass out!" Alice kissed her friend on the cheek, and Susan sat down on the bed. "I'm sorry I didn't call last night. I was coming out of the store and there was the theater showing *Breaking Away* and *Manhattan* and I couldn't resist. I thought of calling you. I'm sorry. And I really didn't realize that the phones were still unplugged when I got home. I was just beat."

"What did you do yesterday?"

"Well, actually," Alice dropped a dress over her head and bit her lip. "I went out to the Botanic Garden in Brooklyn." She smiled.

"I thought you were going to come over to the shop. I looked for you all day."

"Did you? When you didn't say anything about it, I just assumed you'd forgotten and I figured you were busy. . . ." She let her voice fade, but Susan didn't say anything. "I'm sorry." But even while regretting her own clumsiness for the millionth time, Alice felt resentful. To have not spent those hours with Henry? She beat it back, beating back as well the reflexive confession of where she had been, how she had found a new "interest." It would be a good topic of conversation—what he was like, how he was dressed, what he did for a living, how old he was and how experienced. "Hungry?" Alice said, heading for the kitchen. "I'm starved."

"No," replied Susan, an expression of perfect reserve that erased

Alice's own reserve. Instantly Alice wanted to press upon her friend the bagels with all the cream cheese, two grapefruit halves and whatever else she could find—a hard-boiled egg, a banana, a sugar cookie, the jar of artichoke hearts. Susan sipped at a cup of tea and talked coolly about work. Yes she had set up her displays, the clothes were nice, but drab colors, lots of khaki, and even more expensive than the owners had expected. Nubbly cotton sweaters for a hundred dollars, thin white balloon pants for eighty-five. Jeanne, the new salesgirl, hadn't shown up again, they'd caught a fifteen-year-old trying to leave with a French T-shirt under her blouse. Alice said, "These grapefruit are very sweet" and "The cream cheese is Zabar's best," lifting her bagel alluringly.

Although she turned down everything, Susan smiled and said, "Remember that time I took you to Denny's parents' house?"

"His mother made pie for breakfast."

"And one of those nights for dinner there were five plates of chicken on the table, one at each corner and one in the middle."

"And the bowl for gravy was a mixing bowl."

"And there were two mixing bowls full of mashed potatoes."

"Tell me about it," exclaimed Alice. "I mashed them myself with a potato masher."

"Mrs. Minchart has never operated what you might call 'une cuisine,'" laughed Susan, "but there was a whole cabinet set aside for candy and cookies. Do you think it wrecked him?"

"Wrecked whom?"

"Denny."

"How could it have wrecked him?"

Susan tilted back in her chair. "It was so much fun. It was endless fun. I don't think I ever heard about all the things they did, those kids. One year after school, Denny had a job stuffing sausage. I think he must have been only about seven or eight. He'd stuff with this hand crank sausage stuffer for an hour and a half or two after school, and then on Friday he'd take home a great big circle of sausage for dinner. He was such a little breadwinner! And in the summer he fished and took home bass and things for dinner. He was very proud. I knew him for all those years and he never stopped coming up with stories about little things he had done when he was growing up. He was good at telling them, too. I used to think that I made it bad for him, because before he met me, he just sort of accepted his childhood, but I was so amazed and excited by it all that after a while he began to see it as strange, as a sort of golden age. He was much more delighted by it later on than he was when I met him."

"It was interesting. You couldn't help your response. You wouldn't have wanted to, either, would you? You've got to be yourself."

"But what if your self damages the other person? People look so discrete, as if they are a certain way. But obviously, a lot of the time that you're mad at them for being a certain way, it's actually you who's making them be that way."

"But if you tried to separate that tangle every hour of the day, you'd go crazy, and what's worse, everything you did would be self-conscious and false."

After a moment, Susan said, "I don't think Denny thought it was ever as interesting since as it was before."

"Since what? Before what?"

"Since we got together."

"Oh, nonsense." Alice stood up and began vehemently clearing away, in order to express her dismissal of this proposition.

"I'm not blaming myself. I know how you hate for me to blame myself. That's just a convenient watershed. I suppose I'm saying that if I had had his childhood, I would have thought that every-thing since was an anti-climax."

"Noah was here for about forty-five minutes this morning. I realized it was the first time I'd ever really talked to him. Isn't that funny? We've known each other for twelve—"

"I think Denny had a dream childhood, the last Tom Sawyer boyhood in the history of America."

"Let's go outside. It's another nice day."

"Why are you so determined to change the subject?"

"You sound like you're talking out of depression—"

Susan shook her head. "Alice, my dear, you amaze me. How should I talk? What should my voice be coming out of? How should I be seeing everything? You always wait until you think well of something or someone and then you label that the truth."

Stung by both the justice of this remark and by the glimpse of Susan observing and drawing conclusions about her, Alice did not reply. She remembered Henry Mullet. She hadn't slept much the previous night. Tears smarted beneath her eyelids. Susan went on, "What has Denny had for the last five years? A job with no future, a rented apartment, some nice clothes. Big deal."

"A job that he loved, a lover that he adored, an apartment in New York City, and money to spend as he pleased."

"So you say."

"So *he* said. And he didn't think his job had no future. He had lots of hopes."

Susan grimaced. "You know that his father used to make him do farm work in the winter with no gloves because he didn't want his oldest boy ever to like farming? He wanted him to be a doctor or a lawyer or a college professor. He never held that against his father. He never held anything against anyone. Not even Craig."

Not wanting to, Alice exclaimed, "He didn't have to hold anything against Craig, you did that for him!"

Susan shrugged, reached into her bag, and took out a pack of cigarettes.

"I didn't realize you were smoking again."

Susan didn't reply.

"Don't smoke! Eat! I'll go buy you ten pounds of chocolate. You were inhuman when you were giving up smoking."

"You know, I loved smoking in Minneapolis. I loved to go with Denny to the gigs and sit at a table near the front, and watch him and drink beer and smoke. I'd buy a pack of Camels and get a new book of matches, and put them on the table right in front of me, like a magazine or something. Friends would come over and sit down and leave, Denny and Craig would sit down between sets, the waitress would keep topping off my glass, and I would sit there appreciating Denny and *smoking*. That was the key activity. I was secure in the knowledge that at the end of the evening, Denny would get paid, pack up, and then take me home and fuck my brains out. When you had a pack of cigarettes in your hand, you really had something weighty and full."

"You were so determined to give it up."

"Why did we move to Chicago? Why did we move to New York? Time began to push us. Every time a new group came out with a big record, Craig would figure out their average age."

"We grew up."

Susan smiled. "Well, I wouldn't go that far. No one had any kids."

"Can you imagine?" Alice meant, telling a five-year-old about *this*.

"No one ever did. Don't you think that's peculiar?"

"What?"

"You and Jim were married for almost five years. How come you never had any kids? Or even thought about it, as far as I knew."

"Kids in New York—"

"Come on. There're kids all over New York."

"Yes, but think of the awful lives they lead. Mom has to go with you everywhere till you're about fifteen. You're officially indoors, which means behind three locked barriers, or outdoors, which means in some dusty park with five hundred other kids. There's none of that easy drifting through the house, leaving the refrigerator open and banging the screen door that we had. If we'd lived elsewhere, I think we'd have—"

"Really?"

"I don't know. I never thought about it."

"You got to be twenty-seven, and you never thought about it?"

"What room was there for kids? There was always Jim Jim Jim. Can you imagine him modifying his life for kids? Not going out every other night? Getting up at six? Eating hot dogs for dinner? Once when we were at his parents' house, his cousin came over with her baby, and somehow it got on Jim's lap. He didn't hold it at all, and pretty soon, it started to slide off. He didn't even realize it. Finally, Jim's mother jumped up and grabbed it before it fell to the floor. I mean, he didn't have bad intentions, but he didn't even realize it!"

"What about you? Didn't you ever lust after a baby?"

"I lusted after Jim! What was left over to lust after a baby?"

"Well, doesn't all of this seem weird to you? The patterns of our lives formed twelve years ago! And they didn't basically change until *now!*"

"We were happy!"

Susan's eyebrows lifted.

"Well, at least we were going to be happy. I always thought that things with Jim would get smooth and comfortable sometime. When he was around, I felt exposed to something, either danger or embarrassment, every minute, but I knew that would pass, and then we'd do other things."

"Yes, and I always thought that someday Craig would leave, or at least learn to live his own life, and then we'd do other things. Well, let's do something. Aren't you tired of hanging around?"

And something about the way she set her teacup in the saucer and lifted her eyelids reminded Alice that she was with Susan. With Susan! No one was like Susan, after all, no one thought about things as Susan did. Some quality of her mind was unique, attractive but indefinable, inaccessible. Always Alice came around to this sense of something beyond reach, or even comprehension, in her friend. Repeatedly, she had failed to name it: femininity, reserve, integrity, even selfishness, self-reliance, security, but it was larger and more mysterious than any of these, and was something Alice could not help wanting to possess. It was a great talent, this trick of arousing perennial curiosity. Alice put her arm affectionately around Susan's waist and said, "Let's go out to the Statue of Liberty. We've never once been there."

A S I T turned out, they ended up merely in midtown, window shopping. Starting at Bergdorf's, they strolled down Fifth Avenue, looking at store windows. There were high-heeled sandals in alligator-patterned leather, a narrow strap with a tiny gold buckle to set off the bone and tendon of a slender ankle. Chocolates shaped like flowers, spilling from gold boxes. Tablecloths scattered with embroidered violets and appliquéd roses. Cuffed cotton shorts and crisp shirts bearing vivid palm leaves and the faces of tigers and monkeys. Hardbound books with jackets as bizarre and hip as the pictures on record albums. Tight white skirts slit up the front or the back. "I don't think we're with it any more," laughed Susan. They examined their hair and faces in the glittering clean windows.

"I went off to college with a whole new wardrobe," said Alice. "Six square wool dresses with short sleeves, one of which was purple with green vertical bands—"

"I remember that one."

"Two pair of hip-hugging woolen slacks, one gold and one red white and blue plaid, with those funny belts that were longer around the bottom edge than they were around the top edge—"

"Ugh."

"Wait, get this, and a sleeveless wool sweater, also gold, with something in green and blue embroidered in wool across the top. Sleeveless! Hip length—"

"Just long enough to cover the belt."

"Yards of beads."

"I had those apple seeds strung on a string. I could wind them around my neck six times and still get them off over my head. I thought they were the choicest jewels I'd ever seen."

"I was very envious of those. You definitely had more style than the rest of us."

"My favorite period was the Indian cotton period. Calf length."

"Tights and Dr. Scholl's exercise sandals."

"A huge wool sweater."

"With the lanolin still in it, and preferably with little bits of straw and sheep shit to prove it was wool. And hair as long as the bottom edge of the sweater."

"Your hair was beautiful long."

"Peacoat in the winter, with the sweater hanging out beneath."

"That was a good period for you." Alice smiled to think of Susan's hair parted by a pencil line down the center of her head, then brushed smooth and looped over her ears, lifted and twisted once and pinned to her head with a single long silver barrette. Or braided as thick as three fingers down her back.

"Your best period was forties dresses from antique clothing stores."

"Mmmm." Alice nodded. "I still have the sneaking suspicion that those dresses are the hippest of all, that they do so much for your figure they transcend the tides of fashion."

"Dream on."

"Groovy." Alice put her arm through Susan's and stepped off the curb of Fifty-fourth Street. In a moment they stopped to gaze at a tray of glistening preserved fruit: peaches, pineapple, cherries, but also kiwi fruit and sunset-tinted mangoes and lime-colored quinces. Behind them were trays of cakes, mostly varying intensities of chocolate. A sign in the window advertised fifteen varieties of coffee. "Carrot cake is out of fashion, too," said Susan, with a mock sigh.

"Thank God. And honey bran raisin cupcakes."

"And mystical morning lightning herbal tea."

"I loved the clothes but I hated the food."

"Black beans and rice, pinto beans and rice, garbanzo beans and rice."

"Don't forget the water. When you'd finished your beans and rice, there was always a lot of water in the bottom of the bowl. You couldn't really call it broth."

"Yummy."

By now they were laughing. The few passers-by smiled to see them. Alice was amazed at the power of things to raise her spirits so thoroughly, even things she couldn't afford or didn't want. "What's your favorite former fantasy?" she asked.

"Oh, definitely dome-commune-with-radio-station. Don't you remember that one? It was Ray's, I think, first, but he and Denny and Craig talked about it for at least a year. Craig was going to get a first-class broadcaster license. Plots of vegetables next to each dome, chickens, cows, kerosene lamps until we got the hydroelectric generator in, all cars left at the edge of the property. I had the horse plan all ready to go. And goats. Craig saw these people in California who lived in a teepee and kept goats, and he nearly had one shipped out."

"That was a good one. Jim imagined himself getting on a perfectly natural sleep schedule. Whenever it would be dark, he would sleep. He thought you could stockpile it over the winter, and if everything averaged out over the year, you'd be perfectly alert and healthy. We were going to sleep on straw mats and do yoga for an hour before breakfast, which would be entirely fruit, of course."

"Us, too," said Susan. "They must have talked."

"It was a wonderful fantasy. Not my favorite, though."

"What was that?"

"Overland to Nepal."

"You even saved money for that, didn't you?"

"Two or three thousand dollars."

"That was a lot of money, then."

"We never could decide between the Land-Rover idea and the donkey idea. Jim thought if you were going to do it, then you had to go to every extreme, otherwise it wouldn't be a pure experience. He always said that if you thought of something like going by donkey or eating only fruit for breakfast, then you had a moral obligation to do it, because you could lose your soul through compromise."

"Why didn't you ever do it?"

"Well, some guys got ambushed in Afghanistan, remember them? Their donkey was named Willy, which was short for Willimakit. One of them was killed. But basically, we just didn't go, like we just didn't start the dome commune." They walked in silence for a few moments, and a surge of grief struck Alice and drained away. When she could speak coolly again, she said, "Honey seemed surprised that we all moved here together. I guess he was never going to start up a dome commune with his best pals."

"Doesn't seem the type."

"Didn't you love it, really? Didn't friendship seem like the great immensity that would never be exhausted or used up? There was always someone to talk to, always someone attractive, always someone who had a different perspective on your cantankerous spouse."

"Always someone whose food you could eat without asking and whose records and books you could take."

"And whose clothes you could wear."

"And whose bed you could pass out in."

"And whom you didn't have to worry about not touching. Or touching. Don't you miss it?"

Susan stopped and looked at her, thoughtful. "No, not now. It was fun." She walked on. "Everyone did seem so unique and interesting. I don't think that's true any more."

"And familiar. Peculiar, interesting, and familiar. I always thought that was what a big family must be like, except that in a big family, you would be stuck with younger brothers and sisters or babies or boring aunts that you had to show respect for."

"I don't think my mother ever had a dinner party for six people that she actually was fond of. Whether they were relatives or my father's business associates or neighbors or whatever, there were never six that she liked, my father liked, and who liked each other all at the same time. I do remember thinking about our potlucks and feeling very superior about that."

"I thought it would never end. I thought I would never have to eat food with someone I didn't know intimately." Alice laughed.

Susan again lifted her eyebrows. "Did we know each other intimately? I once tried to write down everything I knew about Denny, all his qualities and physical characteristics. I didn't get much beyond a physical description, and even that was pretty general."

Fifty-first Street. They crossed to the east side of Fifth Avenue in order to meet up casually with the windows of Saks. Alice realized with a start that she hadn't thought of Henry Mullet in perhaps half an hour. Thinking of him now seemed unaccustomed, alien. For a moment, a trifle embarrassing. She had told him she was going to spend the day coming to her senses. Perhaps she would. Susan drew her attention to a lovely white summer dress, tucked and ruffled and inset with lace, but Alice's attention slid off the dress and onto Susan, before whom she stood still in absolute love and familiarity. It seemed suddenly true to her that no man would ever do more than kiss her life or her imagination, no man could overcome the quantity of experience she had now accumulated. The labor of explaining everything—not just telling anecdotes, which was rather fun, but explaining strands of thought that stretched over years, habits of perception firmly in place, justifying deeply held views (such discussion bored her even to think about)—seemed as difficult and unrewarding as carrying stones across a stony field. Weren't marriages contracted in later life always shallower than others, more or less parallel, never convergent? And wouldn't Susan's presence always ensure that shallowness, a failure of concentration on the man, perhaps, that would be fatal to a real marriage? No man would ever have more rights over her than Susan did. She could not imagine it. She could imagine Henry kissing her, though. She could see in her mind the drop of his eyes from her face to her moonlit breasts, and experience at once the thud of desire and expectation that his evident desire awakened in her. She closed her eyes. Susan said, "I don't know if I like the skirt and blouse better or the dress, but if Saks were open, I know I'd go spend the rent on one or the other," and the sound of her voice transformed Alice's memory of her own body into a picture of Susan's. It was as if she had thought about it before, except that she hadn't, Susan's pointed chin, her head bent back, exposing her neck and shoulders, the smoothness of her chest and then the swell of her breasts, which Alice suddenly wanted to kiss and suck. Her stomach, never concave, would flow around her navel like water between the banks of her hipbones. Alice imagined her own hand flowing with it. And then her tongue—

"Look at this one," said Susan, and Alice's eyes snapped open. The fantasy had been so startling and complete that she was hardly embarrassed by it, not feeling somehow that she had called it up, only that it expressed itself automatically after a long time of waiting. It could be blamed on the murder, on her arousal by Henry Mullet, on the disorientation of the last week. More importantly, it seemed good, an expression of the depth of their friendship. "It's gorgeous," she said. "I'm starving. Let's find someplace to eat."

H O N E Y was waiting for them on the stoop of Susan's apartment building. "Beautiful evening," he said, and it was, the air so dry that the sinking of the sun and the fading of the light were purely and gently themselves, deepening blue untouched by pinks or oranges or purples. "I hoped I would catch you." He raised the pitch of his sentence slightly, so that they could gracefully state where they had been. Alice complied, as usual, "We were in midtown, just walking and window shopping. We ate." Unable to stop herself, she added, "At New Japan, on Sixth." She stopped herself.

"I just need some information," said Honey.

"Let's go upstairs," suggested Susan, polite but reserved, as if he might sit down, but she wasn't going to offer him refreshment.

"This will be quick," he said. Although it was a Sunday in

May, his tie was tied and his jacket was buttoned. Susan unlocked the door of her apartment and preceded them inside. Honey looked around. Alice saw that he could not help it. She looked around, too. He said, "What do you know about a man named Daniel or David Brick?"

Alice looked at Susan, who appeared as blank as she felt. Susan shrugged. "Never heard of him."

"Tall and extremely thin, shaggy dark hair, occasional goatee, tattoos on—" he consulted his notebook—"left forearm, butterfly, left upper arm, snake, and right hand, musical note."

Susan thought for a moment, gazing across the room toward the big front windows. Alice thought, too, but only as a formality. "Still nothing," said Susan.

Honey looked at Alice, who shook her head, then realized that all the plants were gone. She looked around again. The five-foot *Schefflera*, the giant hanging spider plants, the aloes, the baby's tears, the various ivies that formed a drape around the two windows. The avocado, big plants, little plants, cuttings, trees, all gone. Honey read from his notebook: "Dave or Dan Brick is a fairly well-known character around the musical world of the city. Has been hanging around music clubs, especially those catering to the popular music trade, for six or seven years. Not visibly employed, no known address, between thirty and thirty-five years old." He looked up at them. They shook their heads. "Sometimes carries guitar and calls self a rock guitarist, but not employed by any band in the city. Police record: convicted on drug charges, 1967, served one year of a three-year sentence at Danbury State Prison. Paroled for good behavior. Arrested for passing bad checks, 1972, plea bargained for reduced charge, fined. Picked up on drug charges, 1974, 1978. Released for lack of evidence. Known to be occasionally armed, in spite of felony conviction. Did either Mr. Minehart or Mr. Shellady ever mention anyone like this, who might have hung around with their entourage, doing occasional errands, maybe?"

"They met tons of people," said Susan.

"Okay. Let's see," said Honey. "For a time involved with a woman singer named Nina Slager, or Nina Starlette."

"Nina Starlette is familiar," said Alice. "Isn't she sort of a Patti Smith clone?"

"Denny and Craig might have played at the same place she did once, at a festival or something like that, but Craig hated that sort of musician. He wouldn't have talked to her, and certainly wouldn't have had anything to do with her boyfriend."

"Might Mr. Reschley have known Miss Slager or Mr. Brick?"

"Ray did work for a lot of people," said Alice. "A few years ago, he sometimes hired himself out to groups who were getting ready to make demo tapes. He would do the mixing and producing. When some of the groups got contracts, he got to be well known to the record companies. He wasn't a snob like Craig. He would have worked for Nina Starlette, but he never mentioned her to any of us. She wasn't one of his successes if he did work for her."

"And Mr. Mast?"

Susan laughed. "Noah would have run the other direction at the very sight of someone like Nina Starlette. Noah's sort of a country boy."

"Mrs. Mast?"

"Well, Ryn was a secretary at NBC for a while. She could have met anyone, but she never talked about Nina Starlette or this other guy."

While Susan talked, Alice tried to judge the effect of the missing plants. Susan had always had plants, even in their college dorm. In fact, the university-supplied desk hadn't known a typewriter in the four years of Susan's tenure, but had been pushed against the windows and laden with greenery. The drawers had been pulled out and turned over, so that more plants could sit on them. Now, however, the apartment didn't seem bare, exactly, more— Honey broke into her thoughts. "You feel, then, that there's no likely connection between yourselves and David or Daniel Brick?"

Susan shook her head, as did Alice.

Honey gave a deep sigh. "Well," he said, "Brick was picked up last night on a gambling charge. Since he was a known denizen of the rock and roll milieu, I took the liberty of going through the items in his pockets. On his ring of keys were keys to your apartment."

Alice felt herself vibrate with the shock. Susan had paled. "Someone I've never even heard of? Someone with a police record?"

"I'm afraid so. You can come down to the station, if you'd like, and have a look at him, just to see if you might conceivably recognize him. By the way, Mrs. Ellis, have you had the locks on your apartment changed?"

Alice started. "Should I?"

"It might be wise."

"But—"

Susan interrupted her. "Will he have to see me?"

"He won't see anything, or even know he's being looked at. You could come tomorrow morning; before you go to work would be a good time."

Susan nodded.

Honey snapped his notebook closed, and offered to see Alice to a cab if she was going home. Out the window she could see that it was almost dark. Alice put her arms around Susan and kissed her good night. On the street, as if by magic, Honey had a cab for her inside of a minute, and he was gone, as if by magic, before she had thought again to ask him why she should have her locks changed.

A S S H E let herself in, she could not stop thinking how bizarre it would be to know that a stranger had your keys, had had them for months of nights when you had locked yourself in smugly and gone to bed in perfect trust. Her rooms were pleasantly untidy, demanding the leisurely attention she would be glad to give them while she drank tea, took a bath, thought about

Henry Mullet, and reveled in her present sense of kinship with Susan. Of course she wouldn't have wished it, but one of the effects of the murder had turned out to be a new intimacy between them, not precisely like what they'd had before. Part of it was that they spent more time together, of course, necessary time, for packing and cleaning and doing business, but also idle time, when Alice was more than glad to be a warm comfortable body whose presence in the room might be of some use. Before, Denny would have been that body. Another part of it was that the compelling topics of conversation were new ones, giving their talks a good deal of fresh urgency and, Alice was willing to admit, interest, too. Each evening's conversation held a fascination for her that would be hard to forgo, rather like, but not as demeaning as, the fascination they had held two years ago. What had they talked about since? Books? Movies? Friends? Food? It had all seemed satisfactory at the time, but it was hard for Alice to remember. Now they were talking about their whole lives, and Alice had the sense that they were seeking something, some understanding beyond the solution to the murder mystery, some knowledge of life that only the understanding of an irreducible fact like a murder could give one. This curiosity lent weight to every word they said. Alice sensed that that, too, could be addicting. And Susan needed her. That was most addicting. For the first time in their twelve years of friendship, the balance was nearly equal. In contrast to the last two years, especially, Alice had something to offer and the opportunity to offer it, and, as difficult as it was for her to know just what to offer and just when to offer it, she knew, especially after today, that it was valued. Alice grinned, delighted, and surprised at how delighted she was. She nearly picked up the phone to tell Susan how delighted she was, but it rang. Alice laughed, intending to say at once, "I was thinking of you, too. Did you barricade the door?" but it was Rya, not Susan. Rya hadn't called Alice in months, not since a brief period of closeness around the previous Thanksgiving.

"Is it too late? Are you in bed?" asked Rya.

"No, I just walked in."

"I was afraid you'd be in bed. I always forget what time it is and call people at one or two in the morning. What time is it?"

"A little after nine."

"Is that all?"

"That's all."

"I won't worry about Noah then. He said he wouldn't be in until ten. I was beginning to worry about him, but I won't."

"What's up?"

"Can we have a drink tomorrow evening? I want to talk to you."

"Sure, but why don't we talk now? You're alone and I'm alone."

"Not over the phone. This is across the table in a public place sort of talk."

"Is everything okay?"

"I don't know. That's what I want to talk to you about."

"Just give me some idea."

"It's about what Noah talked to you about this morning."

"That is face-to-face talk, I suppose." Alice wished hers didn't have to be the face.

"You won't stand me up?"

"Of course not." Alice grimaced, thinking that now she couldn't even forget unintentionally.

Rya named a bar on Forty-eighth Street known for its hors d'oeuvres and its noise. Gritting her teeth, Alice committed herself to being there at five-fifteen. After that, the phone was stubborn, silent. Susan didn't call to remind her of their pleasant day or gossip about Honey, and Henry Mullet didn't call to tell her that he had thought about her all day, so that she could admit the same to him. On second thought, however, he probably hadn't thought of her much at all. He wasn't the type. His mind, considering trees and shrubs and "herbaceous plants" (Alice savored the words) would be undivided, wholly concentrated. It was one of his finest qualities. So in spite of the resolute silence of the

phone, Alice smiled and hummed around the seven-room apartment, thinking of Henry's fine qualities. She took a bath, knowing he would call her out of it as soon as she was settled into it
("I just figured you would call now, I'm dripping"), but he didn't.
Nor while she was brushing her teeth, creaming her face, looking
through the drawers and laundry basket for pajama bottoms. Even
as she got into bed and took up her book, the phone didn't ring.
She picked it up to see if it was dead. It sizzled with life. Finally
discouraged, she turned out the light and settled herself to forget
it.

Ringing clattered her out of some dream, more a sense of something, riding in a bus, perhaps, than an actual dramatic situation.
The noise jolted her, almost frightened her, except that the feeling was in her bones and blood rather than in her mind. She was
shocked. She picked up the phone and babbled. "What was that?"
said Henry Mullet.

"I don't know," said Alice. "You tell me. Things always rise
up from the depths if I answer the phone before I'm awake."

"Are you awake now?" His voice was low and rich, as affectionate as she could have wished it to be.

"I think so. Really, what did I say?"

Henry chuckled. Thinking she was about to be teased, Alice
grew annoyed, but Henry only said, "Leave it alone. You said,
'Leave it alone.' "

"I think I was dreaming about a bus." Prepared to be annoyed,
Alice was charmed. Jim Ellis would have made her guess and beg
him and suspect she had embarrassed herself. She said, "Do you
have any sisters?"

"One."

"But you aren't a tease."

"Do you like to be teased?"

"Hate it. Only my grandfather, my mother's father, can get
away with it."

"What else do you hate?"

"Being goosed on the stairs." She laughed.

"Is there anyone who can get away with that? Your other grandfather, maybe?"

"No one gets away with that. I might as well tell you that I haven't preceded a man up the stairs in six or seven years at least."

"I promise never to goose you on the stairs, then."

"What shall I promise you?"

"Promise me to eat dinner over here Wednesday night when I get back from Brooklyn."

"I promise."

"I'll call you when I get home. Seven, seven-fifteen."

Alice was grinning. "What shall I bring?"

"Something delicious and unusual."

"I'll comb the city."

"Alice." From the way he said it, she knew that he had been thinking about her all day, that between the trees and shrubs and herbaceous plants, his thoughts had returned to her like a wave to the ocean. The skin of her forearms began to prickle. It pleased her, but she, of course, had thought at least as much about Susan as she had about him. For a friendship, or even a companionable love affair she was an excellent bet, but for someone who said Alice in just that way? Henry did not go on. She said, "What time is it?"

"About eleven."

"Then I've only been asleep for forty-five minutes."

"Alice." Still he stopped and wouldn't or couldn't go on. Alice was thankful. Perhaps if everything could be put off as long as possible, then the dangers, whatever they were, could be averted. Somehow, in a few weeks or months, she would come up with more time, plenty for Susan and Henry both. Perhaps, in a few months, they would even overlap. That she could not imagine. And she still hadn't told him the salient fact about herself, had she? That she had discovered a murder, reported it to the police, answered probing questions about her relationship to the victims, one of whom had slept with her just as Henry had. Alice coughed.

"You'll come then?"

"Of course."

"Do you mind that I woke you up?"

"Not re—"

"I meant to. I wanted to take you unawares."

"You did that already, last night."

"Mmmm. Last night."

"Henry, do you consider yourself a romantic sort of guy?"

"Nascently so. You?"

"I consider myself the quintessential librarian."

"I'll bet. Good night, Alice."

"Really! I—"

He hung up on her with evident affection. While Alice was cradling the phone in her two palms and smiling, the door buzzer shrilled.

I T W A S Ray with another man, a boy in fact, only about twenty. He was very graceful looking and rather shy. Alice knew at once that this was one of Ray's "homosexual companions," perhaps *the* homosexual companion. She was not really surprised to see them. Ray had cut his hair and was wearing sunglasses, which Alice had to ask him to take off. The boy, Jeff, was hungry. He and Alice sat at the kitchen table while Ray fixed him a sandwich. Alice didn't quite know what to say. Finally Ray said, "Were you in bed? I'm sorry to come by so late."

"I was on the phone. But you're supposed to be in Miami."

Ray and Jeff exchanged glances. "Who says?"

"Detective Honey, as a matter of fact."

"What does he care?"

"I'm not exactly sure, but when you didn't show for work Friday, the police ended up searching your apartment."

"No shit! But I left a god-damned message at Studio Midtown. I had to go up to Massachusetts. Didn't they get the message? I left it with the new kid, and also on the bulletin board."

"No message, and then Honey told Noah that you had been seen in a Miami airport, and that your companions were known to the Miami police."

"What did I look like?"

"I don't have any idea. I haven't talked to him about it."

Jeff finished the sandwich and ate the last bits of lettuce while Ray got up and poured him a glass of milk. He closed the refrigerator door thoughtfully, then said, "Well, do you think I'm under arrest?"

"What would you be under arrest for?"

"Nothing that I did. I didn't kill them. I was with Jeff the whole night."

Jeff nodded.

"I don't think you're under arrest. I just think Honey wants to keep his eye on us."

"Alice, will you put us up for two nights? Just two. Tonight and tomorrow night. After that we've got a place to stay."

"What for? Why don't you go back to your place? Doesn't Jeff have a place?"

"Can't. Can't go to work, either, not for a couple of days. By the end of the week this whole thing will be straightened out, but I need someplace to stay until then."

"Honey knows we're friends. Besides—"

"It's not Honey I'm worried about. Believe me, he's way down the list of priorities. Please, Alice? For old times' sake? Is it such a big deal?"

Alice put her forehead in her hand.

"You've got lots of room. We won't be any trouble. You won't even know we're here."

"Let's get out of here, man," said Jeff, but Ray shushed him.

"I—," said Alice.

"What? Say it."

"It scares me a little, that's all."

"Don't be scared. It's no big deal. You won't get in trouble, really you won't, I promise."

Alice sat back and looked at Ray. He was not looking good. The haircut emphasized the roundness of his cheeks and the pallor of his skin. He reached up to straighten the collar of his shirt and his hands were pudgy and pointed. He was a very nice man. Perhaps Jeff appreciated that. Otherwise they were remarkably mismatched. Jeff had taken off his sandals and turned in his chair, relaxing, sticking out his feet. His feet were slender, with long toes and pronounced definition, high arch and high instep, like the feet of a Donatello. Behind the grace and the self-satisfaction of simply being himself, Alice could see that he, like Ray, was ill at ease and a little worried. She said, "Can I ask you how old you are?"

He glanced at Ray, who shrugged and then said, "Nineteen."

"Where are you from?"

"He's from Tulsa, Oklahoma."

"How long have you been in the city?"

"Are you going to give him the third degree, Alice? Do you want a letter from his priest? It's just going to be a couple of nights. Big deal."

Alice flushed and fixed her eyes on the boy. "When did you come here?"

Jeff shrugged and opened his mouth, but Ray interrupted him. "Don't be such a bitch, Alice. He's my friend. Isn't that enough?"

Alice felt like saying that if he didn't like it they could go elsewhere, but after some effort, she couldn't say it. She jumped up, furious, and went into the living room. After a moment of marshalling her thoughts, she stalked back. "Ray Reschley, you're in trouble and you're going to drag me into it. Maybe you don't think you will, but you will."

"What trouble? We're not in trouble at all, we just have a little matter to settle, and it's going to be settled for sure in a day or so. I guarantee it won't affect you at all." Ray was coaxing. "I thought we were friends. This is nothing. We just need a place to stay. You won't even know we're here, and no one else knows we are, either. There are eight million addresses in the naked city, Alice."

"I doubt it." Alice looked out the bluedark window.

"We'll go if you really want us to. If you really, really don't want us here, we'll be glad to go."

Alice said, "Oh, shit! Okay. Do you hate me for being reluctant?"

"Never!" said Ray, grinning. From the grin, she knew how desperate they were, and she felt a deep misgiving.

In the morning they were gone even before she was up, and their absence (they had made the bed and washed their dishes after eating breakfast) was rather reassuring. Whatever trouble Ray was in, she thought, did not have to be her business right away. The polite remarks she had rehearsed went unspoken, and she realized with a twinge of remorse just how unwilling a hostess she was being. Perhaps if Ray had come alone? But one look at Jeff had let her know that the solitary Ray she was used to was a false Ray; the complications of coupling were as natural to him as to anyone. Of Jeff she did not know what to make, but she hoped he was from a nice family and that his intentions were honorable.

8

R Y A was an assistant publicity director for a recently formed cable TV group. She wore her long blond hair upswept to work, a dazzling white silk shirt, a narrow black skirt slit up the front, and extremely high heels which she managed, when she stepped forward to greet Alice (flat shoes, seersucker A-line skirt, pink cotton blouse) with the neatness of a dancer in the movies, Cyd Charisse, maybe. Alice always wondered what she did at work. Alice smiled.

"Do you think it's better," said Rya, "to sit in the corner or the middle of the room?"

"Definitely booth," said Alice.

"Aren't they always bugged? Isn't it sort of well known that most booths in Manhattan restaurants are bugged by the FBI and the CIA?"

"There's one," said Alice, stepping in front of Rya and moving to claim a high, private booth in beautifully buttoned black leather.

When Alice's plate was piled high with hors d'oeuvres, Rya leaned forward across the table and said, "Tell me what Noah told you yesterday."

"Did you ask him?"

"No."

"Then how do you know he told me anything?"

"He was there for over an hour."

"Does that make you jealous or something?"

Rya shook her head.

"Then why do you want to know what we talked about?" She thought of Rya and Craig and Noah "going on as three." It annoyed her. In addition, she simply couldn't imagine the woman across from her, pretty as she was, having the depth to satisfy Craig as well as Noah. They had been friends, but Alice didn't feel any friendship at the moment.

"You think I just want to pry, but I don't. If Noah was over there making love to you, I wouldn't ask about it and wouldn't want to hear about it."

Alice could not help shrugging, even as she bit down on a hot, juicy, pork-stuffed wonton.

"I need to know what he said to you, because I need to know what is going on."

"Nobody knows what's going on. That's the point. Last night that detective came over to Susan's place and told us that some guy with a prison record that neither of us had ever heard of had a set of keys to her apartment. And—" but it would be best not to mention Ray.

"Who was it?"

"Somebody Brick. David Brick. He used to be Nina Starlette's boyfriend."

"I've heard of her."

Alice shrugged again. It was hard to be sympathetic to someone with Rya's chin. It was a gorgeous chin, pointed and clean. From it her throat swept upward and back, promising decades without flab. It made her face.

"That's only part of it, though. I mean, the murder was awful, and all that." Rya's fingernails, vermilion, speared a shrimp toast from the pile on Alice's plate. "Do you mind? But I don't even know what's going on between myself and Noah. Do you know that we don't even talk to each other when somebody else isn't around?"

Alice shook her head.

"We haven't spoken to one another in six months. Can you believe that?"

Alice wiped her fingers on her napkin and picked up a spoon. "No," she said.

"It's true. I tried for the first month or so to engage him in conversation. Even just about little things like food and stuff. He bought a blackboard. He writes me notes on it, and I write him back."

Alice spoke judiciously. "Maybe you forfeited his trust, Rya."

"Ha!" exclaimed the other woman, triumphantly spearing another wonton. "He told you I was sleeping with Craig, didn't he?"

"I suppose I can admit that, yes. Why don't you get your own?"

"I'm not really hungry. It's not like he said, though. Really it isn't." She blushed. "Or wasn't."

"Were you sleeping with him?"

Rya looked up at the ceiling. "Yes."

"Did Noah like it?"

"No."

"Then the facts speak for themselves, don't you think?"

"Craig was making me."

"Oh, bullshit. Do you want anything? I'll be back."

Picking over the laden steam table, Alice grew angrier and angrier. How could Rya be such a dumb bitch? How could she, Alice, have gotten mixed up in such a stupid tangle? That was exactly what it was, too. Stupid. Not tragic. At this moment, not even sad. Stupid. If people gave out keys to their apartment to ex-cons, they were stupid. If people slept around indiscriminately, flying in the face of long-standing personal and professional relationships, that was stupid. If people bought thousands of dollars' worth of cocaine and didn't worry about paying for it, that was stupid. If you let your life get into the chaos that Craig

Shellady, and now, it appeared, Ray Reschley, had let their lives get into, how could you be surprised at whatever might happen? And Denny. Innocent bystander, yes, but after standing by for fifteen years, mere innocence was the biggest stupidity of all. Alice's spoon jumped, flipping three wontons onto the floor behind the steam table. She put the damned spoon down and began picking them up with her fingers. Rya wasn't the worst. Her dumbness couldn't even be blamed on her. It was probably half inherited and half socialized into her. Alice turned her head and glanced across the room. Rya had pincered the orange slice in her drink between her thumb and fingernails. She pulled it out and stuck the pulpy part in her mouth. Stupid fucking cunt, thought Alice, balancing extra wontons and shrimp toast on her plate, then putting another plate beneath hers. "Here!" she barked, setting it in front of Rya and letting some food slide off her pile onto it. "People in my house, people eating my food!"

"Who's in your house?"

"No one. Forget it." Alice ate furiously.

"Don't be mad at me."

"How can I help it? You tell me these lies."

"They're not lies."

"Then explain everything to me."

"Will you be mad?"

"What do you care?"

Rya was silent.

"Maybe not."

"Okay. Thanks. I was, well—" She looked at the ceiling again. "Did I seem funny on that day that the guys were killed?"

"No."

"Well, I felt funny. I was sorry about Denny, I really was. We didn't talk very much about him, though. And I wasn't sorry about Craig. Noah thought it was just killing me, but I was actually incredibly relieved."

"I'm not going to believe that in 1980 you were Craig Shellady's white slave. I'm just not."

"Well, I wasn't his slave, or anything." Rya seemed genuinely shocked. "I couldn't get out of the relationship, though. And I wanted to. I told Noah I wanted to. He didn't believe me."

"Well, why didn't you just do it?"

"That's what Noah wrote on the blackboard back to me, but it was harder than that."

"You do it, you do it."

"Why do people always say that? People do what they want to, blah blah. You want bullshit, that's bullshit. In the first place, I had to think of Noah's job."

"Noah could have found another job."

"In 1979? 1980? There aren't any other jobs. Nobody's going on the road any more, records aren't selling. Besides, Noah never made anything of himself apart from Craig. You know that."

"Craig told you that if you didn't sleep with him he would kick Noah out of the band? That's positively medieval. Besides, Craig wasn't like that."

"I'm not saying he said it, I just worried about it."

"So what else?"

"I was worried about how Craig would react. To me. I mean, remember Iris North?"

"You thought he would beat you up?"

Rya shrugged.

"Did he ever?"

Rya shrugged again, then nodded. "He gave me a black eye once. And he burned me with a cigarette." She unbuttoned the cuff of her blouse and rolled up the sleeve. On the inside of her arm above the elbow was a white circle the diameter of a cigarette.

Alice inhaled sharply. "Did he threaten you?"

Rya shrugged.

"Did you tell Noah?"

"Sort of. He knew about the burn, and he knew I was afraid, but he thought I could take care of myself."

"There must have been something—"

"You don't understand, Alice. I realize I am sort of a dizzy person. And Noah's been fucked up by so much dope, he really has. Craig knew more than we did, or at least more than I did. All the time. I felt like he was always two steps ahead of me. If I was with him, and wishing to go home, he'd say, 'I know you want to go home, don't you? You can't stand to come here. I love you and you don't love me, and now you want to go home.' "

Alice looked at her.

"He was getting sort of weird, you know. Mad about every-thing, like anything that happened just went to prove something about him, either good or bad. It wasn't like it was when he was with you." Alice smiled coldly. "Anyway, I felt bad about his life. I mean, he seemed to have had such a terrible life, I felt sorry for him. He didn't think anybody really liked him, except maybe Denny, and he always thought Susan was trying to break up Den-ny's friendship with him. I liked him a lot at first. He was exciting to be with, after all that time with Noah. He always had some-thing to say and there was always something to do. He was good in bed. You know that."

Alice nodded.

"I guess I even thought I loved him. At least I told him so. Then I was afraid to take it back. Don't you understand that?"

Alice nodded again.

"He made me feel goofy. I couldn't do anything. I didn't know what I wanted. I wanted everything to be all right, and I guess I thought we would never get away from him, and so if I went along with him, everything would be all right enough. I tried to tell all of that to Noah, but he wouldn't talk to me, and besides, I couldn't say it right. This is the first time I've ever said it right."

Alice didn't know what to say. She pushed her plate away, although there were three samosas and a shrimp toast left. She put out her hand and then put it over Rya's. After a moment, she said, "You didn't kill him to get out of it, did you?"

Rya shook her head.

"Say yes or no and look right at me."

"No." She looked right at her.

"Who did? Noah?"

"Maybe. I don't know. I thought he might have said something to you that would have told you something. I called home that night when he said he was home. About one. There wasn't any answer, and our phone doesn't unplug. I'm scared to death."

"Did you tell Honey that?"

"He didn't ask me. He just asked if I was there, and where I was."

"Noah didn't tell me anything like that."

"What did he tell you?"

"Some stuff. He was confused, I think, about your relationship to Craig."

Rya nodded.

"This is really stupid." But the rush of anger that she had felt was somehow shocked out of her. She said, "I'll buy you another drink, okay?" Rya nodded.

I T T O O K a long time to get rid of Rya, and by the time Alice got home, it was nearly dark. She started when two figures stepped from under the fire escape on the side of her building, but they were only Ray and Jeff. Jeff was in gym shorts. His legs were as nicely shaped as his feet.

"It's been a while," said Ray sarcastically.

"Have you been waiting for me?" exclaimed Alice.

Ray looked at his watch. "Two hours, thirty-seven minutes, ten, no, eleven seconds."

"Why are you waiting for me?"

"No keys."

"I know, but why didn't you go get something to eat or something?"

"Alice, sweetheart, I don't think you understand. We're trying to stay out of sight for a while. That doesn't include dinner at the Automat or pastry at Zabar's."

She let them in. She knew he was going to ask it. He did. "So how about keys?"

"It's just one more night."

"Just for one night, then."

"Are you going out again tonight?"

"As a matter of fact, yes."

"I'll let you in."

"It'll be late."

"I'll stay up."

"Three or four."

"I'll get up."

"Don't trust me?"

"I hate to give out keys."

"Susan has some."

"That's different. Besides, the very thought of Susan makes me even more cautious."

"Just for tonight and tomorrow. We'll be in and out tonight, and then in and out tomorrow. You won't be here to let us in, then."

"Why don't you just stay in, not go out."

"I've got to straighten this tangle out. That means talking to people."

"Call them up."

"Come on, Alice."

"I can't do it. It's not personal, I just can't do it. I'll let you in tonight. We'll figure out something about tomorrow."

"Alice—"

"Let's have something to eat."

Ray made a face. Jeff had slumped back onto the sofa with his feet on the window sill. His eyes were closed. He was uncomfortable to have around, Alice thought, like a tagalong eight-year-old brother who had nothing to say and no toys to play with. His eyes were blank or inward, certainly non-responsive even to Ray, who watched him but was never watched. Alice wondered how long he and Ray had been together. They acted like a well-established couple. After dinner, in the bathtub, she was suddenly sure they had left, taking her keys, but when she put on her robe and came out with her wet hair, they were sitting across the living room from each other. Ray was reading a magazine he had found, and Jeff was staring out the window, his arms crossed over his chest. His boylike quality made him menacing, too, as if his wishes and motives were not susceptible to adult understanding, or contained by adult scruples. Alice had been going to suggest that one of them stay while the other went out, but looking at them, she knew Ray would be the one to leave. Though she couldn't imagine Jeff actually doing anything, she shrank from being alone with him after all. She dried her hair and combed it, and they sat up rather uncomfortably in the living room, hardly speaking. There was no mention of going out, and Alice finally went to bed.

In the morning they were at the breakfast table when she got up. There was a quarter of a cantaloupe at her place, and a hot cup of coffee. Jeff was sitting beside the window with only a towel wrapped around his loins.

"Sit down!" exclaimed Ray. "Here's your coffee. How did you sleep? This is a lovely apartment. I thought all the windows on the street would make it noisy but there's hardly any traffic, is there?"

Alice was alerted. She looked from one to the other and said, "You went out last night, didn't you?"

"I think one of us is going to be here most of the day, but we'll be gone by the time you get home. Thanks a lot for putting us up."

"Did you go out?" She looked at Jeff, who shrugged.

Ray said, "Some people are just more available at night than they are during the day."

"Tell me how you got back in, Ray. I didn't hear the doorbell."

Ray glanced at Jeff, who was gazing down on Eighty-fourth Street. Jeff coughed, then yawned. Ray said, "Well, we really didn't want to wake you. You've done a lot for us already. We didn't get home till after five. That's the worst time to wake up if you want to get back to sleep. The sun was up and everything."

"So how did you get in?"

"We, uh, borrowed your keys when you were in the bathtub."

"Ray!"

Jeff turned and looked at her impassively. It was he who had done the borrowing, Alice could see.

"No harm done," carolled Ray. "They're right back in your purse. It really was better that way."

"If I'd known—"

"But you didn't, and you didn't feel a thing. Look for yourself." He cleared his throat.

"Well, after this, I feel like looking. I feel like counting my money, too." She addressed this to Jeff. "I mean, I don't even know your last name."

"Johnson," said Jeff.

The sarcastic way he spoke infuriated her. She jumped up. "Who are you, anyway? You know something? I don't like you one bit! What do you do? Where do you get your money? Why are you so rude?" But the real insult, the precise devastating indictment of his character that she wanted to make escaped her, and she felt already thwarted.

Ray said, in a neutral voice, "He's a student at Parsons, okay?"

"My whole problem is that I assume everyone else is as in-nocent as I am. I'm really furious with you, Ray. I think you betrayed our friendship and my trust in you."

"Our friendship wasn't so blooming when we asked if we could stay."

"That's different—"

"Is it? You were worried about you, not about me."

"Don't I have good reason to be?"

"Not as far as I'm concerned. I never did anything to you. Look at that desk in there. Who made that for you—"

"You don't know what you're talking about, Ray! And you're a fool to boot! You act like we all still live out in Minnesota, where everything turns out all right! Where nobody really wants to hurt you, even when they're mad! Shit, Ray!" But looking into their two pairs of eyes, one indifferent, one fearful but veiled, she bit her useless tongue and stomped off to her room to get dressed for work.

When she left, Ray kissed her good-bye. From the other side of the living room, Jeff was looking at her quizzically. On the way down in the elevator, she inspected her keys, and then counted her money. It was there, all eight dollars and thirty-seven cents. And her credit cards, too. Still, when she got to work, she took a moment to call up Parsons and ask if a Jeff Johnson was registered for classes there. He was. There were three of him.

THAT morning, Alice decided that the flood of Henry Mullet had largely passed over her. Although taken from time to time by shudders of desire, she was able to think of her work, to talk to Laura and Howard, to anticipate the next evening with Henry (she would wear her white gauze dress, embroidered peasant neck-line, pink and gold Mexican sash, she had already spotted the raspberries she would take on Broadway, and been reassured of a new shipment tomorrow) with pleasure rather than craving. Although she realized that this state of suspension was temporary, she enjoyed it.

About Ray and Rya she refused to think. She always felt secure in the library, secure within the walls (how thick were they? two feet or something?). The murder, of course, had disappeared from the newspapers, and so even from the chance of discussion over coffee or lunch. Laura and Howard and Sidney still had no idea of her involvement, and neither did her parents, for that matter. She had spoken to them once more, and they had mentioned the garden, her grandmother Bovbjerg's knee operation, the microwave oven that might be lost in the mails, and a girl Alice had known in high school who had died in a car accident. In the library, Alice felt detached from the rest of her life, and more than that, permanently, immortally treading the aisles of the stacks, everlastingly answering questions about the *Reader's Guide*, deathlessly sifting through small literary magazines and considering them for order and reorder. Sidney muttered frequently about feeling trapped, Laura schemed over jobs abroad, but Alice embraced her routine, the spar that would float her out of trouble and into a healthy old age. At home, she worried, at work, she hummed.

And Tuesday was a pleasant day, with a well-defined task to engage her attention. In the morning she made a long list of lesser-known American regional poets and their books and chapbooks, and after lunch, because her assistant was out sick, she herself went to look for them in the stacks. Usually Alice hated looking for things in the stacks, since because of the three different cataloguing systems in use in the early years of the library, works of a single author might be scattered over the seven floors. Every volume had to be looked up separately and found. After six years, Alice could not say readily where a given book might be. Almost no one could. Today, however, she didn't mind. It was good exercise. She went from stack to stack and floor to floor, turning on the lights, finding the books, turning out the lights again. It was a fruitful search. Any number of the volumes had never been checked out, never apparently touched. Some of them fell apart in her hands. Others as old, as little used, showed only a faded spine and a film of dust as evidence of their age. Some were lost, had been shelved in the wrong spots for years, had been treated carelessly by clerks and librarians who were long gone to other institutions, to marriage and grandparenthood, to other professions, died, maybe. Alice was almost reluctant to reshelve them, mistakes were tangible marks of the past; she was being sentimental. She reshelved them.

She thought of Henry, she thought of Susan, she thought of Rya and Jim and Noah and Ray and Jeff. She carried a little cloud of thought in her head from stack to stack and floor to floor and she hummed. When she took a pile of books to her desk, she found a note that Susan had the car out to do errands, and that she would pick her up at five. If she really wanted to take the bus, she was to call. Alice looked at the note for a long time, because, oddly, she really did want to take the bus. When she imagined herself calling Susan, though, and expressing such a thing ("Don't be silly! It'll be jammed! We can stop at—") she knew it was impossible. Somehow, though, she didn't want Susan coming there, to the library. Or Honey, either. She lived in dread of Honey's showing up and quizzing her on the steps again. None of them! They had invaded her apartment, and she didn't want a single one of them even looking up a book in her card catalogue. She put down Susan's note and picked up her list of poets. Of course they were obscure, she thought angrily. None of them was any good. When she marched off to find the rest of their works (a waste of paper and shelf space!), she was as angry at them as she had been at Rya the night before.

By four-thirty, her eyes had run over so many books and names and numbers, her fingers had separated so many bindings and pages nearly fused, that she was hardly thinking or feeling anything any more. She idly deplored this disintegration of materials, and said to herself all the clichés about what the library needed. She counted the names on her list and estimated how much of tomorrow her search would use up. She saw, as she turned out the light after herself, a flash of fabric, the heel of a shoe disappearing around one of the white metal bookstacks. It startled her, the presence of another person, no doubt one of the clerks, in someplace so obscure. Although if you thought about it, no place in this cataloguing system could be any obscurer than any other place, since at least the oldest books were arranged according to size and date of acquisition rather than according to subject or author. Alice could not help pausing and catching her breath, listening for the retreat of footsteps. There were no sounds. She walked down the aisle toward the stairs to the floor below. She could not help looking back twice. No lights went on. No one appeared.

On the floor below, she passed a knot of clerks and nodded. Her goal was the far dark end of the dark row of stacks. She would not hesitate, nor would she turn on any lights but the lights above her destined stacks. Not in front of the clerks. But it was strange how nervous she felt, how uneven her breathing. When she came to the book she wanted, she put her hand on it, and then, almost involuntarily, she paused for a long time, staring at the brown binding, absolutely still, making no noise, hearing no noise. She shook herself and then disinterred the book from its place on the shelf. It was 4:45. She would find no more before meeting Susan.

She thought of herself telling Susan, "I'm so paranoid lately! I thought someone was following me in the stacks!" She imagined herself laughing merrily at the very thought, Susan laughing too. She thought of Susan on Sunday, opening Alice's bedroom door with the suddenness of—of what? The only thing that came to her mind was the suddenness of a car wreck. Suzy Soderberg. Car wrecks were on her mind. One last book. It was down another floor. When she stepped off the stairs, she saw that the whole floor was dark. The clerks would have turned off the lights, as there were no evening hours tonight. Alice quailed, but then made herself head down the aisle, turning on only every third light. The book, the last of this particular author, was as far from the steps as it could possibly be. But close to the elevator! But she had to turn off the lights! But the only footsteps she heard were her own. She walked deliberately, thinking of being late for Susan. But she could park. The book was not in its place. She considered. Check-out highly unlikely. Wrongly shelved? She read off the titles of the books above and below, left and right, but she was listening so hard that they made no sense to her. She stopped herself, closed her eyes, read them again. Now it was impossible not to pant, not to think of scary movies in which men came up behind and coshed you over the head, not to think of bullets ricocheting in the stacks, pinging on shelves, sinking into bindings and pages (and who was that clerk, Karen something, who'd been shot at from Bryant Park while she was sitting doing her work on the fourth floor or the fifth floor? The bullet came through the window and went through her hair), and then of larger disasters—flames shooting up through floors, engulfing seven stories of old paper in minutes, seconds, less time than it would take her to get to the stairs. Did she hear footsteps? There was a definite sound, step, step, step. Alice nearly passed out, but the sound receded and then stopped. She came out from behind her stack and looked down the aisle. All of the lights she had turned on had been switched off.

She still had not found her book. She made herself read titles. She longed for the elevator. She nearly groaned. Someone could be coming up behind her. She whipped around. No one. Nothing. They wouldn't find her for years, maybe. She inched over to the end of the stack and turned out the light. Now the floor was entirely dark. She couldn't see, but neither could anyone else. Alice crouched beside the stack, protected, and stared down the long dark aisle. There was no sound, and only the movement of dust gathering. Alice waited.

A N D then, oddly, she came to her senses, or rather her brimming fear drained away, leaving her sheepishly squatting in the bookstacks in the dark, late for her rendezvous. She stood up, shook her hair into place, smoothed her skirt and turned on the light. It was two minutes past five. She would have thought it midnight, or five in the morning. She took a few deep breaths, and exhaled them vigorously, as if thereby blowing out the last weightless but clogging motes of what had possessed her. What had possessed her? Riding up in the elevator she considered the previous few days and it seemed to her that they were comprised of uncontrollable angers, desires, and fears, threaded together like beads on a string of uncontrollable hunger. When she wasn't thinking about Henry, or wasn't angry at something or fearful, she was contemplating her next meal. At night, she planned breakfast. When she ate with someone else, she wanted what they had as well as her own. When she and Susan conversed, if they didn't reminisce or reconsider the murder, they discussed food. The elevator stopped at the ground floor, its tinny doors creaked open, and Alice stepped out. Even the main floor reading room was about deserted. As always it struck Alice as too grand for those who studied there, too grand for term papers on Sarah Orne Jewett and Nathan Hale, too grand for anything human. As she looked at it now it seemed so alien as to be almost funny. For what cause could those eleven men, was it, have possibly died, and wasn't there one still buried in the walls? Not for the great work of preserving books, since as an edifice of book preservation, the library was not ideal. For the greater glory of Lennox, Astor, and Tilden, then? She let herself out of the librarians' station between the reading rooms and glanced up at the spot where men had come once to scrub up the gold leaf of the vault, a vast and dangerous undertaking that trustees in the modern era had rejected as not cost effective. The experimental spot still glowed.

Susan was waiting for her. Even as she pulled open the car door, she was apologizing for being late, explaining that she had been in the stacks. Even as she was getting in, Susan was saying she had just gotten there, had thought she was the one who was late, why she had gotten the car out today in the first place, she couldn't imagine, except that she'd had sort of an urge to drive it. Alice sighed deeply and pleasurably with the relief of ending another workday. Susan turned to back out of her parking spot. It was good to see Susan after all, good not to go home on the bus. "What shall we eat?" Alice said. "And what percentage of the time would you say I talk about food?" Susan stomped on the brake as a motorcycle appeared immediately to her left. "Shit," said Susan. "I'll never get out of here." Alice said nothing about her panic in the stacks.

IN THE end they chose to put the car away and have done with it, then to make an omelet or something, with a spinach salad and a loaf of French bread from Zabar's. Susan was in a good mood. While Alice sat at the table, worn out and therefore, she thought, unusually distant, Susan washed and drained the spinach three times, cut up onions and mushrooms for the omelet, mashed cloves of garlic into half a stick of butter for the French bread. She worked energetically but effortlessly, more interested in what she was talking about, which was Denny, than in what she was doing. Alice thought of other dinner-making conversations they had had, in which the dinner maker always took the lead and the table setter always listened, providing an occasional hum of agreement and encouragement, the price of not helping. Usually such times were special pleasures. Susan was saying, "I think something's been resolved somehow, although I don't know exactly what, or how. I do miss Denny terribly, and I think about him all the time. I mean, I cry at the store and have to go into the back. But I'm more convinced that there's somewhere to get, and that somehow I'm getting there. Do you know what I mean?"

"Not exactly." Alice glanced out the window, hoping for a sudden and miraculous look at Henry Mullet. She was hardly her loyal self, was oddly removed from Susan and the familiar enchantment with her conversation. She thought again and again of her panic in the stacks, and it seemed almost as frightening as a real attack would have been. Fear had paralyzed her, rendered her incapable of thought as well as action. Her only instinct had been to crouch, to cover her head. It was intolerable to anticipate a life whose dangers were immeasurably amplified by such a reaction. But the thought, once thought, slipped away. She was worn out.

"If I knew what I meant, I could tell you, maybe, but I don't. That's the weirdest thing about it. Something about our life was annoying me." She glanced up quickly. "It had nothing to do with anything I was supposed to be feeling. It was like some little barb that kept hooking me. Every time I thought of Denny, or Craig, or all of us together, it hooked me and sank into me, and made me mad and hurt me at the same time. Do you know what I mean?"

"In a way."

"Now I know what the hook is, which doesn't get rid of it, but at least I can see it, whereas before it was invisible. Now I can see that it was a part of things, but then it seemed to infect them, like poison ivy. Everything seemed impossible, the way it does when you have poison ivy all over your body, but now it doesn't. I mean in retrospect. I suppose it's odd that just understanding it should have such an effect on me, since the whole situation is changed now, but it's such a relief to know that something was a certain way and not a certain other way."

"What are you talking about?" Alice sounded rather sharp, but Susan didn't seem to notice.

"What did Craig give you this year for Christmas?"

"Don't you remember? That Halston blouse."

"I remember. And he gave me an ounce of Joy perfume."

"So what?"

"Remember where he said he got the money?"

"They had all those gigs between Thanksgiving and Christmas, and that guy in Bridgeport gave each one a hundred-dollar tip, that drunk guy."

"They did have all those gigs, but Craig spent that money on drugs. Denny told me after Christmas that the weekend before Christmas he 'loaned' Craig a thousand dollars from our joint account, to pay off a debt that was about to get him in real trouble. I didn't dare ask what the trouble was, but I don't think it was drugs. Except that the debt was only partly paid, because Craig had the money in his pocket on Christmas Eve, and he was in midtown, and you know the rest."

"Jesus."

"Now, that doesn't make me mad any more." Susan threw the vegetables into the bubbling butter. "Really it doesn't. We gave him three hundred more, and he paid it off. We used to fight about it, though. We lent a lot of money to Craig, and last night, just as an experiment, I sat down and figured it up, only cash, subtracting all the money he lent us or paid back. It came to fifty-seven hundred dollars. Hand me those eggs, will you?" Alice got up and carried the bowl of lemon-colored eggs over to the stove. "I looked at that figure for a long time. It seems like a lot of money, doesn't it? But we knew him for thirteen years, and that's only just over four hundred a year, or, say, eight-fifty a week. Cigarette money, beer money. And that's where it would have gone if we hadn't lent it to him. Shall I try to flip this?" Still Susan sounded cheerful. Alice had never seen her speak of Craig with such equanimity. "Yes, I like it cooked all through."

There was a pause while Susan slid the omelet to the front of the pan, then eased it over. "Beautiful," said Alice.

"I'd thought I was burning up about that money all these years, but when I added it all up and really looked at the figures, I realized I didn't care."

"Well, it did symbolize your rivalry with Craig. I mean, Denny was giving something of yours to him—"

"No, I thought about that, too." She slipped a table knife through the steaming fold of egg, then separated the two halves. She bent down and took the bread from the oven. Alice reached across the table for the salad, wanting to shake her head furiously to clear it, to fasten her attention with screws or nails to what Susan was saying. Perhaps panic had a chemical effect on the brain, some dissolving of cortical tissue. Susan pulled out her chair and sat down.

"Denny wasn't blindly uncritical of Craig, you know. And he wasn't without a temper, even though nobody saw it except me. About six months after we met, something happened that I should have paid attention to. The three of us were eating dinner. No, there were four. Craig was seeing that Chinese girl whose father was with the embassy, remember her?"

"Helen Huang."

"Right. So the four of us were eating dinner. Craig had the only car, then, and he asked me if I needed it for anything the next day. I thought for a minute, and he asked me again. I opened my mouth to say something, and he asked me again, this time sort of barking. Denny wasn't paying attention, but Helen looked up at me. I think I even managed to say 'I' or something, but Craig interrupted me and said, 'Well, shit, Susan, do you want the fucking car or not? If you do, then this time you can put some fucking gas in it.' I must have inhaled sharply or something, because Denny, who was sitting beside me, looked up and said in a warning voice, 'Susan!' This whole time I'd had my fork in my hand, ready to start eating, and I just turned the fork in my fist and I stabbed Denny right in the arm. It drew blood. I wanted it to draw blood. Well, we jumped up and we screamed at each other and ran into the bedroom and cried, and it was all very dramatic, and Helen, who was raised in a very traditional Chinese family, was floored. At the time it seemed very passionate and exciting, and I cried, though not as much as Denny, and mostly because it felt good to be sort of swept away, you know. I bandaged his arm, and we had this melodramatic reconciliation, and all the ferment seemed to be between Denny and me. But it wasn't. I should have paid attention to that."

Something about this scene Alice vaguely remembered, but the overlay of her present image was far more vivid. The fork turning in Susan's hand, sinking into Denny's arm, the blood spurting (or probably dribbling) out. It was completely believable and there wouldn't be any remorse. Susan was a remarkably pragmatic and not very remorseful person, after all. Alice said, "Did you—"

"There was another time, a few years later, when they had been practicing a bunch of new songs all summer. Nobody had any money, not even you."

Alice wondered if she had always seemed to have money, if she had been generous enough with it.

"They rehearsed day after day, all day, and Denny was mad at Craig because he wouldn't sing this right, or he kept coming in wrong on that, and then blaming their bad sound on Denny. He'd be nice and apologetic to Craig all day, because temper didn't get anywhere with him, and then he'd come home and scream at the cats and scream at me, and once he kicked the glass out of the back door, except he was so embarrassed about it that he told me for weeks that the wind had done it, and then he cried when he told me really he had. I don't know why I didn't—"

"But what does raking all this up teach you?"

"I don't know, but listen. One time last fall I came home late. I remember I was in a terrible mood because Madame and Monsieur had been there all day, half sitting around and half interfering with the salesgirls, and blah blah. Denny was watching some football game on TV, and when I got home, I realized that he'd had about six beers. I was glad to get home, and he was glad to see me, but we started joking around, and he started pulling at my clothes, which he never did, and which I hated. I asked him to stop, and if he hadn't been drinking, he would have, and we would have gone to bed and screwed and gotten a good night's sleep and felt perfect forever after, but instead he got mad and grabbed the front of my shirt and deliberately ripped it open, popping all the buttons. Well, I knew he was drunk, so I was going to put on a show of being indignant and leave it at that when he said, 'You are a cold bitch,' just like that, not as if he'd just thought about it, but as if he'd discussed it with someone. Those weren't his words. He'd never called me any kind of name, even when we were really mad at each other, and now he was calling me somebody else's names, Craig's names, and all of a sudden I had this vision of them discussing me, and it was a vision that went all the way back to the beginning, and it drove me crazy."

"But of course they discussed you. You and I have always discussed them." The food was gone, even the bread. Alice looked toward the refrigerator, wondering what might be in there for dessert.

"But we've never discussed Denny and me, not really. Have

we? You don't know what kind of lover he is, I don't talk about our problems or our fights, do I?"

Alice shook her head.

"That was a conscious decision on my part, you know."

"You have been very discreet, but that doesn't mean I haven't gathered things."

"What you gathered is your own affair."

Alice nodded, remembering occasions, numerous occasions, of approaching delicately about something, of fishing for a confidence if one needed to be given. It was such a pattern with them that she privately referred to it as her "prying with a fork" manner, since she most often did it over a meal. She said, "So what's the conclusion? What did you think was true that you don't think is true now?"

"I'm afraid you'll laugh. I never said it to you then, because every time I said the words aloud, they sounded stupid."

"Well, what?"

"What I thought then was that Craig had some sort of power over us. When we were doing all that astrology, I thought it was because he was a double Scorpio. Later I didn't know why, but it seemed like he was manipulating us, Denny especially. Sometimes Denny was just sort of his creature."

"Last night—" But Alice stopped before divulging Rya's remarks on the same topic. She said, "So what seems true now?"

"That he was just a guy. A pretty compelling guy who usually got his own way, but just a guy."

"That's your revelation?"

"It doesn't sound like much, does it?"

"Not especially."

"Well, now you know how deeply I believed the other thing."

"My dear, you should have slept with him. You would have known he was compelling, but not omnipotent by any means."

Susan laughed. Realizing what she had said, Alice shrugged and began to laugh herself. "Yes, true!" she exclaimed. They sat in their chairs, laughing. When she got up to go to the bathroom, though, closing the door, and sitting on the cold seat, Alice stopped laughing and began to shiver, from the coldness of the seat, she thought. She finished, washed her hands, then washed them again. She washed her face in hot hot water, but she was still shivering. In fact her teeth were chattering. She looked into the mirror, concentrating on her face without seeing it, but not thinking about the stories Susan had just told her. In a moment, she took off her clothes and turned on the shower, very hot. Five minutes of the running water over her head, down her stomach and back, stilled the shivering. She huddled into her warmest robe. When she got back to the kitchen, Susan had finished the dishes. She was sitting at the table smoking a cigarette. According to the ashtray it was her third, and she was no longer laughing, either. Alice said, "I have had the craziest couple of days. I am out of it. When I wake up tomorrow morning, I probably won't even remember you were here."

Susan smiled without showing any teeth. "It's been fun," she said. "Tonight I hate to leave."

"It's still light. I'm really ready for bed, though."

"I can see that." She smiled again, in that funny, rueful, and hardly comradely way.

Alice coughed. "Let me call you tomorrow. At the store. We'll arrange something."

Susan stood up, actually stood up, stubbing out her cigarette thoroughly and thoughtfully. "I've always felt welcome to stay before."

"You would be if anyone was, you know that."

Susan shrugged, but she was, after all, nearly out the door. Alice closed it behind her, and then leaned against it for a long time. A while later, after the fall of complete dark, she pulled on a pair of jeans, took her keys, and went across the street. When Henry Mullet opened his door for her (grinning, Alice noted with relief), she said, "Mind if I'm a little early?"

9

T H E R E was something very agreeable, Alice thought, about waking up in someone else's very private apartment and knowing that you would be back there again, no angling for an invitation, no weighing of his words and looks to detect how welcome you would be, that very evening. Henry was matter of fact, cheery, and handsome in the morning, his rooms were platinum with sunlight. She tottered naked into his bathroom to find that he had set out for her next to the shower a clean yellow towel, folded, a flowered washcloth, and a new bar of soap. She took a shower, not somthing she usually had time for in the morning, and emerged wide awake, a sensation she customarily eased into about an hour into the workday. She had only awakened once in the night to think of Susan in the dark and to be seized with nausea. Washing her face in the sink and helping herself to Henry's toothbrush, she was inclined to view such a reaction as feverish, engendered by their closeness or by her recent roller coaster emotions. Henry embraced her as she came out of the bathroom. "I'm very fond of the way you walk around naked," he said.

"No shame, I admit. Although I'll also admit that I once wondered if you had seen me wandering bareass around my apartment in oblivious splendor. That's the penalty of befriending neighbors in New York, I think."

"I haven't, but I'll certainly keep my eyes peeled."

"I somehow suspect you won't have to."

Henry chuckled happily. He had made coffee. The dishes from the night before, which Alice had seen beside the sink, were washed. A round, cold, golden grapefruit blushed with rose at the stem end sat in the middle of the kitchen table like a bouquet of flowers. At two places were folded paper napkins and grapefruit spoons. Susan seemed a continent away. "I haven't got much," said Henry. "I always eat the same thing for breakfast, and I can't imagine that you'd like it."

"What's that?"

"Grape Nuts."

"I like Grape Nuts."

"Without milk. I don't like milk, and I don't have a drop in the house."

"You're kidding."

As if to demonstrate, he poured out a bowl of little grains, and began to grind them, spoonful by spoonful, between his teeth. Alice said, "That's how the Roman army lost its teeth, you know," but she shivered with delight. She adored him again, and she could adore him all day with the security of getting hungry for a big meal. "Cut the grapefruit," he said. "I had one yesterday, and they're very sweet."

"I won't say what comes to my lips."

"What?"

"Instead, I'll say that I could have you for breakfast, with pleasure."

"And I you." He reached across the table for her hand and kissed her fingers one by one.

"Thank you. What time is it, anyway?"

"Six-thirty."

"Surely you jest."

"Surely not. I have to be on the train by seven."

"I don't think I've ever seen six-thirty with such clarity in my whole life."

"Do you think it's love?"

Alice spoke lightly, sorry he had brought it up. "No. I don't see that with any clarity at all."

Henry continued to grind.

"You don't mind, do you?"

"I don't know. I feel good though."

"Me, too."

By the time he left for work, and Alice left to get clothes at her apartment, it seemed as if they had wedged a whole leisurely Sunday morning into a time that usually wasn't even a part of Alice's day.

At noon one of the other L-2's from the reading room came to find her in the periodicals catalogue and tell her that a man was asking for her at the desk. She could not help assuming it was Henry, but the grin faded when she saw Detective Honey leaning on the desk and surveying the reference room with his professional eye. He looked out of place, as if he felt superior to mere dictionaries and encyclopedias. Annoyed, Alice snapped, "People are waiting to use this desk. We should go outside."

Honey smiled, however, apparently not even noticing her tone. "How are you?"

"Let's go out on the steps." And then, "If you must know, it's irritating to have you come here."

"I just have a few questions."

"Fine." On the steps, Alice crossed her arms in front of her chest and smiled politely.

Honey opened his notebook. "First, you've probably been wondering about Mr. Reschley." Alice nodded. "We still haven't gotten in touch with him, but we are pretty sure he's in Miami, or was yesterday morning. In addition to being recognized almost positively in the airport, he's been reported in a nightclub, and on the street, in the company of a man who is, shall we say, familiar to this department." Alice dared not say a word, but she lifted her eyebrows. Honey went on, "As long as we know where he is, we have no reason to get in touch with him at the moment."

"Oh," said Alice.

"What I need to ask you about, though, has more to do with two other friends of yours, Mr. Mast, for one."

"And the other?"

Honey smiled. "One at a time, okay?"

Alice shrugged, then sat down on the steps. Honey squatted beside her.

"How long have you known the Masts, Mrs. Ellis?"

"Noah about twelve years, Rya about six."

"Would you say that you know them very well?"

"I've seen them a lot, but I've never been close to Noah, and Rya and I have our ups and downs."

"Would you feel confident in judging what sort of persons they are? In characterizing them, say?"

"Didn't we talk about this?"

"I'm interested in what you have to say today."

"Rya works in public relations for a cable TV outfit. I'm not sure what she does, but I get the feeling from her clothes and her general manner that she makes a pretty good salary. She used to be a receptionist and secretary at NBC."

"I am aware of Mrs. Mast's employment history."

"Noah hasn't ever really tried anything with his music outside of the band and away from Craig. He's a pretty average Midwestern boy."

"How's that?"

Alice cleared her throat. "Well, I guess I mean that his reaction on the surface is the same as his reaction in the depths. What you see is what you get."

"Has this always been true of Mr. Mast?"

"Yes."

"And it continues to be true?" He looked at her closely. Alice shifted her weight and looked down, feeling simultaneously that this was just a technique and that he had been following her. She turned away and stared at the facade of the library. All morning she had been a little nervous in the stacks, and had made herself some extra work at her desk. She had offered to take Sidney's shift at the reference desk, because, after all, the only real security was in the flow of traffic. The facade itself seemed different now, not a fortress, but a membrane. The many doors opened and opened. Anyone could go in. That's what the director had said after the attack in the reading room: They were to remember that the library was a public institution in the center of New York, as available in its way as the IRT or the Port Authority building. She thought of Roger Jenks doing his public duty. She thought of her friends. Somehow the square dance had spun into a new figure, and she was at the center, where she had never been before. It was Craig who had been at the center for the last twelve years, Craig whose charm and energy and ambition had supplied a pattern and direction to their lives. Now that he was dead, she had been thrust from the periphery, where she was perfectly contented, and everyone twirled and turned alarmingly toward her.

Honey was inhumanly patient, watching a man playing a violin a few steps down from her. Another man dropped a five-dollar bill into his open case. She thought of Ray and Jeff and Rya and Noah and, of course, Susan. Where did her responsibility lie? Which bundle of information was the least wrong to give, for it was obvious that Honey would not leave without some bundle from her. Which was the most likely for him to get from other sources? She looked at the deceptive edifice of the library and sighed. Honey moved closer. It was uncanny the way he read, not her thoughts, but her feelings. She said, "I suppose I do have something to tell you." Honey turned to a clean page in his notebook and Alice related to him what Noah had said to her Sunday, what Rya had said to her Monday, not leaving out the bit about the unanswered phone call. She did not tell him about Noah's drug habits, but she suspected he knew about that already. She had an odd sensation as she talked, almost a physical sensation of sliding and sliding. Fear and release, shame and relief all at the same time. When it was over her face was hot.

Honey was hardly moved at all. After she had finished, he waited expectantly for more, half smiling, as if she hadn't said the punch line yet. Alice said, "That's all I know. That's the latest."

"Does this seem suspicious to you, Mrs. Ellis?"

"I guess I would have to say so, yes."

"Why?"

"It all seems very fraught with emotion to me."

"Do you think such emotion could result in murder?"

"Don't you?"

"Maybe. But love doesn't always lead to marriage, unless the lover is the marryin' kind."

"Well, since this is all very new to us, or to me, anyway, I couldn't begin to tell you whether Noah or Rya is the murderin' kind."

"What about your other friends?"

"No," she snapped, "none of them."

Honey closed his notebook. He said, "Have you given your key to anyone, Mrs. Ellis?"

"Only to Susan."

"Miss Gabriel has full access to your residence?"

"She's the only one."

"But she does have full access, downstairs key, elevator key, apartment key?"

"There isn't an elevator key."

"It was very trusting of you to give away a key."

"She would never give it to anyone else."

"Probably not."

"You think I should get it back." Alice spoke accusingly.

"As a general rule, lending keys is a very unwise practice, Mrs. Ellis, as this recent experience must show you."

"She's my best friend!"

Honey put the notebook in his pocket. They parted with the

usual formalities, and Alice turned to go back to work. The detective was moving quickly down the steps, his burly torso straining the seams and vents of his jacket. Alice opened her mouth. Why couldn't she just let all of her fears out, as she had let out all of her suspicions of Rya and Noah? Though she had betrayed their confidence, and the unaccustomed feeling of telling secrets had been demeaning, there was a seductive momentum to it. If she spilled her fears and confusions, he might extend the security of his power over her. But he was down the steps, didn't look back. She could not call out. The library. A janitor she did not know was wedging the doors open to catch the breeze.

A L L afternoon Alice imagined herself confiding in Henry. Not in bed, not formally, over coffee in his living room, but in his tiny kitchen, doing dishes, or at the breakfast bar, a time-out between their romantic dinner and their romantic bedding, a hermetically sealed interval that would affect neither. She imagined herself doing what she hadn't done yet—describing the scene of the murder, the silent chaos, the smell, her sense of being quietly but exactly beside herself as she gazed upon the remains of Craig (her one-time lover) and his friend, Denny. Her friend. Then she would describe Ray, what he had built for her and how he had talked to her, how they were from the same town, and had bought penny candy at the same corner market and spent summers at the same public swimming pool. Ray she would describe very carefully, so that Henry would know from the description itself what Ray had and had not done, what Ray was capable of doing. Then, as carefully, but of course not at such length, she would characterize Noah and Rya, both what she had thought of them and what she thought of them now. In the very disjuncture between before and after, Henry might see the truth about them, too. Of course she would treat Denny and Craig in detail, and for once there would be no slighting of Denny in favor of Craig. Perhaps she would even tell him about Susan. She would narrate it all to him, and her story would be so orderly and so detailed and so complete that Henry's clear, trained eye (the eye that glimpsed a spider web at twenty feet) would see as she could not see. Thinking of telling him, her heart pounded and the skin of her forearms stood away from the flesh. She could not tell whether it excited or terrified her. Undoubtedly both. But then Henry himself excited and terrified her, or rather, there was Henry, good-natured, handsome, and there was herself, excited and terrified. She left work early and walked up Fifth Avenue, ready to buy a new dress, her fingertips in her pocket running over the raised letters of her Master Charge card that she was ready to fling at the salesgirl the moment she spotted the right vestment for the evening. Twice she thought she saw Susan, and made herself stare at the figure until it resolved itself into a stranger. They were all strangers. That was a palpable relief.

In the end, she arrived on his doorstep in her white dress with the Mexican sash, raspberries in one hand and cream in the other. Henry opened the door in a wash of beefy aromas and embraced her crushingly before she had time to say anything. Then he ate a raspberry, the one she had balanced for him at the very apex of the mound. "All we can eat," she said, "red and black both. I realize that raspberries aren't so rare, but all you can eat is." Even as she spoke, before setting anything down or taking her first sip of champagne, it was clear that Henry's was the sort of apartment where it would be difficult to speak of such things as murder and suspicion. It was the sort of apartment where the easiest thing to do was adore Henry.

Henry smelled of witch hazel, baby powder, the laundry that did his shirts, shampoo, and meat juices. He had been crumbling rosemary in his hands, garlic with the wooden spoon he held. The air was solid with his presence, driving all other presences away. Always she liked the way people's quarters gave evidence of their lives, but Henry's apartment was not an idle collection of books and knickknacks and clothes. It seemed only his, exclusive.

He propelled Alice toward the stove and exposed the stew for her. Beside it were arrayed the Brie, the arrow of bread, the crisp head of broccoli beaded with moisture, a mound of breadcrumbs, her bowl of raspberries, which he had set down, and thick cream the color of sunlight. Unable to simultaneously devour it all in one gulp (including Henry) and sink tinily into it, Alice stood with her hands at her sides, half unconscious, thinking that she should say something but unable to speak. She did not want to say anything about love, but some remark about it was at the very gates. He put a glass of champagne into her fingers and she took a biting sip. "I'm glad you're here," said Henry.

"Me, too."

"Actually, you seem amazingly here, if you know what I mean."

"I would have said the same thing about you if my wits weren't blasted by your very presence."

Henry turned red and stifled a grin, leaning over the broccolli. "At the risk of making you self-conscious," he said, "I'll say that I've never known anyone with such a disconcerting combination of reserve and frankness before. There's a kind of absolute silence about you that you keep shattering."

Alice took a sip of her champagne, fear and desire rising in one fountain within. Throwing herself at him, leading him on, was irresistible. "How far along in the dinner are you? What does the stew have to do?"

"Simmer a while. I just have to cut up the broccoli, really. It's not time to steam it."

"Let's go to bed."

Henry put down his knife and began to untie his apron.

Alice could have crawled to the bed, but in fact she stepped rather lightly over the floor, air and doorways and objects breaking to either side of her like waves. Henry's hand at her back was unfastening the Mexican belt. It fell with a clank to the threshold of the bedroom. The ribs of the down comforter lay over his bed like a plowed field, and Alice had the sensation of planting herself

in it or spreading herself over it in her white dress like a stand
of wild carrot. Henry slipped his hands under the straps and the
white batiste slid down over her breasts. Her nipples were rigid
with expectation but Henry didn't touch them. Instead he put
his hands on her buttocks, inside her pantyhose, which he peeled
down her legs, one at a time. She stood up and her dress fell to
the floor. She could feel her vagina moisten and swell, feel the
space there that was usually insensate. She groaned. Even so,
Henry did not turn her around or come around in front of her.
He was looking at her from the back, at her neck, her spine, the
weaving of muscles that tapered to her waist, the round jut of
her hips. His looking made her see them. They were perfectly
still for a long time. Outside the open window, a dog barked and
was angrily hushed, cars swished by. When she turned to look at
him, he was intent upon her. His pulse pounded visibly in his
neck. Alice reached up one finger to feel the rush. Sometimes
Alice was taken aback by male flesh. Its firmness seemed numb
to her, as if only poking could penetrate to the nerves, or only
slapping could set up a reverberation that the man might dis-
tantly feel. Henry did not tempt her to hurt him, in fact she was
barely able to touch him, so explosive did he seem, so electrified
with neurons.

It seemed safe to take his hand, run her fingers over the mounts
and callouses. She shivered, and he pulled her closer. "Alice," he
said. She stopped his mouth with a kiss. It was a kiss she could
not give up or bring to an end. When his hands ran over her skin,
melting it, it was in addition to the kiss. When his chest rubbed
against her breasts, turning the nipples to points of fire, it was
in addition to her greed for the workings of his lips and tongue.
When he entered the space that had opened and seemed to probe
it and stretch it, still it was in addition to the mouth she could
hardly give him a moment to breathe with. He dove and dove,
groaning. Alice writhed beneath him as if to escape, but Henry
pressed inescapably upon her. Inside her he grew and she realized·

he was coming, felt his wetness and came with a great shivering herself. Immediately she closed her eyes, afraid of seeing anything differently, with less desire and delight, than she had before.

A transition to tales of murder was impossible. They sat at Henry's neatly set dinner table, Henry in his bathrobe and Alice in one of his shirts. The braised beef was delicious, the broccoli a little overdone, although Alice didn't say anything. "This is not what I imagined," said Alice. "I mean, I just put that dress on an hour ago. I could have at least spilled something on it before taking it off."

Henry's grin matched hers. "Not me," he said. "I dared to dream. You should see my list: set table, put on meat, answer doorbell, do it on the living-room floor, wash broccoli. Everything."

"I'll bet." Now? How did one start? Can I talk to you? But she *was* talking to him.

He helped her to another stalk of broccoli, then went into the kitchen for the second bottle of champagne. Alice looked around the room for something to help her begin. The pale pedestrian furniture, bought second-hand, no doubt, and without any eye for form, was saved by the boldly painted walls, cream with slate blue moldings, and by the plethora of dried and mounted specimens that covered the walls and all the flat surfaces. Many of them, she could see, were antiques, purchased, perhaps, from the estate of some ancient doctor or botanist. Others Henry had done himself. Where the walls weren't hung with the plants and butterflies themselves, they were covered with sketches of flowers and ferns and insects and spiders and birds. Indeed, just above her head, framed and set off by a little horizontal lamp, was a hand-colored engraving of a harlequin duck, obviously the pride of Henry's collection. The unsigned sketches, which were a little stiff but not bad, Alice suspected were by Henry himself. She was tempted to get up and look closely, but was also afraid of seeming nosy and making Henry self-conscious. She enjoyed the sense of being surrounded by things. It gave her the pleasure of endless possibilities. She sat still and ate the flower of her broccoli stalk.

As a rule she hated clutter. It had been one of the sorest points between herself and Jim Ellis, who gathered objects and brought them home to write poems about, who always preferred alleys to streets because he couldn't resist a row of trash barrels, and whose addiction to garage sales had to be strictly controlled. His accusation that Alice was a librarian in her soul was true insofar as her fantasy house had a multitude of drawers and cupboards built into the walls like a card catalogue, and no surfaces for the reception of anything. She found Henry's objects pleasing, though. They seemed to grow from and express him. Jim's had seemed to demand that he express them. Alice stood up and walked around the table, wanting to exclaim at her insight. She had thought that insights about Jim Ellis were behind her. Feeling intelligent, and perceptibly freer from her former marriage, she stopped at the window and looked out. It was still light on Eighty-fourth Street, but the shadows from the trees in Riverside Park stretched almost halfway up the street. An old woman from the apartment building next to Alice's was dawdling at the corner with her dog, a tiny ratlike beast with bug eyes. The doorman of the Riverside Drive building was taking a delivery, and a woman with a D'AG BAG was hurrying home, her eyes down and her purse slapping against her leg. The view was slightly depressing. And she could see into her windows. Although the light of the sunset reflected off the glazing, she could make out her round kitchen table, her square dining-room table, and the corner of the washing machine in the laundry room. That was depressing, too. She turned back to Henry's busy refuge with a sigh. There's something you don't know about me? There's something I'd like to tell you?

A cork popped in the kitchen, and then the mere sight of Henry with the bottle smoking in his hand, his feet bare and bony on the hardwood floor, his robe pale blue against his tanned skin lifted her spirits. Later, she thought, later there would be a good time.

It was frightening the way her adoration seemed to flow out of her like ink into water, staining everything, hiding everything.

She thought of Rya saying that she had declared her love to Craig and then been afraid to take it back. Was that what Jim Ellis felt about her? "Christ, Henry," she said, holding out her glass. "Where did you get all this stuff?"

They went back to bed in the dusk, taking champagne and the remains of the raspberries, leaving their forks on their plates, their water glasses half full, even the bowl of cream on the table, spent lemon halves, a stick of butter, unstoppered bottles of herbs on the kitchen counter. Henry did manage to turn off the lights. Alice kept close to him, some part of her body continually touching some part of his. Now was the time. They didn't have to make love at once. "Hen—," she began. He didn't hear her.

"You know what I found out today?" he said. "That shit and science come from the same Indo-European root. No kidding. Also discern, shin, ski, shield, squire, and shiver."

"Henry, you make all this up."

"No, really. The word means to cut or split. And we all know that shitting is most basically a process of separation."

"Henry, I want to tell y—"

"Alice, I love you." He said it quickly, while she was not looking. Her mouth dropped open. She said, "It's only been since Saturday. You don't know anything about me," but in spite of her best intentions, she failed to sound brisk or businesslike.

"I was in love with you Sunday morning."

"Oh, Henry. Come on. I catalogue books. I don't know how to dress. I talk too much about my first husband. My hobbies are uncreative. I wasn't smart enough to go to medical school or even law school."

"You can't talk me out of it."

"I don't know if I can reciprocate."

"That's partly what I love about you. You consider things. I just do things, like I'm driving a train, or something. The tracks are down, the engine gets stoked up, and off I go, eating up the miles, never turning aside, hardly ever looking out the window. I love the way you eat, and the way you talk to me at the table.

You take a bite, and then you sit back and chew it, and then you swallow it and take another one. I say something to you and I can see you listening and thinking about it, you lift one finger, as if for silence, and then you speak very consideringly. When I was a senior in high school, my mother used to make me eat everything with chopsticks because I was eating so fast. Even birthday cake. I ate birthday cake at my eighteenth birthday with chopsticks. Except I got proficient enough with them to eat too fast after a while."

"But I don't know if I can reciprocate."

"But when you do know, you really will."

"But what if I never do know? This scares me."

"You'll know."

"You sound very self-confident."

"One of my compelling qualities."

"Yes, yes, you're right." Alice was panting. Henry pushed the hair off her forehead and kissed her hard.

I T   W A S   one of those long nights of awaking into desire, making love, falling asleep, bumping into one another, and awaking into desire again. When Alice's eyes opened permanently, it was still dark. Henry was in love with her. Food was out all over the house. Alice got up as carefully as possible and went into the living room. She seemed to have been at Henry's for ten years. It was ten after three. With the best of intentions about clearing the table and putting the food away, she stood idly by the window, not trying to sort out her thoughts, for that would be impossible, but trying to think them one at a time. The moon, which must have been above and behind Henry's building, shone with penetrating whiteness upon the windows of her apartment, into them, in fact. She could make out any number of things, including the sandals she had worn to work, which she had left on the kitchen floor while washing the raspberries. From this angle, with this full moon, her apartment was wide open. It was

disconcerting, but not nearly so disconcerting as Henry's decla-
ration of love. The possibility of his friendship, of his good advice,
of a concentrated focus on her tangle of ignorance now seemed
hopelessly remote. While she talked he would look at her hair or
her breasts. His advice would be too quick and enthusiastic, too
colored by the vividness of his new feelings and his wish to protect them. It was not a matter of trying. Henry would try hard
to be calm and objective, but in Alice's limited experience, lovers
were as often adversaries of a sort as they were friends. In addition, there was her undutiful self, who could think with some
perspective, who could panic and hesitate under the weight of
someone's love, but only if the lover was not in the room. She
was doomed to reciprocate on the first eligible occasion. Whether
or not it was Henry she adored, it was certain that she did adore,
that she shivered with delight every time she thought of Henry
actually saying, "Alice, I love you."

And then there was something else. There was no way of
knowing whether Henry loved something permanent, some knob
of her being that was her forever, or whether he loved a mood
engendered in her by recent events. She and Henry had lived on
the same block for a year at least and he couldn't remember
seeing her before. Maybe the murder was a sort of isotope that
made her transiently visible, that would halve its life and fade.
She was different in many ways these last ten days—more emo-
tional, more afraid, less routine, but when the events washed off,
she was sure that their dye would, too. Henry would perhaps be
disappointed at the paler Alice, the Alice that really did work at
the library and visit museums and talk to her parents every two
weeks and spend whole days thinking about books and food.

And what did she think of Henry?

There was a movement in her apartment. She stood up in surprise and leaned against the windowpane. There certainly had
been a movement in her apartment, something white above the
floor had moved from the dining room to the kitchen. Whatever
it was stayed back from the window and Alice didn't see it again.

Her body had gone cold, and now was covered with goosebumps. There was something in her apartment! Someone, really. Someone in a white shirt that reflected the moonlight. She looked in each window systematically, starting in the laundry room, then the living room, then the dining room, then the kitchen. Whoever it was didn't appear again, but there had been something odd— the sandals. The sandals in the kitchen that had been right in the middle of the floor were off to one side and separated. Whoever it was had stumbled over them and kicked them. Alice put her hand on the window frame and gripped it tightly. The clock on Henry's coffeetable read 3:25. Alice dragged her eyes from the clock and back to the darkened windows across the street. She watched for a long time. There were no lights, no movements, but also no appearances at the street entrance, the only way besides the fire escape of getting out of her building.

After a while of staring, what she had seen came to seem impossible, and she couldn't remember where the sandals had really been. She made herself look again for the glint of white through the kitchen window, but the moon had moved. Now it reflected off the glass. She glanced at the clock, then regretted it, certain she had missed something. The downstairs entrance opened and Alice inhaled deeply, but it was no one, some man from upstairs she had seen with his wife half a dozen times. He was wearing a dark suit, anyway, and carrying an overnight bag.

She longed to creep back to bed and snuggle up to Henry's back, to abandon her apartment and everything in it, but the sense that the scene had not yet played itself out kept her where she was. Something would appear, above or below. She leaned her elbows on the glass and yawned, then made herself look for the pale shape of the sandals again, to shock herself awake, but she could see nothing. How could they know she wouldn't be there? No one knew that except Henry.

Inexorably, the stillness across the street grew boring, and her concentration began to fail. The buildings in her peripheral vision began to change shape, first expanding, then contracting. Her corneas seemed to dry out. She closed her eyes for a second and then opened them without knowing how long she had failed to watch. When she opened them, she understood. Obviously, her night-time visitor was Susan, the only person with a key. It was almost light. She had fallen asleep. She turned to the clock, which read five minutes of five, took a deep breath of relief, and began to pick up items from the table and carry them into the kitchen.

At ten-thirty, she called Susan at the store and fished for an admission that she had come over in the night and stayed, or looked for her, or anything. But Susan was cool and innocent, and by eleven, perched at the reference desk, Alice was inclined to view the separated sandals as the result of too little sleep, too much champagne, or a trick of the moonlight. The phone rang at her elbow, and when she picked it up, Rya's voice asked for her. "This is me, Rya, what's up?"

"Alice."

"What's the matter, Rya, are you crying?"

"That guy went over, that detective, and they took Noah and arrested him. He called me from the station." She sniffled.

Alice made sympathetic noises, but was afraid to speak, her spirits lifting by the moment. Then she remembered to say, "What are the charges?"

"I'm not sure," Rya was whispering, "but I think murder." Alice could barely hear her, but even so the words made her skin tingle. She said, "They've got to have evidence. They surely don't have any evidence."

"They had something. Honey came to my office yesterday and asked me about whether I'd tried to call home that night."

Alice flushed. He would have gone immediately from her to Rya. "That seems like pretty slim evidence."

"There's something else. They didn't say what it was. Anyway, they're moving him around, but maybe Honey would let you see him, and Noah would see you. I don't think he wants to see me."

"Why me? I don't see that it's any more my business than anyone else's."

"Please?"

"I don't want to, Rya. I just don't want to. I'm sure they won't let me see him anyway. They never want people to get together on their alibis."

"Maybe Noah doesn't have an alibi. But please? I can't think of anyone else."

"I'll think about it."

"How did I get myself into this?"

"I ask myself that every day, Rya."

"Will you call me?"

"After I've thought about it. But I'm sure they won't let me."

She was right. At the Twentieth Precinct, they wouldn't even tell her where Noah was, and Honey was out and would be for the rest of the day. Alice tried to imagine him authoritative, making an arrest, clamping on the cuffs. It was easy. He could have done it to her, to Susan, to anyone. He had done it to Noah. That was a relief. Even if he got convicted, and with the sort of evidence Rya knew about that was unlikely, he would surely be out in ten years or so. Good behavior would be automatic to Noah, and supposedly the prisons were full of dope. They obviously wouldn't send him to someplace like Attica; he was harmless. She would testify to that herself. He could start a prison music program, gain a social consciousness. It wouldn't be so bad. People thought that prison was the end of life, but really it was just a new life, with its own interests and concerns. Noah might be good at it, better at it than, say, Susan. She thanked the officer at the desk, left a message for Honey, and went out. It was another beautiful day, she inhaled deeply, she turned toward the park, Henry was in love with her, he couldn't see her tonight but Saturday they would have the whole day. By Central Park West (the light changed, she stepped into the street), she was so despondent that she could hardly breathe. She thought of lying down in the center of the road, doing it suddenly, before any oncoming car would have time to brake, before she would have time to think about it or feel it. But of course her foot lifted onto the curb without even a hitch in rhythm, and her steps carried her in the sunlight down toward Columbus Circle, where she could get something to eat. She thought of herself in the last ten or twelve days, borne on the flood of thought, anxious, angry, upset, but alive. Now she felt dead, thoughtless, a walking paralytic, all feelings, all concerns locked immobile like gears forced together within. She bought a hot dog with sauerkraut and walked down Fifty-ninth Street.

10

W H E N she got back to her apartment at the usual time, Susan was there, and she was carrying a bag of groceries. Actually, she was not in Alice's apartment, Alice noticed, merely in the hall, as if she had just arrived. She seemed rather ebullient, showing Alice the food she had bought, exclaiming about how hungry she was, complimenting Alice on her skirt and blouse, marvelling at the continued good weather. "Did you hear about Noah?" Alice said, but Susan was preceding her through the door and Alice couldn't see her face.

"Rya called me. She said you were going over to see him. I told her to come by, but she said she couldn't make it until after dinner."

"I couldn't see him. I couldn't even see Honey."

"I'll make a hollandaise for this."

"Do you think he did it?"

"No."

Alice began to be afraid again. "I've been terribly depressed all afternoon." She raised her voice slightly at the end, to encourage Susan to confide the same thing. All Susan said was "Really?"

"Haven't you?"

"Should I be?"

"Our friend has been arrested!"

"Honestly, that doesn't depress me. It's irrelevant. He'll be out sooner or later. Honey obviously doesn't know what he's doing, which rather depresses me, but Noah I'm not worried about. He's been crazy lately. Something concrete, some kind of action from outside will perk him up. People are always happy when they're actually being victimized."

"But what if he did it?"

"Impossible."

"Rya doesn't think so."

"Rya has always attributed a lot of force to Noah's character that just isn't there. Here, wash these." She handed Alice a package of chicken breasts. Alice tore off the wrappings. "He would never have the self-assurance, especially to face down Craig." She began rolling the washed breasts in flour. Alice's head was throbbing with pain. She sat down.

Susan went on. "I've figured out a lot of things."

"What?"

"I've figured out why they never got big."

"What does that have to do with anything?"

"Well, I'm convinced that if they'd ever gotten as successful as Craig wanted to get, they would never have been killed. I've thought a lot about it, the relationship of their murder to their exact degree of success. I'm sure it wasn't random or inevitable, but maybe it was unavoidable."

"I'm so tired of talking about it and thinking about it."

"That's because you're having only a welter of thoughts. If you—"

"It's because I can't bear that it happened!"

Susan looked at her, then went back to sautéing the chicken. It was Alice's favorite recipe, one Jim Ellis had taught her and she had taught Susan. Boned chicken breasts floured and sautéed in butter, then smothered in a sauce of cream, chicken drippings, and lemon juice. Very simple. Susan was bribing her. Also in the bag were chocolate pastries from Zabar's, one of her weaknesses. Alice closed her eyes. In a moment she heard the clink of a glass on the table, and opened them upon a glass of white wine. She took a sip. Susan lifted the last golden piece of meat out of the pan and turned off the flame. Then she turned to Alice and put her hands on her hips. "You seem to think that this means nothing to me."

"I don't mean to imply that. I'm sorry if—"

"Denny's mother calls me nearly every day. Did I send the clothes? The clothes got there. Do I mind who gets what, isn't there anything else that I want to keep, there are some letters of mine from way back that Denny had at home, every little thing, but mostly she, or one of the sisters or brothers, just wants to hear it again. They can't believe it. Well, I can't believe it either. It only sinks in bit by bit, as I think about why it was, and what might have led up to it. Some guy off the street didn't just come in and blow them away. Whatever happened was the culmination of something."

"Yes, I—"

"It's not crazy or senseless, that's the point! Things led up to it, step by logical step. Every detail is significant. And it's not just significant in terms of what happened, it's significant to me, to my peace of mind, to my being able to go on from this. I'm the one who's got to know why it happened, I'm the one who's got to think about it. I can't wait for Honey to file a report!"

"Actually, today when Rya called and told me that they had arrested Noah, I was almost happy. I couldn't bear being happy, or feeling good that Noah had done it, or at least that they thought Noah had done it. I was so sure that the result of the investigation would be worse. Much worse. And it seemed almost appropriate that Noah should be the one, if you know what I mean. I could survive Noah."

"Who couldn't you survive?"

"Well." Alice looked steadily at her friend. "When, uh, Honey first talked to me after I found them, I thought it was going to be me. I thought he could convince me of anything." She laughed, Susan did not. Alice began to eat.

After a few seconds, Susan cleared her throat and said, "I think that the first year after we got here was the worst. I thought it was great then, but now I remember it, and all I can picture is sitting around the living room with these greasy guys from the record company, planning out a strategy. Craig and Denny were horribly enthusiastic. Craig used to sit practically on top of the guy and stare into his face. Denny wasn't much better. There were the Eagles on the Coast and there were the guys, two bands, dueling it out for national primacy. Even though he'd never met the Eagles, Craig used to call them by their first names. I hated it, and teased him about it, but he couldn't help it. Once I said, 'None of the Eagles calls you by your first names!' but he didn't bat an eyelid, just said, 'They will by Christmas.' "

"The record company was very encouraging. How could they help being hopeful?"

Susan scowled. "And then they got booked into smaller and smaller gigs. Oh, yeah, first it was the Bottom Line and all that, with the company making the deals, but then it was supper clubs out in New Rochelle, playing for the country set, and then it was towns in Connecticut and Pennsylvania, and the guys were doing their own hustling. By then everyone realized that good old Dinah was off the charts, not even in the top hundred, and that the album had shot only to sixty-nine anyway, before plummeting. Who cared, the next one would burn everybody up. They made up songs around the dinner table. Denny kept a pad for lines of songs by the bed. They got stoned, they didn't get stoned, they got drunk, they didn't get drunk, they composed by themselves and they brainstormed with each other and Noah and even Ray. Denny practiced new riffs by the hour, except that he *got them off other people's records!* He'd practice it and get it right, but it wasn't new, it wasn't his. I felt sick all the time. When they walked in the door, my chest would get tight and my heart would start pounding or I'd want to throw up for fear of what they were going to say. I've never seen two people have so much hope about anything! And then the record company was rude to Craig, and he broke the contract, and they didn't even get to finish recording the second album. But of course they could get something with another company, no problem, all these guys were interested, all these guys had approached them, except it was like magic. There was no one. No matter what they did or how hard they worked, no one was going to record them again. It was like one of those old movies where someone says, I'll see that you never have a job in this town again. I couldn't believe it at first. And they never did believe it. Or, they believed it, but they acted like it *was* magic. Craig always thought it could turn around at any moment. Just the right move, something as simple as wearing the right shirt to a gig could turn it around. Going to Studio Midtown on the right afternoon and falling into conversation with the right guy, coming up with the right kind of lyric, just one line, something with real punch. Craig always thought that it was a tiny little thing that was keeping him out, and if he only found it, then he would be in again. And it wasn't just the music business, it was the cosmos, or luck, or karma. Anything could get him back in, like being a vegetarian, and anything could keep him out, like being a vegetarian."

"I remember when he was a vegetarian."

"Shit, we went round and round about that one. He was bad to eat the flesh of animals, evil. His whole system was contaminated and he lived on a polluted plane of being. But then he changed his mind. Rock and roll demanded a certain destructive energy that could only come from eating meat. He thought if he matched his being perfectly to the spirit of rock and roll, they would meld, and he would get another recording contract."

"He was a little crazy about it."

"He thought it was just around the corner. Months and years elapsed and still it was just around the corner. Before I left for the Adirondacks, one of the last conversations I heard him have with Denny was about how giving up their first contract had really been the right thing to do, they couldn't let those bastards treat him like that, just like it happened the day before, not five years before. Can you believe it? It made my skin creep."

"Craig was definitely a little monomaniacal."

Susan went back to dipping artichoke leaves into the hollandaise and scraping them on her teeth. Alice was breathing heavily. Susan was not finished, however. "I don't blame them any more, though," she said. "I blamed them all those years for playing the wrong sort of music or learning the wrong riffs or writing bad songs. And of course I blamed them for being so never say die about everything. For caring so much every time they ran into a producer at a party or met someone who might be able to help them. There was a way that Craig said certain names, always first names, that was a sure signal that he was counting on this person, adoring this person. It always ended with the person being a shit after all. I don't know which was worse, the hope or the disappointment. And even when I vowed to myself not to pay any attention it was like water rising and falling around me. I couldn't vow not to get wet."

"You paint this in such vivid colors! I remember that they wanted to get ahead. Jim wanted to have his poems in *The New Yorker*, too—" She trailed off skeptically.

"You weren't there, you weren't around. You had your own life. Besides, this was for inside the house only. Do you think our Craig Shellady would have admitted failure on the street? Especially when Jim did get a poem in *The New Yorker* and Ray did start to get a lot of work with better-known bands?" She pushed the bowl of spent artichoke leaves away from her and went on. "But now I see it wasn't their fault! They couldn't have done anything. They were behind the tip of the wave for their style of music, and the time had passed, even before we got here, when every good band was going to be recorded. It all shrank, and they were left out. It was a historical force! Inflation! Oil! Changing tastes! So what that they were good and wanted success more than life itself!"

"How did that kill them?"

"You can't understand it. The very air of the apartment was thick. It was like walking through mayonnaise, trying to breathe mayonnaise. Craig was there incessantly. I'd make Denny promise not to talk about it for one night, or one morning, but Craig would just hammer at him until he fell apart. Talking to Denny was like talking to himself, and I'd been around so long that I wasn't even there." The sound of the downstairs buzzer startled them and the bustle of Rya's overwrought arrival prevented Susan from going on, rather to Alice's relief. Rya was carrying a suitcase. "I can't stay," she said. "I have a late plane to Houston." She thrust out her chin. "I've just got to get away. Noah won't talk to me. I can't stand it. Anyway, Detective Honey said I could go see my parents for a week, and I got on the plane. It was the last seat until Saturday, so I thought I'd better take it. Noah's being arraigned or indicted or one of those tomorrow afternoon. Do you hate me?"

Susan stood up and began taking the dishes to the sink. Alice said, "I thought you hadn't spoken to your parents in six months."

"I called them this morning. My daddy would rather have me home, anyway."

"What about work?" Susan spoke coolly, as if she disapproved. Alice didn't disapprove.

"They gave me time off. David's been wonderful. He even offered to get Noah a lawyer."

"Well, why not go?" said Susan. "Why the hell not?"

"The weather's going to be awful, and under normal circumstances, of course, I'd rather be with Noah, but he won't see me. I don't see what good staying around would do."

Alice shrugged.

"Well, I've got to catch the plane. There should be a cab on West End."

"What airport?"

"Kennedy, but I'll be glad to drop you. It's late."

Susan wiped her hands on a dish towel and then they were gone.

THE first time Alice let herself think about the possible visitor of the night before was when she woke up in the middle of the night and couldn't help it. It was then, when she was trying to recall the exact shape and character of the whiteness she thought she had detected through the window—the laundry room window—that the full realization that Susan had done the murders floated into her thoughts. It was not Denny who had been murdered with Craig, but Craig who had been murdered with Denny. In Denny's apartment, Denny was the intended victim. The knowledge came so smoothly, so much like old business, that Alice stretched, turned over, and rearranged the blanket before beginning to react, to feel sick, to tremble and fidget, to perspire. She pushed back the covers and went into the bathroom.

Getting it down was like swallowing a whole boiled egg, extra large, with the shell on. She would do anything, think of anything (Hugh and Doreen, each of her four grandparents, Henry, Noah, her obscure poets, whether there was enough on her Master Charge to buy a lot of new clothes) rather than choke it down. She stood by the bathroom window, looking down on the empty street.

The insane thing was that it didn't make her admire Susan less. It was not like discovering some new friend had supported the Vietnam War to the end, or really believed that black people were inferior. And it seemed that nothing about her revelation could impel her to extricate herself from the friendship. Could a tree of its own volition pull itself up, root hair by root hair? What did Susan say, that Noah didn't have the force of character to confront Craig? And did Susan?

The hard-boiled egg only half swallowed, she turned on the light and got into the shower. It was not even dawn yet. She longed to be at the library. As the water poured over her, she imagined herself a little house in the inner court, two little rooms, one on top of the other with a ladder between them that could be pulled after herself when she was upstairs. Thick carpets the color of grass on the floors and bright flowered wallpaper, stacks of yarn for knitting and fabric for sewing and books for reading and symphonies, string quartets, concertos, sonatas, cantatas, oratorios to listen to, something mindless to work at like making license plates and the library rising around her, cutting off her view like a thorny thick forest.

When she got out of the shower, she looked out the window at Henry's apartment. He hadn't called after Susan's departure. She had known he would not and now the telepathy didn't work as it had. No lights came on; he would be asleep, fortifying himself for grafting trees or pruning them or something else equally guiltless. She went naked into her bedroom and picked up the phone, but then put it down. It was not until then that she began to wonder about the practicalities of Susan's act, about the practical side of the act itself. She had been there, she had even walked around, but in a daze, seeing only the spectacle, unable to comprehend the scene. No wonder Honey had been exasperated. She thought of Susan with him, self-assured, unimpressed. Did Honey find it as easy as Alice did to imagine Susan carrying out the details of her plan: purchasing the weapon, arranging gasoline for the car, covering her entrance into the city and her exit with the anonymous comings and goings all around her, using her very familiarity with the apartment and with the habits of Denny and Craig as her most deadly weapon. Or did that vision only come with years of experiencing her friend, watching how neatly and patiently she arranged things, the deftness of her fingers, and her plans, always precise and unhurried, unfidgeted, unaffected by frustration or boredom, so that she could unpick a complicated seam two or three times and still hum to herself, so that she could arrange nearly a whole window full of clothes, and then change her mind and do it over without wanting to smash the glass. And could Susan actually have bought and held and finally fired such a gun, a gun that created the mess that Alice found? Alice tried to imagine the feeling of that black-edged thing coming into her hand but she could not. Into Susan's hand? Yes. Susan's hands were as big as hers, and wider, stronger, although perhaps you didn't have to be particularly strong to fire one, only to have the intention of firing one.

She sat down on her bed, then slumped backward, thinking of the last party she had given in this very apartment. Everywhere she looked she had seen an intimate. Susan, Denny, Craig, Ray, Noah, Rya, distributed about the gathering like ripe peaches, a richness, comfortable, handsome, interesting. Craig had brought her some daffodils, snitched from the park or someone's private bed, but yellow and sweet. Denny had smacked her on the butt. Were any of the others less lost than these dead ones? She felt herself being sucked friendless into the future, against her will, almost as she had felt when she first realized Jim would leave her for Mariana, except that in this case there was no promised relief, no wound for time to heal. These difficulties were both drier and more permanent, and they made her feel older than mere betrayal had, permanently older. But who cared about that? This she hated about herself, this sea of self-absorption, out of which her intelligence rose only sometimes, like a periscope. After a long numb interval, she stood and began to dress.

There was still no seeing Noah. The unknown officers at the Twentieth Precinct didn't even know where he was, or said they didn't. Honey would be in touch with her, they thought. She left her name and phone number.

AT WORK she was not unhappy. She was sure the evidence against Noah, however it might distract Honey, could not be sufficient for a conviction. Against Susan there was no evidence, only a feeling on Alice's part borne of confusing conversations and 3 a.m. hallucinations. Every time she thought of the scene, of the motive, of the opportunity, nothing told against Susan, no fact damned her, nothing about her threw all the fragments into alignment. Although Alice's conviction of Susan's guilt remained unshaken, everything ameliorated it. After work she ran into Henry on the corner of Eighty-fourth and West End, and he embraced her as a matter of course and kissed her with perfect self-confidence, as if he expected his kisses to be welcome. They were, but only in retrospect. She felt him notice her coldness and elect to ignore it. To make up, she put her arm around his waist, but resolved not to go back to his apartment with him. There she would be unable to think at all.

"I wanted to call you last night, but we had to take down part of a tree. It was enormous, and we had to do it after the garden was pretty much cleared out. I didn't get home until one. Your windows were so peacefully dark that I didn't have the heart. Just wait until November, though. Nine to five, I swear, and lots of days off for exploring the countryside and finding specimens."

"Will that matter in November? November is a long way away."

"It will be life and death to you in November, my dear. Haven't you noticed my fungal personality?"

"You intend to grow on me?" Alice laughed in spite of her mood. "Disgusting." But she resisted his pressure toward the silver and glass door of his apartment building. He noticed that, too, but only paused for the briefest second before continuing down the street toward the dusty green of the park.

"And how was your week? I missed you. The irises are beginning to bloom."

"Did they remind you of me?"

"Everything reminds me of you."

Now she stopped. Henry stopped, too, kindly, affectionately, adorably. Resolute, Alice said, "Can we not see each other for about a week?" but as she said it, desire overwhelmed her, and she could feel her pulse throbbing in her neck and temples. "Why do you have this effect on me?"

"What effect is that?"

"I won't answer. I didn't intend to say that."

He turned to face her and put his open hand under her hair, over her cheek and ear. "What effect?"

"Someday you're going to be intolerable, Henry. You lean on me, you push me around. I'm used to being alone. I like being alone, with lots of space around me. And I have a whole other life besides this one!"

Henry's hand dropped. Alice wondered if she looked as aghast as she felt. He turned away, saying, "I'll call you later," and stalked down the street. The renewal of Alice's longing and desire was immediate and inevitable, like the resumption of music after a rest. She chased him and grabbed his elbow. "Henry, listen, I'm not going to talk, because I can't predict what I'm going to say, but the effect is one of intense desire. Whenever I see you, I start dying to be with you."

"Have you had dinner?" His voice was carefully neutral, and the difference piqued Alice in spite of herself. "No, let's!" she said, brightly, falsely. She could sense that the bulkheads separating the murder from Henry from her job from her parents were beginning to crack and leak, and in unexpected ways. She clutched Henry's arm tightly. Why not tell him the whole story? Why not say, I have something to confide in you, Henry, or Listen to this! She did not have to begin with the perfect phrase, it would not be an artistic exercise. But even the remote possibility of speaking seemed to close her throat and stop her breathing. Henry was hurrying toward Broadway. She said, "Henry, I am falling in love with you. I always react badly when I'm falling in love." This she had not meant to say, since it might not be true, and when he made the desired response, of unbending and taking her under his arm, of smiling warmly and kissing her on the hair, she was so irritated as to actively dislike him. Turning down Broadway, she burst into tears of frustration. Henry stood her on the corner and surveyed her, proprietary. "You're a mess," he said. "I'm going to Zabar's to get some food. You stand right here. After that we'll go back to my place and eat and take things one at a time, all right?" Here was her invitation. Alice nodded. Henry disappeared through the always promising doors of the delicatessen, and Alice stood among the umber-strollers and the passersby, the future unreeling before her as palpably as the frames of a movie. Henry would lead somehow to Honey which would lead, of course, to the machinery of courts and laws. No decisions would seem to have been made—the two of them would talk about only possibilities and nuances, theories and likelihoods. It would be a relief. It was a relief already, just to think about it. Everybody slowed as they passed Zabar's, if not to notice the bargains or the lady grinding out red pasta, then to ogle the slices of chocolate torte in the newly opened bakery. No one seemed to pay attention to the good weather any more, perhaps because it had changed imperceptibly from good to tedious. Alice bent down and wiped her eyes on the hem of her skirt, wishing she were the sort of person who always carried a handkerchief, or at least a wadded Kleenex. And approaching from the south was Susan, the smile of pleased recognition already fixed on her face. Inside the store, Alice thought that she could just make out Henry's head at the end of a long line for the cashier. She hoped that the five people in front of him all had baskets full of little items. She raised her arm and waved to Susan.

Susan kissed her. "Did you see Noah, then? I called you a couple of times this afternoon, but you were away from your desk."

"No, they wouldn't let me. I talked to Honey, though." She said it rather quickly.

"What's happening? They can't just hold him there."

"He was arraigned this afternoon." That's what Rya had said, at any rate.

"Is he getting out on bail? Does he have a lawyer? Does he know a lawyer?" Susan had settled herself in, and it became apparent to Alice that she thought they would go home together. Henry, thankfully, had made little progress in his line.

"I didn't ask that. And I can't remember if Rya said her boss got him a lawyer, or offered. Maybe we should call him. What's his last name?"

"Don't ask me. Levine? Loewy?"

"What a bitch she is!" exclaimed Alice. Two people stood in front of Henry. He hoisted and shifted his basket. It was piled high. Fifty dollars' worth of stuff, maybe.

"I think we ought to call her up and make her come back."

"Would it be worth it? She'd be around all the time."

"Even so—"

Henry moved closer to the counter. "Listen," said Alice, taking Susan's arm and turning her away from Zabar's. "There's more. This is too crowded. Walk down the street with me." She glanced back; Henry was at the counter, arm raised to point out rolls and croissants. She sighed. In a moment he would be out on the street, looking for her. She propelled Susan down Eighty-first Street. "What?" said Susan. "What? I have to work tonight. I was going to go in and get some cheese."

"No, listen. We'll come back. Just walk around the block with me, I have something to tell you." She looked behind. No Henry, indignant, out of love, followed them. She said, "It's solved. He did it. He confessed and Honey's convinced."

"You're kidding."

Alice peered into Susan's face, trying to detect the exact degree of surprise and elation there. The other woman was impassive. Alice pressed her. "I'm not kidding. And Honey says he has direct evidence."

"I can't believe it."

Really? thought Alice. But disbelief was a condition Susan often expressed. "Me, neither, actually," she said.

"But then why would he confess?"

Alice coughed, pretending to think of Noah, but really preparing herself to lie again. Finally she said, "Maybe he's just trying it out. Maybe he thinks it's a way out of something. But maybe he did do it. He could have."

"He could have stood up to Craig?" Susan smiled.

"Everyone has depths, don't you think? On the face of it, yes, it seems unlikely, but who can say?"

"He never stood up to Craig. In twelve years of playing music, he just took orders, even when they were contradictory, wrong, spiteful, or stupid. He never even argued."

Alice forced conviction into her voice. "It could accumulate. Honey thinks he did it, anyway."

"He's convinced?"

In vain Alice looked for something telling in Susan's face, listened for something revealing in her voice. There was no relief, no budding gladness. "What are we going to do?"

"What do you mean?" answered Susan. "It looks to me like we're done doing."

They had turned the corner of Eighty-second Street, and were walking back toward Broadway. Alice walked without speaking, listening to the confident rhythm of Susan's clogs on the pavement, back to Broadway and then toward Zabar's again. "Wait here," said Susan. "Then you can walk me back to work. Want anything?" Alice shook her head. Henry was long gone, or maybe only briefly gone, but a miss was as insulting as a mile, wasn't it?

She looked down at her shoes, Top-Siders, the lace knotted where it had broken, and even as she looked she seemed to grow distant from them. She lifted her eyes and fixed them on the Zabar's window, and then she turned her head and looked across the street. Everything had grown smaller, more distinct, and Alice marvelled that she wasn't afraid, only wildly, violently annoyed. A man bumped her, nicely dressed, preciously dressed in tight jeans and the sort of imported cotton shirt that Susan sold. Alice wanted to destroy him. She watched him step into Eighty-first Street and disappear into the crowd and wanted to shout, "What's the matter with you? Can't you excuse yourself? You bumped me! You slob!" Her anger seemed to lift her off the ground. She closed her eyes and put her hands on her head. She was perspiring at the hair-line and breathing hard. She wondered why anger didn't break people, split them open like figs, explode them. At her elbow, Susan said, "You look awful. Why don't you open this and have some." Into Alice's grasp she put a large cold bottle, sparkling cider. Alice touched the bottle to her forehead. Everything resumed its normal size. "Are you hot?" she said. "I think this weather is awful. Maybe I'm coming down with something." She closed her eyes and took another deep breath while Susan struggled with the cap to the cider. "I'm sure I'm sick. It must be the flu. We've been leading such a strange life. It would obviously make you more susceptible to things." Susan handed her the bottle and she put it to her lips. The sharpness of the carbonation was startling, delicious and repellent at the same time. A sense of panic that had ignited within her was quenched for a moment. She wiped her mouth after a long drink and handed the bottle back to Susan. Susan. Susan held out a piece of Brie cheese to her, then a large ripe strawberry. Susan who was familiar, kind, competent, habitually loved. Alice ate the strawberry, then another hunk of cheese, this one balanced on a cracker. "Feel better?" said Susan.

"Much."

"Come back to the shop with me. It's nice and cool, and everything is new. Sometimes I think that's the only good thing about the shop, that nothing belongs to anyone."

11

T H E three salesgirls at Chops all had something of Susan's
air of peace. Like her, they were attractive, but not in the usual
fashion. Jane, although slender, had broad shoulders and wide
hips. Karen was short and round, Louie had the wide-apart eyes
and oddly shaped teeth of someone from the West Virginia min-
ing country. And yet they were all superbly dressed and graceful,
as if the shop owners hoped to prove to prospective customers
that anyone could be transformed by Chops clothing into the
ideal New Yorker. The girls were enormously polite, not only to
customers, but also to Alice, Susan, and each other. Their personal lives were unimaginable, and Chops, with its white walls,
dark woodwork, and neutral carpeting that flowed up steps, into
dressing rooms, and over the various levels of the window display
area, seemed to exist apart from personal lives. Customers entered smiling, already casting their eyes at the clothing displays.
They gave out little noises of pleasure at the freshness of the air,
and they seemed to relax visibly into the renewal of possibility
that Chops presented. The mirrors were along the south wall,
silvering the air. It worked on her, too. She was no longer ill or

even afraid. She lounged in a chair behind the sales counter and watched the customers wander in, try on clothes, and wander out. People were watched, but left alone for their vanity to flower in peace.

Susan, the author of this orderly world, was her best self. She arranged clothes on hangers, folded and piled sweaters so that red, blue, green, and yellow glittered off one another and drew the eye to that expensive corner of the store. She complimented customers on their choices, but only if they had shown some taste, thanked Jane and Karen for taking care of difficult customers, and apologized instantly for a suspected overcharge, thanking the customer for coming back and telling them about it. She vacuumed; she looked at the books; she showed Alice new designs that she thought Alice might like or might marvel at the expense of.

To someone like this, Alice thought, a life like Craig's would of course become unbearable. Susan glanced over at her and Alice made an ostentatious sigh of relief. Susan smiled. And if you were involuntarily attached to that life, the fear of being sucked into it would be constant, wouldn't it? An action to close off that possibility was at least understandable. And now they were saved. Noah, after all, was a mess. Even if he didn't get off (and innocent, how could he not get off?), prison might be good for him. He could remake his life there. Get out for good behavior before he was forty-five. Forty-five was hardly middle-aged any more. But he would be acquitted, Alice was sure of that. And that would be the end. There were new murders every day. Once Honey had brought in his suspect, he would have other things to do.

It was only momentum that kept Alice's gears of thought and analysis grinding past any practical application. The mystery was over, and everyone, as befitted life in New York City in 1980, could have what he wanted. She looked across the room. What she wanted was to have her life arranged by Susan for months and years to come. The fears she had had of Susan earlier in the week, the glimpse she had seemed to see of Susan in her apartment, were her knowledge of the murder rising to the surface, and adjustment to the facts, while curiously physical, hadn't been especially hard. Susan disappeared into the back of the store and reappeared carrying a large carton. When she opened it, white blouses spilled forth, gauze, lace, luxury. The odor of cotton wafted in Alice's direction. When Susan began to pick them up and button them onto hangers, Alice stood up and went over to her.

ALICE stuck her card into the Citibank money machine and was informed that she could withdraw a hundred dollars or less. She took a hundred. Behind her, Susan was gazing downtown. Alice smiled, and stuck the money in her purse. "Now," she said, "let's go to your place and change clothes."

"What for? It's after nine."

"You'll see. Leave it to me." Susan walked along with complete docility, her clogs tapping the pavement. Alice took her hand off the other woman's elbow and put it around her waist. "I'm starving," she said. "I'll take you out to dinner. I'm tired of living my life as if I were a librarian." The inside of her mouth ached with hunger.

After calling Gallagher's and making sure that Susan was in the shower, Alice dialed Henry. For once he answered. She let his open, alluring tones ring in her ear for a moment before speaking, since she knew that the sound of her voice would close them up. "Hi!" she exclaimed.

"Oh," said Henry.

"You think I abandoned you, don't you?"

"You might say that."

Alice took a deep breath. "I got sick, or rather, I knew I was about to get sick, and I had to find a restaurant to throw up in. When I came back you were gone."

"Are you all right now?"

"Well, actually, when I got there, I didn't throw up after all. Why didn't you wait for a minute?"

"I did."

"Henry—"

"Do you want to come over?"

"I do, but I can't. I'm at a girlfriend's place, and we've got to go out."

"Fine, I'll call you."

"Henry—"

"I have to get off."

"I'm thinking of you."

"Fine." He hung up. The shower was no longer running. Alice put the phone on the hook. "Who was that?" said Susan, suddenly behind her.

"I called Gallagher's," answered Alice. "I made a reservation."

Susan grinned. "Funny kind of reservation." Alice grinned back at her.

There wasn't much to say, really. Their cab ride, the seats they took, their preliminary exchanges with the waitress about drinks and dinner, all these were like companionable silence. Alice's spirits rose fearsomely, or were turned up, like the volume on a television set. This is it, Alice thought, bouncing a little in her chair. The sensation of having moved into a new relationship with Susan had grown vigorously since the afternoon and now was so bulky that it crowded out their customary conversational ease. Leaving Henry at Zabar's, probing Susan so unsuccessfully that her convictions were somehow confirmed, spending the evening at Chops, sitting here, every moment carried the quality of arrested importance, so that the mechanism by which they had given way to one another was incomprehensible. This vividness confirmed her suspicion that this was it, while her knowledge that this was *it* enhanced the color of every moment, including the present one. Susan said, "My father always thought that the only good dinner was a steak dinner. Medium steak with salt and pepper, baked potato with butter and salt and pepper, three leaves of lettuce and a wedge of tomato with oil and vinegar and salt and pepper." She chuckled.

"The cuisine of the Midwest," said Alice. They could talk about food forever. "There were some Chinese dignitaries that visited Rochester last summer and my mother sent me the menu of the dinner they gave. Roast beef, ham, broccoli, potatoes au gratin, corn on the cob, salad, homemade ice cream and chocolate cake. They must have spent days in the bathroom."

"Here it is." Before them were set warm oval plates of dark, fragrant steak. The meat to be eaten, simple, familiar, savory, filled Alice with a sense of abundance. She pressed it with her fork and juice spurted. Susan took a bite. "It is delicious," she said. It was. Alice ordered a bottle of wine and poured two glasses full to the top. Susan smiled slightly. Because, perhaps, of the money, or the meat, or the wine, Alice felt pleasingly unlike herself, less constricted and taller, able to survey the room, judge the meal, make demands of the waitress. Susan, in her crisp white dress, her hair smoothed back by a toothed band, seemed a pristine treasure. That their fondness, or even love, was mutual, seemed astonishing. There are men, Alice thought, who never get over the luck of their wives, the luck of having such women in their arms or their rooms. Alice could never be that kind of woman, but Susan was. Denny must surely have felt that way about her. Susan said, "When I was in grammar school, there was a family down the street. I didn't like their little girl much, but the mother served the best cakes. They were always colored the most extraordinary colors—orange with blue icing, pink with green icing. One kid was allowed to color the cake batter, the second kid could do the icing, the third could decorate, and they were always covered with things like cut-up gum drops or had red hots in the batter or something. I couldn't believe the way my mother always stuck to chocolate cake with chocolate icing or white cake with white icing."

"Susan—"

"Hmm?" It was a polite sound, as if from a distance, telling Alice not to broach anything important.

Alice acquiesced, and said something about the pink and white checkerboard cakes her grandmother had made for her birthdays, but her fresh understanding of Susan and her fresh feeling for her pressed to come out. Successfully, for once, perceptively for once, and quickly, for perhaps the first time ever, she had put together the gist of their talk since the murders. And this in spite of her roller coaster sweep of emotions and her usual fears of doing and thinking the wrong thing. She glanced at Susan and realized that the knowledge itself left her strangely unrepelled, as one was unrepelled by the deaths in *Hamlet* or *Macbeth*. Craig seemed, in retrospect, to have been as much the agent of his end, and Denny's, as Susan was. Hadn't his every risk with drugs or motorcycles or money always seemed invited, his every escape the effect of luck or the kindness of others? And Denny, as perceptive as any of them about Craig's proclivities, had never stepped back once, had never even tried to untie the knot that bound them so closely. *Having* the knowledge, however, was somehow exhilarating, although perhaps Susan wouldn't see it that way. They cut, speared and ate. Alice drained her wine glass and filled it again. She filled Susan's again. Susan stirred sour cream and butter into her baked potato, then closed it together to preserve the heat. She said, "All these memories of my childhood have been booming over me lately. I don't think I know how to be an adult without Denny."

"I felt a little that way after Jim, and I was nearly twenty-one when I met him."

"I think a lot about my grandparents' farm. There was a pump handle by the sink. How can I be old enough for that? I spent the summer there with Sarah when my mother had rheumatic fever. We spent the whole time wading in the drainage ditches. When I couldn't get to sleep last night, I tried counting the number of things each of my grandparents would have touched in the course of a single day. Everything they talked about had weight: how much the pigs were gaining, how many pounds of milk the cows were giving, how many tons of seed or feed they would need or had used. When the weather was bad, my grandmother would always say that the air was so heavy you couldn't lift it with a pitchfork. And she was heavy. You could always hear her upstairs, and follow her progress from room to room. And she always sighed when she had to climb the stairs, or even get out of a deep chair. My grandfather was thin, but his tools were heavy, his clothes were heavy, his boots were heavy. It sounds unpleasant, I suppose, but it was very physical and substantial. If something weighed a lot, it had value." Susan pressed open her baked potato.

A man came in who looked from the back like Henry, but wasn't Henry. Alice's heart jumped, but only once, and only, she thought, because the prospect of Henry and Susan meeting struck her so bizarrely. She hadn't thought about Henry all evening, and now, when she did, the usual sexual vibration, as of a bell struck, was absent, subsumed in her present enthusiasm for Susan. There was not the energy for both, she thought. As she sat there, Henry began to seem fantastic; that she had slept with him, eaten with him, wanted to confide in him seemed aberrant and mindless behavior. Her passion for him, which she remembered now as a fact, not as a feeling, was rather embarrassing, not herself, a bolt from the blue. She squirmed in her chair. Looking at Susan reassured her, but at the same time reminded her of the danger their friendship was in. The circumstances themselves put it in danger, in spite of Honey's incompetence and the evidence, whatever it was, against Noah. And Susan herself might inadvertently expose something. Alice said, "Have you thought any more about leaving your apartment? Or even leaving the city? Maybe we should move on. We've been here six years, and God knows, I'm firmly wedged into the L-Two trap. I would love to find something at a university library, and with your taste and experience, you would obviously be snapped up by a department store in the hinterlands. We aren't unemployable any more, you know, or even beginners." Susan did not look receptive, but Alice went on, "We're being exploited now. We could make more and live for less almost anywhere else."

"I hadn't thought about moving."

"You don't have to live at the scene of the crime!"

"I'd rather drop the subject."

"Of course." Her second glass of wine nearly finished, Alice drained it and ordered another bottle.

"Are you hoping to get me drunk? Talking me into living with you without benefit of clergy?"

"Is that the way to do it? Anyway, I'm hoping to get me drunk."

"What for?"

"I don't know." Alice smiled. "Like I said, I'm tired of living in that pale librarianly way. I have no debts, I eat plenty of fruit, I come home every night and read. A big day for me is seeing old leftist movies at the Bleecker Street Cinema. I've never dissipated anything, even a free afternoon. This is New York: It's time I did something that was costly. I'm tired of going to all the cheap things and counting every nickel. I'm tired of worrying about the abyss, you know? Yes, you have to be careful in order to live by yourself in Manhattan on seventeen thousand a year, but I've been careful careful careful. Nobody else has. Now I'm not going to be careful for a while."

"So you're going to get drunk?"

"How clichéd, right? You know something, when I met Jim, he had absolutely no talent for having a good time. His family were avid Presbyterians, no dancing, no drinking, no playing cards, the whole schtick." Susan smiled. "And no Yiddish. Anyway, he set out to become bad. He started smoking, he started drinking beer and gin and then whiskey, he smoked dope, he took acid. I knew more about sex than he did, and that was just necking. I thought it was hilarious. It worked, though. Now he has fun. I bet he has only fun. He left me behind in more ways than just the one."

"Why do you always think that he went on to something better?"

"Because he thinks that he went on to something better."

"Don't you realize that what he went on to was another twenty-two-year-old? So now she's twenty-four. I give her four more years at the outside."

"That's what you've always said, but look at her. She looks like Sophia Loren, more or less."

"So, the next one will look like someone else. He likes twenty-two-year-olds. He was crazy about you when you were twenty-two."

"Was he?"

"Yes!"

"I could never see it."

"Well, I could."

"Did you ever tell me that?"

"Over and over."

"Why don't I remember? I just remember being his slave. He was crazy about me?"

"Yes! I can never get over the way you're so certain of what you think that it becomes the only reality for you. It's like you don't even sense any other possibilities."

"What do you mean, I'm narrow-minded, or I'm self-confident?"

"Neither, only that you're very loyal, to notions as well as to people."

"Wrong notions?"

"Sometimes. I think this is a perfect example."

Alice considered, then said, "But why do you think I was always extraneous to the matter at hand, then? I always felt like Jim's sidekick. Good enough company but not the focus of his attention."

Susan lifted a mouthful of peas on her fork, looked at them, and put them down on her plate again. "Partly I think they were all like that. They were all twenty-two just like we were. If you wanted something very badly, it was best to ignore it, you know?"

Alice nodded. "And Jim seemed to want girls much more badly than anyone else, I always thought. That's why he was always jumping up and down; it was like he could hardly contain himself."

"Did you ever tell me this before?"

"Something like it, but you wouldn't listen, or you didn't listen. You were very convinced that that woman was the love of his life."

"So was he!"

"Not until you suggested it to him."

"Oh, bullshit."

Susan leaned forward. "No, really! There was a point when Jim was ready for his grand passion to go either way. He could abandon everything for it, or he could do the right thing and abandon it. I think that each course of action appealed to him." She hesitated, looked at Alice, and ate the peas still balanced on her fork. After another moment, she said, "But you were so taken by the idea that this was the love of his life that you made it hard for him not to abandon everything for her."

"You don't think he wanted to?"

"Not at first. Then he got pretty fired up."

"I can't believe this! When he came back, he was so dutiful and sad."

"But I'm sure he came back because he really was ambivalent, because he couldn't decide which woman was better or which life was better. And then you were so certain that he was going to leave that he had to play it out."

"Well, yes I was certain, but that was the fruit of observation. I didn't want it to be that way."

"Obviously. I don't think you had this neurotic instinct for a failed marriage, and I do think that we've all suffered from mating ourselves so early in life. I think we set up structures out of ignorance, and then it was almost impossible to break out of them, even when we could see them. I mean, if you were in the habit of bitterly challenging him to be affectionate, how could he turn around and be affectionate without feeling defeated?"

Alice was shocked and silenced, but not entirely displeased.

While she had been stupid and had driven away someone she needed and cared for, at least she had been desirable.

Susan went on, "I'm sure that's why he calls you. He really isn't being patronizing. I think sometimes he really longs to have you back. Sometimes it must be hard to be eight years older than your mate, don't you think?"

"She would have been seven for the Beatles."

"Weird, huh?"

"And Jim is crazy for the Beatles." Alice put the last bite of steak in her mouth and chewed on it. It was bitterly delicious, full of the welter of feelings she was experiencing while eating it. One of these was the pleasant image of herself stubbornly wrong about the murder and Honey right: There was nothing to prove Susan had done it but her own blind conviction. She ate as she might have tied a knot around her finger, so that every future steak would submerge her in these revelations. She did not speak for a long time, then she said, "What structures did you and Denny make? You were even younger than we were."

Susan sighed. "I think I was always challenging him to make it with his music. I don't think I ever gave him a graceful way out of the business, or a chance not to defend Craig. I let myself be the south pole to Craig's north pole. Denny could only travel back and forth between us. He couldn't triangulate." She smiled ruefully. "At least, that's what I think when I'm feeling powerful. When I'm not feeling powerful, I see us all, the three of us, dog-paddling blindly in circles, and every time we meet up with one of the other ones, we try desperately to climb up whoever it is and get some breaths of air."

"Do we know any relationships that haven't become awful?"

"In our generation?"

"Yes. I don't know what my parents and grandparents are doing."

"Maybe they don't do anything. Maybe that's the point."

"But I'm happy."

"Are you?"

Alice said, "Our friendship hasn't become awful, do you think?

Maybe it was each other we should have married to begin with.
I do love you."

Susan smiled in acknowledgment, but seemed to retreat, as
always, before the onslaught of intimacy. Alice wanted to embrace her.

T H E cab dropped Susan after midnight; Alice didn't dare
look at her watch when she got into her place. Because of the
wine, her eyes opened for good at six, but she didn't feel ill, or
even disoriented. She awoke knowing everything was settled. Two
weeks ago, the murder had exploded underneath them all like a
landmine, scattering them aloft. Now they had all come down
where Alice wanted them to be—Noah on a permanent vacation,
maybe, Rya at leisure with her parents, Susan safe in her apartment, and Alice safe with Susan. The way Henry's presence had
divided her, even for only a week, had been a strain. She saw now
that things had changed since Jim—that although she had plenty
of time and energy for dates, there was just no room for someone
as consuming as Henry. She looked out her bathroom window at
his three quiet ones, experienced a moment of pleasurable regret,
then turned away humming. She felt unusually alert, as fresh as
the cool dry air blowing from the west. She went into her bedroom and opened the closet door. There was a muslin sundress
back from the cleaners that she had been saving for some date
with Henry. She ripped off the plastic bag with both hands, pulled
it off the hanger and slipped it over her head. It fit better than
last year. She closed the closet door, took clean underpants out
of her drawer and stepped into them, then made the bed and
turned the two spider plants in the windows, as she did every
month or so. Usually she was proud of her plants, but the new,
pristine bare look of Susan's apartment made them seem scraggy
and old-fashioned. Henry, too, would probably sneer at them. She
went to the laundry room and got the dustmop. Just then the
downstairs door buzzed, which made her drop the mop, but she

felt no intimation of danger, though it was not yet seven in the morning. She pressed the talk button and said, "Who is it?" then, "Who's there?"

No answer. She turned with the dustmop toward her room, and the buzz came again, this time longer and more insistently.

"Well, who is it?"

Nothing. In college people would play jokes on you—buzzing your room when they knew you had just taken a shower. Again the buzz. Alice hesitated a second, then pressed the talk button down firmly. "WHO IS IT?" she demanded.

She was answered with a groan.

Her reluctance to do anything, to acknowledge in any way that she should go downstairs and see what was going on, was immediate and potent. She felt herself being drawn in again. What she had thought was a thread around her wrist was really a rope around her waist, or her neck. Her instinct was to fight it. Instead, she dropped her hand down the handle of the dustmop, gripped it like a club and opened the door. Nothing there. Afraid to enter the solitary cubicle of the elevator, she began to descend the stairs. It was cooler than she expected, and she shivered. The elevator passed her, going up. She took the steps carefully but steadily, holding the dustmop in the air. Last flight. She leaned over the banister and peered into the tiny lobby. Nothing. But then, there couldn't be. It had been the outside buzzer. She crept toward the inner door, trying both to see and not to. She took a deep breath, then saw the wino. A wino on the doorstep. She stood up straight and put down the mop, then she tapped sharply on the window, thinking that she would gesture that she was going to get help. The wino, reclining, began to lift himself up and turn toward her. She could see that there was something wrong with him and wondered if she should open the door after all and let him inside. He moved very slowly, and she waited, a little aghast. And then it wasn't a wino. It was Ray, and his face and shoulder were covered with blood. She pulled open the door and he sort of melted through the doorway slowly, like Silly

Putty, then he lay at her feet, with his eyes closed. There was blood all over him, and Alice felt the old disbelief freezing her, as it had two weeks before. But then she stamped her foot and sourly said, "Stupid bitch!" She grasped the dustmop more firmly, stepped carefully over Ray, and looked out the door. Up and down the street. No one. Out of danger, she dropped the dustmop and bent down to Ray. She unbuttoned his shirt, getting an impossible amount of blood on her fingers, and put her hand on his heart. It was still beating. After that, she opened his shirt completely and looked at his chest, to see if the blood was coming from there. It was not, although his chest and abdomen were discolored with bruises. It would have come from his face, then. She swallowed hard and sat back on her heels. Fresh, in the sunlight and open air, it didn't seem like blood, didn't have the odor of two weeks ago. She wiped the sweat off her forehead with her elbow, then looked carefully at Ray's face. His eyelids, closed, seemed intact, if about to turn black and blue. His nose was a mess, and his jaw was broken. Some of the blood had been coming from his mouth, and she could see one small tear in his lower lip. Most of the blood, though, had come from his ear. His right ear. Alice bit her lip, then leaned backward around the doorjamb and rang for the super. After she had identified herself and told him as clearly as she could to come to the front entrance, she put her hand inside Ray's shirt again, and sat there feeling his heart beat for forty-five minutes until the ambulance came. From the hospital she called Detective Honey, then went over to where they were working on Ray. He was conscious now, and she took his hand. The doctor and nurse worked around him matter-of-factly, without panic. Alice deduced from this that he wasn't in lethal danger, and smiled at him. Another nurse came over with forms for her to fill out, and the doctor told her that Ray would have to stay under observation for at least a day. Alice looked at Ray, who looked relieved, and then sat down in a nearby chair to fill out the forms. They were amazingly complex. She put down that he had Blue Cross, although she didn't know. Things could be straightened out after he was better. Finally the resident came over and sat down.

"Miss Ellis," he said.

"Mrs. Ellis."

"Are you engaged to Mr. Reschley or anything?"

"No, I'm an old friend. We're from the same hometown. I take it he looks worse than he is?"

"Not exactly, but he's not in danger of his life. Mrs. Ellis, I've, um—"

"Is there something besides cuts and bruises?"

"Dr. Lee can talk to you about that, but I wanted to tell you that I—"

"About what? Who is Dr. Lee?"

"Dr. Lee is a staff otolaryngologist, he should be down again in a little while. But also, Mrs. Ellis, I called the police."

"So what? I called the police myself. But tell me why you called Dr. Lee." Alice spoke briskly, but she shrank to hear. The resident looked around, then clutched his clipboard more tightly. Finally, he said, "Mr. Reschley's right eardrum was repeatedly pierced with a sharp object, Miss Ellis." Alice looked away, toward the nurses' station, then back at the doctor. His own ears were rather prominent, she thought. She licked her lips, then said, "Would that hurt a lot, Doctor?"

The resident nodded.

12

DETECTIVE Honey was much brisker than usual. For once he seemed to be agitated, annoyed with Alice and with her friends. What time had the first buzz come, how long had it taken her to get downstairs, had she seen anyone, no matter how remote, on the street, had Mr. Reschley said anything, had Mr. Reschley been conscious at any time. Alice's replies were monosyllabic; Honey hadn't the time for anything else. Finally, he said, "Is there any reason why Mr. Reschley should be deposited on your front step?"

It was impossible not to answer candidly. "I don't really know, except that he stayed with me earlier in the week."

"When the department was under the impression that Mr. Reschley was away from the city?"

Alice nodded.

"Mrs. Ellis, you didn't inform me that you had seen Mr. Reschley this week."

"You didn't ask me."

Honey's eyebrows lowered. "Mrs. Ellis, I'm not going to tell you about the penalties for giving misinformation in an investigation. You know that there are such penalties. I'm going to talk to you about something more personal." Someone had drifted toward them. Honey looked up and glared; the man scurried away. "I realized before this, Mrs. Ellis, that you were not being very co-operative in this matter. As I look back on the past two weeks, I see a reluctance on your part to participate in the investigation, even when you seemed to be co-operating.

"In a professional sense, this reluctance is neither very unusual nor very inconvenient, which is why I have overlooked it up until now. At first I thought the problem was mine, that you might have co-operated more enthusiastically with another detective on the force."

"Ray wasn't under arrest. How was I to know that the stuff about him being in Miami wasn't just a trick on your part? I assume you know what you're doing."

Honey ignored her. "Do you know what a violent crime is, Mrs. Ellis? Among other things, a violent crime is the beginning of a train of events, and a sign that whatever balance a given social network has achieved is strained. The crime is a change, and the change is always sudden and profound, affecting every member of the network in unforeseen ways and often violently. Sometimes the murderer kills again, and other times violence simply happens again, through other agents. Something else is always true. The parties to the violence, whether guilty or not, always assume that they know what is going on and can predict what will happen and can make their own judgments about what to do, when nine times out of ten, they don't, can't, and shouldn't. In the end, the investigating officer, whose job is to try and see the larger picture, is blocked and hindered by the ignorant confidence of these parties, and violence that might not have erupted does, and another person is hurt or killed. Do you understand?"

Lectured, Alice snapped back, "Are you blaming me for this beating?"

"Should I?"

"What do you want me to do?"

"I want you to tell me everything you know. I want you to understand that you have to gain by the investigation, not to lose by it. I want you to take precautionary measures for your own safety, such as having your locks changed, and I want you to understand that your relationship to every associate has changed in ways you can't even guess." He looked at his watch. In spite of her aggressive tone, she felt dumbfounded.

"Now, Mrs. Ellis, is there anything else that you haven't told me about your activities or the activities of your friends?"

"Do you want to know about Jeff Johnson, Ray's friend? He was there with Ray at my place before."

"I have interviewed Mr. Johnson, although not in this matter." Honey made some marks in his notebook. "Anything else?"

Alice shook her head.

"Do you understand my remarks about candor, Alice?"

Alice nodded. Honey stood up with a sigh and called over the doctor, who said that Ray might be able to talk late that afternoon, and in a moment the detective was gone. Alice sat quietly, her head against the wall, for a short time.

W H E N she walked into her apartment, her phone was already ringing. Assuming it was Honey, Alice picked it up gingerly. It was the voice of Jim Ellis, deep, breathy, forever intimate. "Alice?" he said. "What's happening? I was hoping you would call me."

"I'm sorry, I—"

"There hasn't been anything about it out here, and nothing in the *Times* that I could find, either. Who did it? Did they find anyone?"

"It just happened this morning. It was awful. There was blood everywhere, in fact there still is. I haven't even had a chance to take off my dress, can I—"

"Alice, what are you talking about? The murder was two weeks ago."

"Oh, that! I'm sorry—"

"What are you talking about?"

"I found Ray beat up on my doorstep this morning. They punctured his eardrum on purpose, over and over. The doctors are afraid—"

"Who punctured his eardrum?"

"He hasn't been able to talk. I'm not sure. There was this weird guy he was hanging around with earlier this week. No affect. That's where he got the coke, I'm sure, but I haven't talked to Ray. He was unconscious. I'm not exactly sure what is going on." Her voice petered out. She could hear Jim smoking. Finally he said, "Don't hang up, but go change your clothes and get yourself something to drink, whatever you have."

"There's some brandy."

"Good, get that. I'll hold. Take your time."

Alice put down the phone and did as she was told. Five minutes later, she came back to it and sat down with a cup of the bitter, vaporous liquor. When she picked up the phone, Jim said, "Now take two deep breaths and tell me what's been going on."

"The other thing is that they arrested Noah."

"Noah!"

"Yes."

"Noah Mast actually killed Denny and Craig, actually killed Craig? Did that have to do with cocaine, too? What is going on there?"

"Craig was sleeping with Rya."

"Bitch!"

"Well, it's not exactly clear how voluntary it was on her part. You know Craig. Sometimes it was easier to do what he wanted than what you wanted."

"But it doesn't make sense that he killed Denny, too. And how does Ray fit in?"

"I don't know if he does. He's the only one with an alibi, but also the only one with a real motive. He got the guys some cocaine. Ten thousand dollars' worth. It wasn't paid for, as far as we know."

"Where is it?"

"That's the sixty-four-dollar question. At least, I'm sure that Ray doesn't know, and I don't know. And Susan doesn't know."

"What the fuck is going on back there? What's happened to everyone?"

"I wish I knew. I'm fully aware of how bizarre it all is, believe me." She was waiting for him to ask how Susan fit in, but he did not, rather to her relief. He said, "How do you feel?"

"I don't know. Swirling. Like I've been spinning around and around and am going to fall down and break my neck. I don't want to talk about it."

"Susan—"

"How are you?"

"Me?" he barked.

"You! Your family! Mariana!" She said it easily, without even the ghost of a stammer.

"Oh, fine. We're fine. I've just been terribly concerned. That city is a hole, you know. You don't realize it until you get away from it. I told Craig—"

"I don't know. We've had beautiful weather, and there are flowers everywhere."

"You should have—"

"Nothing bizarre ever happens in California, right?"

"That's beside the point. When you get away, you can see things in perspective."

"Perspective! Perspective is thinking that parallel lines meet!"

"Why are you mad?"

"You're a snot! You haven't been here, you don't know what's going on, and you've still got loads of opinions about it—"

"Alice—"

"And why do you always say my name in that patronizing affectionate way, as if I had to be led gently back to my senses?"

"Let's not argue right now."

"Let's do argue! There's nothing we can do about Ray or Denny or Craig. I think we'd better argue."

"I'm sorry about the tone of my voice, but whenever I talk to you, I feel like I have to be careful."

"Or what?"

"Or something will happen."

"What could happen? Really, what could happen? It's already happened. Our relationship was severed two years ago."

"That's not what I mean."

"Well, what do you mean? That I would go crazy or commit suicide or something?"

"I think we should leave this discussion for a more appropriate time."

Alice imagined Jim and Mariana worrying about her. His evasion told her that they had, that they had titillated themselves with worry about her. If she did commit suicide, then their marriage would attain real dramatic grandeur. She said, "I never once thought of committing suicide, even the very day you disappeared without a word. It didn't make me want to *kill* myself."

"I'm sure—"

"You know, George Sand was always afraid some lover was going to die in her arms, actually die from delight at being her lover."

"You have to admit that you've always acted very—"

"Very what?"

He weighed his words. "Very obsessed. You were very dependent."

"Yes, I was."

The sun behind Alice cast her shadow over the yellow and green tablecloth. She wondered what would be said next and who would say it. She heard Jim eat something. After that he sighed a couple of times. Alice said, "Did you love me? This time I'll believe you." And was Mariana listening now?

Jim said, "Yes, very much." He said it dully, truthfully. She believed him, possibly for the first time in her life.

"Why didn't our marriage last, then?"

"I think because I felt like I was throwing it into a bottomless pit. You didn't appreciate it."

"I appreciated you."

"But you were also the great lover and giver. The only one."

Alice winced. "That's what Susan said. We talked about you last night."

"Susan—"

"Well, how is Mariana? You didn't answer me."

"Actually, she's pregnant again. She's at the church."

Alice's eyebrows lifted at the notion of religion in the life of James Calvin Ellis but she only said, "When's the baby due?"

"Middle of January."

"Is she really at church?" Alice laughed.

"Why is that funny?"

"Well, it's Saturday, for one thing. And I've always thought she was listening whenever we talked. I've never called you or talked to you without imagining her on the extension, being very quiet."

"I don't think she's ever been here when we've talked, except the last time when you called to tell me about the guys."

"Will you forgive me for imagining it?"

"Will you forgive me for worrying that you might commit suicide?"

"Do you think they're equal insults?"

"Do they have to be?"

"I guess not."

"I forgive."

"Me, too." Then she said, "Can I say something else possibly insulting?"

"Why not?"

"I can't imagine you two as parents, only as participants in a grand passion, or as California sybarites."

"We're very domestic. I'm actually reminded rather often of your parents. More than of mine."

"What kind of baby do you want?"

"A healthy one."

"Was it awful with the other one?"

"Very."

"I was really sorry about that, though I didn't know how to tell you."

"Thanks."

"Do you want to get off now?"

"Do you?"

"I should." Alice looked at her watch. "I should make some calls. Everything is a mess here."

"Let me know about Ray. Are you in danger?"

"Of course not. None of this really concerns me, except as an unlucky bystander. The detective thinks I should get my locks changed, but I can't see—"

"Do it. Pay attention to him. Get a twenty-four-hour guy and I'll send you the money."

"It isn't that. Do you really think I should? No one has my key except—"

"Do it anyway."

"Okay." Alice hung up with a pleasant feeling of mutual affection. Across the street, Henry's windows were shadowed and blank.

T H E locksmith said that he would be there about two. At four-thirty he rang the buzzer, awakening Alice from a deep, blank, timeless sleep. When she leaned against the wall and tried to gather herself together, he said, "Hey, the locksmith, man. I came to change your locks."

"Okay." But it took her an age with the locks she had. Her thick fingers seemed to slide off them without effecting any movement. She put her face in her hands and rested. Then he was there, behind the door, knocking. Alice bit her lip, and at last opened the door. "I was taking a nap," she told him. All he needed to complete his costume as the last derelict hippy was a mongrel dog on a piece of string. Alice estimated that he had not washed his hair in three months and not combed it in six. He picked up his tool box and she stepped back to let him at the door.

"You have a robbery or something?" he said, squatting and unscrewing things.

"Not exactly. Some people have keys."

"Bad shit," he replied.

"Yes, that's what I understand."

"You want me just to change the tumblers in this one, or you want something new? I got these French babies. They go more toward the middle of the door, and are kind of ugly, but they never get broken into, how about that?"

"How much is that?"

"A hundred, regularly, but I got a special deal on the last order. Eighty-nine fifty."

"That seems like a lot."

"Hey, you got a glass of water or something? I'm dying."

"Sure."

When she came back with the water, he was sitting on the couch, his feet on the window sill. "Shit," he said, "that's great. New York's got the greatest water, you know. There was this guy that was selling it. Fuck, I've been working. Guess how long I've been working."

"I couldn't imagine."

"I am beat. I started work yesterday about noon, and I haven't been to bed since. This is a great gig, you know. You could do this all day and all night if you had the right substances. First the junkies break in, then the cops come, then us. And junkies never sleep."

"I'm sure they don't."

"Some guys charge extra for late night deals, but not me. I charge extra during business hours. That's when I like to sleep."

"One of those French locks would probably be good, but I would have to give you a check."

"No checks. You kidding, man?"

"I don't have that much cash."

"Sorry, lady."

"Well, how much would it cost to change the tumblers?"

"About twenty, but I won't do that. This lock is about fifty years old. It's not going to stand up to that."

"Is there anything else?"

"I can put another lock of this type in. It won't be all that safe, compared to other stuff I got, but you could put in a good second bolt."

"How much would that be?"

"Fifty, sixty."

"You really won't take a check?"

"You want to make it out to the IRS for me?"

"Why don't you do the work, and I'll go out and get the cash for you."

He looked reluctant, then shrugged. "Yeah—"

"No, forget it. Thanks for coming by. I'm going to think about it some more."

"Look, lady. I'll take a check, all right?"

But the more willing he became, the more determined Alice became not to do it. "No. I don't want to do this. I don't see how I'm going to keep that person from having my key again, anyway, so it won't do any good. It's a waste of money. We'll just leave it like it is, okay?"

"It's up to you, man."

"That's right." She held out her hand for his glass and he stood up. "I've got ten dollars. Will you take ten dollars to put the screws back in?"

"Yeah, why not."

"Will it be just like it was?"

"Hey, lady. It's fifty years old!"

"Okay, forget it." She handed him ten dollars, and he put back the screws. After he left she went into the kitchen and looked for something to eat. There didn't seem to be anything.

A R O U N D dinner time, Alice went to Susan's, taking an Entenmann's chocolate chip cake. She was fully determined to broach the topic of possibly changing her locks, but said, "Did you get to see Ray?" instead.

Susan shook her head. "They're keeping him sedated today, but they thought tomorrow would be better. Honey was there when I got there, but I don't know if he talked to Ray or not."

"I think he thinks we got into all of this by being careless. He gave me a big lecture this morning."

"He was polite to me." Susan shrugged. "It's always tempting to think that he doesn't know what he's doing."

Alice thought, Thank God for that, and said, "What do you want for dinner?"

"Cake."

"I feel like popcorn."

"And a six-pack of Coke."

"Sounds delicious." She sat down at the table. "Really, Susan, do you think Ray's going to be all right? I never did even see this Dr. Lee, much less get to talk to him."

"That must be the Oriental guy. I did talk to him, as a matter of fact. I told him Ray was my brother."

"I told the hospital he had insurance up the wazoo."

"They think there's going to be substantial hearing loss in that ear. There was no damage to the other one, though."

"No more perfect pitch."

"I forgot to ask about that. I don't know. I don't think it's like eyes. I don't think you have to have two to do it together."

"Still, his ears are his living."

"I'm sure whoever did it was perfectly cognizant of that fact."

"Are you scared?"

"No."

"I'm having my—" But Alice couldn't go on. She would mention it later, when she had figured out a way not to imply a lack of trust. She said, "Jim called today, too. He thinks we're all nuts."

"How was it otherwise?"

"Well, the phone didn't glow or vibrate. He sounded sort of dull. I even started remembering when he used to come home from class and give me the blow by blow—how Deedee in the front row objected to the use of ellipses and Mark over by the wall wanted to re-write the entire poem in seven-syllable lines. Talk about boring." She lifted her eyes to Susan's. "I like you better than him now, anyway, and you're here and he's there."

"And?"

"And you were right, he said loving me was like throwing it into a bottomless pit."

"I do think that you never saw the truth, that Jim was a little reserved, or even shy about expressing affection, whereas that sort of thing comes very easily to you."

"I guess."

"Let's have some cake." This is how they would go on, Alice was tempted to think, certainly for the rest of the evening and maybe for years, maintaining separate residences, perhaps, but living as close together as a pair of shoes. Soon, sometime in the next ten minutes, the night's conversation would take root. First, two or three topics would be begun and discarded as boring or worn out. This would happen automatically, a result of the cake or the newspaper open on the floor or the view of a neighbor passing across the street. Inevitably, though, something would take root, then grow and branch and exfoliate into a whole evening's talk. Susan rolled over and reached under the coffeetable for the Arts and Leisure section of last Sunday's paper. Alice smiled and wandered over to the chair across from her. Weren't they set for life, with steady jobs, enough money, no commitments, couldn't this last for years, in a way that marriage could never last, without effort, without swings in desire, or mistakes in translation, or the balancing of needs that marriages always demanded? People stayed home for passion and went out for companionship, when actually the reverse would work much better. Alice picked up the book review and glanced over the poetry reviews. Susan said, "There's a free concert of medieval consort music at the Cloisters. Eight o'clock."

"That would be nice."

"Long ride on the bus."

"That's true." As if on cue they settled themselves more deeply into their chairs.

"My favorite time to go to the Cloisters is Christmas, anyway." And here they would be at Christmas, Alice thought, crossing her fingers, except with the windows closed and slacks and sweaters on. Between now and then, what a wealth of time! She sat forward and threw down the paper. "Don't you think time passes differently now than it did three or four years ago?"

"How do you mean?" Susan's eyes continued to scan the Calendar of Events.

"Well, I remember being really impressed when we moved here that four whole years had gone by since college, and five for Noah. Now I've lived in my apartment for the same length of time that I lived in Minneapolis, but the two experiences aren't equal at all. This, in spite of everything, has a much smoother quality to it."

"I know what you mean. It used to be that every season broke over you like a big wave at the beach. The passage of time itself sort of bowled you over and changed you. You're right, it's not like that now. I could see turning around in thirty years and wondering where it all went."

"It feels different. It doesn't seem to be going anywhere. There's a woman at the library who had a baby a few years ago. Sometimes she brings him in. It seems almost odd, because he's obviously growing up, learning to walk and talk, wearing little oxfords and shorts with flies, but she seems permanent. Even her hair doesn't grow in any visible way."

"Maybe that's being an adult." Susan sat up. "Maybe that's the only truth about being an adult, that in some basic, visceral way, time stops."

"It's kind of nice."

"Do you think so?" Susan dropped the paper and picked up her cake plate. After forking off two or three bits of the frosted square, she said, "It scares me. Once you're out past the breakers, the sea may be very flat, but there's no bottom. Even talking about it scares me. I want those seasons and Christmases and birthdays and school years to add up the way they did when we were kids."

"I know what you mean, but I still prefer the serenity."

Susan sighed, picked up the paper, threw it down again. "I guess I don't know what to think, actually, since the thing about Craig that drove me most to insane fury was the constant springing of his adolescent hopes. He always thought it was going to add up sooner or later. It makes me mad to think about it. *I* was the one who was always telling him to grow up. And telling Denny, too, I'm sorry to say."

Alice waited expectantly, but Susan did not go on. Alice looked over her shoulder. She was reading an article about videodisc recorders as they compared to videotape recorders. Alice smiled. Susan's television, a twelve-inch black and white with a broken aerial, was so infrequently used that they were always surprised when they turned it on and it actually worked. She picked up the magazine section, which she opened first to food, then to fashion, then to the double-crostic. Susan said, "Do you think I loved Denny?"

"What?"

"Did it seem to you that I loved Denny? Did we look like people who were in love?"

"Yes. You *were* in love."

"I don't know that. I can't remember. On the one hand, I loved to sleep with him. I loved everything about it from talking to him in bed to making love and sleeping next to him. He was very good in bed, from the beginning to the end. I mean, aside from knowing what to do, he was perfectly desirous, and his desire expressed itself in an attractive, natural way. I've been trying to say to myself just how he was, but there aren't any expressions that give the flavor of it. He was self-confident, and passionate, and pleased with my body. I also liked being with him, when we were alone, and sometimes when Craig was around. For a long time I thought that if we could just get this problem of his professional life solved, then everything would be fine. It was a problem, in a box, manageable. Later on, I saw it differently, but at first it was just an addendum, detachable from the general perfection. But right alongside my love for him and my sense of permanence and my complete inability to look at or desire other men was this utter conviction that it just couldn't go on. The conviction was instinctual and irrational, so I didn't pay much attention to it, or tried not to, but it was there from the beginning, like a Siamese twin to my love for him. I think I toyed with the idea of walking out the door every day for twelve years. We would argue about buying milk and I would say to myself, This is intolerable, it can't be borne, I'm packing my bag, but at the same time I would be planning his favorite dinner, or buying him some little present to make up. I don't see how I could have entertained two mutually exclusive certainties at the same time."

"Ambivalence—"

"Do you think that's what it was? Just a kind of inherent ambivalence, stuck to me but not to us?"

"Did you ever tell him about it?"

"I don't think that's something you tell men. Would you have told Jim?"

"Believe me, it would have been a relief to both of us if I'd ever had a moment of ambivalence."

"You are terribly absolute." She said it as if it really were terrible.

Trying not to be sensitive, Alice laughed. "I think of myself as the ultimate waffler."

"Never! Never! You don't know how frightening you are sometimes."

"Then the ultimate wimp. You may be right about my absoluteness, but maybe I'm really absolutely prostrate, resolutely prostrate, militantly prostrate."

"You're thinking of Jim, but I don't think you really were like that."

Alice said, "You know, I really love you. I love our friendship. I can't imagine what I would do without you."

Susan smiled, but her face instantly filmed over and it seemed to Alice that her skin would be cold to the touch. After a moment, she said, "But did you think Denny and I were in love?"

"Yes, I did. I was so sure of it that I never thought about it."

"I wish I had a videotape of everything, twelve years long, unedited, or at least a tape recording. If I could stand back and look at us together, I might know what was going on."

"I should have been a better eyewitness." Thinking of Henry, she added, "How do people learn to notice things?"

"Well, you did have your own life to live, you know."

"But I feel like the view is always partially blocked, or even completely blocked, by a mirror."

"And I feel like the view is always partially blurred by a mist of resentment."

"It would be lovely to see clearly, wouldn't it? To know something for sure, just once."

"Would it?" Susan picked up the News of the Week in Review and settled back onto the sofa. Alice got up to make popcorn.

Alice had left before eleven, still unwilling to actually sleep in that apartment, and was now sitting naked and freshly bathed in her dark kitchen, drinking a glass of milk. In a detached but interested way, as if scientifically, she was considering the fact of the murder, and Susan's identity as the murderer. It hardly moved her at all any more. She had thought Thursday night that the surprise would never leave her, that without wishing to she would never look at Susan and not sense those two corpses in close proximity. But she had apparently overestimated her capacity for moral outrage. Homicidal drunk drivers and cheating landlords that she saw on the news outraged her more. Everything about her upbringing and education had prepared her for a grand repudiation of this wrong: Susan had taken two lives, and two lives that Alice was close to and cared about. Nonetheless, Alice knew that her adoration of her friend, and her anticipation of lasting, comfortable intimacy were greater than ever. The evening before, she could have sent Susan back to Chops and gone off with Henry, but she had not. Although monumentally confused just at the moment, she had not acted confused at all. Part of her had wanted to be polite and careful and conventional, but the rest of her had simply acted. Alice smiled.

IN HENRY'S apartment, the lights went on, one, two three. He did not appear, but the knowledge that he was there filled her with such sudden longing and desire that her throat contracted. She sat silent in the kitchen, watching, staring after him, but he didn't appear, not even the top of his bushy head. He obviously had no interest in her apartment. After a few minutes, his lights went out, one, two, three. Alice wanted to cry.

The intensity of her feeling surprised her, abolishing all her thoughts of only a minute before. The evening with Susan and her nagging worries about Ray faded to insignificance beside the fact that Henry had not even glanced out his window at her, had not even checked to see if her windows were dark. For a moment, she thought that she dared not go over to see him. It was nearly twelve, he would already be in bed, but even as she thought it, she was struggling with her jeans and looking for a casual but attractive shirt. Keys? Keys? Keys were on the dining-room table.

Did she need anything else? She ran back to her bedroom for flip-flops, and in a few moments was on the street.

It was another fragrant night, but warmer, the twenty-third of May. Sometime in the previous week, in the round of identical, ideal days, the boundary of summer had been crossed. Summer in New York. It was almost threatening. But the breeze off the river, though warm, was dry and refreshing, evocative not of flowers but of truck gardens—tomatoes, zucchini, cucumbers. Her fingers found the button beside the name "H. Mullet," and pressed.

Henry was wearing his terrycloth robe, tightly and modestly tied around the waist. He did not step from the door when she got off the elevator, nor did he greet her. The elevator doors closed behind her, and in the silence between them there fell only the sound of whirring gears and clacking cables. It occurred to her for the first time that he might have someone in the apartment with him. That issue they had not had time to clarify. If an innocent curious voice were to call out "Henry?" she could—

"What's up?" said Henry. Serious and closed, his face was not as handsome as she remembered, not young, the sort of face that had belonged to the fathers of her friends when she was a child, would belong to Henry in Brooklyn, when he was a father of little girls. She said, "I saw your lights go on and off. I wanted to see you."

He waited for her to go on, his determination not to help her, and his anger, apparent.

Unable to help herself, she said, "You angry at me?" and her own voice sounded annoyed, although she didn't think she was annoyed in the least.

Henry bristled, pulling his belt tighter with a jerk, and then saying, "Irritated, but not for long."

"What do you mean by that?" Aghast, Alice sensed the hardness of her tone, but it seemed to float away from her, out of reach. Her hand, that should have gone over her mouth, thrust aggressively into the pocket of her jeans.

Henry said, "I don't understand you. You give me the run around in the street yesterday, then call me up in the middle of dinner just to turn me down for the evening, and then you stomp over here at midnight, and glare at me. This I do not understand."

"I'm not glaring at you!"

"You're glaring at me."

"Don't tell me what I am doing!" Finally she closed her mouth with a snap, tight over her uncontrollable tongue. If she was lucky, Henry would take a deep breath and start them over again, invite her into his welcoming apartment, elicit the cause of her temper. Yes, he looked old, but wonderful. Warm and solid and insulted. A hank of hair on the crown of his head was standing straight up, blond whiskers glinted over his chin and cheeks. It was possible that she did love him.

He did not smile or step back, which would have been invitation enough. The slightest, most casual question would do for an opening, but his lips were closed. She said, "I know what I'm doing! I'm not glaring at you!" words that were somehow tied to their conversation, but not to her thoughts. Henry's face grew perceptibly more distant. She saw in the change how receptive he had been only a moment before, how trivially conciliatory the proper words might have been when she stepped off the elevator. He had gone from being annoyed with her to thinking she was boorish. He retreated a step. Appalled, Alice remained motionless, the glare, for that's what it was, she admitted, still plastered across her face. Hardworking, passionate about his profession, interesting to be with, solid, wonderful in bed. The door closed in her face, and she heard his bare feet retreat down the short hallway, the bedsprings creak. She turned and poked the elevator button, thinking of Susan, then waited quite a time, staring at her face in the wavy glass, reflected off the empty darkness of the elevator shaft.

13

I N T H E morning Ray told them through wired jaws that he was selling his co-op and going back to Minnesota. His father was considering going into the solar energy business. Ray was interested in that. He winced when he talked, and they sat to his left. "I've been thinking about it for a month," he said. "This has made up my mind."

Susan had come reluctantly, and Alice could see that Ray's injuries did little to soften her resentment. She responded to his announcement with a laugh.

"What's so funny?"

"Are you going to marry some nice girl and settle down? Come on."

"It's unlikely but not impossible."

"Won't you miss the old gang?"

"I'll miss Noah and Alice."

"Not our old gang."

"I don't know. I've thought about it."

"The passion, the danger—"

He spoke carefully. "I don't know what I'll miss. I don't know anything. I've got to try something else. Don't you know that all of us have reached the point where every choice is a compromise? That would be better than this. Anyway, it's none of your business."

"Ray," said Alice. "Do you need some magazines?"

Ray shrugged. Alice leaned toward Susan and took her hand. "There's a newsstand downstairs." She lifted her eyebrows. Susan scowled, but then nodded. Ray said, "There's money in the drawer." Susan went out without taking it. Before the door swished closed, they listened to the click of her heels in the corridor, then there was silence. Ray squirmed painfully in his bed and then winced. Alice said, "I shouldn't have brought her. I'm sorry."

Ray lifted his hand and dropped it.

"Is there anything you need from outside for the next few days? I can come back this evening, maybe."

Ray lifted his hand again, dropped it again, and then, after a moment, turned on the television, checked two or three channels, and turned it off. At last he said, "Alice, I feel very badly that I got you mixed up in this. Especially after you said—"

"Better my doorstep than a stranger's."

"For my sake, yeah."

"It's okay, I'm just glad—"

"It isn't okay."

He was about to say something awful or frightening. Alice sighed. Sure enough, he said, "My former friend Jeff duplicated the keys to your apartment. He gave them to me, but I'm not so sure that he didn't make some for himself."

"Why should he? I don't have anything of value."

"I'm sure it's nothing. I shouldn't have said anything. A person shouldn't have keys out, that's all."

"I can have the locks changed."

"You could."

"I was going to anyway."

"How come?"

"I don't know. Spooked, I guess. This stuff has spooked me. Last week I thought someone was following me in the stacks, and then later I thought I saw—uh—traces that someone had been in my apartment one night when I was out."

"Which night?"

"I don't know. Some night. Wednesday, I guess."

"What kind of traces?"

"Nothing. Some shoes that I thought were one place were another. Stuff like that. It was stupid."

"No, it wasn't. That was me. I was in your apartment Wednesday night. I let myself in with the duplicate keys."

"What for?"

"I wanted to borrow something, but you had it with you."

"What did you want to borrow, Ray?"

"I didn't borrow it and I didn't hurt anything, and Jeff stayed outside, so let's just forget it, all right?"

"I don't want to forget it! What did you want that you couldn't ask me for?"

With his good hand Ray pushed the sheet down and then pulled it up again. Alice exclaimed, "Don't be so mysterious! If there's something going on, and in my apartment, I deserve to know what it is!"

"I wanted your keys to Susan's apartment. Remember she made the rest of us give ours back suddenly, and there was no way I could avoid it."

"Why did you want the keys to Susan's apartment?"

"Well, as a matter of fact, I wanted to go over there while she was at work one day and look for something."

"The cocaine?"

"Well—" Ray nodded. "I had to just make sure that the police had it. Looking for myself was the only way."

"But I had my keys with me, so you didn't get to look, and somehow that's related to your getting beaten up, isn't it?"

"A couple of guys want either their drugs or their money."

"Ray, how could you get into this?"

"Actually, it seemed like a good deal at the time. Everybody felt very lucky." His lips spread in a clenched-teeth grimace.

"So what are you going to do now?"

"I should make plenty from selling the co-op. I bought it four years ago, and the couple below me know someone who's already interested."

"Are they going to wait that long? The people who want their money?"

"Someone they know is a realtor."

"Oh."

The door opened and Susan came in. She was carrying an *Esquire*, a *Gentlemen's Quarterly* and a *People*. She set them down on the nightstand. She was breathing heavily. "Ray—," she began.

"Well," said Alice, standing up. "We had probably better be going!"

"Sit down," said Susan. "I'm going to say what I have to say anyway." Ray looked at her fearfully. The tirade had obviously been readied and polished while she was going for the magazines. Ray turned his head, winced, and slowly turned it back to where it had been before. "I—," Susan began. "Oh, screw it!" She grabbed her purse and clattered out of the room.

When Alice caught up with her, she said, "Is there any good place to eat near here?" and Alice felt reprieved.

She ordered wine with her shrimp salad, and when it came, golden and dewy, she was moved by the esthetic perfection of her green meal on the beige tablecloth. Once she had begun, though, she realized her mistake, for everything was warring. The effects did not take place in her stomach; there was no nausea or pain. In her bloodstream and her head, though, there was a series of alternating sensations—elation and exhaustion—that made her hands tremble and her lips twitch while she ate. She was starving. She couldn't not eat. Susan said, "Are you all right?"

"It's been a bizarre weekend."

"To say the least."

"I'm glad you didn't berate Ray. You have every right to be—"

"Madame had to wait on a customer herself yesterday. She was positively shocked. This slender gray-haired woman who practically swam in the sixes came out of her dressing room and handed Madame a pile of things and told her to go look for smaller sizes, and while Madame was marshalling her English to say no without losing a sale, the woman went back into her dressing room and handed out another set that she didn't want and said that Madame needn't bother with those, they were hideous, and would she please—"

"He's gotten himself into an incredible mess and—"

"Hurry, as she was due somewhere in half an hour. It was masterful. And then she bought one little handkerchief for thirteen dollars and said everything else was just so badly made and the whole time she was writing out the check she had to stand on her toes to get her elbow onto the counter. Madame tried to explain that we don't take checks, but the woman—"

Alice sighed.

"Kept interrupting her with remarks about how she never carried cash in the city and the credit card companies always cheated you and a check was the only way, and Madame was so flustered that she took the check without asking for identification, and she couldn't remember any English for about ten minutes after the woman left."

"Yes, I realize that you don't want me to talk about Ray any more."

"He always did everything Craig ever wanted him to."

"If he hadn't gotten them the cocaine, they would have gotten it through someone else."

"I know." But Susan said it reluctantly, loath to relinquish her resentment.

"Did Honey ever approach you about it?"

"Actually, I approached him. I told him it had been there when I left, and that I thought Ray had been the contact."

In spite of herself, Alice was shocked. Some residual reflex was alarmed at the notion of confessing any knowledge of drugs to a policeman. Susan eyed her a second, then laughed. "I know. It was a week before I could bring myself to say anything. But really." She frowned. "Isn't it awful? I hate that lingering hippy shit."

Alice offered, "Then you're pretty sure that it was friends of Ray?"

Susan's eyebrows lifted quizzically. "Who else?"

"What about Noah?"

"Isn't some unknown dope dealer more plausible? Maybe the convolutions of all our jealousies and anxieties are irrelevant after all. Maybe the answer is just money or revenge."

"And that's why you're pissed at Ray?"

"I guess. Mainly, though, I'm just pissed. Ray, as an idiot, seems as good an object as any. Or I'm not pissed. I don't know. Are you leading a secret life?"

Alice jumped.

"I called you late last night, after I got home, and no one answered."

"Well, I was going to—"

"I have a secret. Would you like to know it?"

Alice looked just briefly at her food and at the table next to them, composing herself. Now that the time had come, she wasn't exactly sure she did want a confession. Unspoken knowledge had more grace, left them each more room for privacy and thought. And such a confidence was legally unwise. There was that to consider. "Of course, but—" Alice looked meaningfully around the room, but actually there was no one within earshot. This was as good a place and time as any. "I feel so odd. Light-headed and jangly."

"Tell me the truth. How have I seemed to you these last two weeks?"

"I don't know. It's hard to say—"

"Brave, jaunty, a little insensitive?"

"Not exactly—"

"Too analytical, not prostrate enough?"

"I never knew anyone who died before—"

"Died?"

"Certainly not anyone that was murdered." Alice found herself whispering.

Susan wiped her mouth and gazed at Alice speculatively, for a long time. At last, she said, "Do you feel like you're made of the same material all the way through?"

"What?"

"Not literally, but spiritually. I don't. I feel like no matter what I say or what my intentions are, I literally cannot express myself, what is true about myself."

"Everybody thinks—"

"Do they? You too? You feel this transforming interface, like an electric grid, between yourself and your appearance? It can't be tricked or turned off and must censor and distort or cancel every communication? Do you really?"

"Well, language is a very clumsy tool—"

"Here's a fact. Yesterday before I came over, I stood beside my window for a long time. I'm going to tell you I wanted to jump. Did I tell you I wanted to jump?"

"Yes, but—"

"I don't know for sure that I wanted to jump, because I didn't jump, of course, but it may be that I wanted to jump."

"Susan!"

"One time I got out the car and took it up Route 9W, on the other side of the river. There are all sorts of drop-offs and curves over there, but I was afraid of making a mess. Also that it would start to burn. I'm going to tell you that I wanted to get myself into a fatal accident, but that's not really what I mean, maybe, since I didn't do it."

Alice shuddered. "When was that?"

"The day I picked you up at work. But this is what I mean. Inside me there's one intention. Outside me, there's another action. The one doesn't seem to bear any relationship to the other.

Inside, there's me, feeling a certain way about the murders, and outside, there's Susan, going to work, cooking, eating, walking, talking, bearing up without any visible strain. Any observer would think it was your boyfriend that got it, not mine."

Alice took a deep breath, sat back in her chair, and cast her eyes around the restaurant. The darkness of the room disoriented her, and her arms and hands still seemed to be trembling, although when she looked at them, the trembling wasn't visible. She clasped her fingers together and rested them in her lap. She opened her mouth once or twice in the hopes that something instinctive and helpful would come out, but nothing did. She stared for a moment at a spot of dressing she had spilt on the tablecloth, then looked up at Susan. It was then that she perceived the exact degree of Susan's independence from any efforts she might make. Erect between the arms of her chair, sinking her fork with precision into her quiche with one hand, the other hand calm in her lap, Susan looked untouchable, clean, as if she had attained a kind of solitary perfection that she had always been aiming for. Alice did not for a moment doubt the depths of her despair, the profound grief, chagrin, remorse, and whatever else that went to make up the aftermath of Susan's murderous act. She saw, however, that events had had a concentrating effect on her friend, that in some way she was more completely herself than she had ever been. Suicide was a persuasive consequence to such an implosion. She said coaxingly, "Do you want to talk about it? You know you don't have to."

Susan looked at her watch in her usual businesslike fashion, then smiled companionably. The realms of mystery in her were suddenly unfathomable to Alice, who smiled companionably back.

"Obviously," she said, "there's no satisfactory response. Denny and I had this problem for years. I blamed him, I blamed Craig, I blamed myself, I blamed astrology. There was no conceivable avenue of communication. And it got worse, or else the full extent of the problem gradually unfolded. I don't know which. There was no way I could express a truth about myself in a way that he could understand. I could tell by his response, which was usually sweet and well intentioned and always aimed at some spot just beside me or above my head. You're the same, but different. The problem is in me, obviously."

"But—," said Alice. But nothing.

"Now, I am going to try and tell you how I've been feeling since the big day. In a way, I'm rather surprised whenever I move and act and breathe, because my body doesn't seem like a human body any more, it seems like a solid block of granite with an attached skin. No hollows, not even any cracks or fault-lines, you know. That's why there's no change. When I was in high school once in Latin class, we had this ex-priest who taught us, and he was more interested, sometimes, in talking about theology than about Cicero or whoever. It was pretty boring, but I remember that he gave us his definition of eternity. He said for us to imagine a block of granite a mile high, a mile long, and a mile wide. Every hundred years a bird would fly by and drag a feather over that block of granite. When the feather wore down the block of granite to nothing, that would be one moment of eternity. Well, it feels like that block of granite is in me, and that the bird hasn't even come by with the feather the first time."

"But doesn't everybody feel more or less like that when someone they love, uh, dies?"

"I don't know."

"Susan! Listen to me. Those tacky, time-worn remedies are true. They work. Time does heal all things. Getting it off your chest does make it less monumental. Sharing your burdens does ease them. Escaping the scene of the crime does get it off your mind. This image of a granite block is an idea. It has no reality. You can get help from someone, and someone can succeed in helping you."

Susan smiled, and even as Alice finished speaking she doubted her own words. She looked away, across the room again, so aware of her own body as a hollow, slippery thing, a confusion of moving surfaces and independent enterprises that when she looked back, Susan seemed to recede. Friendship after all was a paltry thing, the bumping together of two round objects. She put her elbow on the table and her forehead in her hand.

Susan went on. "If I did kill myself, it wouldn't be like killing a person." She smiled again. "It's hard for me to even think of it as dramatic or significant, and then when I make myself, it's only from your point of view or the point of view of the store or my mother or something. But that point of view is a hard one to maintain, and also seems wrong somehow. Not morally wrong, mistaken."

"Now that we've talked about it, do you feel any less inclined to do it?"

"No. I told you. There's no change. You've got to try to imagine that. No change." For the first time during the conversation she looked momentarily distressed, as if permanence were the worst feature of the whole problem. Perhaps it was.

Alice tried again. "But life is change. If you continue to exist, then things will change. This is a fact, a true fact."

"Maybe. Who's to say?"

"Everybody. Human experience. Scientific observations of the universe."

Susan lifted her eyebrows coolly but skeptically, then said, "I want to go home."

"I hate this."

"People who are talked to want to make a difference."

"I love you."

"I know. I've thought about that phrase a lot. It flew around my apartment, I must say, with complete abandon. It never made a difference, never stood up to anything. Usually it meant 'you owe it to me to do what I say' or maybe, 'thanks for doing what I said.' I couldn't figure out what love was, or why anyone wanted it, even when I was saying it."

"Susan! Is there anything else to your secret? You could have just left him!"

Susan's eyebrows lifted and she shook her head. With a smile, she replied, "We were in love. Let's go, really."

They let themselves out onto the bright street, and had to pause for a bit to adjust to the sun and the crowd. Susan took Alice's arm. "Let's not go there again. Too dark. It was creepy."

W H E N she got off the phone with the locksmith, who said he would be over as soon as he could make it, the phone rang at once. It was Rya. "I've been calling you all morning," she said irritably. "Where were you?"

"I was out for a walk."

But Rya really didn't care. "I'm going crazy here. What's going on there?"

"Well—"

"Did that woman get Noah out? I've tried our apartment twelve times."

"Noah's in custody somewhere. I'm not sure where."

"David promised they would get him out."

"He might be at Riker's Island. That's where they go to await trial."

"Trial! What's going on? David said this woman was the best in New York City. That's what they always say, though."

"I haven't been able to see him. Honey's being cagey, somehow. There's some kind of evidence."

"My God."

"I think you should come home. There's something else, too. Ray got beat up and left on my doorstep."

"You're kidding. Well, I was going to come anyway, because it's just awful here. I told my brother about Noah being in jail, but I don't dare tell my parents. My father's all set for me to move back to Houston. He's even found me a job at a local TV station. I think they think I'm getting a divorce."

"I can't imagine where they got that idea. Look, I don't know what's going on between you and Noah, or what's in Noah's mind, but I do think that you'd better be here, and Susan thinks so, too."

"So he did it, huh?"

"I don't—"

"That's very weird." Rya didn't sound particularly upset.

"It's not—"

"I was scared sometimes that Craig would drive him to do something bizarre, but why Denny? He was never mad at Denny. You couldn't get mad at Denny."

"Maybe."

"I even said to Craig once that he didn't know the effect that he had on people. I couldn't explain it very well so I'm sure he just ignored everything I said, but he really drove you crazy. You were always doing stuff that he wanted you to do that you didn't want to do, but he didn't know that after all you really didn't want to do it. Once you'd done it, then he went on to the next thing that he wanted you to do, whether it was to pick up the tempo, or whatever, and he never realized that you hadn't been convinced. I still can't explain it. It made me want to strangle him more than once, but Denny, I still can't understand Denny. I guess I don't understand Noah very well, either."

"You don't sound very upset, I must say."

"Don't I? It seems far away. It seems like just a thing that happened. This life is unreal. All these girls from my high school have six kids. I can't explain. What's going to happen?"

Alice, annoyed, only wanted to get off the phone. "That I don't know."

"Well, I'll be there tomorrow. Can I stay with you?"

Rudely, Alice said, "If you care enough to come."

Rya did not take offense, but then she rarely did. She said, "I don't know if I do, but I suppose I'll find out in the next few days, huh?"

IT WAS seven before the locksmith managed to be there. Alice had a hundred dollars in cash secreted in a drawer and a nervous feeling that had he known where it was, he would steal it without changing her lock. Once she allowed herself to think that, then there was no stopping a flood of other suspicions— primarily variations on the theme of the power and ubiquity of Ray's "friends." If some of them were in real estate, then why not others in locks? Who was more likely to have duplicate keys to all the attractive residences in town than a smart locksmith? Or keys to the apartments of unsuspecting women? You had people at your mercy if you had keys to their apartments. Did locksmiths have to be licensed? Could locksmithing be as profitable as systematic stealing? What would keep a locksmith honest besides a moral decision? Was the population as a whole, of which locksmiths would be a fair sample, more honest than not? She was shaking, not with fear, but the peculiarity and excitement of her speculations. What she really wanted to know, what she felt she could not exist without knowing, was whether Ray's "friends" were a knot of deviants on Christopher Street, or whether they formed a pervasive network that included the locksmith or Detective Honey or even other people—Henry? Henry had appeared awfully suspiciously the very night of the murder, hadn't he? The buzzer rang and the locksmith announced himself. When he got upstairs, Alice made him tell her his name slowly, so that she could remember. While he was inspecting the door again, she wandered with apparent idleness into the kitchen and wrote it down next to the phone—5/24/80—Don Dorfmann—7 PM. When she came back he had removed the chain, which he held up to her, shaking his head. "Shit, man, I bet you make sure the last thing you do every night is put on this chain, right?" Alice nodded. Don Dorfmann laughed, which made his hair jiggle in one clump. Alice noticed that he had put the back part of it in something of a braid. "What's wrong with it?" said Alice.

"Nothing, except for the fact that a seventy- or eighty-pound kid could break it, no sweat, in about a minute."

"Oh."

"I took it off."

"I see. How much is a new one?"

"A good one? The kind I have on my door? Fifteen bucks. Not much when you look at it. Okay, now this is what I'm going to do." He rummaged for a moment through his tool box. "I'm going to put this kind of new lock in your door, up above the other one. I'll leave that one there. That plus a new chain, ninety bucks. It's a pretty fair lock, not the French job, but all brass, penetration proof, all that shit. Good lock for the money, fine for this neighborhood." Alice calculated the tax and the tip, then nodded. He started to appraise the door and she went back into the kitchen, where she added another line of information to her note. CityWide Locksmiths 545-9922. She turned on the flame under the kettle and sat down where she could appear to be minding her own business, but actually watch Don. He was rummaging through his tool box again. When he leaned over, his two workshirts, one a ragged plaid and one blue, separated from his pants and exposed his pale but hirsute lower back. Certainly there had been a time when she would have greeted someone of his appearance with a sigh of relief, assuming without a second thought that he could be trusted. Now she would have preferred an older man, the father of six or eight kids, in neat blue overalls with his name stitched in a nice oval over the front pocket, someone who had lived in Astoria for thirty years. Don Dorfmann rummaged once again through his tool box, this time with annoyance, and said, "That asshole!"

"What?" said Alice.

"Ah, this asshole that works one of the other trucks, he's always borrowing my tools. You don't have a needlenose pliers around the house, do you?"

Alice longed to be able to say yes, but she shook her head. He rummaged again, found a long nail, and began to poke at the door. After a moment, he threw down the nail. "Fucker!" he exclaimed. "You got a phone?"

Alice went into the kitchen, tore off the sheet of paper, and said, "It's in here."

Dorfmann dialed. "Hey, Gene. Where's that asshole Bosworth. He's got my needlenose. Well, see if you can find him on the radio. Yeah, I'll wait. Keep trying. Yeah, I got this chick's door all torn apart." While he was waiting, Alice stood in the doorway and closed her eyes. She knew with perfect conviction that Bosworth would never be found. After a long time, during which Don Dorfmann fidgeted and cursed, he exclaimed, "What the fuck's he out by Coney Island for? They got locksmiths out there. Shit. Two whole new doors, huh? Well, what am I going to do for needlenose? Nah, that place is closed. Yeah, there's that supply place in Long Island City. Anybody around over there? Well, who's closest? I'm on the Upper West Side. Yorkville? I could get there. Okay, thanks, Gene, and if that asshole calls in, you tell him I'm going to have his butt in a sling." He hung up and turned to Alice, who was already nodding in resignation. "Back in an hour, at the most, if I can get this guy across the park. If not, there's a tool supply place over in Queens. Meantime, you got no problems. You're no worse off than you were before. God, that fucker!" He tucked in his shirts. "Look lady, I'll even leave my tools here. You got nothing to worry about." Alice was still nodding. Finally, she said, "Well, it's been that kind of weekend all around."

"Me, too," said Don Dorfmann, and then he was gone. Alice picked up the phone and called Henry. His windows were dark, so she hadn't much hope. Susan, apparently, was out, too. She entertained the suspicion that they were out together, just as, in junior high, when she called two friends and both their lines were busy, she had entertained the suspicion that they were talking to each other, about her. She sighed. It was after eight and she hadn't eaten yet. Thinking of food made her think of her lunch with Susan. Then she entertained the suspicion that Susan had jumped, after all, and the temptation to call the Twentieth Precinct and find out. But anything like that would come to her immediately from Honey. She shook her head violently, cried "Ack!" in a loud, harsh voice, and went into the kitchen, where she smoothed the piece of paper with Dorfmann's name on it and slipped it half under the phone. After that, she entertained a picture of Honey finding it and being posthumously proud of her.

14

AFTER eating Alice could think more clearly, and she felt
almost sanguine about the future. Actually, events had worked
themselves out remarkably well. Ray had suffered the most, but
he had also risked the most, and now he had been jerked roughly
back to normality. She hadn't seen him so serene in years as she
had seen him that morning, a man who had learned his lesson
and knew it. In addition, his beating would surely throw enough
doubt on the evidence against Noah that his release, somehow,
would be insured, and how could he fail to have been shaken up
by his experience, how could he fail to start a new life or even a
new marriage, with someone brighter and more sensitive than
Rya? That Susan should finally react appropriately to what she
had done was good, unequivocally good, sufficient punishment,
in Alice's view. If she could preserve Susan long enough, Susan
would understand that. Ray's beating would cover her, too, lead
Honey's suspicions toward the Westside Highway, where perpe-
trators vanished, or turned up with any number of sins to account
for. For them, Alice had no sympathy. Denny and Craig? They
glimmered in the distance. It was odd, she thought, how readily

people cut their losses. The shock and horror she had felt that first weekend at the deaths of her friends and the shattering of her group could not be recovered. This, she thought, was how avalanche victims felt, who gladly left fingers and feet in the snow as a payment for their lives. It was how she herself had felt when Jim agreed to come back and try again—no, he didn't love her as she'd thought he had, but he wanted to come back, that was enough, that was wonderful. In the end, you were pragmatic, weren't you, and the relief and joy of attaining your compromise goals were as delirious as if you had gotten everything.

By the time she had washed her dishes and swept the kitchen floor, it was nine-thirty, and she was thinking about bed. To despair of the locksmith, she thought, would be to suggest that, tools or no, she had ever expected his return. If there was one thing she had learned about New York in her six years there, it was that you couldn't simply run an errand, meet someone, drop over to the hardware store. Tomorrow he would get the pliers, at nine or ten, no matter how much he wanted to get them before then. And how was it that she, only daughter of a tool addict, was expecting a microwave in the mails and not a full set of everything her father carried?

She flopped down on the couch with an old *Newsweek*, giving him another hour. At ten the phone rang. "Hey, man, I can't put anything together for a couple of hours yet. I can give you one of two choices. I can send another twenty-four-hour guy over there sometime tonight, when he finishes the job he's working on, or I can come myself around midnight."

"Then how long would it take you to do the work?"

"Hour, maybe."

That was one o'clock. Adding another three hours to compensate for his optimism, that had Alice in bed by four. The very thought made her yawn. "Look," she said. "It doesn't seem so important to me now. I mean, I don't even know for sure that this person has my key. If I start to worry, I'll go stay somewhere else. But what about your tools?"

"Fuck 'em, man. I've had it. I haven't taken a night off in three months. You keep 'em, and I'll be there by seven-thirty, eight for sure."

"I'll be up."

"Look, lady, you can call another locksmith, if you're worried, but the boss said he'd give you twenty-five percent off for your patience."

"I'm not worried. I'll see you tomorrow."

And she wasn't. She marched right into the bathroom and took a shower without once, she realized afterward, thinking of the shower scene in *Psycho*, then she got out, dried herself vigorously with her largest blue towel, put on a T-shirt and underpants, and called up Susan, who answered with perfect calm and no suicidal intent in her voice that Alice could detect. She said, "I want to ask you a question."

"Anything."

"Does what you told me today mean that I can worry about you and check up on you?"

"I don't know. Try it and see what happens."

"What are you doing this evening?"

"Watching television and writing letters."

"What kind of letters?"

"Business correspondence to clothing wholesalers."

"Sounds innocent enough. Can I come over?"

"It's nearly eleven. You don't need to worry about me." Her tone was extremely firm.

"It's not—"

"I don't think I would do it tonight." Her voice rose a little, but she suppressed it. Alice could tell that her concern was already tiresome to the other woman, and she could not bring herself to press any further. Whatever she might say now about fears for her own safety would sound made up. "Okay."

"Don't worry about me."

"I won't."

"Promise?"

"Well, I won't apologize."

"All of this will be over soon."

"I hope so."

Down on Eighty-fourth Street, a cab pulled up in front of her building, but then Henry's building, too. A woman got out, slender, well dressed in the sort of purple silk dress that Alice never could find but always wished she had. The man behind her, who waited a second to pay the cabby and receive his change, was Henry. The woman, who was nicely made up, with dark lipstick and a daring, fashionable hairdo, smiled confidently at him. Henry's reaction was not visible, but going up the step to his door, he took her arm at the elbow, so firmly that Alice could feel it herself. Suddenly exhausted, she finished her milk and put the glass in the sink. Then, though she had planned to look at the news for a moment, she went straight to bed, detouring only to put up the chain. But the chain was on the floor. Alice looked at it for a long moment, perplexed, then kicked it angrily down the hallway, exclaiming, "Well, it never did me any good, anyway!"

ALICE didn't know where she was. In the first place, the bed was angled oddly to the window. That should have been to the right, opposite the bed's foot, but it was to the left and behind her. And the bed seemed to point in the wrong direction. Alice had the sensation for a moment of being on a train that was beginning to move backward. She shook her head and came more fully awake, then remembered that she was sleeping in her second bedroom, because the sheets in her bedroom were dirty and she had been too lazy and depressed to change them. Alice sighed and turned over on her stomach, arranging the sheet over her back and holding her eyes tightly closed. So that she would not think of anything that might keep her awake (Henry, Susan), she made herself think the words, Go back to sleep, in a monotonous chant. Just then a sound from the outer rooms of the apartment wakened her completely. She turned her head so that one ear was free of the pillow, and held her breath. The sound, a very small one, came again. It was a familiar sound, or at least, a fragment of a familiar sound, but Alice could not place it. After hearing it the second time, she did not hear it again. In a few minutes, she began to doubt that she had heard it at all. She took a deep breath and settled herself once more for sleep. The twin bed in the second bedroom was very comfortable, firm and without lumps. She liked the sheets she had for it, too, old and all cotton, slick and limp even after washing. Doreen had given her the comforter from her childhood bed. It was light but warm, perfect for Alice, who slept cold even in the middle of summer, but also sometimes broke into a sweat in winter and had to throw off her gown in the middle of the night. The sound came again, quickly, a hair louder. Alice, nearly asleep, was inclined to dismiss it. If it was so familiar, she had obviously heard it hundreds of times before, and it was undoubtedly some sound of the apartment building. She stretched herself into a comfortable X and pushed her nose into the pillow, thinking, Go back to sleep, go back to sleep. Everything was quiet. Even the sirens on Broadway sounded distant, without urgency. She thrust her arm under the pillow.

She was nearly asleep when she realized what the sound had been—the scrape of a key being removed from a lock—and the knowledge woke her completely, although she did not move from her hitherto utterly relaxed position. She was inclined to think that she had imagined or dreamt the sound, especially since it was unaccompanied by the closing of the door or the creak of footsteps. Her cowardly panic in the library stacks recurred to her and she grimaced, embarrassed, but even as she reassured herself, she could not help listening. And the door to the hallway was open. And she was only wearing a T-shirt. She closed her eyes, which seemed pasted open, and lay very still, waiting for the next hour or two to pass.

Sometime while she was waiting, the next sound came, an even smaller sound, the movement of the door in its frame, arrested. That was the frightening thing about it, the human thing about it, that the swing of the door had been arrested. Alice's eyes popped open and she eased herself over onto her back with the smoothness and silence of a seal in water.

There could not be anyone in the apartment. It was too bizarre. After thirty-one years of safety, of there never being anyone there no matter how strongly she feared or believed that there was, that there should be now was literally unbelievable, and she could not make herself believe it. The clearest, and the most tempting, course of action was not to act, but to go back to sleep. She was not one of those people who feared sleep. She loved sleep. In sleep she was safe, warm, possessed only by dreams, and her dreams were always innocuous. And if there was someone in the apartment, wouldn't they be more likely to hurt her if she was threateningly awake than if she was peacefully asleep? And if they did hurt, or even kill her, did she want to know about it beforehand? Any action, even the small action of putting her foot on the floor, seemed dangerous, ghastly, and impossible, as if the noise she had possibly heard indicated writhing snakes on the floor, not a human presence. Her bed, as long as she stayed meekly in it, would serve as a raft to float her through whatever was going on. She heard the creak of a step and then another step. She made herself release her fingers from the side of the mattress and put them limply on her stomach. She made herself feign deep, relaxed breathing. She was determined not to give away the fact that she knew anything was going on. After all, who could hurt a defenseless sleeper, eyes closed, mouth open, the quintessence of vulnerability? There was another step. Whoever was stepping was doing so slowly, carefully, with full knowledge of the old floor and its tendency to sound. The forty-four-foot hallway. The stepper would be just passing the kitchen now. Alice's pupils had adjusted, so that the room where she lay was completely visible to her, but the hallway was without light. For a moment she stared helplessly at the doorway, dreading that some monster face would appear there, something inhuman, with snout and fangs and only a single, central eye. She lay there enthralled by the imaged horror of that shock, wishing, as she had in the stacks, to close her eyes and cover her head, wondering if she would ever be able to move, and not really caring.

That the stepper was Jeff Johnson was obvious after she made herself think it. Ray, of course, had known for sure that he had a key, but had hesitated to tell her, and contented himself with a suggestion. There were two more steps. Alice took a deep silent breath, feeling her paralysis drain away as she imagined more and more vividly Jeff Johnson, with his oddly affectless air of being eight years old, but also human and familiar, sneaking down her forty-four-foot hallway in the middle of the night. With an enormous effort, she slipped one foot out onto the floor, slid between the sheets, then put the other foot on the floor. The rustling of skin against cotton and of ball in socket sounded so loud to her that she couldn't tell if she was making noise or not. She paused, tempted again to forget it and go back to bed. There was another step. Jeff would be almost to the dining room by now. The most important thing was to get her underpants on. She could see them hanging with her shorts over the chair across the room, but to get there, she would have to cross the doorway, would have, possibly, to expose herself to Jeff Johnson's gaze, and Jeff Johnson's knowledge of her knowledge.

What did he want? That was the most frightening thing about him. Since he seemed to feel and want nothing, he might feel and want anything. As a child, she had never understood cartoons about the cruelty of little boys to animals—the tying of cans or firecrackers to the tails of cats, for instance. Thinking of Jeff Johnson lying on the couch, his feet up on the sill, she understood them. His primary interest in all things would be to see what would happen. But it seemed absolutely true that she could do nothing without her underpants. There was another step. The steps were very slow. You couldn't tell, though, how big they were. Alice took one giant step toward her underpants, grabbed them, and swung herself as silently as possible back toward the bed. She put on the filmy and incandescent bikinis, then cast her eyes around for a weapon. Jeff, of course, would have something, maybe even a gun. Ray's beating showed that he wasn't afraid of injury being done. All Alice could see was a yardstick. She could not imagine a yardstick doing anyone harm. She looked out the window at the light rising from the streetlamps. The window! The *open*, screenless, barless window! She crept to it and peered out. It was impossible. She was better off in bed. The drop was straight. No balcony or third floor roof miraculously appeared. The fire escape was around the corner, outside the other bedroom. Only a little granite ledge, about four inches wide and a foot above the window sill offered any possibility of escape, and it was not a possibility that Alice considered realistic. Across the street, Henry's windows were open and dark, but Alice dared not shout, dared not, actually, even turn around for fear that she would encounter Jeff's juvenile stare, watching her escape.

Alice crouched on the window sill, grabbing the casement, and then slowly, looking up so that she wouldn't fall, brought her foot around and placed it on the four-inch ledge. The ball of her foot and her toes were firmly there, but nothing else. She turned her foot so that it paralleled the wall and slowly straightened, inching her hand up the casement and letting her other foot come out and join the first foot. With her free hand, she felt above her head for another ledge or some sort of ornament. There was another ledge. She grasped it, let go of the casement, grabbed the ledge with the hand that had just held the casement, and began to straighten her body, pulling herself up with her fingers. With both feet on the lower ledge and both hands gripping the higher one, which ran about forehead level, she felt almost secure. She took a deep breath, but not one that expanded her too much or threw her center of gravity away from the wall. Then she began to creep away from the window. The brick was old, pitted, rough, and scraped her knees and thighs. That she was there astonished her. She seemed to have done it magically, without volition.

Although when she was inside, she had imagined herself safe once she got out, now that she was out, she could only envision

Jeff making an instinctive beeline to the window and espying her, lifting a gun—tensing her toes like a ballerina Alice crept toward the corner of the building. There would be the ledge of the bathroom window to hold on to, at least. Other than that, she had somehow to creep what looked like fifteen or sixteen feet along the ledge, and then, somehow, to go around the corner of the building, and creep another ten or twelve feet to the fire escape, where Jeff could be waiting for her, or where she could escape, perhaps, run to Henry or Honey or somewhere, but she couldn't think where. She tried to get comfortable, turning her feet carefully, one by one, first with the toes apart, then with the toes pointing the same direction, but she couldn't get her heels onto the narrow ledge. She imagined Jeff entering the bedroom, seeing the disturbed but empty bed and stood on her toes to sidle toward the bathroom window. The ledge under her fingers was covered with grit and pigeon feces, endangering her grip, but she discovered that she could brush the ledge off a little as she moved. Although she could not force out of her mind the image of Jeff at the window looking at her, watching out for him was impossible. Alice did not even dare to turn her head. If the shot was going to come, it would have to come unexpectedly. Alice closed her eyes, trying not to think of what a shot would do to her. Even a flesh wound, maybe even the sound of the shot, could startle her enough to make her fall. Four floors. She closed her eyes again until the urge to look down had faded. She slid her left foot carefully along the ledge, then her right foot. The roughness of the brick snagged her T-shirt, startled her, let her go. She dared not lose her balance, because there was no way to compensate. Friction, the greatest surface of her skin against the greatest surface of the wall, was her only hope. She slid her left foot again, then her hand, brushing off the ledge, careful of her grip, took another breath, slid her right hand, then her right foot. The high, small window of the bathroom was almost within reach—too low, something she would have to duck carefully below, but something to hold on to. There were no shots, no exclamations, no noises from inside the apartment. Alice grabbed tightly to the sill of the window and bent her knees. In a long moment she had ducked under, at least ducked her eyes under. It was impossible to know if Jeff had seen her fingers or the top of her head, was even now standing in the bathroom, contemplating the miraculous appearance of his quarry just when he had despaired. Alice stood up and breathed deeply two or three times. With her right hand on the casement of the bathroom window, she had about three feet to the corner. Whether she would be able to turn the corner was one question. Her calves were beginning to tremble, although not yet to hurt. And the ledges were another question. She could not remember if the ledges even went around the corner. She stretched out the fingers of her left hand, trying to feel around the corner, but she wasn't close enough. And then, even if she got around the corner, and the ledges were there, perhaps Jeff would be there, too, waiting shockingly on the fire escape for Alice to inch right into his arms. Alice's heart began to pound so hard that it seemed to beat the skin of her chest against the brick. It was odd the way what she feared to see panicked her more thoroughly than anything else. She inched her left foot toward the corner, then her left hand, took a breath, then closed up with the right. The safety of the bathroom window sill seemed distant already. She reached carefully around the corner. And where was Jeff, now? Down on the street, frustrated, on the verge of looking up and seeing Alice in her luminous underpants, the bull's-eye of a huge target, bigger than the broad side of a barn, how good was Jeff's aim, what sort of practice had he had, what sort of weapon did he carry? Around the corner the ledge continued, at least the ledge for her hands. She inched toward it, the image of Jeff down on the street looking up at her warring with the image of Jeff squatting on the fire escape, waiting for her. It seemed impossible both to go on and not to go on. Insanely, she wanted to lie down and go to sleep. At the corner, on the very verge of the turn, she looked back. At least he was not looking out the window.

And how would she, how could she make the turn? The angle, which had seemed huggable in prospect, seemed in actuality to fold dangerously away from her, as if she were lying on a dropleaf table and the leaf suddenly dropped. She breathed very carefully, and made herself think of Jeff pointing that gun at her, and looked up instead of down, but no tricks were of any use. The impossibility of turning the corner immobilized her, expanded in her mind like a balloon, pushing every other more reasonable thought away.

She was going to fall, she was going to fall. Dreams of falling came back to her vividly, not as prophecies of this particular experience, but as certain knowledge of the sensation of falling, of the absolute loss of her grip, unreclaimable, a mistake never set right. Alice groaned. It seemed not that the building turned a corner, but that it disappeared entirely. Once again, for a split second, she felt herself not standing against the wall, but lying on it, at the edge of it, where it dropped into a bottomless pit. When the split second disorientation was over, a repetition of it was what she feared the most, suspecting that any unconscious movement to correct it would precipitate her off the wall. She said, "I am standing up. I am standing up. My head is up, my feet are down. Time to go around." She felt for the ledge around the corner, gripped it, but it seemed unattainable. She was stuck.

Then, like an inevitable rising tide, came her self disgust at being stuck. Forever she had been stuck in one thing or another. She could never get past being stuck! What was wrong with her? And then, without thinking, she was struck by the absurdity of being about to die, of which she was certain, and yet wondering right to the end how she had failed this time and how she could improve. At once, the corner seemed possible, and she inched her way right up to it, put her foot around it, and then dragged her head under the cornice, and planted her crotch right on the angle of the brick. She took a deep breath, tightened the grip of her left hand, and then brought her body flat around, scraping her thigh painfully, but there it was, her foot, and here came her hand. She was around the corner. The fire escape, about twelve or thirteen feet ahead, was dark, shadowed by the building next door. Alice stilled herself and listened. It was impossible to tell if Jeff was there. She inched toward it, one hand, one foot at a time. Soon she herself was in the dark, which was frightening. Now her feet were trembling as well as her calves, and her wrists, too. Six feet to go. She paused and listened for breathing. There was none. Perhaps, after all, Jeff could not find the key to the fire escape bars, bars Jim had made them install five years ago. It was right in the lock, but the lock was out of the way. Alice put out her left hand and touched the iron railing of the fire escape and gripped it tightly. After a moment, she put out her foot, and then her other hand. Almost at once she was on it, ready to go down.

Afraid still of any clanging or noise from the fire escape that might resound to listening ears in the apartment, Alice squatted and put her foot on the first step of the down staircase. It was rusted and rough, but made no creaks or groans. Gradually, she shifted her weight to the foot. Still no noise, still no Jeff in the window. Then, just as she was about to straighten up and put her other foot on the step below, the first step crumbled into dust, and her foot went through into empty space. Alice took a deep breath and gripped more tightly to the railing, then began to put weight on her other foot, on its step. Only the greatest effort had kept her from crying out in surprise at the breaking away of the step, but now she was better prepared, saying to herself, "No noise! No noise!" The transfer of weight was painfully gradual. If only she could see the steps, see what shape they were in, but the shadow of the building next door was too black, and the steps themselves too darkly rusted or painted. The second step bent, then it, too, split and fell apart. Alice hoisted herself back onto the fire escape, glad that she had never had to escape from the apartment in the last five years. She paused and thought of herself going hand over hand down four flights of railings, but that she could not even imagine as she had imagined herself on the ledge. At last she tip-toed across the fire escape to the steps upward and began to test them. From her apartment, anyway, Jeff would have no ready access to the roof, and, perhaps, no reason to go there. The first of the upward steps bent, too, under her foot, but the prospect of an ascent was somehow easier than the prospect of a descent into nothingness, so she rested her weight mostly on her two hands on the railing, and began slowly to climb, quiet and holding her breath, up the ten rusted steps. Only one, at the top and the least protected from the rain, threatened to break and fall noisily onto the fire escape below, but as soon as Alice felt it begin to go, she lifted her foot off it and swung up to the fifth floor platform. There, to catch her breath, she crouched in silence.

It was then that a kind of fog, comprised of fear and fatigue, began to invade her. The steeply pitched tin roof seemed to recede, to become, in fact, rather unattractive as well as impossible. Even as she disapproved of herself, she began to feel safe enough here, and no amount of self-disgust could prevail on her to go any farther. Her body, her whole being began to feel kind of shocked, numb, drained of adrenaline, so what if it was too soon. But the fire escape was very dark, and furnished with two large potted plants. Alice wedged herself behind one of them, against the wall, and waited for conviction or fear to move her upward toward the roof.

Instead, she must have dozed, because she had the sensation of waking up suddenly and of not knowing for a second where she was. She might even have dreamt of going around that corner again, because the sensation of being about to fall was an immediate one. Her feet were asleep. She moved the left one very carefully, and wiggled the toes, then the right one. She lifted her shoulders one by one. Still there was no sign from the apartment below that it was inhabited in any way. Perhaps, after all, the initial sounds that impelled her escape were natural to the apartment, or were even a dream. Perhaps she had sneaked out of her window and around the apartment building for nothing. Perhaps Jeff was home, innocent in his own bed, not really a psychopath, dreaming of cocaine, looking forward to breakfast. Alice rolled her head around on her neck and opened her mouth, trying to stretch and relax the jaw that had been clenched and tense. Then she opened her hands and fluttered her fingers. It was all she could do not to sigh. She couldn't even remember the noises now, remember if the silence that surrounded them was the silence of her mind or the silence of her apartment. On the other hand, it was not worth the risk, after all this effort, to check. She waited. It seemed like she had waited for about an hour.

It was like waiting for rain to let up, when after a while, and it is still raining hard, you just go out into it, your concern about getting wet dissipated, your adjustment complete. Alice stood up, and heard the scrape of metal. She stopped still, thinking at first that the sound had come from her, but it came again. It came from below. As quietly as possible, she squatted down and peered through the grating of the floor. At first there was nothing, just the empty blackness of the lower fire escape, but then a figure appeared, a head leaning and then moving out of the window of her apartment. Head, then shoulders, then arms, like a baby. Then the figure twisted, and out came the hips and the legs, one by one. The silhouette, substantial, athletic, shapely, was unmistakably Susan's and when she lifted her hands from the window sill and turned around, there was a gun in one hand. Alice nearly gasped.

But she did not. In the end, she did not gasp or make any kind of a sound, and she had the courage to keep watching, watching Susan's head, turning left then right, then back toward the apartment. Susan stood quietly for a long time, then put her free hand back on the window sill, preparatory to going back in. Alice nearly breathed. First Susan's left foot went over the sill, then she began to lift the right, but she put it down again. She had thought of something, and she did it. She looked upward, peering right at Alice, right into her face with her own shaded eyes that Alice could imagine but not see. She peered for a long time, and then she lifted her right foot and climbed back into Alice's apartment.

Conscientiously, she closed the window and then the metallic bars. No doubt she locked them. Alice let her head roll back against the wall, but otherwise dared not move for a long time.

T H E next sound Alice heard was the sound of an alarm clock, muffled, but nearby, as near as her ear. She opened her eyes and found herself crouched on the fire escape, not in sunlight, but in full day. When she opened her eyes, the first thing she saw was her upstairs neighbors in glorious naked splendor. When the hand of her neighbor arrived at and stilled the alarm clock, his eyes opened as well, on her. He gave a bark of surprise, muffled by the closed window. Alice smiled politely and stood up. Her neighbor, Gardiner she thought his name was, she had only spoken to him once in the lobby, covered his wife with one hand and motioned a question to Alice concerning her desire to come in. Alice, still smiling, nodded. The wife turned lazily over, determined not to wake up, and uncovered herself again. He spoke to her. She woke up.

On the street an hour later, in Phil Gardiner's sandals and Rose Gardiner's clothing, Alice grew immediately jumpy in a way that she hadn't been in the Gardiners' apartment. Susan seemed imminent everywhere, and the seven blocks to the Twentieth Precinct house endless and dangerous. Oddly, though, she felt only a little appalled by Susan's pursuit of her, and very anxious to see Honey.

Honey, of course, was not there, although he had checked in already and would surely turn up soon. She turned down a cup of coffee and sat across from the empty cell in the detective's common room. She tried to imagine Susan there, and could not. It was very difficult, nw that she was sitting and thinking, to relinquish her habitual picture of Susan, her habitual appreciation of Susan's competence and warmth. Perhaps Honey would tell her she had had a nightmare and send her home. Phones on the detectives' desks rang continually. Alice was grateful for the

way that they broke up and scattered her thoughts. Honey did
not come. Alice waited. Called the library, made some excuse,
turned down another cup of coffee. It was nearly eleven. The
locksmith would have come and gone. She should have called
him. Just then Honey appeared.

He showed her politely to his office, offered her still another
cup of coffee. He was wearing the same gray suit he had worn
the first day she met him, and three or four times since. In every
other way, too, he was unchanged, and Alice had a strong sense
of herself in a stranger's clothes, changed utterly. To such a
monolith it was nearly impossible to speak. Courteous concern
played over his surface like little whitecaps. "You look like you've
had some sort of accident, Mrs. Ellis."

"I'm just scraped up a little. If I begin, you won't believe me."
But she knew that he would. He got up and closed the door.

"Does your visit have anything to do with these abrasions?"

"Yes."

"Can you tell me about it?" He took out his pad, and Alice felt
herself sinking back onto the usual couch, opening her mouth.
She closed her mouth. She said, "Maybe you can tell me about
it."

"I don't understand you."

"Really?"

Honey swivelled in his desk chair and leaned it back until it
groaned under his solid weight. Finally, he said, "Why are you so
suspicious, Mrs. Ellis? I'm not. I've never thought ill of you, never
suspected you of the murder, for example."

"Are these observations personal or professional?"

"Personally, I find your reticence intriguing. Professionally, I
find it annoying and obstructive. And unnecessary, as far as I can
tell." He swivelled back to her. Alice said, "In the first place,
please believe me, I can't help it. In the second place, I want you
to talk to me. I want to know the truth, too. I feel like I tell you
what you want to know, and then you shut up your book without
giving me the diagnosis. I do think you have some idea what's

going on, and I really do want to talk to you. I came here of my own accord, and I waited for two and a half hours, without a magazine, I might add, but I don't want to leave here without knowing. I have had a very bizarre experience, much more bizarre and strange to me than it has been for you, and I find the ignorance I've been floundering around in intolerable."

"So?"

"So, I'm offering you a bribe. In exchange for my telling you what I know and think, I want the same from you. I want to question you."

Honey laughed. "Who goes first?"

"I'll show you my good faith. I'll tell first." Honey nodded, and Alice recited her experiences of the previous twenty-four hours, beginning with Ray in the hospital and Susan at lunch, ending with Susan's dark and silent appearance on the fire escape, gun in hand. Honey was appreciative of her exploits on the four-inch ledge, but she waved him off. When he had gotten it all down, Alice said, "Now, I want to ask you the first question. Where do you think Susan is now?"

"At her shop. Minding her business."

Alice sat forward. "Am I still in danger?"

"I don't know. I rather think so."

"Have I been in danger all along?"

He said it without hesitation. "I've thought so, yes."

"From Susan?"

Honey nodded.

"You sound like you think she did it."

"I've thought so for a long time."

"Why?"

"Motive. Poor alibi. Psychological outlook. All circumstantial, really."

"Then why did you arrest Noah?"

Honey smiled ruefully. "Extremely bad luck. In the first place, he lied. In the second place, we had a witness who heard the shots and placed Mr. Mast at the scene of the crime, or near it, while it was being committed. And Mr. Mast, too, had a motive in the affair that his wife was having with Mr. Shellady. Finally, Mr. Mast was in possession of three and a half ounces of cocaine, which is a felony offense in this state, and it was for that I had to arrest him."

"Rya said the charge was murder."

"I never explicitly stated that Mr. Mast was being arrested on a homicide charge."

"But you let her believe it, and tell it to us."

Honey shrugged.

"Who was the witness?"

"Daniel Brick. He and Mr. Mast had been in the apartment with the victims, and he had left the group and gone down the elevator. While he was in the elevator, he heard shots, and then about ten minutes later, Mr. Mast came down." Honey inspected his pencil, then looked at Alice. "The exact scenario isn't quite clear."

"When did you figure all of this out?"

"Shortly after we arrested Brick. He was bursting with it, in fact."

"But when did you decide it was Susan?"

"Some time ago."

"Why didn't you arrest her, then?"

"Absolutely no evidence. No weapon. No witnesses to put her at the scene of the crime. Dan Brick, who got a look at her when she came to look at him, had never seen her before. No fresh traces of her presence in the apartment, such as used water glasses or anything, no hairs, no telling cigarette ash." He smiled. "She could have gotten there by any means, but even our investigations into bus schedules and toll takers have yielded nothing. I didn't expect they would. A homicide arrest is a legal procedure. If there's no hope of an indictment, much less a conviction, then an arrest is futile."

"What did you think would happen?"

"I hoped she would show herself somehow. I kept people upstate looking for the weapon, or evidence of where she purchased the weapon. That may turn up. It usually does, even if it's unregistered, but often it takes a while."

"But she's still got the weapon."

"I doubt it's the same one, frankly."

"So now she's shown herself?"

Honey smiled again. "Yes, she has."

"By trying to kill me?"

"Your testimony will be invaluable as evidence."

"The *sine qua non* of a conviction?"

"In a manner of speaking, yes."

Alice felt a large anger take shape in her chest, but repressed it. "You thought she would show herself by doing something to me."

"Yes, I thought it was a good possibility, Mrs. Ellis, especially if you manifested any certain knowledge of the murder."

Nearly throbbing with fury, Alice managed to utter, "What if she'd actually killed me?"

Opaque and unmoved as ever, Honey said, "I considered that relatively unlikely, Mrs. Ellis, although I did think it worthwhile to put you on your guard."

"Just tell me one thing more. Was anyone watching over me? Was anyone aware of when Susan and I were together, when I might be in danger?"

"I know what you mean," said Honey. "Someone shadowing you to protect you, like in the movies. No. No, we haven't that kind of manpower."

Alice closed her eyes, actually seeing red, a kind of large red oval spot, like the giant red spot on Jupiter, crossing the back of her eyelids. Then she gripped her right hand over the end of the arm of her chair and pulled. There was a ripping noise of nails in wood, and the arm of the chair came up in her hand. She was panting. "Detective Honey," she said. "I don't think I am capable of expressing to you how angry I am at what could have happened to me."

"I suggested to you repeatedly—"

"Don't speak! Just don't speak for a while, and please don't go out of the office. I would like not to destroy every item in this room."

Honey nodded and Alice closed her eyes again.

15

IT WAS after one when Alice and Detective Honey arrived at Chops, but Susan was not there. Jane, always polite and professional, informed them that Miss Gabriel had taken the day off and would be back in the morning. She seemed to look at Detective Honey suspiciously, but when Alice turned and inspected him, he did not look extraordinarily like a policeman. When they left the store, Alice said, "Do you think she left town?"

"It's possible, but I don't think so. After all, she has no reason to suppose that you knew she was at your apartment. She never saw you."

Alice still felt weak from her fury at the police station, and rather distant from what she was doing—accompanying Honey to Susan's apartment to have what Honey called "a conversation." It was peculiar that she should be with him instead of with Susan, profoundly peculiar that she had finally assisted him in laying hands on Susan after all of her resolutions to stay away from him. Oh, yes, but Susan had tried to attack her the night before, in the middle of the night. She had thought so hard and completely about that, she seemed almost not able to remember it.

At Susan's entrance, Alice took out her keys. "Shall I let us in, or do you want to ring?"

It was when he said that they should ring that it came completely to Alice that this visit was a procedure, hedged about with legal rules and police protocol. Honey rang. Susan's calm voice spoke through the intercom. "Who is it, please?"

Detective Honey, as calm, said, "Detective Honey, Miss Gabriel."

The door buzzed at once, and they went in. Alice hoped that Susan would not come down to them, and when the elevator appeared, she was not on it. Alice realized that she had been holding her breath when she began to breathe again. Going up the six floors, Honey moved in front of Alice and took his gun from the holster. Alice felt her eyes widen and her jaw drop. When the elevator doors opened, however, there was no one in the hallway, and the door to Susan's apartment was still closed. Honey rang the bell, and his arm came across Alice's stomach, holding her firmly against the wall. His gun was pointing at the ceiling. Alice said, "Do you really—" but then the door opened, and Susan was standing there as usual, in her yellow terrycloth bathrobe with a cup of coffee in her hand. She was smiling politely, and saying, "I just got up—" when she saw first the gun, and then Alice. The trembling of the coffee cup in her hand for a second and a long silence were her only reactions. Then she smiled again and said, "Do come in." She gave Alice no special greeting or glance. Her eyes slid past her without warmth, and she motioned them to the two orange chairs, herself taking a seat on the couch. Honey holstered his weapon, but did not snap the lock.

Though Alice had been almost comfortable in the apartment since the murder, the murder now seemed hugely present to her, as if no time had intervened since the moment of her discovery. She seemed to herself both in the chair and looking at the chair with Craig in it. She shifted uncomfortably. Never at a loss, Honey said, "I'd like to have a few words with you, Miss Gabriel. I brought along Mrs. Ellis in order to fill in some pieces of information and to corroborate some details." Still Susan did not look at her. She put her hand in the pocket of her robe, and Alice jumped, but then she took it out again with only a Kleenex. She wiped her nose. It was terrible, worse in a way than the night before, out on the ledge. Whatever hope Alice had had that the experience was a dream or a hallucination vanished. She sighed.

Honey said, "I gather that you are ill, Miss Gabriel?"

"Just a cold. Mostly tired."

"You were up late, then?"

"Yes." Now she looked at Alice. "I watched two late movies and didn't get to bed until about three."

"Really. Which ones were they?"

"Let's see. *Dark Victory* was one, that Bette Davis movie, and some war movie about the Battle of Bataan, with Claudette Colbert and Superman."

"Was anyone with you while you were watching these movies?"

"Of course not."

Honey looked at Alice. "Mrs. Ellis thinks that you were at her apartment last night."

Susan looked at her. "Was anyone with her at her apartment then?"

"No," said Alice, hopefully.

"Then it's just a matter of deciding between us, isn't it?"

"In some sense, yes," said Honey. "Miss Gabriel, are you registered to own a handgun?"

"I'm sure you've checked on that."

"Then, do you own an unregistered handgun, or a handgun registered to another party?"

He looked her straight in the eye, and Susan did not answer.

"Miss Gabriel, exactly when did you return from your vacation? Was it in the evening of Saturday, May tenth, or perhaps,

the evening of Friday, May ninth?" Still Susan did not say anything, and Alice wondered how Honey could break her silence.
There was, of course, still no real evidence, and it was, after all,
her word against Alice's own that she had "exposed herself," in
Honey's words. Alice saw that this exposure was primarily a conversational gambit for Honey, a way of surprising Susan into a
telling reaction. As such, it had apparently failed. Honey asked,
"Did you buy the gun upstate, Miss Gabriel, or have you had it
for a long time? Perhaps it was purchased when you first came
to New York, for personal protection?" Susan turned her head
and looked toward the kitchen. Her copper-colored hair, blunt
and shining, swung gently with the movement. Then she looked
back at Honey, but still did not speak. It was probably apparent
that Honey was bluffing. Honey said, "When you returned to
Manhattan on Friday night, did you park in New Jersey and take
a subway or a bus to New York, or did you drive straight in?"

Silence.

"You came, perhaps, down the Westside Highway, turned off
at Seventy-ninth Street, found yourself a spot to park around the
corner on Riverside, and came to the apartment building. At approximately twelve o'clock, or a little later? When the band
members were still out and hadn't came home yet?"

Silence.

"You would have been carrying only your keys and the loaded
gun, to avoid leaving anything behind by mistake that would give
away your presence here, and you even, perhaps, took off your
shoes before you came in and put them in a plastic bag, so as not
to bring in any tell-tale signs of upstate vegetation or soil?"

Silence.

"Let's see. Possibly, when you came in, you went into the
bedroom, or the bathroom, and waited there for Mr. Minehart
and Mr. Shellady. You would have been here for as long as two
hours before they came home, but perhaps you sat quietly and
patiently, without even touching a book for fear of giving yourself

away. I have noticed that you are remarkably calm, Miss Gabriel."

Silence.

"At about one, then, Miss Gabriel, you heard Mr. Minehart and Mr. Shellady come in, accompanied by Mr. Mast, and also by a fourth person, whose voice you did not recognize. That would be Mr. Brick, who was unknown to you, and who has told the department that he never saw you at any time."

Silence. Susan stared straight ahead. It was hard for Alice to tell if she was breathing.

"Perhaps, and this is merely speculation, the four men had had a few too many beers at the bars. A little high, and a little set up, then, perhaps the men were arguing, or rather, perhaps Mr. Mast and Mr. Shellady were arguing. Can you surmise the subject of the argument, Miss Gabriel?"

Silence.

"My suggestion would be that the subject of the argument was Mrs. Mast, and that the argument was a loud and extremely angry one, at least on the part of Mr. Mast, in whom there had built up a great deal of resentment toward Mr. Shellady. Perhaps the other two had some trouble calming them down? But they did, finally. In the end, Mr. Mast was unable to sustain opposition to Mr. Shellady, who, everyone has agreed, could be both persuasive and abusive, and on whom Mr. Mast depended for his job."

Silence.

"But then it was business that brought the four men back to the apartment, wasn't it? The business of the cocaine. Perhaps you could tell us in your own words how the business negotiations went?"

Silence.

"I would suggest, but you may correct me, that the negotiations did not go as Mr. Shellady had imagined they would. The sale to Mr. Brick, who is fairly well known as a dabbler in cocaine distribution among the musicians of the city, fell through, and, with no other reason for staying, Mr. Brick soon left. Mr. Shellady and Mr. Minehart now knew two things: that they were unlikely to pay off their debt to their suppliers by selling the remaining cocaine in their possession, and that they had made a mistake in trying to doctor the powder with Manitol to make it appear to weigh more than it really did. The supplier, perhaps, was becoming anxious for his money. What happened next, Miss Gabriel?"

Susan licked her lips.

"Perhaps there ensued a conversation between Mr. Minehart and Mr. Mast, in which, as a favor, Mr. Minehart asked Mr. Mast to take the coke to his apartment until another contact was made. This favor was granted, and Mr. Mast soon took himself and the cocaine off, leaving the other two men alone, as far as they knew, in the apartment. Mr. Mast then, might have stood in the hall for a few minutes, himself waiting for the elevator, or doing something else."

Alice imagined Noah, breathing hard and with trembling fingers, rolling and then lighting a joint.

"The bedrooms and the kitchen were dark. Mr. Minehart and Mr. Shellady sat down in these two chairs that Mrs. Ellis and I are sitting in, and, counting on their intoxication and perhaps their distraction by the argument and the negotiations they had just been involved in, you came to the living-room door with your gun raised, and you shot them each once in the head. Since they had both turned to look at you, the shots entered from the front. Then you returned to the bedroom and waited until you were sure of the departure of Mr. Mast and Mr. Brick, and you retrieved your shoes in the bag and your keys, went down the back stairs so as to miss anyone who might recognize you. You were lucky. You did miss everyone, and soon you were in your car, back on the Westside Highway. What you did with the gun, I have been unable to find out, but otherwise you were extremely successful in leaving no evidence of your presence at the scene, so that even though your alibi was weak, there was no positive reason to suspect you."

Susan had not moved for hours, it seemed to Alice. Now she turned her head and looked at Honey, her eyes still calm. "Setting aside the truth or falsity of what you have said," she declared, "and viewing matters from a purely legal standpoint, you still have no evidence that I was even present at such a scene, whereas you do have evidence that Noah and this other guy were there, and that each of them had a motive."

Alice looked at Susan and then at Honey. The sunlight was streaming in the windows now, brightening the beige carpet and bleaching out the brownish stains that Alice could not help but be aware of, as pale as they were. On the floor beside the couch was the morning paper. On the coffeetable a peach pit, the hulls of four or five strawberries, and some toast crumbs. Motes of dust floated in the sunlight. After what seemed like hours, Alice said, "I know one thing she did while she was waiting. She watered the plants."

A small smile stretched Susan's lips. After a moment, she suppressed it.

Alice said, "When I got here Saturday morning, I had missed a day, but the plants were damp. There was one, especially, a piggy-back plant that was very sensitive to dryness, and would have begun to look wilted. After the police came, I remembered that I had originally come over to water them, and I felt them. They didn't need it. Everything was damp."

Susan sat back in her chair.

Alice went on. "And then you got rid of them. That struck me, but I didn't realize why."

Susan said, "You never notice anything. I can't believe you noticed that."

Alice bit her lip, stung by the other woman's tone.

Honey said, "Let me add something, Miss Gabriel. Mr. Mast, who has been in my custody for felony possession of a controlled substance with intent to sell, is of the opinion that Mr. Minehart and Mr. Shellady killed each other, or that one killed the other and then killed himself. The evidence at the scene of the crime did point rather more in that direction than in any other, except for the factor of the missing weapon. Without the weapon, the evidence is merely confused, and doesn't point anywhere. You, it is true, did an excellent job of concealing your presence in the apartment, and no judge will convict you on the strength of what Mrs. Ellis has just said, unless the prosecutor is very deft. Let me suggest, however, that what you were unable or unwilling to conceal was your anger at the victims. For some reason, you wanted it known that they were murdered, that there had been an intention to kill them. Perhaps, at one time, you hoped the blame would fall on the suppliers of the cocaine, but that, after all, was secondary. What was primary was your determination that Mr. Minehart and Mr. Shellady would be known as murder victims, and I think, frankly, that closing off other options was your first mistake."

Susan pulled the lapels of her robe more tightly together, and said, "Is this still a conversation?"

Honey replied, "Yes, but I do have Mrs. Ellis here as a witness, and you are entitled to a lawyer at this point."

"Well." She looked at the ceiling. "I guess I don't care. I would like to say something, mostly to Alice."

"I'm afraid I can't really leave you alone, Miss Gabriel."

"You can hear, too. And you don't have to tell me that thing about my rights. I don't care."

Alice looked at Honey. They waited for a minute or so, and then Susan sat up and began to speak. "Let me tell you about the day before I left for my vacation. I was here all day getting ready, and they were here all day, too. I got up about eight and made some coffee. I was looking forward to the vacation, and feeling pretty good. I had finally decided to leave Denny, and I thought of the vacation as a practice session. I hadn't lived alone since I was nineteen, remember. It was very quiet in the apartment, I didn't even have any music on. Craig came out of the second bedroom about nine, which was sort of a surprise, since they'd come in late, and Denny hadn't told me that Craig was staying."

Her voice was reasonable, nicely modulated. "Denny got up a few minutes later. They started talking right away. They called to each other from the bathroom, went at it over breakfast, over the dishes. It was obviously a conversation continued from the night before, from all the nights before, and they simply couldn't drop the subject."

"Were they talking about the cocaine?"

"Oh, they wouldn't have talked about that in front of me." Susan reached across the debris of her breakfast and picked up a red book on Alice's side of the coffeetable. Susan said, "This is a guide to records that was put out by *Rolling Stone* about a year ago." She opened it. "Page ninety-eight. You see how it falls open at the page? '*Deep Six;* two stars. Sole album by the band that recorded the hit single "Dinah's Eyes." "Dinah's Eyes" had a mildly interesting riff by guitarist and band leader Dennis Minchart, and the wavering voice of lead singer Craig Shellady attains a kind of gravelly substance, but the rest of the album is pallid stuff, imitating almost everything else that had a vogue in the early seventies. Both sides are short (thirty-four minutes combined playing time) but they seem twice as long. Too long. Now deleted.' That was the subject."

"Miss—"

"You have to understand They talked about that review for almost a year. Both of them knew it by heart. I knew it by heart. I also knew by heart every remark they had to make about the review. That *Rolling Stone* always hated their kind of music. That you had to be black and play jazz to get four stars, or be produced by an editor at the *Rolling Stone.* That at least they'd gotten two stars. Look at John Denver, he only got one and sometimes none. But then look at what they said, those fuckers. 'Imitating almost everything else.' They'd been trying some stuff out, but not imitating, not copying. They went through the whole book and counted how many records got no stars or one, how many got two, how many got three or more. Then they went through again leaving out the jazz section. It seems like it took days. But at least, this particular discussion of that six-line passage took another whole day out of my life. Believe me, I'd stopped telling them not to worry about it, that it was only one guy's opinion, or that they couldn't control what people thought, they just had to do their best. Now I kept quiet, and hoped they would go on to something else, and finally they did. They went on to a discussion of whether Craig had been right in breaking their contract for a second album. That was a discussion they'd been having for four years. I could just envision both discussions going on for the rest of my life, and never going anywhere. They repeated themselves so much that they were even using the same phrases. Well, about dinner time, they stopped talking about the contract, and there was about a half an hour of silence, and then they started talking again, and damn if it wasn't about the review. Craig compared it to the original review of the album in *Rolling Stone*, which had been better. He decided for the umpteenth time that the two reviews balanced each other out, and then he went over to the framed clipping on the wall of the article about them in *Rolling Stone*, and he read it, even though he knew that by heart, and then the both of them began talking about those fuckers. I mean I could see what they were doing. They were trying to make sense. They were trying to make these two reviews and this article into the word of God, into some kind of oracle that would tell them once and for all whether they were any good, but they couldn't do it, and I knew that even if they had, even if a real voice from the sky said, 'Stop playing music, you aren't going to make it,' they would have talked their way around it. That night I thought truly for the first time that they needed to be killed. Or rather, that if they had an accident or something, they would be a lot better off. And I would too."

"Susan—"

"Let me finish. I used to think that if I could get Denny away from Craig then Denny and I could go on and do something else, and have a grown-up life with kids and jobs. When Craig was out on the Coast those eight months, it almost happened. Denny was ready to do something else, and was thinking hard about what he wanted to do. He even called Craig and told him what he was thinking about, and Craig said he thought it was a good idea and maybe things weren't going to work out after all. That was what I should have been suspicious of, that permission, because sure enough, about three weeks later, this woman in L.A. calls and says that Craig is in really rough shape with heroin and that he nearly died and was in the hospital. Denny was the only person he had in the world, and could Denny come out and get him when they let him out of the hospital? Well, we left that day. How could we not? They were like brothers. I didn't even dare start a fight over it. The trip out was terrific, but as soon as we got Craig, everything changed. The first day, Denny talked a little about what he was thinking of doing, and then the second day he didn't talk about it at all, but they talked about what Noah was doing and Ray, and how much fun the band had been, and the third day, they talked about what they would do differently if they had it to do over again, and by the time we were back to New York, they were figuring out how to get a few gigs here and there. I screamed at Denny over that, and he said he was just humoring Craig till he felt better and got back on his feet, because they were brothers, you know, just like brothers, they'd slept in the same bed as kids, and before we knew it we were back in the same old shit. I realized that I didn't have a chance. As long as I was with Denny, Craig would be there, too, robbing him of every bit of will power, every bit of real ambition, always supplying him with wishes. He could talk you into a tizzy, Craig could. After that, it got so that every time I even disagreed with something they wanted to do, Denny would say, 'Why do you hate Shellady so much? You'd cut off your own arm rather than give him anything with it.' "

"So why didn't you just leave him?" exclaimed Alice.

"I was going to, as I said." Susan's voice had taken on a slight hollowness. "I really had made up my mind that morning, and even though I was angry by the time I left for the Adirondacks, that was still my intention. But you've got to understand what it's like hearing the same conversations over and over for years. Musicians are home all day. They never have to be anywhere. This apartment was never quiet. It was always the scene of endless chatter, and all they talked about was themselves and their careers and their ambitions and what they would do with the money when they got it. It hurt me. It literally made my skin prickle and my heart pound. I dreaded for them to get up in the morning, I dreaded coming home from work, I dreaded for them to come back from the store or wherever, I dared not be awake when they got back from a gig. The knowledge that they were going to talk about this made me want to jump out of my skin. When I went away, I expected there would be relief, silence and relief, but there wasn't. Everything they were doing was engraved on my brain. I dreamt about it, I thought about it during the day, I thought I heard their voices. At one point I was sure I could hear them coming through the woods, that they had found me. I was so sure that I just sat down on the front step and waited. I could hear the crashing of their boots and the eternal conversation about 'those fuckers.' I must have sat there for an hour. And it didn't subside until I started thinking about silencing them, and I couldn't think of any other way. Each time I did one little thing, like finding the plastic bag for my shoes, or learning how to load the gun, it seemed like the noise was just a little closer to being silenced, that I was just a little closer to finally communicating the truth to them. And I thought I was doing them a favor. Even if I left them and my life went on, their lives would never go on. Their lives would be like listening to a scratched record play the same three notes over and over forever. I thought that even if I left them, it could take years before I stopped hearing it all. I couldn't stand that. I really couldn't. Anyway, I didn't think I would really do it until the moment I pulled the trigger. And I have to say that when they saw me in the doorway, there was dead silence, and they weren't thinking for one second about their careers." She put her chin in her hand and gazed toward the kitchen.

"So it went like he said, the night of the, uh, murder?"

Susan glanced at Honey. "Pretty much. The stuff about the dope was rather annoying to overhear, since Denny had promised and promised and sworn up and down that they had a buyer and they were going to be rid of it and paid off the very weekend I left. The first thing the guy did when they brought it out was weigh it on his own scales. It weighed three point two ounces, and they had had five. Even when I left, they'd had almost five, so I knew that they'd been into it the whole time I was gone, that only my presence and irritation had kept them out of it before. And then he did some kind of purity test, and he said that he guessed that the stuff they had was only about seventy percent pure, so he would only pay them for a little over two ounces, and that was doing them a favor. After he left, the first thing Craig asked Denny was whether I had any money, and how much Denny could get from me. Denny said that I had some shares of stock, he didn't know how much. Then Craig said that Rya's old man was rich, but Noah said that Rya hadn't talked to her folks since before Thanksgiving, and that had been a fight about money. So they were stuck, and the next thing I heard was Denny saying that I would be home tomorrow and I would have a shit fit if this stuff was still around, and Craig dismissed him, and then he apologized for me, as if I were crazy or something. Noah was still pissed and said he wouldn't take the stuff, even though they promised to have it out of his place by Monday. I always did wonder what happened to it. I was furious, I was just furious, and then they settled down to drink some more beer and plan how they were going to spend their first million when this guy at A and M they'd just met played their tape for someone, and that's when I came out of the bedroom."

It was a seductive story, and Alice, as always, was seduced. She could imagine everything perfectly, and she hardly blamed Susan at all. She half thought Honey would get up and leave, giving Susan an hour to leave the country or at least change her name and disappear into Brooklyn, but Honey said, "I'm not clear, Miss Gabriel, about your motive for attacking Mrs. Ellis." There was that. Alice had nearly forgotten.

"Oh," said Susan.

Looking at her, Alice's spirits began to sink.

In a more subdued voice, Susan said, "I couldn't figure out where you were last night. I knew you were there. I had a strong feeling of your being there, especially when I saw that the bed of the second bedroom was mussed, but it was like magic. You were invisible. That spooked me."

"Actually," said Alice, "I was out on the ledge, crawling around the building."

"Mrs. Ellis did a very amazing thing—" put in Honey.

"I did go out on the fire escape."

"I saw you. I was one floor up. I saw you come out. I saw the gun, too."

"I remember looking up, but I didn't see you. All I saw was plants."

"I was wedged behind a pot, next to the wall. It was so dark." Alice thrust her hands between her knees. "Were you going to shoot me?" She was as afraid to hear the answer as she had been to round the corner of the building, except that no adrenaline buoyed her up now.

Susan wrinkled her brow. "I really don't know. I had the gun, and I was looking for you, but I didn't know until I shot Denny that I was going to shoot them, either. I felt very separated from everything the whole time it was going on. I suppose the evidence is that I would have shot you like I shot them, but as I told you yesterday, I can't really tell."

"But why did you want to kill me? I love you! I wasn't going to hurt you! Why me?"

Susan tried to smile. "Don't you always have to kill anyone who knows? I mean, you are a faithful voter, you lick stamps for the Democratic Party, you worry about the state of the union. Wasn't this scene inevitable?"

"I didn't feel in danger! I didn't even blame you! If you hadn't scared me half to death last night—" Alice's voice trailed off. There was no telling, after all, what Honey would overlook and what he would not. Finally, she said, "And they've got Noah. The least practical thing would have been to kill me." She turned to the detective. "I mean, you told me yourself that you were waiting for something like that."

Susan tried to attain a light tone. "None of this has been exactly practical, has it?"

"But—"

"Don't ask! Can't we just talk about it some other time?"

Alice looked down at the scratches on her arms and knees. They no longer stung very much, but the skin felt tight and grated. She said, "Well, I think you should tell me." Even as she said it, she was amazed at how determined she sounded.

Susan looked out the window rather than at Alice. After a long pause, she said, "I don't think I was really afraid of your turning me in, even though I was sure that once you knew you would turn me in. Maybe I was afraid of your not turning me in. I was afraid of your knowing! I was afraid of the closeness you would feel to me once you knew, of the unspoken kinship. And I was right! Over the weekend it was like being married. It felt like you were practically in my clothes with me, and there would never be any end to it. You would wear me down about living together, and then we'd eat and sleep and breathe this intimacy for the rest of our lives! How could I get away from that? I wanted to be alone! I wanted there to be silence! For thirteen years I worried about all the permutations of three people's feelings about each other. And for a while after they—after that night, I was sad and horrified but I was also relieved! It was over! Really over! And then you started preying on me!"

Alice must have looked shocked, because Susan exclaimed, "I know you don't see it like that, but I did! You were like an animal circling closer and closer, and when you got to me, you weren't going to devour me, you were going to sit on me, all over me, affectionately, forever. Your intentions were great. I realize that. But that was what was wrong. People with good intentions never give up! Denny had good intentions. Denny was a kind man. He was superhumanly kind. He never gave up on anything, not Craig, not me, not the music business. Good intentions are wicked! As far as I can see, all they lead to are lies and delusions. Oh, God!"

It was Alice's turn to sit as still as possible, hoping that her face didn't give away the turmoil and pain of her feelings. It was all too easy to see herself from Susan's point of view, hovering, enfolding, suffocating, smiling. She closed her eyes. Susan went on. "You were going to act normal forever, pretending that I hadn't done anything, pretending that nothing bound us except simple friendship. Denny was like that. Most of the time he pretended that Craig and I really liked each other, but we hated each other! And Noah, and Rya, and Ray! Everybody was always pretending something!"

"But we did like each other. We made compromises, that's all. That's life! You can't get to be thirty without disapproving of your friends sometimes, or being hurt or offended by their bad taste and bad judgment. We all knew pretty much where we stood with each other. That was the pleasure in it!"

"Was it?"

Honey looked at his watch. Susan sat up, and Honey said, "Mrs. Ellis will get you some clothes from the bedroom. I would rather you sat here with me."

Alice stood up and Susan leaned forward, reaching under the couch. In a second the gun was in her hand and she was pointing it at Honey. Alice inhaled sharply. Susan said, "Were you afraid I would get this?"

Honey smiled, but Alice could tell he was nonplussed. After a moment, he said, "You may not be aware that there is a mandatory death sentence in this state for shooting an officer of the law."

Alice gripped the cushion of her chair as Susan squeezed the trigger. There was a click. "Not loaded," said Susan with a smile. "The bullets are in the bedroom." She turned the gun in her hand and gave it to the detective. Honey said, "You are a remarkably calm woman, Miss Gabriel."

"Only on the surface, Detective Honey."

"Mrs. Ellis," said Honey, "would you get Miss Gabriel some clothing, please." Alice stood up, her knees knocking, and went into the bedroom. When she came out, the clothes she was carrying were her own, lent to Susan at various times over the past months. Susan smiled as she put them on. As they were leaving the apartment, Alice said, trying to make her voice as casual as possible, "Say, can I have your keys to my place? I'm locked out."

"Take them all," said Susan, thumping the heavy bunch into her hand. Honey fitted her wrists with handcuffs, although Alice didn't see that this was necessary. Susan watched for a moment, then looked at Alice. Finally, she said, "You thought too well of me. It was galling."

R Y A, who had shown up close to midnight Wednesday night and gone to bed at once in Alice's spare room, was not inclined to rise, even though Alice had told her that Noah was to be set free that day, and that it was she, Rya, who ought to go out and get him. "Come on!" exclaimed Alice. "Honey said he might be out by ten, and it's going to take you a while to get there!" Rya rolled over so that her face was to the wall, and groaned. Alice, who hadn't yet put on her shoes, kicked the other woman on the derriere with her stockinged foot and went on, "Get up! I have to go to work today, and it's nearly time for me to leave."

Rya sat up. "I thought you were going with me! Shit, I'm beat."

"I can't go with you. I missed all those days, and yesterday I was way behind. But you've got to go!"

Even dishevelled from inadequate sleep on a hot night, Rya was pretty, almost elegant. Her twenty-six-year-old face was rosy and smooth, and the fluid hair was too heavy to have tangled in the night. "But he doesn't even expect me! He probably doesn't even want me to come! Oh, shit!" She lifted her legs and rolled backward onto the bed.

"What is the matter with you? Don't you want to see him?" A picture of Noah making his solitary and unwelcomed way back from Riker's Island seemed not to have even occurred to Rya, or at least not to have affected her. "Don't go back to sleep!"

"Please go with me! Can't you take another day off? They won't mind."

"I can't and I won't. I have too much to do. I'm going to bring you a cup of coffee. Don't go back to sleep."

She was enraged when she returned and found Rya prone with her nose in the pillow. She put down the hot cup she was holding, grabbed the other woman's shoulders, and yanked her up. "Ow!" cried Rya.

"Sit up! You've got to get up! Don't you want to see him? *I* want to see him, and he's *your* husband!"

Rya reached for the coffee. "So your relationship isn't as complicated as mine is. No, I don't know that I want to see him. I don't know anything! Don't you understand that? Three nights ago, you told me that he had killed Craig and Denny because of me. Last night, when I was falling asleep on my feet, you told me that no, it was Susan who killed them for some reason that I still don't understand, and that we had to go out and get him this morning."

"You had to."

"That's worse, anyway. What if I'm not ready to see him? What if the whole prospect of starting up our marriage again scares me to death? Don't you realize that we haven't spoken to each other, or at least he hasn't spoken to me, in six months? You've got this good wife trip that you're laying on me, and I can't stand it."

Alice walked out of the room.

A minute later she walked back in. "Look," she said. "I don't care what happens between you and Noah. In my opinion, you don't deserve for anything good to happen because you've made such a terrible mess of everything. In my opinion, you've both been so stupid that it boggles the mind. But I also think that what is happening to Noah today has nothing to do with your relationship. A man who has been accused of a crime, and who is pretty confused himself, is getting out of jail. He deserves to have his wife, and not just some girl he knows, meet him, and take him home. You can pick up where you left off or you can get a divorce after you get home, but this event of leaving jail is a public thing, like getting married or buried. You have to meet him because it's the human thing to do."

With her finger, Rya pushed her hair behind her ear. "Then you come with me. That's the human thing to do, too."

"I won't!" Alice was vehement. "Why don't you be brave for once! Why don't you rise all the way to the occasion this time!"

"Please?"

"I've got to go to work!" Alice grabbed the now empty coffee cup from Rya's hand and turned on her heel and went down the long hallway. She was determined not to accompany Rya to Riker's Island, determined not to get anywhere within Susan's orbit. The attack of Sunday night, like a narrowly averted accident, had become far more real to her in retrospect than it had been at the time. Her thoughts swung between the dark mystery of seeing Susan step out onto the fire escape and the sunlit bitterness of having everything spelled out the following afternoon. Everything was fresh again. She did not seem to have accepted the murders, Susan's planning of them, Ray's injuries, the attack on herself, or Susan's opinion of her at all. Whatever composure she remembered having attained over the weekend was false, and had vanished anyway. Even the Fifty-ninth Street Bridge, where you caught the bus for Riker's Island, seemed dangerous ground. She rinsed Rya's cup and set it in the drainer. Rya herself appeared in the kitchen doorway. "I can't go!" she wailed. "I can't go! He's just going to have to take a cab by himself. He won't mind. He'd be embarrassed to have me out there, I'm sure."

Alice screamed, "Why are you such a bitch! Such a selfish bitch! Think of somebody else for once! How he's managed to put up with you for six years, I'll never know!"

"If you went with me, it would be all right!"

"I won't go with you! I just won't. Don't nag me!"

Rya thrust out her chin. "It's because Susan's out there, isn't it? I bet Susan's out there. Otherwise, you'd go. You were willing to try and see him, but you're not willing to do this. I know it's because Susan's out there."

"I want to keep my job!" But Rya was already down the hall, disappearing into the second bedroom. Alice looked at the telephone and looked away. It was impossible. She picked it up. After all, it was rather easy. She said, "Howard. I've got to miss work again today. I'm not sick. I've been involved in a murder."

"Jesus!" said Howard.

"Just peripherally, and actually, it's been going on for a couple of weeks, but there are some things I have to do."

"Take the rest of the week, Alice."

"I couldn't stand it. Today is enough. I'll see you tomorrow." She heard Howard put down the phone and imagined the entire library lighting up instantly like a neon sign with the news. Rya entered the kitchen, her hair pinned up. "What should I wear?" she said meekly. "Do you think a dress is appropriate? Do I have to take the subway? God, I hate taking the subway alone. But I guess I'll have to."

Alice put down the receiver. "I think anything Noah likes is appropriate. And we take a bus over to the Fifty-ninth Street Bridge. Honey gave me the information. I'll go with you."

"Thank God! But listen. Sometime, you will tell him I was ready to go alone?"

Alice nodded, feeling doomed.

THE trip was briefer than Alice expected, into Queens, then Astoria. The neighborhood was middle class, nearly up to the bridge. With the recent weather, Alice was reminded forcibly of the beach. The robin's egg sky and the sapphire water made the perfect Cape Cod contrast. Yes, they had heard of Noah, which somehow surprised Alice, as if they had come to retrieve him from a trashbin instead of a modern, automated prison facility, and he would be ready in about an hour and a half. They were instructed to wait with the other visitors in the army tent behind the parking lot. Alice craned her neck, but the white-trimmed group of buildings on the island looked only like a college.

The temptation to ask after Susan was almost irresistible, only to ask how she was, not to see her, but even that Alice feared and hated to do. Rya said, "Is Susan here? You ought to go see her."

Alice snapped, "Forget it!" and it was Rya's turn to smile. Alice cleared her throat angrily and sat in her seat with great determination, but it didn't matter. Soon enough she had crossed the parking lot again, asking after a recent arrival, "Susan Lynn Gabriel."

The uniformed guard dialed some numbers and repeated Susan's name into the phone, then he turned to Alice. "Was she brought in last night?"

"Yes, but—"

"That's the one. Can she have visitors? I'll send her over."

"I don't —I'm not—"

He hung up. "Just get on that bus, and ask the driver to take you to the women's area."

"I don't want to go to the women's area! I just wanted to find out how she was!"

"Well, ask her yourself."

Rya was watching her. Alice decided to get on the bus and go over the bridge, and maybe even get out at the women's area, but then, even though she wasn't going to see Susan, she began to perspire and get frightened, as if she were. The bus rolled over the beautiful blue of the bay, turned left, stopped here and there. People got off much too quickly. "Well?" said the driver, and he seemed so weary and irritable that she got off. She stood immobile for a few minutes, then went in. She was not going to speak, but an authoritative black woman asked who she was, and she did it, named herself and asked to see Susan Gabriel, who was a new arrival. Alice was told to check her purse. Then, too committed to turn back, she was led to a room and invited to sit down. Everyone was polite, but this was not a place where you waffled or changed your mind or acted bizarre in any way. She dreaded the sight of Susan as much as, on the ledge outside her building, she had dreaded the appearance of some monster face around the sash of the window. In the midst of her dread, Susan was brought in, looking much as usual.

She smiled knowingly when she saw Alice, rendering Alice unable to speak. After a minute or so, the wardress prompted them. They had ten minutes. Susan said, "How did you get here? But you're magic. You always turn up."

"Not necessarily. Anyway, there are regular buses. You go through Queens. The bus doesn't penetrate a time warp or anything."

"You should use the car."

"It's impounded."

"Oh. I guess it would be. How about the apartment?"

"They went over it yesterday. Starting today I can go in and out again."

"It's all very practical, isn't it? Like moving to Europe."

"Except that they do a lot of it for you."

"I suppose."

The tone of their voices was familiar to Alice, and after a second she realized that Jim and she had spoken just this way, with affectionate but distant politeness, after the divorce. She also had the same desire to proclaim one last consummate accusation, to make her position known forever, and the same inability to do it. She said, "We came out to get Noah, actually. He's in the men's part. Honey reduced his charge to a misdemeanor. Rya got back last night."

"I can just see Rya at a prison."

"She's okay."

There was another long pause. Susan looked at her with the old amused directness and said, "Do you hate me?"

Alice thought about the word "hate" and compared it to her feelings of the past two days. She looked up. "Yes." After a moment, she said, "For now."

"How's Ray?"

"Feeling better. Honey dropped around his place the night he got out of the hospital and said that he should go back to Minnesota and gave him a good talking to about lifestyle and companionship. I guess Ray's going to do it."

"Five minutes," said the wardress, halting all conversation once again. Alice coughed.

Susan said, "Can I say something? Don't be so dependent. You don't have to be."

Alice opened then closed her mouth, then chuckled.

Susan said, "What?"

"I was just about to say, How will I know what to do without you telling me?"

"You will. You knew what to do the other night. I would never have thought of that."

"True." And here was another thing like the divorce, the harsh habit of being in love that inflamed every exchange. Alice looked directly at Susan for a moment. Susan didn't feel it. That was clear. She was merely being kind. Alice stood up. "It's almost time. Can you get packages? Can I send you anything?"

Susan shrugged. The wardress approached, and Susan stood up. The wardress led her away. As she was about to disappear, though, she stopped and looked at Alice. And Alice was betrayed by the furious desire for some loving word that would change the situation from horrible to tragic. Susan said, "Some of those long bobby pins. Send me a package of those long bobby pins, okay?"

Alice nodded.

BENEATH his casual manner, Noah seemed a little startled when he came to meet them, but the distracted way he greeted Rya made it clear that it was not precisely she who startled him, that his surprise was a personal condition only tenuously related to his exact circumstances. He seemed glad to see them, although even as he looked at them affectionately, he seemed not to be listening to what they had to say. He declared at once that he was fine, before they asked him, and complimented Rya idly on her dress, which he hadn't seen since last summer, but still he seemed startled. Alice thought that such a condition might last for a long time, even become permanent. She gave him a sisterly kiss on the cheek, and he hugged her suddenly, tightly, with real feeling. She had not always liked Noah. Tears came to her eyes.

As they looked for a taxi that was going to take them back to Manhattan, Noah reminded Alice very much of a little boy of a certain age, perhaps eleven or twelve, elated and confused, but determined not to show either. His face was arranged, his gait was arranged, his remarks were arranged to give no evidence that his arrest, indictment, arraignment, and confinement had been any different from a gig in Bridgeport or a weekend in the Catskills. This air of false resolution made him look very handsome, both older and younger than usual. Alice glanced at Rya, wondering if she noticed. Rya looked small, stooped slightly by the weight of the scenery. She was not looking at Noah. Alice pursed her lips and shook her head. "Another beautiful day," said Noah. "Especially out here near the water."

"The air is lovely," said Alice.

"So," he said, "it was Susan."

"Yes," said Alice.

"I didn't think of that. I heard the shots, you know, when I was outside the door. I didn't think of Susan. I thought one of them did it. I thought sure that was it."

"Who did you think it was?"

Noah shrugged. "I thought Craig was crazy enough to do it, but I guess I thought Denny would have a motive."

"But what about the weapon? The police never found a weapon."

Noah smiled and shrugged. "I don't know. Besides, you never know what the police have found." Thinking of Honey, Alice nodded, and said, "How did they find the cocaine at your place?"

"By process of elimination, I suppose. I just grabbed it at the last minute, because I didn't want Denny to get in trouble."

"With Susan?"

"Who else?"

There were no cabs, and so they sat on an old bench, waiting for the bus. A breeze blew briskly off the water. "This smells great," said Noah. He was grinning. Rya took some pins out of her hair and put them back in. Noah looked at her, then looked toward Manhattan, or what would be the Bronx, Alice guessed, then took Alice's hand. Alice shivered, suddenly afraid, and looked quickly toward Rya, who was gazing at the planes coming into LaGuardia and taking off. Noah's hand tightened on Alice's, became painful. After a long moment, Noah groaned, "Oh, God!" and then burst into tears. Alice bit her lip and blinked. Rya, as if viewing everything from a distance, slowly turned her head and watched in amazement.

Noah cried for a long time, holding tightly to Alice's hand, only to Alice's hand. The bus did not come. Rya sat perfectly still and Alice tried not to look at her, tried not to signal in any way what she thought Rya should do. Once Rya opened her mouth and closed it again, then, after a few minutes, she spoke. "Why are you crying, Noah?"

Noah perfectly took her meaning, which Alice saw was really to inquire, not to challenge. Of course he would be crying, but it was important to know what aspect of his recent experience was most vivid to him. Noah caught his breath, was unable to speak, caught his breath again. Finally, he said, "It's intolerable to be alone like this."

Neither Rya nor Alice exclaimed that he was not alone, that they were with him. They exchanged a glance, and Alice realized that Rya, too, acknowledged the depth of their threefold solitude, and had no answer for it. Alice looked toward the Bronx, and she felt suddenly like a stone, about to be carried with a great show of purpose toward millions of other stones. In fact, though, belying her movement, there would be nothing among those stones for her, and no promise that she would ever again cease being a stone herself.

A cab came, carrying a woman and a small boy. Rya stood up first and stepped forward, then turned halfway to wait for them. Alice bent down to retrieve her purse, which had slid under the bench. The sun was shining brightly, and it was almost hot. Noah took a deep shuddering breath and stood up. Just then there was a piece of broken pavement, and Noah stumbled. Alice put her hand out, but it was Rya who grabbed his elbow so that he didn't fall down. Noah smiled. Alice was suspicious of any hope for them, but on the other hand, never before had she seen Rya even notice anyone else's problems, much less try to help with one. The woman assisted her little boy out of the cab and looked around suspiciously. Alice smiled at her, and then they were in the cab, speeding back to Manhattan.

S O O N enough she was at the gate of the Brooklyn Botanic Garden. She was not willing to say that it was Henry she wanted to see—she would not, for example, have gone over to his apartment, but when she catalogued her alternatives for the empty afternoon, shopping reminded her too much of Susan, work seemed a bore, there were no movies she wanted to see, and she had no friends to visit. Only the Botanic Garden, with its deserted paths and grandly organized exotica seemed alluring. She stood at the gate, though, for a long time, unable to go in, although she could see that there was no Henry weeding or pruning among the ivies and crab apples of the formal walk. She was not merely afraid of an embarrassing encounter, although, standing there, she strongly felt the garden to be Henry's preserve, she was more afraid, oddly afraid, of intruding upon the garden itself, as if she would be unwelcome. A group was going in: an older black man in work clothes carrying his lunch, an extremely fat woman who had to be helped through the turnstile, a teenager with a baby. Alice followed them. Anyone, after all, could go in. The man sat down on one of the benches and a truck full of equipment drove by, but otherwise the upper walks were empty. It was not until she had strolled there for a while that Alice realized how populated and jangling her life had been for the last few weeks. More importantly, it was she herself who seemed an intrusion upon it. A discomfort she had felt, like a burr in her side, had goaded her closer and closer to Susan, closer and closer to Honey, so that, in the end, she had succeeded in inserting herself in the picture. When she thought about Susan, her embarrassment was so profound that almost any other pain seemed preferable to it. And embarrassment was exactly what she had always assumed their friendship would preserve her from.

At the end of the formal walk, she turned sharply left, along the upper walk, where she and Henry had not gone. Spread below, as in an amphitheater, were the rows of cherry trees, fully leafed out now, the lilacs, almost faded, and straight ahead, the rose garden, surrounded by a picket fence, which was just coming into bloom. The roses were so profuse, so colorful, and so fragrant, even a hundred feet away, that it seemed startling that no one was viewing them, that they should have such a self-contained existence even here, in the middle of millions of people. Alice was not a particular lover of roses. Usually she found them fragrant, but too garish, too full of blooms or too blank without them, unable to bear up their own richness. Her favorite flowers were more modest—daffodils, lilacs, lavender—but from this distance, the velvety reds, flashing yellows, and glassy whites seemed to break up the light of the summer sun into its various elements and cast it back far more brilliantly than any other flower ever could, seemed not exactly of the earth, but of space and air itself. Alice stood still for a long time, until a man came and sat near her on the bench. Afraid that he would say, "Pretty, huh?" or something equally compromising, she turned and walked down the hill toward the lilac bushes.

Maybe Doreen and Hugh and the grandparents were right after all. If she went back to Rochester, where she at least had relatives, if not friends, and relatives she got along with, she would be eating fresh strawberries right now, and the first oakleaf lettuce. Later in the summer, she could go fishing with Hugh and Doc, who still had the confidence to eat what they caught. Going home wasn't necessarily a defeat. Thirty-year-olds settled near their parents every day, and viewed it as a matter of coming to their senses, bolstering up the disintegrating American family, or even out-growing all of those spurious resentments that had driven them away in the first place. If you could freely return to the geography of your parents, after embracing to your heart's content the most dangerous, exciting, and alien landscape imaginable, didn't you thereafter have everything? Weren't you then forever both small town and cosmopolitan, experienced, and yet reaping the abundant fruits of innocence? They seemed very alluring just then, the lives that her living ancestors had led; not just Doc, who had spent three years in Europe during the First World War, two of them before the Americans came in, patching up the wounded, and then come back to Minnesota to practice, and become a friend of the Mayos, but Pop, too, who'd had a little fortune once, only an inconsiderable, small town accumulation, but he'd lost it by speculation, and then made some of it back again by his dogged but hungering avoidance of speculation. Her grandmothers had their own stories, more personal and more shadowy, since the essence of being a grandmother is to have been perfectly virtuous and a sterling example for a little girl all of your life, but after all, their lives were of a piece, as were those of Doreen and Hugh, lives that lasted so long and were so continuous that every subterranean force set in motion by inheritance or chance had the opportunity to grow, flower, and subside. Her relatives seemed actually to have learned something from their long existences, which was perhaps why Alice had always liked them. They had not been battered by random events into numbness, as Alice felt in danger of being. Each of her forebears had a peculiar and fully branched inner life. Maybe that was the great compensation for living in the Midwest, in a climate as routinely cruel as Minnesota's.

It was then that she saw Henry's back as he disappeared into the brush of the native plant collection. She didn't think he had seen her, but she turned quickly and hurried toward the Japanese garden and the promenades of the greenhouse. About Henry she was also embarrassed, although it was the commoner embarrassment of having met kindness with rudeness, of having acted inconsistently and probably stupidly. Obviously it was only right to apologize to him sometime, and it would be all too easy to put off such an apology until the interval itself would amount to still another discourtesy. It now seemed bizarre that Henry had offered her such quick and passionate love only a few days ago. It probably seemed bizarre to him, too. It was marvellous in a way how completely her passion for him had been a part of the murder. At least, she didn't feel it now. She surveyed the water lilies, not liking them particularly, but struck by the luminosity of the pale lavender ones. In the annual beds, varieties of marigolds, nicotiana, and begonias had been set out, just as they would soon be in her mother's and grandmother's flower gardens at home. Alice wondered if Henry had helped. She thought of Susan that morning, of her kindness that was merely kindness, and her toes curled with mortification. Still, such embarrassment was good if it served as a prophylactic against another abject relationship. Wasn't it better, for the time being, to be loveless than to do it again a third time? She contemplated calling Jim Ellis for a moment, but finally didn't want to do that either. That, too, was a relationship she was finally out of, that should be left to grow and branch and vine freely without even a shadow of her presence. And there was nothing exotic or especially interesting about it, after all, was there? It was just a marriage like millions of others. Jim's most recent poems hadn't even been concerned with it.

Alice wandered past the children's garden and out the zoo entrance. She had begun to feel hungry enough to think of lunch, but not hungry enough to yearn for it. Still, there was a diner across the street.

Although the pastrami was lean and its juice had seeped tangily, with the mustard, into the fresh, warm rye bread, she pushed it away after the first half, wiped her mouth, and concentrated on her Coke. It had plenty of ice, and after sucking off all the sweet syrup, she began to crunch the pieces of ice one by one. The waitress came by and offered her dessert, but she shook her head and pointed to the sandwich. "Take that, too. It's good, but I'm just not hungry." She smiled, and the waitress smiled back at her. She looked out the window and wondered what to do with the rest of the afternoon. It was only three-twenty.

Behind her, Henry's voice said, "I thought that was you. What are you doing out our way?" Without an invitation, he sat down. He was carrying a cup of coffee. Alice said, "No lunch?"

"I ate around eleven."

"I was in the garden, actually. I didn't see you."

"You must have seen the roses."

"They're lovely." He was wearing dirt-covered overalls and he saw her looking at them. He seemed, after all, very familiar, and their affair, though dreamlike in retrospect, bore all the self-consciousness and constraint of a real and no longer new relationship. Alice said, "I ought to apologize—"

"Me, too."

The last thing Alice wanted Henry to do was apologize. She said, "What for?"

He looked at her, not exactly enthusiastic about going on. "Well. For being pushy, like you said."

"I don't know that I said that very seriously. Besides, I hang back more than most people do, I think. And why apologize for being the way you are? I'm sorry for something much more concrete. I stood you up and slighted you and was rude and stupid." As she spoke, a wave of real regret passed over her. "It's worse, though. I've been pushy before. Every time, in fact. I've had this habit of pushing people toward commitments and then sort of going blank after they were made. This made me realize it."

"Well, I—"

"I was angry with you. I did feel slighted and foolish and disappointed."

"I'm sure you did. I—"

"I don't feel that way any more."

"I'm glad, but you shouldn't anyway. Someday I'll tell you all about it. Not now. Maybe in November." Alice smiled, feeling rather impish.

Henry shifted in his seat and peered uncomfortably in his coffee cup. Unable to resist, Alice went on. "You said that you loved me."

Henry's face turned a decided shade of red, and it was Alice's turn to peer into the bottom of her glass. Finally, he said, "Can I, uh, take it back?"

Alice's smile broadened. "You know what? All things considered, even those you don't know about, I rather wish you would."

"You do?"

"Consider it never said."

"I don't want to do that."

"I guess I don't want you to, either." Alice's ice was now gone, but they seemed permanently seated. She wondered what they would talk about next. Henry said, "In November, I'll probably be living in Brooklyn. I've been looking for a place. I may even buy something."

"What about your trip to China?"

"Actually, I withdrew my application. I decided that putting it in had been just a habit. New York is really pretty interesting."

"Are you speaking sociologically?"

"Not at all. You could spend years studying parts of the Bronx, and more years out in Jamaica Bay. Speaking botanically, a lot has happened here, and rather quickly, too. The hand of man has been heavy, but pretty obvious. Europeans tend to stampede through the china shop in a destructive rush, but they always leave shards and scraps and untouched corners. There aren't any untouched corners in most of the Orient, and the shards and scraps have been put to use long ago. I'm ready for years of weekly field trips, I think."

"May I go along sometimes?"

"Of course."

The waitress came by with the coffeepot, but Henry waved her away. When she gestured toward Alice's empty glass, Alice shook her head. Still, though, they couldn't seem to stand up. Henry sighed. "We aren't very well suited, are we?"

"No."

"I—" He stopped.

"But we'd be good for each other's faults."

"You mean my rushing into things."

"Yes, and my never seeing things. Besides." Alice smiled, but did not go on. After a moment, Henry smiled, too. "Yes," he said. "There is that!" In a moment, they stood up. As they left the restaurant, his arm came around Alice's shoulders, and he squeezed. Alice lifted her chin and kissed him lightly on the cheek.

AFTERWORD

I would like to thank the following people and institutions for their generous help when I was researching this novel: The Brooklyn Botanic Garden; The New York Public Library; Detective P. Hoffman of Manhattan's 20th Precinct; Captain Edward Steinberg of Riker's Island and Staten Island; David Vladek of Washington, D.C.; Paul Greenough, Adrienne Drapkin, and Beth Nugent of Iowa City, Iowa; and Jerry Becker of Chicago. To Marc Silag, for his expertise on the music business, I am very grateful. I would also like to thank Bill Silag for his willingness to make all those calls, for his huge fund of information about every subject, and for his patience. Any mistakes in the work are, of course, entirely the fault of the author.

A NOTE ON THE AUTHOR

Jane Smiley was born in Los Angeles, grew
up in St. Louis, and studied at Vassar and
the University of Iowa, where she received
her Ph D. She now teaches at Iowa State
University. She is the author of two previous novels, *Barn Blind* and *At Paradise
Gate*. She lives in Ames, Iowa, with her
husband, a historian, and their
two daughters.

A NOTE ON THE TYPE

The text of this book was set via computer-driven cathode-ray tube in Trump Mediæval. Designed by Professor Georg Trump in the mid 1950s, Trump Mediæval was cut and cast by the C. E. Weber Type Foundry of Stuttgart, West Germany. The roman letter forms are based on classical prototypes, but Professor Trump has imbued them with his own unmistakable style. The italic letter forms, unlike those of so many other type faces, are closely related to their roman counterparts. The result is a truly contemporary type, notable for both its legibility and its versatility.

Composed by Waldman Graphics, Inc., Pennsauken, New Jersey Printed and bound by R. R. Donnelley & Sons, Co., Harrisonburg, Virginia

Designed by Sara Reynolds